'A new contender for the Great Chinese-American Novel ... Davies has gathered the threads of Chinese American identity and woven a brilliant, ambitious and indelible tale.'

South China Morning Post

'An intense and dreamlike new novel ... What makes *The Fortunes* so hopeful, the type of novel that could have only been written now, is its willingness to take liberties with that past – to rearrange its details and indulge in speculation, in order to help us imagine a different way forward.'

Hua Hsu, *New Yorker*

'Haunting ... Davies, ever deft, points us into the messy complexity of identity with compassion and nuance'

San Francisco Chronicle

'Davies' nuanced contemplation of how America has affected the Chinese (and vice versa) forces the reader to confront what is both singular and similar about all cross-cultural transactions.'

Kirkus Reviews

'A resplendent, inventive, heartbreaking chronicle of the Chinese-American experience'

Washington Independent Review of Books

'It's doing what a great novel should do: revealing what there is to care about and to think about. Even better, it's revealing those questions about a slice of history that America needs to be dealing with.'

Huffington Post

The FORTUNES

PETER HO DAVIES

SCEPTRE

First published in USA in 2016 by Houghton Mifflin Harcourt

First published in Great Britain in 2016 by Sceptre
An imprint of Hodder & Stoughton
An Hachette UK company

First published in paperback in 2017

1

"Kung Fu Fighting"
Written by Carlton Douglas
© Edition Carren
All Rights Reserved. Used by Permission

"Half Caste Woman"
Words and Music by Noel Coward
Copyright © 1931 (Renewed) WB Music Corp.
All Rights Reserved
Used By Permission of Alfred Music

"These Foolish Things"
Words by Eric Maschwitz and Music by Jack Strachey
Copyright © 1936 by Lafleur Music Ltd
International Copyright Secured
All Rights Reserved

A CIP catalogue record for this title is available from the British Library

ISBN 978 0 340 98025 5

Typeset in Sabon MT by Hewer Text UK Ltd, Edinburgh
Printed and bound by Clays Ltd, St Ives plc

Hodder & Stoughton policy is to use papers that are natural, renewable and recyclable
products and made from wood grown in sustainable forests. The logging and manufacturing
processes are expected to conform to the environmental regulations of the country of origin.

Hodder & Stoughton Ltd
Carmelite House
50 Victoria Embankment
London EC4Y 0DZ

www.sceptrebooks.com

for Owen and Olanne

Truth becomes fiction when the fiction's true;
Real becomes not-real where the unreal's real.
 —*Cao Xueqin*, The Story of the Stone

Tell all the truth but tell it slant.
 —*Emily Dickinson*

—*Anon.*, Oriental riff

Contents

Gold

Celestial Railroad

Beset by labor shortages, Crocker chanced one morn to remark his houseboy, a slight but perdurable youth named Ah Ling. And it came to him that herein lay his answer.

—American Titan, *K. Clifford Stanton*

1.

It was like riding in a treasure chest, Ling thought. Or one of the mistress's velvet jewel cases. The glinting brasswork, the twinkling, tinkling chandelier dangling like a teardrop from the inlaid walnut ceiling, the etched glass and flocked wallpaper and pendulous silk. And the jewel at the center of the box—Charles Crocker, Esquire, *Mister Charley,* biggest of the Big Four barons of the Central Pacific Railroad, resting on the plump brocaded upholstery, massive as a Buddha, snoring in time to the panting, puffing engine hauling them uphill.

It was more than two years since the end of the war and the shooting of the president—the skinny one, with the whiskery, wizened face of a wise ape—who had first decreed the overland railroad. His body had been carried home in a palace car much like this, Ling had heard Crocker boast. Ling pictured one long thin box laid inside

another, the dead man's tall black hat perched atop it like a funnel. People had lined the tracks, bareheaded even in the rain, it was said, torches held aloft in the night. Like joss sticks, he reflected.

For a moment he fancied Crocker dead, the carriage swagged in black, and himself keeping vigil beside the body, but it was impossible with the snores alternately sighing and stuttering from the prone form. "Locomotion is a soporific to me," Crocker had confessed dryly as they boarded, and sure enough, his eyes had grown heavy before they reached Roseville. By the time the track began to rise at Auburn, the low white haze of the flats giving way to a receding blue, vegetal humidity to mineral chill, his huge head had begun to roll and bob, and he'd presently stretched himself out, as if to stop it crashing to the floor. Yet even asleep Crocker seemed inexorable, his chest surging and settling profoundly as an ocean swell, the watch chain draped across it so weighty it must have an anchor at one end. Carried to the Sierra summit, he looked set to rumble down the lee side into Nevada and Utah, bowling across the plains, sweeping all before him.

Ling knew he should be looking out the window, taking the chance to see the country, to see if the mountains really were gold, but he hadn't been able to take his eyes off the steep slope of his master's girth. *My gold mountain,* he thought, entertaining a fleeting vision of himself — tiny — scaling Crocker's imposing bulk, pickaxe in hand, following the glittering vein of his watch chain toward the snug cave of his vest pocket.

Ling didn't own a watch himself, of course, but shortly after he entered service Crocker had had him outfitted

with a new suit from his dry goods store, picking it out himself. The storekeep had been peddling a more modest rig—"a fustian bargain, as it were!"—that the big man dismissed out of hand as shoddy. He settled on a brown plaid walking suit instead, waving aside the aproned clerk to yank the coat sharp over Ling's narrow shoulders. "There now!" Crocker declared, beaming at him in the glass. "Every inch a gentleman's valet." He taught Ling how to fasten only the top button of the jacket, leaving the rest undone, to "show the vest to advantage," and advised him he needn't bother with a necktie so long as he buttoned his shirt collar. "Clothes make the man," the circling clerk opined, sucking his teeth. "Even a Chinaman." And then, of course, there must be a hat, a tall derby, which Ling balanced like a crown, eyes upturned. As a finishing touch Crocker had tucked a gold coin, a half eagle, into Ling's vest pocket—a gift, though the cost of the outfit itself would come out of his wages—where Ling could swear the thing actually seemed to tick against his ribs like a heartbeat: *rich, rich, rich.*

He patted it now, as he finally turned to take in the scenery—the pale halo of sere grass along a ridge, the stiff flame of a cypress, the veiled peaks beyond—wondering despite himself if the mountains might glister through the flickering pines.

2.

Gold Mountain. *Gum Shan.* Ling had never even laid eyes on gold before he left Fragrant Harbor. It had made him feel furtively foolish. There he was, sent to find it and he'd

never seen it in his life. What if he didn't recognize it? How yellow was it? How heavy? What if he walked right by it? "How can you miss it, lah!" Aunty Bao had snapped, over the snick of her abacus. "There'll be a mountain of it, stupid egg!" But Ling wasn't so sure. They came from Pearl River. If it were really full of pearls, he wanted to tell her, he wouldn't be sailing to Gold Mountain.

"Besides," Big Uncle insisted, "you *have* seen gold before." They were in his cabin on the "flower boat," the moored junk that housed the brothel Big Uncle owned and Aunty Bao—palely plump as the pork buns she was named after—managed for him. Yes, Big Uncle was saying, a grandfather had made his fortune prospecting in Nanyang. The old man had had a mouthful of gold teeth. As an infant, Ling had even been given gold tea, a concoction made by pouring boiling water over a piece of gold, supposed to ensure luck. Didn't he remember? Ling tried. For a second a vast, bared smile, glistening wetly, rose up before him and with it a feeling of fear, an impression, as the lips drew back, that beneath the flesh the man himself was made all of gold, that behind the gold teeth lay a gold tongue clanging in a gold throat. But the only "grandfather" he could actually recall was a broken-down old head swabbing the decks who had already lost those teeth, pulled, one by one, to pay for his opium habit. All that was left was a fleshy hole, the old man's lips hanging loose as an ox's, his tongue constantly licking his bruised-looking gums.

Still, Big Uncle pressed, "Gold is in your blood, boy!"

Perhaps, Ling thought, but he'd learned to doubt his blood.

His people were of that reviled tribe of sea gypsies known as Tanka, "egg folk," after the rounded rattan shelters of their sampans. Forbidden by imperial edict to live on land and only grudgingly tolerated in ports and coastal villages, for generations they'd made a thin living as fishermen, mocked for their stink by the Han Chinese. Latterly they'd made an even more odious, if also more lucrative, reputation smuggling opium for the British and pimping out their women to them for good measure. Ling's mother had been one of these *haam-sui-mui,* or "saltwater girls." "A lucky one," Aunty Bao observed with a moue of envy, a beauty plucked from the brothel by a wealthy foreigner and established in her own household. Only his mother's luck had run out fast. She'd died in childbirth, and her protector, Ling's father, had settled a generous sum on Big Uncle to take the infant off his hands. All Ling had left of her was her name. He had grown up on board the flower boat along with the other bastards, a clutch of them grudgingly provided for until they could be disposed of profitably, the girls as whores, the boys as coolies (a *C* or *P* daubed on their chests in pitch for Cuba or Peru, where they'd labor in the sugar plantations or mine guano).

The only children Big Uncle kept were his lawful sons by Aunty Bao. Their father styled himself a respectable Chinese comprador—frogged brocade jacket over ankle-length changshan, silk cap smoothed tight over shaven head—grooming his boys to run the family business, even if that business consisted of a brothel, an opium den, a smuggling fleet. Big Uncle's sons were plump and well dressed—on land they could pass for Cantonese—but more than anything Ling envied them their father's

name. As a small child he would watch them following the big man, listening as he taught them his trade ("Opium and sex belong together; the one enhances the other." "Or at least prolongs it," Aunty Bao pouted) and Ling began to trail them in turn, imitating their deference, their attentiveness, until the oldest boy, thinking he mocked them, shoved him to the deck with a thud. Big Uncle had turned at the sound and casually, as if stretching, struck the bully about the head. Ling recalled glimpsing the heavy leather wrist guards of a hatchet man beneath his silk sleeves. "They're worthless if they're crippled," Big Uncle noted calmly over Elder Brother's sobs, patting Ling's shoulders and examining him. "How are you?" he asked, and Ling, eyes wide but dry, piped up, "Well . . . father!" And the man smiled on him from beneath his sleek mustache.

Young Ling had no hope, even as he searched the faces of the white ghosts who frequented the brothel, of finding his own father. The man had given him up, after all. But he still wanted *a* father, needed one. To be fatherless in China, he understood, was to be poorer than the hungriest peasant.

He had made himself useful about the boat, running errands for the girls, waiting on their customers. His specialty was preparing opium for the men: pinching and rolling the doughy pills between his small fingers, holding them over the lamp on the needle until they began to smoke and bubble, then deftly depositing them in the bowl of the waiting pipe. Over time, squatting at their feet, he began to pick up shreds of their language—English mostly, but also phrases of Portuguese and French, Italian

and Spanish—to go along with his Cantonese. It got to be a performance, men calling him "little parrot" and tipping him in coin (from which Aunty Bao took her customary cut). Once he saw Big Uncle watching him, and a few days later the man gave him a gift, a pet cricket folded up in a tiny cage made from a carved bamboo cylinder. He cherished it, peering in at it though the narrow bars, falling asleep to its ringing song, like a prayer or a promise. He wept when it fell silent, hiding for days, thinking he'd be beaten for letting it die (though Big Uncle never asked about it again).

Aunty Bao must have seen his hopes in his face. When he grew taller, she insisted he leave—"He'll fall in love with one of the girls, lah! Bad for business!"—and so Big Uncle sent him on his way, though not to Peru or Cuba but to "Big City," San Francisco. He already sold girls from his nursery to supply the brothels on Gold Mountain. The boy with his pocketful of English might do well there too, he reasoned.

"Off to your own kind," Aunty Bao crowed, but Ling, despite his misgivings, went willingly enough, eager to prove himself a dutiful son. "Your passage is paid," Big Uncle told him, "a position arranged." Ling had bowed, promised to send money, and the old gangster nodded complacently. That was when he'd told him gold was in his blood. Ling was fourteen years old. He knew nothing of America, nothing of mining—pictured himself drawing gold from the dirt like the apothecary straining over that old grandfather, yanking the gold from its roots, brandishing a nugget in a pair of pliers, wet and a little bloody—but he vowed to strike it rich and return in

triumph. (His ideas of gold were to be even more confused when, on the voyage out, the captain had lowered the dory to recover an odd floating rock, as it seemed, the color of pale tea. *Ambergris!* the crew exulted. *Floating gold!* Though later Ling was to learn it was whale puke.)

Outside the carriage window, the trees — sharp firs poking through their layered foliage like the spike impaling receipts on Crocker's desk — fell away as the train ascended a ridge and the view opened before him. The distant peaks shone in the morning light, not gold, of course, but brilliant white, and as they climbed he watched the flakes tumbling past the window, mixed with sparks and smut from the smokestack.

Snow, and it was June.

The flurry whipped and twisted like a swarm, so blithely nimble, even as he felt the train grow taut, girding against gravity. And then an updraft swooped in and sent it spiraling back into the sky.

Beneath the thunderous thrill of it all — Ling was used to accompanying Crocker about town, but never before into the field — lay a thrum of unease. He contemplated the idle men waiting at the end of the line, the striking Chinese, and wondered why Mister Charley had brought him along.

3.

He'd been with Crocker for a little over two years by then, since 1865. His first job off the paddle steamer in Yee Fow — Second City, as the Chinese knew Sacramento — had

been at a laundry on I Street, one of the shanties backing onto China Slough, hauling boiling kettles from the stove to the great half-barrel tubs where his boss, Uncle Ng, a wiry Cantonese, sat smoking and working the soaking linens between his red callused feet, every so often tapping the ash from his pipe—"soo-*dah!*" as he pronounced it —into the suds like so much seasoning.

Ng wore a wispy beard and a sleepy mien, heavy-lidded, his head seemingly propped on the long-stemmed pipe clamped between his teeth, but he had a dark mole the size of a pea above the bridge of his nose, a third eye that seemed to squint whenever he furrowed his brow. His queue he coiled around his head to keep out of the laundry water (at first glance, vision bleary from lye, Ling had been scandalized to think Ng had cut his hair, imperial law requiring the queue as a mark of fealty), but he let a single strand sprouting from his mole grow long and silky, believing after the Chinese tradition, if against all experience, that it brought him luck.

Ng was an inveterate gambler, tucking his coins into his ears for safekeeping and absenting himself each evening and part of most days to play the lottery or dominoes or "precious dice," whatever he could find. He'd bet on which starling would rise off a roof first, back one cockroach over another in a race, so long as there was someone to wager against. He would return invariably with tales of perspicacious wins and unforeseeable reverses, but it seemed to Ling as if they mostly evened out, which might have been the extent of Ng's luck.

Not surprisingly, he was an indulgent boss, often leaving Ling unsupervised as if he were a partner, not an

employee. Even when he was present during the day he was often stretched out, snoring, on an ironing platform, catching up on sleep from the night before. Ling took him for a fool—easy to see why he'd never amounted to more than a laundryman—but the old man's neglect was mostly benign. Early on, with a sly show of solemnity, he confided his "mystery"—a few crumbs of blue from an ink block added to the rinse water to make the "white whiter"—but otherwise he offered little direction beyond a couple of quick stabs with his pipe stem, once at the wall of tightly wrapped parcels stacked like bricks, then at the heap of plump, sagging bundles tied up in sheets, their knotted corners twitching in the breeze like ears. "These clean, those dirty. You . . ." The pipe stem swung from one to the other. But when he found Ling a few days after he started with his hands blistered from washing, he clucked over them, dressed the wounds himself. "Why. You. Think. I. Use. My. Feet?" he asked, punctuating each word with a tacky dab of salve.

The other member of their household was a surly young woman who told him to call her Little Sister, though she seemed two or three years his senior. "Or I could call you Little Brother," she offered pertly, seeing his hesitation. He blushed at the slang for penis. "Pleased to meet you," he said, and she smiled thinly. Her hair was parted in the middle, swooping down over her ears in two glossy black wings after the Tanka fashion, but when he asked, *Haam-sui-mui?* she grimaced.

"They call us 'soiled doves' here." Not Tanka then, by her accent, which was the same as Ng's, but at least her profession was familiar.

"Half the laundries are brothels," Ng explained cheerily. "Good business! There's a dozen fellows to every woman in the state." Ling thought of the ship he'd arrived on, packed so tightly with men they shared their bunks —three tiers, eighteen inches between—in shifts. He'd heard one sailor joke, *Add some oil and they'd be sardines.* And yet his abiding memory of his passage was of loneliness, despite (or perhaps because of) the cramped quarters, shunned as he was by many of the other sojourners for being Tanka. In San Francisco, though, surrounded by ghosts, he'd felt the disembarking crowd of Chinese draw tight together, himself among them, Han and Tanka, Cantonese, Hakka and Hoklo all as one.

Little Sister slept past noon, but when she emerged on Ling's first day, Ng set her to teaching him the "eight-pound living"—ironing—which she consented to, grumpily.

"You?" Ling asked, surprised.

"Who you think had your job first?" she snapped, winding her hair into a tight bun and securing it with a chopstick.

"Then why not just get another girl?"

"Girls are expensive. You're cheap!" The mannish jaw that clenched gave her face a sullen cast, unhinged into a wide, wanton grin when she laughed.

"Very funny."

Her face closed, and she went back to lining up the flat-irons on the stove, hefting them one at a time to spit on their shiny surfaces until the saliva skittered on the hot metal and she was ready to apply it to the shirt stretched out across the board before her.

"You see?"

He nodded.

She pressed the iron back and forth firmly, shoving the wrinkles along like waves until they fell off the edge of the board.

"See, lah?"

He nodded again.

She took a dainty sip from the bamboo beaker at her side and blew a fine spray of water onto the cloth before her, the iron sweeping over it with a little sigh of steam.

"I thought we were supposed to clean them," Ling joked, but she ignored him, directed another jet of water at a stubborn crease. He caught a pink flicker of tongue between her teeth.

She moved forcefully but gracefully in her loose clothes, with a slight swinging rhythm that carried from her wrist to her hips and down to her dainty feet. She had rolled back her wide sleeve and he could see the sinews in her forearm—as taut as a man's—rolling under the skin. When he looked up she was staring at him, and the next time she spat with greater vehemence. She made the work look easy, handling the hot irons so nimbly that they seemed to glide over the clothes, her body behind them swaying and fluid.

He would never have imagined that someone could iron lewdly, and yet he couldn't help as he watched her thinking how else she used those hips, those forearm muscles, that mouth.

"Your turn," she said, clanking her iron back on the stove.

The irons were heavier and hotter than he'd thought watching her—he cried out when he grazed his knuckles on a plate, stuffed them in his mouth to suck; she held out a rag for him to bind around his hand—and within minutes he was sweating, the drops dripping down his nose onto the linen, where he erased them with the hot iron, embarrassed to seem weaker than her. She had taken up a needle and thread.

"Too slow!" she scolded, without seeming to look up from her stitching. "Keep moving or the shirt will scorch."

He felt his cheeks burning, heated with the work and the shame of it. Women's work; but surely that should make it beneath him, not beyond him. When he paused to take a gulp of water, she shook her head. "You're supposed to spit." But when he tried the water just dribbled down his chin, or erupted from his mouth, not as a spray but as if he'd thrown up.

Wiping his chin, he thought he caught a smile on her face, but a moment later it was gone, like a wrinkle pressed away, her face smoothly indifferent.

"Here!"

She bit off the thread she was sewing, took the iron from him, and set to work again, drawing in a mouthful of water and expelling it with a little puff.

"How do you *do* that?"

"What? This?" And this time she hit him squarely between the eyes.

"Ai-ya!" He wiped his face on his sleeve. When he was done he found her standing on tiptoes before him, mouth open for him to study her tongue, her lips. He examined

how she pursed them, the lithe curl of her tongue between them, and rehearsed the same motion tentatively inside his own mouth, all the time aware of her warm breath on his face, moist and honeyed like steam off tea.

"Now you." She dropped back onto her heels with a little thud.

He worked on until his arm and back ached, but with concentration, by the time the pile was done he was able to direct a spurt of water in the approximate direction he intended. He looked over at her, but she was lying back among the dry clothes, eyes shut, asleep he thought, though when he flopped down beside her she leapt up at once.

"What are you doing?" she demanded.

"I'm finished."

"Finished?" She pointed to the clothes all around them. "There's no finished."

He unwound the strip of cloth from his hand, clawed from gripping the iron, and massaged his fingers. "But I'm tired." His palm smelled sourly of metal.

In answer she pointed to the ceiling, where among the rough beams he saw a metal hook gleaming dully.

"That's for when you're tired." It took him a moment to understand; he'd been studying the faint spray of freckles across her cheeks. He'd heard of scholars tying their queues to such hooks, so that if they fell asleep over their books they'd be jerked awake. Uncle Ng must have heard the same story.

"Aren't you going to help?" he asked.

"You need the practice. Besides," she said, closing her eyes again, "I earn my keep."

He had thought they were becoming friends, but when Ng returned and asked about his progress she gave a scathing report of him — lazy and weak, a shirker. He felt betrayed, leapt to his own defense. "See," the old man cried. "He's a good boy." And then he struck her across the face. "You teach him better." Ling took a step back, but the girl stood fast, one cheek white, the freckles stark as a constellation, the other flushed red, freckles vanished as if struck off by the blow, until Ng dismissed her. "Go do *your* work."

She entertained each evening in a narrow lean-to adjoining the laundry, a door with a shutter in it — closed if she was engaged, open for viewing if she was available — leading to the alley alongside. Ling slipped out back late that night after Ng had headed off to his regular appointment at a gambling den and approached it, his mouth dry. He meant to apologize for getting her in trouble. The wicket was open, a smoldering square of lamplight in the gloom. After a glance up and down the alley he crept forward and peered in. She was sitting on the side of her bed in a white shift — silk, from the ivory glow of it, and so finely embroidered he knew she must have "borrowed" it from a customer. The walls around her had been papered at some point with old newspapers for insulation, the indecipherable headlines surrounding her. She was still sewing, making alterations and repairs to cleaned clothes during the lull between customers, hunching low over the work — her hair untied, swinging forward like a dark curtain around her face to meet the swoop of her needle — as if to make it out in the greasy light. He could see the ridges of her backbone through the thin cover of the gown, and

then she cried out softly and put her finger to her mouth. In doing so she glanced over at the shutter, her face accusatory as if he'd made her do it, and he fled.

He hadn't known her for a moment. She had painted her face, a dainty red bow in the center of her wide mouth making her lips seem pursed in anger. He wondered, fleetingly, if it resembled his mother's face.

He wandered the streets, trembling, his skin tight and feverish, for what seemed like hours, meeting nothing but male faces until he persuaded himself she couldn't have recognized him. When he returned the moon had risen like a button in the sky and the shutter in her door was closed.

Ling's own "room" was a splintery corner screened by hanging laundry. He'd lain awake, watching the clothes sway back and forth in the breeze until they rocked him to sleep, and even when he woke in the dingy morning light he thought he was still dreaming. From his pallet he could see a pair of bound feet and calves beneath the drifting hems and tails. He watched her—for it *was* her—move around, start a fire, set a kettle to boil (its stiff iron spout reminding him of his erection), and fill one of the laundry tubs until steam billowed from it. He figured she was preparing for the first load of wash until she dropped her shift—he saw it crumple around her clenched feet before she kicked it into the laundry pile—and stepped into the water. It must have been very hot, because she lowered herself slowly—dimpled thighs, flaring buttocks (*Look away*, he thought, but he couldn't), slim back and bony shoulders speckled with moles—until her round face came into view, shiny with sweat and tight with pain. He

held his breath in secret sympathy. She set about herself roughly then, with a washcloth, shoving it first between her legs and over her breasts as if they belonged to someone else, pummeling her body as if — already he couldn't think of it any other way — it were a load of laundry. He wanted to go to her suddenly, to stay her hand, take the cloth from her and use it more gently.

Only after she had dashed scoops of water over herself from a bamboo dipper did she allow herself a moment to lean her head back on the edge of the tub, silken ribbons of lank hair dripping on the boards. The tightness around her eyes and mouth eased, like creases loosened by steam, and he saw how young she was. When she rose from the water, glistening like silver, he found himself looking away at last, even before she wrapped herself in towels, helped herself to a bowl of rice porridge, and retreated to her room.

He lay back and stared at the shivering spangles of light reflected off the slough onto the sheets around him.

He'd seen women naked before, of course. He used to spy on the girls with their men at the brothel, but he never imagined himself with any of them. They'd mothered him when he was small, bossed him when he was older, stirred no desire in him (though he missed being surrounded by women in this bachelor city). He watched them in an effort to picture his mother and father together. The men rarely had a face, though. It was just the back of their heads he saw, their hair light brown or blond or tinged with red, tied off in the short, tarred ponytail of a sailor.

He ladled porridge for himself and ate it staring at the new stack of coins set next to the ashy stems of incense on

the faded red shelf they used as a shrine. Little Sister had left a kettle on the fire, and when the steam began gushing from its spout he set about filling the first of the morning's laundry tubs, grating soap into it. He soaked and scrubbed and rinsed and wrung half a dozen more loads under Uncle Ng's cloudy eyes (the old man had stumbled in shortly after Little Sister had retired and swept the offering of coins into his hand) before his boss loaded him with string-and-brown-paper parcels of clean laundry and beckoned him — "Come, boy" — to follow him out into the city on his delivery route.

Ling had been thrilled at first by the bright bustle of the streets — the hollow thunder of boots on boardwalks, the shivery jangle of harness, or spurs, or coin, and over them all, momentarily seeming to silence every other sound, the steam whistles of the paddle wheelers announcing a fresh surge of disembarking passengers through the streets like a foaming tide. Everything seemed to shine under the high white sun. He craned his neck to squint up at the three-story buildings, marveled at the plate glass, the names of stores and businesses emblazoned in gold as if on the very air, alongside his own gape-mouthed reflection. But most of all he stared at the white ghosts striding or riding by: "So many it's like Yu Lan," as someone had said when they'd arrived in San Francisco, meaning the Ghost Festival, when the gates of hell swung open for hungry spirits to walk abroad. Ever since he'd learned his father's race, Ling had found himself shy around foreigners and yet drawn to them in the streets or in Big Uncle's opium den, staring at them as if he might guess at what his father

looked like, what he might have inherited from him. For years he'd studied his nose in the mirror, wondering if it would grow big as a devil's, but it had remained small and flat, to his relief; it was at best a dubious distinction to be Eurasian. Only in the hinges of his eyes, where the lids folded, he fancied he saw a crease of his heritage. He felt the same fascination now, except at home he'd been invisible, one face in the crowd; here he felt as if he were subject to stares himself, the ghosts meeting his gaze and scowling, until Uncle Ng cuffed him and told him to keep his eyes to himself.

Ling had concentrated on the packages clutched to his chest—Ng had a baying pole slung over his shoulders with more parcels dangling from it—cradling the laundered clothes from the filth of the city, the glossy clods of horse manure, the dust lacing the warm air. If he had owned such linens, he thought, he would never have worn them. But he had trudged back to the laundry more circumspectly at the end of the day, staggering under the pole himself now, malodorous sacks of dirty washing hooked on notches at either end, swaying heavily with each step.

That had been only mildly humiliating, though, compared to the gauntlet of ghost boys he and Ng had had to run. They capered alongside, holding their noses or making monkey noises, pelting the two Chinese with horse apples from the roadway. Most of all they enjoyed darting close to tug on Ling's queue—Ng, he noticed too late, had tucked his in his collar—sometimes so hard that Ling found himself toppling. *A Yankee yank,* they called it, never mind their Irish accents. It was as if they were

mocking his foolish notions of kinship. He wanted to fight back—Ng had a laundry bat tucked in his belt like a truncheon—or at least shout back, but Ng hissed at him to be quiet, to keep his head down and put the end of his queue in his pocket, and he had to content himself with swinging his carry pole in wary circles to ward them off.

"Don't let them provoke you," Ng advised, waving a hand before his face. "They're only flies."

Which makes us dung, Ling thought, getting a whiff of his burden.

4.

And so this was his life. Washing in the mornings, deliveries every afternoon while the clothes dried, ironing at night. And always, always thinking of Little Sister, especially evenings when Ng set him to watch the shop. He'd shown him the cleaver he kept under the counter in case of trouble, a confidence that had made Ling swell with importance, though Little Sister herself had only sneered. "You in charge? Wa!" She fingered the chopstick holding up her hair. "I can look out for myself." Many of her clients saw so few women that they were shy and mannerly with her. Besides, she reminded him, she peddled opium in addition to her other services, which settled the more boisterous among them, though he had seen her in her bath scrubbing at bruises as if they were stains. Still, Ng's behest made Ling feel protective of her, obliged him to listen to the noises from her crib—fleshy smacks, low chuckles, and a panting giggle that must have been hers —hefting the cleaver, as if hoping for a scream, an excuse

to burst in. He never heard her laugh like that during the day, and he couldn't help but imagine those muffled, complicit sniggers directed at him. He pressed his hands to his ears, the blade of the cleaver cool at his temple. Every night of his childhood he'd nodded off to the slap of skin, indistinguishable from the lap of water against the hull of the flower boat, but he couldn't sleep now until her work was done and she slipped out of her room to urinate softly — "So-*dah!*" — into the latest tub of stained clothes they were soaking (an idle defiance, since all their laundry water came from the slough that served as sewer for half the town).

The glimpse of her bathing, repeated most mornings, made him feel he knew something of her, something secret — he still watched, though he looked away whenever she gave Ng her earnings, handing them over brusquely as if *she* were paying for something — and it made him tender toward her, even as she continued to be surly with him, surlier, if anything, in response to his efforts at friendship. Ng didn't allow her out — not safe for females on the streets, he claimed — and Ling figured she envied him his freedom. Not that she could have gone far on her bound feet. He tried to bring her small gifts, mooncakes or the sour plums she favored, and citrus, which he plucked from the trees. Oranges she placed on the little kitchen shrine, but lemons she especially prized (only later did he grasp that she used slices of them as a contraceptive; he could never eat lemon chicken again). In the evening, bent into the steam of a mutton broth, their faces flushed, or gnawing on fried chicken feet, he told her stories of the operas he saw and dreamed of

taking her to, until she roused herself reluctantly and went in to her work.

He ironed at night, when it was cooler — she'd deemed him tolerably skilled after a few days, and he'd straightened with pride until he realized there'd be no more call for her instruction — working until the ache in his shoulders seeped into his soles. But when he still couldn't sleep he sat up sometimes trying to fashion a kite by candlelight from the brown paper they wrapped the clean laundry in. It tore too easily, or his hands, so accustomed now to the heavy iron, were too clumsy for the delicate work. But then he hit on the idea of fitting a light frame inside an unclaimed shirt, starched for stiffness.

Little Sister watched him launch it one morning from the plank jetty behind the laundry, snorting at his efforts. But when he finally got it aloft, the breeze off the slough catching it, he was pleased to see her head tilt up to the light, her long pale neck exposed.

"Ah, the Chinese flag," she mocked, but when he teased the line to make the kite dip, a perilous maneuver, and it almost plunged to the water, he heard her cry out. He arrested the swoop with a sharp tug and was rewarded by her relieved laugh.

He waited until it climbed high enough for the wind to fill it again, the kite pulling on the line like a fish.

"Here," he called, and held out the reel of thread to her.

She came forward — hesitantly, he saw from the corner of his eye. They both watched the kite, the shirt dancing as if a ghost possessed it, arms streaming in the wind, and he felt her hand groping for his, taking the reel.

He'd run a stick through the hole in the center of the bobbin and she let the spool spin free, the wind taking the kite higher and higher. It shone so brightly in the sunlight he had to squint to follow it. Ling wondered if Uncle Ng, wherever he was in the city streets, staggering back from a night of gaming, might see it and guess where it came from. He imagined himself wearing the shirt, gazing down on the city from above. Further along the bank, a distant figure, no more than a shimmering silhouette against the dazzle of the water, practiced tai chi, oblivious.

And then she gave a little sigh and Ling saw that the thread had run out and snapped, the loose end swirling up into the air like a thin skein of incense. Far above, the shirt, carried away on the breeze, dwindled, its empty arms flailing against the sky.

"I'm sorry," she said, but when he tore his eyes from the kite and looked at her she was trembling with excitement, her face alight. "Where will it fly?" she breathed, but all he could think was that it would eventually flutter into the dirt.

He lingered, reluctant to draw the morning's water and head back into the dank fug of the laundry.

"Why do you stay?" he asked abruptly.

She shrugged. "Even if I could run, even if he didn't send a hatchet man after me? All Chinese girls on Gold Mountain are whores. There's nowhere to go." She glanced at him. He was watching the turbid water lick the pilings of the pier. "The question is why *you* stay."

"I'm not," he assured her. "I'm going to find gold. As soon as I've made my stake."

She made a face.

"What?"

"Nothing. Just be sure you do."

"I will!"

"Good!"

She was still gazing intently after the kite, a hand shielding her eyes from the glare off the slough, and he stayed with her, staring, even though he could no longer pick it out against the sky.

When he answered her hungry questions about the world beyond the laundry, he told her of the city as if it were a great adventure, but in reality the streets alternately scared and enraged him. Uncle Ng had been only too glad, he noticed, to let him take over the delivery route, sending him out by himself within a few days. "You have good English," Ng noted, which was true at least relatively: Ling was always adding to his modest (if also profane) vocabulary picked up around the flower boat's customers, whereas Uncle Ng's English was so poor that he still kept a sign on the counter with different-sized circles carved into it (half cent, cent, three cents, half dime, dime, quarter, half dollar), which he pointed to with the stem of his pipe to tell his customers how much they owed him. "Better you go," the old man concluded. Ling wasn't so sure; his English seemed good to him only for understanding the epithets hurled at him by insolent boys — *Chink, heathen, Celestial, slant-eyed son of a bitch, pigtailed bastard*. At least he couldn't understand the barks of the stray dogs that chased him down the streets, snapping at his queue or the sacks of laundry hanging from his pole.

It bothered him too that he must step down off the boardwalk and into the muddy street whenever he saw a ghost coming toward him. The same street that they spat tobacco in, that their horses and mules pissed and shat in. His "thousand-layer" shoes grew spongy and clotted. He dodged buggy drivers' whips, not knowing if their cries of "Go on!" were meant for him or their animals. He wanted to explain that he was carrying ghost laundry, he was trying to keep it clean for them. He wanted to say that his father was a ghost. But he held his tongue — at least until he got back to the laundry.

"More dirt mountain than gold mountain," he grumbled one night as he sorted the rancid washing into piles. He knew he needed the job, at least until he had saved the price of a pick and a pan, but that might take months on his paltry wage, and his patience was wearing thin. The closest he'd come to the diggings so far was the occasional miner who paid for his laundry with a pinch of dust.

"What you think prospecting is?" Ng chuckled as he ironed. He didn't trust anyone else with the finest linens and lace. "Ankle-deep in a cold stream, bent over like a paddy farmer, washing more dirt. At least *we* use warm water!" He had won at "heaven-and-nine" the night before and was still in an expansive mood.

Ng had "seen the elephant," as the old-timers liked to say, meaning he'd seen it all, everything the mother lode had to offer. He'd been an original forty-niner, made a small fortune at placer mining near Youbet and (appropriately enough) lost it at fan-tan, made another and learned his lesson only so far as to lose it at poker (the whites had barred his entry to the saloon at first, "But once I had

some gold about me they became more sociable"). By then the easy pickings were played out and the Chinese were being driven out, pushed off claims at gunpoint or by ruinous foreign miner taxes, likewise often collected at gunpoint. Ng had seen one dead Chinaman shot in the back, "the end of his queue dipped in blood like a brush in ink." He frowned at the recollection, his middle eye beady with rage. Others, Ling had heard, had been lynched with their own queues.

"If I were you I wouldn't be in such a hurry," the old man counseled, setting his iron down on the stovetop so hard that sparks flew, to which Ling wanted to cry, *Don't you know they call it a Gold* Rush? Already he felt himself falling behind the ghosts.

He contented himself with pointing out sulkily, "You found gold."

"Gold found him, more like," Little Sister chimed in. She was folding the ironed clothes with deft little flicks while Ling parceled and bound them with twine, the bundles still warm from the iron, like packets of sticky rice.

Ng raised his hand halfheartedly. "Shut it, fox spirit!"

"How?" Ling pressed.

In '54 or '55, Ng explained, licking his fingertip and smoothing the lone hair from his mole across his brow, he'd been playing out a hand of poker with a stocky little Frenchman—a Keskadee, in the parlance of the camps. The two of them were down to their last few cents when the Frenchman, named Philippe but known universally around town as the Celebrated Frog, had ceremoniously shrugged the shirt from his back and thrown it on the

table. "Made en Paree," he'd declared, slipping his suspenders back over his union suit with a prideful snap. The shirt was filthy and sour-smelling, ruffles yellow as wilted lettuce, but it was worth more than Uncle Ng had left to his name, and he looked at his hand—two pair, kings over threes—and had an inspiration. "Call," he said, and when the Frog sneered, "*Avec quoi?*" Ng told him, "You bet shirt. I bet I wash it if I lose. Deal?" And the Frog, who was celebrated for, among other things, sending his shirts to San Francisco in flush times, from where they were shipped to Hawaii or even Hong Kong to be laundered, at a price of ten dollars apiece, hoisted up his shoulders in assent.

"Ten dollars?" Ling cried in disbelief.

"Yes! Back then there weren't even enough women in the state to take in washing."

"Or anything else," Little Sister scoffed.

"Hong Kong," Ng sighed, laying his iron down more gently this time, seemingly transfixed by the oily curls of hot air swimming over the stove. "How I used to envy that laundry in my homesickness."

"But what about the game?"

"Oh." Ng blinked. "Lost."

Afterward he understood that the Frog had only accepted the bet because he was sure he would win, as he duly did with a full house, yet the loss had been the making of Ng. It had cleaned him out, but Philippe had so enjoyed strutting around camp in his pressed and gleaming shirt and telling the story of the bet that Uncle Ng's services were soon in high demand. He'd set up shop using a couple of long toms, or sluice boxes: "And that's how I got my start."

"But you never found gold again!"

"I did so! All those miners, see here, they'd not washed for months—years, some of them. What did they care with no women for fifty miles? The stink on them." He wrinkled his nose. "But when I drained that dirty water, why, there was flake caught in the riffles of the sluice like carp in a paddy field, gold dust from out the cuffs and pockets and seams of all those reeking clothes! How do you think I bought my own business? I gathered up all those pinches and drifts of color until those boys were *picked clean*!" He delivered the pun in English with a toothy grimace, and sat back teasing the hair from his mole as if to confirm his luck. But he must have seen the disappointment in Ling's face.

"Gold is gold, however you make it," he said, holding up a coin and clenching it between his teeth as if it were a clinker he'd just plucked from a pan. "Man swills it out of the mud, he gets dirty, gives you some to wash his clothes."

"And then you gamble it on 'white pigeon ticket,'" Little Sister added tartly.

"But he makes so much *more* money if he finds gold," Ling insisted, eyes on the coin. He had caught his first glimpse of gold by then, flashing from the corner of a sailor's grin on the voyage out like a hook in a fish's lip. *So that was gold,* he'd thought as the ship plowed through the waves: a sharp tug in the flesh, hauling you toward land. But this was the first gold coin he'd seen, and he felt a pang of lust. Ng was turning it in his puckered fingers, balancing the glint between his thumb and forefinger. They called it a yellow eagle in Chinese, and Ling could

see the wings of the embossed bird beating gently as the light slid back and forth.

Then Ng's hand dropped, his long sleeve covering it. "One in ten finds gold, all ten get dirty."

Ling nodded, but he felt cheated somehow.

And yet he liked that phrase *See the elephant*. Felt an affinity for the beast.

His mother had left him nothing excepting a child's cap. He'd seen children, children rich with parents, wearing them at New Year's, caps sewn with eyes and ears, teeth and tongues, to look like tigers or lions, dragons, or pigs or rabbits.

"You had one of those," Aunty Bao had told him once. "Only thing you came with. Shape of an elephant."

"What happened to it?" he asked.

"What?" She'd already forgotten him. "Pah! Who knows?"

He might have felt robbed of his birthright, but in fact he felt buoyed up. It didn't matter that it was gone, that he'd never seen it. He already knew he had nothing. But that his mother had given him something once, imagined him wearing it, felt like a gift (it never occurred to him that it might have come from his father). He didn't know if she'd bought it or received it as an offering, but either way, he resolved, the elephant must have meant something to her, not merely to ward off demons or bring luck, as all the caps were supposed to, but because *elephant* sounded the same as *sign,* or *things to come,* even if he couldn't guess what.

It was just an expression, of course, but he couldn't help picturing an actual elephant—he'd seen a

daguerreotype of one in a newspaper—at the end of the trail, its soft leathery bulk rising before him like a cliff. It seemed at once more wondrous and more tangible than gold. And what would it feel like to ride one?

He pictured the great beast approaching, kneeling heavily for him to mount, and carrying him, swaying, away, stepping over mountain ranges and even the ocean, which it drained with its trunk to wade while ships steamed around its knees, their funnels just clearing its drooping belly. It carried him home, of course, plucking him from its back with its trunk and depositing him gently on the ground, then daintily backing out of the light to reveal his old home and family—Big Uncle, even Aunty Bao, marveling at his triumphant return—from its vast shadow.

"What are you smiling about?" Little Sister asked him, and when he told her she smirked lewdly, drew his queue forward over his shoulder, smoothed it down his front, batting it gently so it swung before him. "Oh, I've seen my share of elephants," she breathed.

"Have you no shame?" he snapped, and she told him coldly, "'Gold is gold.' You'd know if you ever made any."

I have money! he wanted to call after her when she turned away.

He knew what she cost—*two bit touchee, four bit fuckee,* she crooned into the night—less than a clean shirt. "Less than a clean pair of drawers," as she put it herself. "Not that many of them *have* a clean pair of drawers" (or any drawers at all, as Ling knew, most considering their long shirttails sufficient underclothes).

He traced the circles carved into the counter with his fingertip.

Since his first payday, he had had coins of that size jangling in his pocket, and when he held them in his hand, growing warm from his flesh, they seemed filled with possibility.

That evening he approached her door again, the glimmering window in it. But as he did so he felt a hand on his shoulder.

"'Cuse me, John. You comin' or goin'?"

Ling stared at the hand—a prospector's, by the dark sickles of dirt under the nails. He didn't dare speak, just stumbled back as the other brushed past him and pressed his face to the hatch.

"Evenin', missy. You dancin'?"

Ling heard the bolt drag back, and the door swung wide, light opening like a fan into the alley. The fellow smoothed the tips of his mustache with thumb and forefinger, then stepped inside, and the fan folded shut. A moment later the shutter snapped closed and the alley was completely dark, but even in the blackness Ling could see the afterimage of the ghost's face, pale above the brambles of his beard, glowing in the dusk.

He stalked the streets past other cribs, some with girls beckoning listlessly from their windows, but he shied away, veering into the street out of their faint light.

It was very late when he finally returned. Her lamp out, the stove cold, ash piled softly in the grate. Soon it would be time to scrape it out, run water through it to make lye. But first he slept . . . and dreamt of the elephant. In the streets, forced off the boardwalk, he was obliged to dodge not only piles of horseshit but the animals themselves, the clods of mud thrown up by their hooves and the flick of

their reeking, flailing tails. Once one had farted in front of him so loudly that Ling reared back and lost his hat, which looked for all the world as if it had been blown off by the horse. But an elephant might trample such horses, and the whites, laughing or indifferent, who spurred them past him on the street. An elephant, he figured, might just shit on *them*, or blast their hats from their heads with its trunk if they tried to jostle him aside.

It came to him now, sitting beside Crocker all these years later, that a locomotive was the nearest he'd come to an elephant. The first time he'd seen one it had spooked horses, thrown a man sprawling. He'd been making deliveries. Men were running and then he was running—*from them* for a panicked instant, then, as they drew level and passed him, *with them,* parcels jumping wildly at the end of his carry pole. He'd thought it was a fire at first; there was a pillar of smoke over the rooftops. He wasn't the only one; others were coming with buckets slopping. Then he heard the shrill of steam and he knew, even before he rounded the corner.

Ng had described an engine to him once—"a great hot iron come to smooth the earth"—but Ng had been doing laundry too long; an iron horse on an iron road wasn't iron*ing* (even if the engine with its pilot did resemble a flatiron). To Ling the engine seemed like a live thing, scaled with soot, snorting and shuddering and shivering the ground. When it lurched into motion, men fell back. The great brass bell yawned so wide he could see the tongue dangling in its throat, like a cry of "Gold!" Describing it later to Little Sister ("You're making it up."

"No, no!" he swore), he said it was like a New Year's parade—the crowds, the raucous clanging racket, and at the heart of it the train, bedecked in red-white-and-blue rosettes and crepe streamers, like a dragon, its fiery face and lantern eyes and long, trailing body. He'd actually glanced down to see if there were feet beneath it, arms supporting it.

And now I'm riding in one, he thought, watching the trail of cindery smoke widening in their wake like a rent in the very sky. How he wished she could see him.

All those weeks he had assumed that she didn't know he was there behind the laundry line while she bathed, but the morning after he snapped at her she dropped her soap and, when she bent to look for it, their eyes met beneath the sodden edge of the drying clothes.

"Did I wake you?" she asked matter-of-factly.

He nodded dumbly.

"Don't look so worried. *No money lookee.* But since you're up, you might help."

He parted the sheets between them, their wet corners licking at his calves, and ducked under the line, remaining stooped to disguise his erection. A fresh kettle boiled on the stove, filling the air with steam like incense in a temple. She was holding a cloth behind her back and he took it and began, gingerly, to wash her. "Harder," she instructed, and when he hesitated, she begged him, giggling, "Harder, harder," and he rubbed her firmly, angry at the mockery, until her flesh turned fiery beneath the cloth.

"Thank you," she said simply when he was done. She had been sitting up, her knees drawn to her chest and her

arms encircling them. Now she lay back slowly, her neck on the edge of the tub, her eyes closed. He watched the soap scum drift across the water like clouds until the surface was still and clear. Her breasts seemed to float just beneath, the water lapping her throat gently with each breath.

"I don't mind it so much, if I can have a bath every day." She opened an eye, pinched her arm, her cheek. "See, good as new."

Still, she must have sensed his pity. He was thinking of the frayed shirts, the torn and mended pieces he washed and ironed.

With a splash she stood up, dripping so that he fell back. She let him look for a moment, her skin flushed and untouchable, then she wrapped herself tightly in a towel. "It's only work, after all. Everyone works. I make sheets dirty, you wash them." She was hardened, he decided— such an odd contrast to her smooth, soft flesh. "At least I don't do laundry now. All I wash is myself."

Perhaps he was thinking of her jibes, or maybe her ghost lovers—the irony was that because of her cleanliness, she had more custom than the typical tart, who might bathe but once a week—but that afternoon, when he was harassed by the local urchins, he lost his composure, lashed out. They'd been waiting for him earlier than usual, and when they'd pulled his hair he'd stumbled, gone down on one knee in a runnel of horse piss, still warm. He'd been even more enraged at the thought that the clean laundry might have been dragged through the mud, and when they'd come after him again, he'd swung his pole sharply. He'd only meant to bowl one of them over with

the soft weight of a laundry sack, perhaps spill a cap into the dirt, but he misjudged and cracked a rawboned boy about the ear. The amusement of his fellows had faded quickly when the lad took his hand away to show them the blood. He wiped it off on his shirt, and Ling had wanted to tell him *Don't!* They'd set on him in earnest then, the lot of them piling on so that Ling was knocked down, his face clawed and cut, his queue yanked and stamped into the mud, his packages strewn about. They looped his queue around his neck twice, like a noose, and pulled him to his feet, led him like a dog up and down the street. When he broke away they tripped him again, set about him with their boots this time, until he could only curl up, clutching the dirt as if to burrow into it. They drew a pair of drawers over his head like a bag, sat on him, stuffed the foul thing into his mouth—"Lick it clean!"—until he gagged. Finally, pulling him to his feet, they drew his queue up between his legs to hobble him, proclaiming to the laughter of the gathering crowd their intent to "send him home with his tail atween his legs." They only lost their nerve at the edge of Chinatown, releasing him but flinging his pole and laundry after for good measure.

He'd been spitting with rage, had run into the laundry for the cleaver when Little Sister put a hand on his arm. He made to pull away, inhaled a wince. "Ribs," she pronounced, stilling him with a touch. He held his ragged breath while her fingers traced his sides. "Just cracked, I think." She pulled him over to a stool and filled a basin and cleaned his face as best she could while he turned it from her (and yet followed her shivering reflection in the basin water). Only when she'd sewn up the gash over his

eyebrow did he steal a direct look at her: the purse of her lips as she tugged the thread through his flesh the same as when she repaired any other ripped item, except this time when she bit the thread, she leaned in close to his brow and he felt the brush of her lips, or perhaps her teeth, before the thread snapped.

She told him about the time that ghost women had burst into the laundry, complaining about the prices, that they were too low ("Too high?" Ling had corrected her automatically. "No, too low for them to compete!"), and put Ng's queue in the mangle. "Made him kowtow! To women!" She shook her head, smiling. "He'd be there still, thinking about gnawing it off, if I hadn't freed him. He's lucky they didn't throw him in the slough to drown. Those boys are the sons of those women, some of them."

She handled his queue gently as she told him the story, rinsing it with warm water—"A wash always helps," she crooned—then unplaiting it so that the hair slipped through her fingers and covered her hands, and then replaiting it until it felt as strong and heavy as rope. And by then he was still.

He turned slowly, feeling his queue run through her hands. She was still close, her head bent low, and he leaned in slowly to kiss her. But she drew back.

He stared at her, and then very deliberately tipped over the basin, so that she cried out.

He watched the water seep into the boards.

"I have money," he said, and he stumbled to his pallet, rummaged for the change knotted in a rag, thrust the coins under her nose. "See!"

She pushed his hand away, and when he shoved it back in her face, she knocked it aside so roughly that the coins scattered, one of them rolling across the floor until it tumbled through a crack in the floorboards to fall into the slough.

They both stilled as if listening for the splash.

Ling knew that some Chinese refused to sleep with whores who slept with ghosts. "I'm not like those others," he told her softly, and would have told her of his parentage, except she shook him off.

"You think they won't have *me*? I won't have *them,* any of you." Her eyes flashed.

He pressed a hand to his side, suddenly winded. "But why?"

"It's like they say. *Chinamen*"—she snarled the word learned from her customers—"only brought their womenfolk here so someone could be lower than them. So they'd have someone to look down on. You left us the only job you couldn't do for the ghosts."

"But how can you hate your own people?" *How can you hate me?* he meant. And yet, he calculated, would she sleep with him if she knew he was half white? Would half be enough?

"How? I tell you how! You know who sold me to Ng?" She paused to catch her breath. "My father! You know why? So he could send a brother to Gold Mountain to make the family fortune." She nodded heavily. "That's right. Chinamen love gold more than girls. The same brother who knocked on my door once. Yes! He didn't recognize me until he was in the room." She laughed sourly. "Probably wasn't looking at my face! And you

know what he does now? He's a laundryman, just like you. So my father, you see, sells me as a whore for my brother to come to Gold Mountain to do women's work." She spat, a frothing gob of spittle that seemed to sizzle on the floorboard between Ling's feet. "So no, I don't sleep with laundry boys. You stink of other men's sweat. Your fingers are wrinkled like old women's hands. I won't have you touching me. At least you don't see *them* selling their women to *you*. But that's Chinamen for you! You all want wives, lovers, but none of you want daughters. Daughters are bad luck, daughters are shameful, dirty, to be drowned like wash in a tub." She was sobbing now. "Well, this is what you deserve, the lot of you. You send all your girls away, one day you find there's no women for you. Just men, men, men, as far as the eye can see."

He thought of her teaching him once to starch collars, how to make the creases sharp. "This one," she had said, holding up a band with the triangular wings standing stiff and proud, "this is my favorite. They call it 'patricide.' The story goes a son came home one time wearing this kind of collar and when his father embraced him the wings cut the old man's throat!" She had grinned wickedly. It was just a story, Ling knew, but she told it with such relish he couldn't help imagine blood on the pointed tips of the collar.

"I'll show you," Ling tried now. "I'll be rich."

"Not if you spend your savings on me!"

For a moment the only sound between them was the drip of laundry.

"I will be," he muttered, fingering his stitches warily.

"And what will you do?" She sniffed, humoring him. "When you're rich?"

"Come back for you!"

"Ha!" But he could see she was touched, as if he'd stroked some bruise of hers.

"What else?"

"Why, go home. Of course."

"Of course!" She laughed rancorously. "You think *I* can ever go home? Chinamen are sojourners here. Even if you die, someone from your clan or company will send your bones home. I *live* here now, and I'll die here, and no one will bother with my bones. I'm a Melican now. Why shouldn't I fuck them?" She bared her teeth in a smile. "Don't look so sad. I'll get rich too! See if I don't. You know where gold comes from, yes?"

He began to explain, but she shook her head and thrust a hand into her pants. "Here's my mine, my rich seam. What do the Melicans call it? The *mother* lode? Women are like dirt in China, but not here. Here we're rare as gold. And men are dirt."

He took a step toward her, but she pulled away, held up a finger before him. "Not for you, laundryman! Go back to your washee-washee, your women's work!"

5.

Crocker's place was on his delivery route, but he'd never seen him, only his huge shirts billowing like sails from the line outside Ng's (the best linen hung on the line, the lesser Ling spread on the roof, weighed down with stones), leaping and snapping as if they'd haul the whole shack out onto Sutter Lake. Once Ling had pulled one of those shirts over his head—it hung down to his calves, the cuffs

flapping like wings beyond his fingertips—to make Little Sister laugh. "I'll take it for a tent when I go prospecting!" She shook her head, but he could see she was amused, and as he stared at her she took the challenge, shimmying into a petticoat and shirtwaist. They stood side by side, looking at each other in the cheap mirror Uncle Ng had bought and carefully positioned for good feng shui. "We look like proper Americans," he laughed, but she shook her head, abruptly deflated. "We look like mourners." She was right. Ling imagined himself for an instant at his mother's funeral—not that he'd attended it—the too-big shirt evoking the mourning clothes of a child. Little Sister shrugged her borrowed clothes off quickly, and he pulled Crocker's shirt over his head with a shudder.

And then a few days after his beating, still bruised, he was delivering a bundle of fresh laundry and the big man himself met him on the back porch in his undershirt— "About time!"—yanking the top shirt from the brown paper parcel and shaking it out with a crack and a puff of starch. Ling had imagined a fearsome giant from those prodigious garments, a man who could pull up trees with his bare hands and flatten mountains with a stamp, but here was Crocker struggling into his shirt, circling like a dog after its own tail, suspenders flapping around his knees, until Ling caught the sleeve and held it for the big man to punch his arm through.

"Obliged," Crocker grunted, shrugging his suspenders on as if he were shouldering a pack and hunting in his pockets for a tip. He rummaged for loose change like a man scratching his balls, but all he could come up with was a single gold dollar. The big man considered the

coin, not much larger than the nail on his thumb, then he snorted and flipped it to Ling, who caught it with a clap of his hands. He'd bowed low to the ground, unable to believe his luck, figuring to run before Crocker bethought himself, when he heard an exasperated sigh. Crocker was fumbling with the collar, trying to pinch it together at his throat, but the small stud kept squirting from his thick fingers. "You there!" He'd said no more, just raised his chin and let his arms fall to his side. Crocker's cheeks and upper lip were clean-shaven, but he wore a thick beard, fanned below his jaw like a cravat. Ling would remember the rasp of it on the back of his hands as he worked, and the way the man's Adam's apple had throbbed beneath the tight linen. When he was done, Crocker rolled his vast head around on his neck, collar creaking, and nodded. Silently he proffered his wrists for Ling to attach cuffs and stuck out his chest for his shirt-front, stiff and gleaming as armor. "Obliged," he said again at last, and perhaps because he'd already tipped Ling once, or perhaps because Charles Crocker was not a man who liked to be obliged to a Chinaman, he offered him a job there on the spot as live-in laundryman and manservant. "At least I'll get my consarned shirts washed faster."

It was a gruff, almost begrudging offer, but to Ling it was as if he'd struck gold.

Uncle Ng was ironing when Ling told him of Crocker's proposal. "Bird matters," the old head opined, waving them away. But he paused for a long moment, the smell of hot cotton, with its sweet trace of burnt sweat, rising

around them, until Ling thought the shirt must be scorched.

"I have been meaning to speak to you," Ng said at last, as if to the shirt he was smoothing again. "You know I have no son. I would adopt you."

"I have a father," Ling began.

"The man who sold you to me?" Ng sipped, spat. "Or the one who sold you to him? Who sells a son? A daughter maybe, not a son."

"I don't believe you," Ling cried. Big Uncle had favored him, he was sure.

Ng shook his head without lifting his eyes from his work.

"The girl came of age to work. You cost less than another girl. Also, you spoke Melican."

"It's not true!" But he knew it was; he could already feel the tears rearing in his eyes, clamped his jaw to stanch them.

"If you were *my* son," Ng went on, working the iron in circles now as if polishing the cloth, "you would inherit the business when I die."

And tend to your spirit, Ling thought dismally.

Ng was folding the shirt now into a neat square of cloth with just his fingertips, the movements suddenly nimble after the clenched effort of the ironing. He pulled another shirt from the pile and set to it with a fresh iron. Over his bowed head, among the rough beams, Ling saw the metal hook gleaming dully.

"But . . . I mean to be rich."

The old man bent once more to his ironing, the board groaning under the pressure.

"The girl," Ng added presently. "You would own her too, of course."

Ling was wrapping his few clothes tightly into his bedroll. Now he paused.

"Did she know about me?"

Ng shrugged. "She's a whore, not a fool."

Both of them sold, Ling thought. But her as a prostitute, him as a son. He secured the roll with twine, slung it on his back.

"I don't want," he managed at last, "to own her."

"Love, is it?" Ng spat on the shirt before him, as if the issue were no more than a particularly obstinate crease.

"You don't believe in it."

"Of course I do. Men love gold, don't they? But gold can't love them back. Only a damned asshole thinks that."

They stared at each other then, the old man's knuckles whitening around the handle of his iron.

"Don't try to stop me," Ling warned. "I'll drown you in your own dirty water."

"I never told you," Ng said at last, setting the iron down and lighting his pipe from the stove with a spill of paper. "That Frenchman, the Frog, the one with the shirt? He was my friend before. His claim was next to mine. Neither of us had any luck. Not in the creek, not in town. The Melicans called him foreigner too, made fun of his English. Same as me. Once when I caught two fish I gave one to him. Another time we shared a rabbit he trapped. We both enjoyed frogs' legs. No gold, maybe, but plenty frogs in that creek." He took a long draw on his pipe, exhaled smoke. "I called him friend. He called me brother. *Fraternité*, he taught me this. And he was the one said they

should let me in the saloon, join the game. *Egalité,* that was another of his words. But after, when he beat me, made a fool of me, strutting around in his clean white shirt, calling me *Madame,* washerwoman, he was one of *them.* You understand?" Ng looked up at last, all three of his eyes narrowing. "I might as well have washed *him,* I made him so white."

"So?"

"So." Ng unclamped his teeth from his pipe, blew the fine hair from his mole aside. "You'll be back."

Ling had flung out the door. He stood panting in the street for a long moment, then turned on his heel, marched to her lean-to, and knocked heavily.

"Crocker?" she asked when he told her breathlessly about the new job. She stretched her arms wide. He nodded. "Seen your elephant, I reckon."

In answer, he put the gold piece Crocker had given him in her hand.

For a moment they both stared at it on her palm — a woman in profile, as if looking away — and then Little Sister's hand closed over it like something naked to be covered. With her other, she pulled him into her crib. He heard the shutter snap closed behind him.

She smelled of lye and lemon, so clean he hesitated to touch her. When he did reach for her, he couldn't help but examine her for marks, as if he might have smudged her. He started with her blemishes, the puckered spots on her arm where she had burnt herself with the iron. He kissed them. He had those scars; she touched him back. Her hands were soft, except for the pad of her index finger, swollen purple from the pinpricks of mending. She winced

slightly when she closed her hand around him. *I'll buy you a thimble,* he vowed, and she lowered her head, her hair lapping across his thighs.

Afterward they were silent, lying side by side, staring at the dark ceiling. When he tried to pull her close, she seemed limp and heavy in his arms, as if waterlogged. He thought of his coin again, where it had been — in whose hands, whose pockets and purses, before it came into his, and into whose it would now pass. It made him feel flimsy, insubstantial, this small gold piece. It made him want more, so many that no one coin could ever be so important to him again. And he wondered if he'd spent it wisely (certainly he'd spent it quickly, he reflected with chagrin). He had thought he'd been courting her, but perhaps it was really the coin he'd courted.

Courted? A nice word for it.

He pictured the coins of his home, the holes at their center so that they could be threaded on a braid for safekeeping. American coins had no such hole and they seemed always to be slipping away.

He wished she'd give it back, and when she didn't, when she rose and rinsed and dressed and still didn't give it back, he hated her a little. He could ask for it, but he was afraid of being refused. *She wasn't worth it,* he thought abruptly, though even now he knew he'd give her another coin when he earned one, and another after that, though he'd never save them long enough to buy her outright.

And she knew it too, he could tell. Suddenly he could feel the anger emanating from her, shimmering like heat from an iron. It was there in the stiffness of her movements as she brushed the tangles from her hair, the

determination with which she avoided looking at him or talking to him, except to say, "Time's up." She wound her hair into a tight knot, jabbed a chopstick through it. He'd roused himself then, leapt from the bed really, and pulled on his clothes so roughly that he'd torn the stitches under the arm of his shirt. They'd both stopped at that sound of tearing, for just a moment. He might have asked her to mend it, she might have said yes, but then it was too late.

"Don't look at me like that," she told him at the door.

"Like what?"

"Like I cheat you. Like I got cards up my cunt, a finger on the scale. Can't I make money too?"

"You wanted me to go," he reminded her softly.

She was shutting the door on him. "I want you to go now."

"I'll be back," he whispered through the gap.

"I'll be here," she replied bitterly.

In the morning, he thought in the dark alley, she'd wash him off, and he was glad he wouldn't be there to watch.

6.

The Crocker household consisted of Crocker himself, Mrs. Crocker—a pale, grave presence—and their three children, but on that first day Ling was greeted at the back door by the maid-of-all-work, a florid Irish girl called Bridey. She had been waiting for him on the back porch, arms crossed stoutly over her bosom like a barred gate. Ling had mistaken her for the lady of the house at first, bowed and called her Madame Crocker, and she'd snorted, though a hand had loosened from the knot across her

chest, floating up to pat her hair coquettishly. She wasn't
flirting with him so much as admiring herself in the mirror
of his error, as if he were no more than a puddle or a
window she'd caught sight of herself in.

"Well," she offered waspishly, "I see they won't be need-
ing me no more. Nor the puss to catch the mice, so!"

Bridey was the girl he was replacing, a trade, she gave
him to understand, that was greatly, pitiably, to the
Crockers' disadvantage (her contempt for Ling was
merely the long shadow of her starchy resentment against
her employers). Bridey shared the bristling umbrage of
many Irish girls toward the Chinese who were displacing
them from work, but in her case the general animus was
tempered by her own good fortune. She was to be married
and had given her notice, hence a place had opened. So
fluffed up was she with her nuptial prospects that Ling at
first took "Bridey" to be her title and not her name. She
looked down on him from this lofty matrimonial height
but also took a kind of glee in lumbering the Crockers
with him, though — as Ling would come to know — they
were just as delighted to see the back of her, such were the
liberties she'd taken: refusing to do laundry "as scullion
work" and entertaining her "cousin"-cum-beau, Sean, a
beanpole of a boy seemingly always on the verge of
toppling, in the kitchen and at the Crockers' expense.
"I'm not no nagur, nor no Chink neither, to take orders,"
the girl had declared roundly to Sean on one of his visits
while she was teaching Ling to cook (he took to it swiftly,
since most everything in Bridey's economy, from eggs to
cabbage to potatoes to meat, was to be boiled like so
much laundry, and anything else fried with fatback). She

huffed on a silver spoon she was polishing, rubbed it on her sleeve, and studied her reflection in it. "I'm as white as 'em, ain't I?"

Bridey had shown Ling where to find the buckets and brushes and brooms. Shown him where to dispose of the chamberpots and how to make the beds so tight that a coin would bounce on them (she caught the coin), and even how to do the laundry, despite his assurances that he knew. She'd begun to show him how to iron—pummeling rather than smoothing the linen as if into submission—until he'd taken over impatiently and she'd nodded. "Well, I never. They do say your sort pick up a thing right quick." Though to his surprise, she'd later set a newspaper on the ironing board and given it a brisk pressing. It was to become one of his preferred tasks (once he remembered not to spit on it), poring over the headlines as he ironed in an effort to parse out new English words before carrying the paper in to breakfast. He got a second chance to practice his reading later, while ripping the old pages into strips to serve in the privy.

Bridey had sailed out of the house a week after Ling arrived, Sean meeting her at the garden gate, doffing his hat so low that Ling feared he might snap in two like a reed.

"She might have been a papist, that one, but her staunchest faith was in manifest domesticity," Crocker had grumbled after her departure. "Let the Fenians have their home rule, by all means, just not in my home!"

It was more women's work, but Ling felt a modest thrill in knowing that he was preferred to a white woman. That might have seemed like faint praise, to be the lesser (and

cheaper) of two evils — on his arrival he'd overheard
Crocker murmur to his wife, "The best difference between
your Chink and your Cat-lick is that one doesn't have
enough English to back-talk" (indeed, it had taken Ling a
moment to gather that Crocker meant *Catholic*) — except
that on his second day, trussed into an apron, duster in
hand, Bridey had shown him into the parlor, her braying
voice falling to a hush in the presence of such polished
solidity, while Ling had found himself, as if transported,
at home. The Crockers, he saw, were followers of the
modish fad for chinoiserie: rosewood furniture and tall
silk screens filled the room, which was dominated by an
ornately carved altar. Big Uncle had a much smaller
though still sumptuous altar in his cabin on the flower
boat, a shrine on which to burn incense and leave offerings
of fruit to the ancestors and before which the old gangster
would bow, as he did before no living man. The Crockers'
was used as a breakfront of sorts, displaying ornaments
and silverware, the only venerable dead on show vases of
dried flowers and a stuffed songbird in a vitrine. And yet
something of the altar's dignity clung to it. To Ling it
suggested the value the Crockers put on things Chinese,
and he felt touched, if also a little homesick, as if he had
been "collected" in the same spirit of connoisseurship, as
if he too might be polished to a high gloss in their home
(even if he did the polishing himself).

When he took the job — not that Crocker's vast
certainty had allowed any room to decline it, in retrospect
— Ling told himself it would be temporary. He was still
bound for the mother lode to make his fortune. Yet after
three months, when he had enough to buy a pan and even

a burro, he closed his fist around the money. He knew all about a Chinaman's chance in the goldfields—as thin and wispy as a lucky hair—from Uncle Ng. But around Crocker he saw how even ghosts were disappointed, drifting back to town hungry and hollow-eyed, the only gold on them their rotted teeth. Crocker liked to watch such wrecks from his office, men he'd once outfitted at his store, their ragged clothes faded to the color of the dust in the street hanging loose around them. "One in a thousand strikes it rich," Crocker told him when Ling shyly revealed his own plans. "But every man jack needs a shovel, a winter coat, good boots. You've heard of fool's gold— pyrites?" Ling nodded. "Here's the secret, son: it's all fool's gold."

And so Ling had stayed, struck by how much his new employer sounded like his last. He didn't like being called a fool—though he felt a strange shiver when Crocker called him *son*—and suspected that Crocker simply didn't want to trouble himself with finding another new servant, but it had already occurred to him that Mister Charley might be the next best thing to gold. He knew from the way Crocker's chest swelled tautly at the sight of the defeated that the man had his own designs on striking it rich. Once, he'd grasped Ling's arm and pointed out the wagon ruts crisscrossing the dusty street: "Someday there'll be rail lines covering this whole land like that." And then who knew what wealth might not roll down the mountain?

Without a room to rent or food to buy, and even discounting what he spent on Little Sister (for he continued to visit her weekly), Ling was able for the first time to

send money home, hoping that by making good on his vow to Big Uncle he might negate Ng's claim. Even if it was true, he thought the old gangster might yet embrace him if he proved his worth. He found a round-shouldered scribe in Chinatown to write a letter for him. Something, though, warned him not to confess his new line of work; he had promised Big Uncle to make his fortune in gold, not as a servant. They knew about servants at home, it turned out. Her sons all had them now, Aunty Bao wrote back gaily, and then complained about one in particular, Ah Poy, his insolence, his laziness. Never mind being a son; by the time he'd read her letter over, Ling felt stung, not to be a servant but that he might be a bad one. He redoubled his efforts at work, and only occasionally as he held a frock coat for Crocker, or knelt to button his boots, or bowed to fasten the fob of his watch (an action that felt like chaining a gate against a herd) did he feel as if he were serving his family.

They couldn't notice such efforts, of course, but Crocker did.

Six months after he'd hired Ling, Crocker had fallen into a black mood, his railroad enterprise stalled, the tracks not much farther than the outskirts of town. Part of Crocker's disdain for the failed miners was that they made such lousy workers. He'd hire them on at the start of the month, and by the end half of them would have defected, riding the rails to the end of the line for free and then lighting out for the diggings again. "And those that don't spend their wage on new rigs spend it on drink, so that I'm left with the worser half!" he thundered. Now these fellows had had the temerity to demand a pay raise.

It had happened once before, three months earlier. Then Crocker had duped them—called their leaders to the office over his store and, once they were spotted coming down the street, ordered Ling to walk in the front door, hustle out back, down the alley, then hell-for-leather it round the front again. "Over and over, mind," Crocker had instructed. "As many times as you can before those fellows arrive. And see here, take your hat on and off betimes," he called after him.

Ling had managed a half-dozen breathless circuits before Crocker welcomed the delegation on the boardwalk.

"What's all the palaver?" he heard a mutton-chopped Irishman ask Crocker as they shook hands. "You running an opium den, is it now, Captain?"

"Hiring," Crocker told him serenely, nodding curtly to Ling as he led the men upstairs to his office. "Plenty more where he came from too, so I hear."

The men had been back to work within the day. "Credulous bog-trotters!" Crocker had guffawed, watching them go, his chain and fob jiggling with mirth. Ling had allowed himself to join the laughter, marveling that anyone could be so stupid as to mistake one man for a multitude, delighted by the thought of the men's ignorance, their inability to tell one Chinaman in his bamboo hat and baggy cotton suit from another, being turned against them. He thought he'd be able to smile now whenever a ghost called him John (though shortly he'd start to hear a new epithet in the streets: *scab*).

And then Crocker had added, clapping him heartily across the back, "As if you little Chinaboys could under-

take such hard labor." Ling had staggered a little under his meaty paw, making Crocker bark with laughter.

But now these same fellows were calling Crocker's bluff.

One morning a few days after the new year, Crocker had come prowling into the kitchen before sunup. Ling had been preoccupied, thinking of the long-ago cricket the old gangster had given him, the dry rattle of it in its bamboo cage after it died. Big Uncle was a spirit, Aunty Bao had written, "dead of a curse," and then reminded him of the outstanding debt be owed for his passage. Ling had immediately dispatched a sum — asking for a paper servant to be burnt at Qingming so that the dead man might be well attended in the afterlife — and realized he'd never write home again (nor send another cent; his debt was to the dead man, he figured, and he knew himself to be untouchable under Crocker's roof). He was free, and yet he'd wept, so silently he'd hardly been sensible he was doing it, until he heard the household waking, and then he'd scuffed the tears away as if ashamed.

He roused himself when Crocker appeared. The big man, restless and irritable, had been looking for coffee, and Ling hurried to set the pot on the stove. But even after he'd set a cup before his employer, Crocker had merely sat and watched, the wooden chair creaking under him as he rocked, while Ling tended the laundry kettles, hauled in firewood, all the time terrified the chair would give way and Crocker crash to the floor, splashing coffee on his clean shirt. Ling was in a sweat worrying what the man wanted, but after slowly slurping his coffee, pursing his lips as if to draw the last of it from his beard, Crocker

merely slapped his thighs and bustled out. Ling had sunk into the chair in silent relief.

The next morning, though, Crocker had come out onto the back porch, two of his business associates with him: Stanford, the former governor, a frequent dinner guest, as sleekly plump in his nankeen trousers and morning coat as one of his prized thoroughbreds, and another gentleman in a sack suit, leaner and with a leather eye patch, whom Ling didn't know. They talked among themselves, smoking—"The Metropolitan Railway already has four miles of tunnels under London, for Pete's sake!" "Underground ain't the same as under mountains, boss" —but Ling could feel their eyes on him, appraising, as he chopped wood. Once, on the stump, Stanford had called the Chinese "a degraded race" and "the dregs of Asia" (Uncle Ng had liked to quote the phrase whenever they emptied their laundry tubs), vowed to drive them out of California, declaiming an animosity that Crocker confided went back to the gold camps. "Leland took it as an affront that some of your brethren struck pay dirt when he didn't: American gold for American pockets is his view." Ling always stood a little straighter around him, at once haughty and trying to impress the man, though as far as he knew Stanford had never noticed him before (at dinner the man's conversation was only of horses, once contending against all the rest that a galloping steed took veritable flight, all four hooves off the ground. *Imbecile,* Ling had concluded).

And then finally one of the three—the fellow with the eye patch—told him to come forth. The man— Strobridge, Crocker called him—planted himself before

Ling, pummeled his shoulders, pinched his arms. It felt odd to Ling to look a one-eyed man in the face, especially as the fellow cocked his head to one side, as if listening rather than looking. Ling stared at the man's jaw instead, the wad of tobacco bulging and bobbing in his cheek, until he started to imagine it was the missing eye rolling around in there. He made himself focus on the sole good eye then, and it felt like gazing down a long tunnel. Strobridge finally thrust a bushel basket into his arms, piled it high with billets, then made Ling totter around the yard with it. But after a single staggering circuit Ling had lowered the burden and the other two men had looked at Crocker pityingly, the one-eyed man hawking in the dirt, his dusty ball of juice rolling between Ling's feet.

"Know what the men call 'em? Wongs. On account, two Wongs don't make a white."

Stanford, beneath his top hat, chortled into his beard —"Don't look to me, Charles. My competence is horse-flesh, though by that measure I'd say you're trying to sell us a nag"—and Ling wished he'd choke on it. He began to empty the basket to puzzlement, then outright laughter as he transferred a portion of logs to a second basket. "Who's he think's going to carry that 'un?" Strobridge snorted, pushing his straw skimmer off his brow. "I told ye they're not worth half a man. Beats me how they built that there Great Wall." But Ling had pulled his old bamboo carry pole from beneath the porch and threaded the handles of first one and then the second basket onto it, crouched between them, and raised the balanced load across his shoulders. The baskets bounced lightly in time with his strides, giving a little spring to his step as he

circled the yard. You'd have thought he'd produced the Monkey King's golden-clasped rod, such was the astonishment. Crocker nodded vigorously while Strobridge and even Stanford clustered around and tossed more wood into both baskets. "Stand fast," Crocker told Ling, and so he had, even when pearls of sweat had sprung from his brow.

"Are all coolies strong as you, boy?" Stanford asked. The man had recently had a giant sequoia named for him, before that a mountain. Up close he smelled faintly of horse.

"Yessir," Ling began. "*K'u-li* is Chinese for—"

"Coolie," Stanford repeated slowly. "Coo-*lie*."

He's correcting my pronunciation, Ling realized.

"Yessir. Most Chinese strong as me."

He had wanted to explain that *k'u-li* in Chinese meant "hard strength."

Strobridge and Crocker exchanged a glance. The former rubbed his hands together and the latter, thumbs hooked in his vest pockets, cried, "Bravo! What did I say, Stro? They're *from* China, not made of it!" And Ling, muscles still braced under his load, had trembled with pride.

Crocker told him Strobridge, his foreman, had hired "fifty Celestials" the very next morning. "You're a credit to your race, my boy." (And to Crocker, it seemed; he'd won a tidy wager with Stanford in the process, he confided cheerfully.) It felt like a vindication to Ling. Tanka were looked down on by the Han Chinese, Eurasians viewed with suspicion. Yet here he was proving himself the best of them. It was the Year of the Ox, of hard work. He went about his duties in the Crocker home, even his ironing,

with greater gravity, as if every load of laundry lifted required stiff-backed dignity.

Ling had boasted to Little Sister about his new significance. They were lying together after coupling, her head on his chest so that he felt he was breathing for them both —a fleeting tenderness she might end at any moment, since it wasn't part of her price, and which he tried to draw out with talk.

"Credit to your race?" She twisted her neck to eye him. "How do you spend that?"

He tried to settle her, stroking her hair, but now it seemed as if he were pushing her away with each inhalation.

"Besides, what's he pay these new workers?"

Ling had to admit that it hadn't occurred to him to ask.

"No head for business, lah," she berated him, sitting up.

"As if you have!" He'd been teasing, reaching for her, but her eyes sparked.

"What do you think? I have an ass for business, tits for business only?" Slapping at those parts, and not gently.

And she told him the story of Ah Toy, the first Chinese courtesan in California, so beautiful—*ho leng*—men paid just to look at her. "Her face, I mean!" Little Sister shook her head at the wonder of it. "And you know what she did with her money? Bought her own brothel!" she added approvingly. "Now that's what I'd do if I could." She brightened suddenly. "That's what we could do if you get more than credit! Sure. You make enough money, buy a brothel, I'll run it for you. *Partners!*" She said the last in English and he'd laughed it off, but later, walking back to

Crocker's through the quiet streets, he'd whispered the word to himself over and over, as if correcting her: *Pardners*.

7.

He was improving his English, training his tongue to roll his *r*'s so that *Crocker* didn't sound like *Clocker*. He lingered at the door when the little Crockers—Master Fred, Miss Harriet (his favorite: she was fascinated by his queue. *How long did it take to grow?* she asked once, wide-eyed), and little William—were at their lessons, and forced himself to practice his English when on errands, wincing to hear other Chinese with their accented *Engrish* and *Melican*. Several times he leaned in to "interpret" between a countryman and a white, easing the way, as he saw it, and setting a good example.

But one morning he came across a stooped Chinese in a standoff with a blowzy ghost woman. She was barring his way on the boardwalk, a knot of passersby tangling around them.

"Go on!" the woman was demanding, her face ruddy. "Cat got your tongue?"

"More like t'other way round," someone hollered from the crowd.

It was the laughter that made Ling worm his way to the front.

"May I be of assistance?" he offered soberly, but the woman regarded him with frank repugnance—"'arken to 'im!"—fanning herself with her hand as if to shoo him away.

Up close, she reminded him of Bridey, albeit much reduced, hair wild beneath her bonnet, face chapped and wan. He almost called her by name, yet she didn't seem to know him, and he thought he must be mistook.

Instead he quietly asked the other fellow in Cantonese what was going on, but the wretch only shrugged. "The mistress turned her down for a job. Now she blames me!"

"W'as he say?" the woman demanded of Ling, lurching between them. "W'as 'is answer?"

"Let it be," the other Chinese muttered, eyes down.

"Sing-song," the woman jeered. "Bing-bong, ning-nong-nang!"

"What is it you wish to know?" Ling asked punctiliously.

"Just this! What's so blasted special about him, eh? About your lot, that they hire you afore me and mine?"

Ling stared at her blankly, as if it were a trick question, as if she couldn't see they were Chinese. He remembered how Uncle Ng dealt with untoward customers, giving no indication of understanding, smiling and chattering away in Chinese—insults mostly—until they threw up their hands. Ling regretted it was too late for him to take the same tack.

He tried to leave instead, turning away from her, and she yanked his queue, snapping his head back so hard he bobbled the package he was holding. But it was the laughter—even the other Chinese smirked—more than anything that set him off. He whirled on her, snatching his hair away, causing her to fall back.

"Unhand me, you trollop!"

There was an appalled hush, broken only by the woman's choked sob.

"Couldn't even get hired for *that*, damn you!" Too late he grasped how drunk she was. "Chinks even got that market cornered."

The other Chinese made to bolt, there was a scuffle of boots on boards, and Ling felt hands laid on him. He struggled, but then he heard the cold snick of a blade being drawn, felt the bright line of it at his throat, and went limp.

"What do you want us to do with them, darling?" he heard someone drawl over his head, but the young woman was inconsolable, hurrying off in tears.

The tears were coming to Ling's eyes too. A hand was pulling his head back by the queue so that his neck was bared, the knife so hard against his Adam's apple he didn't think he could swallow. The pain from his scalp was excruciating. He felt a fumbling behind him and then he was released, the knife scraping his chin as it withdrew so that he touched the spot at once, as if feeling for a shaving cut, in case he bled into his collar. But when he started to move off he felt his hair pulled again. Twisting, he found himself face-to-face with the other Chinese, their queues knotted tight together.

"A real pair of Siam twins!" someone ballyhooed.

Ling tried to turn away again, but the other man set off in the opposite direction and almost pulled Ling off his feet. The crowd howled.

"This way," Ling hissed.

"No, this!"

And now when they set off, they clashed, the brim of the man's hat catching Ling above the eye.

"Let me—" Ling began, picking at the knot before it got any tighter, but the man slapped his hands away.

"Who asked you to interfere? You're asking to be kicked!"

"Son of a dog!" Ling snapped back.

The other man raised his leg—as if to stamp, Ling thought—and drew a gleaming cleaver from his boot top. Ling closed his eyes, braced himself for the blow.

He felt himself struck, a momentary searing pain, and then nothing.

"Scalped him, by God!" he heard someone hoot. "Bloody savages!" And when he opened his eyes he saw the other Chinese holding up a severed queue like a snake. Ling only recognized it by the royal blue ribbon at the end, given him by Miss Harriet.

He tried to snatch it back, but the fellow jerked away, Ling's queue still knotted to his own, trailing in the dust.

Ling crooked his neck, felt the odd weightlessness, then shook his head more swiftly. It felt like it might fly off altogether, and he stopped, suddenly dizzied. Golden motes of dust kicked up in the melee and lit by the sun swirled around him.

"Quite the queue-riosity, you might say," some wag joked. "A rat without his tail."

"Go on with you," another of the ghosts said, not ungently, and Ling nodded—once, as he meant to, and then two, three times, as if his head were loose on his neck. He put a hand there and felt the thick, loose brush of hair at his nape. It ran like water through his fingers. Like a mane, he thought. A breeze stirred across his shoulders, and then he was running, chasing the other Chinese,

heedless of the blade flashing in the man's hand, his own queue skittering ahead of him just out of reach. He could have caught it too—the running came effortlessly, as it seemed to him, as if he were flying, with no flailing weight of hair at his back—but what was the point? They were approaching Chinatown, but at the end of an alley he veered off from the chase, headed back to Crocker's instead, still running, as if untethered, with nothing to hold him back.

"Cut your hair, I see," Crocker said when he met him. He nodded, too shamed to speak. "Much better that way. You look like a man at last."

It was the next day Crocker had suggested he outfit Ling "like a civilized fellow." He'd walked out of the store feeling a head taller, less Crocker's servant than his muse, his prototype, even perhaps his protégé.

He had a little mirror in his room, an old pier glass, the silver backing cracked and peeling so that looking in it he saw himself bent like a stick in water. He admired his new attire in it and decided he cut a fine figure, even if the flawed glass made him seem always to be bowing slightly to himself. (Only little Harriet, who had liked to follow him about clutching the end of his queue in her tiny fist, missed it, staining her pinafore with tears until he promised to grow it back.)

He had shown Little Sister the clothes. He showed her his hat, he showed her his collars and cuffs, starched and ironed. And she had stroked them gently, taken them off one by one. She ran her fingers through his hair when she'd lifted off the derby, then caught it—what was left of it—together at his nape. "Short as a boy's," she breathed.

He closed his eyes, remembering her washing and plaiting his hair. He had been planning to tell her it had been his idea to cut it, but she didn't ask, and he felt cheated somehow. He was already in a foul mood from having to wait for her. He'd stormed up and down the boardwalk, the heels of his new boots thundering. In his Western suit and hat, he must have looked like a ghost in the night, and startled Chinese had stepped aside for him, cursed him in Cantonese under their breath. But he had said nothing in return, just as he had said nothing to the ghost boys who had once taunted him. Why? he wondered now, in her arms. What was he ashamed of?

He'd come to see it as a trade, losing a queue, gaining a handsome outfit—an advantageous one, at that. He'd taken to wearing his new hat tilted forward, low over his eyes, to disguise his shaved forehead. It was the look of a rake, a young tough, and he marveled that now he could stride along the boardwalks of town without anyone expecting him to step aside. It wasn't only Chinese who mistook him for a white, nor only at night. Once in broad daylight when one urchin shoved another into his path, the one who trod on his toes, besmirching his boots, actually apologized, and Ling found himself clipping the offender around the ear as heartily as he might clap a fellow on the back. He hooked his thumbs in his vest as he'd seen Crocker do, threw his shoulders back as he strode, had to remind himself to round them again as he went about his household duties. When his queue began to grow back, he'd already determined, he'd bind it up under his hat, perhaps even lop it off himself (never mind his promise

to Miss Harriet). Time enough later to grow it out before he returned home.

After they had lain together he had produced a gift for Little Sister—"I almost forgot"—a silver thimble. He had studied the choices in the little haberdashery in a sweat, the storekeep eyeing him narrowly, and finally opted for one with a scrolling band around the base. She held out her hand and he slipped it on, stubbing her finger slightly. She twirled it between them, watching it catch the light. She was laughing, the same low snigger he remembered hearing through her door so many nights. Now he realized it was sobbing.

He reached for her, but she rolled away, hunching her shoulders, the bones of her back rising and whitening like the knuckles of a fist. His hand hovered over her, stroking the air.

Finally she started to speak, as if to the wall. "My father said he was taking me to visit my grandmother. I believed him, but my mother must have known. She wept when he took me, called me back, hugged me tight. I said she was being silly—I was a pert one—'Silly, Ma, I'm only going for the day.' She didn't tell me. I used to hate her for that. But I think she just wanted me to be happy for one last hour."

He stared at his hands in his lap. He was thinking of the first coin he'd given her, Crocker's gold piece with the woman's head on it: Liberty, he'd lately learned. He climbed heavily to his feet, began to dress.

"How much money do you have now?" she asked, as if she'd read his mind.

"Some," he hedged. "Not much."

But she'd looked at the clothes and not believed him.

"I thought we were partners."

He told her he didn't have enough for that, but she wasn't satisfied. "I'm a good earner, aren't I? A hard worker. I have some savings too."

"You?"

She nodded, and he knew she'd been holding out on Ng.

"How much?"

But she just shook her head, and he was relieved, in fact. He'd had the sudden fear that she'd saved more than him, that she'd saved every cent he'd ever spent on her. He had to fight the impulse to tear the place apart for it, shake her until her teeth snapped and she told him where it was hidden.

"If you don't have enough," she said now, "get your friend Crocker to extend you some of that famous credit. Or better yet, buy me himself."

"Never!"

"Not like that," she whispered. "But couldn't he give me a job, like you? I can clean, sew. Don't they need a maid?"

"You'd do laundry again? Ironing?" He was trying to jolly her along; he couldn't imagine taking her to the Crockers. He already saw to their needs. But mostly he couldn't imagine presenting her to Crocker.

"You could say I'm your wife," she implored him, but she saw in his face that he couldn't. "Ah, at last," she said, lying back as if satisfied. "You're ashamed of me."

He started to deny it, but she shrugged sulkily. "I'm happy for you. You've done well. Risen so high, you've left

me behind. From women's work to *man*servant. Good for you. Or does he call you his China*boy*?"

She hadn't bothered to cover herself, and in the dim light her areolas seemed to lie on her chest like dull copper coins.

"But why now?" he asked. "Why do you want to leave now?"

She squinted, sighting along her body; tapped the thimble against her belly.

"If it's a boy, he'll be all right, I suppose, but if it's a girl? What life for her?" She closed her eyes. "Listen to me, even I don't want to bring a girl into this world."

He fastened his collar, picturing her for a moment in her bath, scrubbing herself raw until the water turned pink.

"Isn't there any . . . remedy?"

"What? Cathartic pills, or preventive powders? Perhaps you were thinking of a button hook, a chopstick."

He winced.

"You're lying. Aren't you lying?"

"It could be yours," she'd said then from the bed, the thimble pointing at him like a gun barrel, but it didn't sound as if even she believed it. "Would you deny it a father?"

He paused at the door, confounded. It was so peculiar to wonder if he was a father, after wondering for so long who his own was.

"Better that than a father who doesn't want it," he offered at last.

"There are worse things."

"How can *you* say that?"

She stared into the candle, her eyes shining with flame. "Oh, that. That *was* a lie," she whispered. "My father didn't sell me to Ng."

Ling shook his head wearily. "So?"

"When we left, we left together, he and I. He had come back for me, you see, my father, from Gold Mountain. He had made money, and now he wanted me to help him make more."

"What are you saying?"

She looked at Ling like he was a fool.

And he was, he thought, slumping against the wall. It was why she couldn't run off, why the old man never lay with her, why he absented himself every night.

"How could he?" Ling began, but she spoke across him. "It was easy. As soon as he had someone else to do my work around the laundry."

"I didn't know," he breathed. As if it were an excuse.

She shook her head. "It's nothing. Filial duty. The money helps feed my mother and sisters at home. That's the truth." She smiled tightly. "I remember this one girl, on the voyage out. She thought she was getting married. She was a vain, stupid, happy little thing. She told me all about her wedding plans and her fiancé who was bringing her back to Gold Mountain. Someone must have gotten sick of her bragging. They told her she was going to be a whore, and when she asked the fiancé, he just laughed. "When I said I'd make you a wife, I meant a hundred men's wife!" She jumped overboard the next day. I remember seeing her in the water. She was Tanka, you know. She could swim. I thought we'd go back for her, but we sailed on, and all the men just stood there at the rail watching

her get smaller and smaller. Someone said later she was a real saltwater girl."

She stared at Ling's stricken face as if at a distant horizon, and he backed away. He was still clutching his hat, crushing the brim in his fist.

She nodded as if to herself. "Who would marry into such a family?"

He stumbled out into the alley as if pushed.

"You think too much about fathers," she called after him. "What about your mother? Do you ever give her a thought? Do you?"

Afterward, he couldn't recall her wiping her tears away. She'd let them dry on her face like a man.

She was just a two-bit whore, he told himself, but something about the very epithet nagged him. Two bits, he knew, made a quarter, but he'd never seen a single bit. There wasn't even a circle for one carved on Uncle Ng's counter. Something about the absence vexed him, as if the American money he handled weren't quite honest, the transactions conducted with it not to be trusted. He studied the quarters in his palm, coins he would have spent on her. When and how, he mused, had two bits become indivisible, so that there was no separating them?

He stayed away a few weeks, thinking she'd deal with it, but when he finally went back she was gone.

"Sold," Ng said peevishly. "More trouble than she was worth, that one," though apparently she'd been worth at least what he owed in gambling debts.

"To who?"

"Someone who could afford the bride price." Ng cackled.

"Who?" Ling had demanded, and Ng had given him the name of a notorious highbinder.

"Try asking *him* his business," the old man sneered, making a palsied chopping gesture. "You had your chance."

Gone, Ling couldn't help thinking later, like a stain washed away. He never heard what happened to a child, if there was a child.

It was the first time he'd seen Ng in months, though Little Sister had told him the laundryman asked after him. His former employer barely acknowledged him until Ling addressed him by name and the old man, the queue coiled around his head now threaded with gray, had startled, his hooded lids widening. "I thought you were a ghost," he explained, looking Ling up and down in his suit.

Ling was eyeing Ng too. How wrinkled he seemed, the tendons in his jaw rising like stubborn creases, the sallow flesh of his fingers and wrists shrunk tight to the bone, as if he'd been left in his own laundry water too long. Only his right arm, the one he used for ironing, seemed unwithered, as if it belonged to a much younger man. Not gambling debt, Ling thought. Ng reminded him suddenly of the grandfather on the flower boat, that other prospector-turned-opium addict, face permanently pinched from sucking on a pipe. He shuddered.

"You rich now?" the old man asked.

Ling shrugged inside his new suit coat. He guessed the old head was going to ask him for money.

"Look rich." Ng nodded. "Look proud."

"Why not? Should I be proud to be poor?"

Ng shook his head like a dog. "Money doesn't make

you proud. They pay you *for* your pride, I think." He took a long wet draw on his pipe. "Only, what if you don't have enough pride? Eh? What if you sell it all and are still not rich? What then?"

He scattered a handful of salt on the counter before him, scraped an iron back and forth across it to clean the metal.

"Or perhaps you're too proud to be Chinese," he murmured. "So proud you need to be white."

Ling had been thinking of doing the old man a favor, bringing him some business. Now that Crocker had dressed him, he liked to have Ling with him, in attendance, which meant Ling had less time for work around the home. A new cook had already been hired and the household laundry was to be sent out once more. But now he saw that he couldn't come back here again, that he'd only thought of using the laundry as an excuse to impress Ng.

"And to think," the old man sneered, "you were nothing but a pair of empty hands when you came."

"She told me what you did," Ling hissed.

"So?" Ng jerked his bony shoulders. "This is normal for poor girls. How else you think they live? It could be worse."

Ling tried to ignore the echo of Little Sister. "How worse?"

Ng's eyes clouded. "You know, *I* had a little sister. Not now, but once. Baby sister. In the time of big famine in Guangdong, before you were born. Lucky boy. No rice, no taro, no meat. People dying in the streets. With my own eyes, I've seen that. I and my brothers would have died for sure."

"What are you saying?" Ling frowned. "Are you saying you . . . ? Your own *sister*?"

"*No!* Who could do that?" Ng hung his head. "But my baba, he knew another family, also starving, also with a baby. And so the families . . . helped each other."

"But that's—"

"*What?*" Ng roared. "Worse than being whore? Yes, I think so. I think so very much."

Ling found his eyes drawn reluctantly to a skinny string of Chinese sausages, even more desiccated than the old man, hanging from the rafters like a shorn queue.

"I don't believe it," he managed, looking away.

"You think no one could be so desperate? Yet all around you, thousands of Chinese come so far from home to risk everything. To get rich, you think, for gold? No! For *food*, for life. It's not hungry spirits you should pray for, it's the hungry living."

"But no father would do that!"

"What do *you* know of fathers? He did it so the family would *live*."

"Wasn't she family too?" Ling began, but Ng was shouting over him: "If you'd ever had a family, you'd understand."

They were the old man's last words to him, spoken like a curse, and flecked with so much spit that Ling had backed away, expecting the iron to follow. Only after he left did he realize the lucky hair from Ng's mole was neither plastered to his brow nor waving silkily in the air before him, but plucked or fallen out. Little Sister, Ling remembered, had always promised to snip the loose thread on that button one day.

Months later—Uncle Ng dead of an overdose or debts, it wasn't clear which, and the laundry under new management (a fellow called Two Nose on account of a fleshy mole on one nostril, who seemed to have converted the lean-to into an opium den)—he heard a rumor that Little Sister was dead: by her own hand, a chopstick thrust through her ear, someone said; in childbirth another. He refused to believe it, and yet his eyes stung as if from the lye of the laundry.

In his bed that night he dreamt of a secret hoard of coins, hundreds and thousands of bits, a veritable treasure. He could see them—gold, of course, with an elephant embossed on one side—but not grasp one. All those lost coins! He woke with his hands balled so tightly his palms bled.

He'd not been back to Chinatown since, but a few months later he'd spied a headline in the newspaper he was ironing for Crocker: "The Chinese Question." As far as he could make out, it was an announcement for a meeting. He knew the place from his delivery rounds—a stockyard near the river. Something compelled him to go. He didn't know the question and yet it felt asked of him personally. He might even speak, he imagined, show himself as an example, doffing his hat and bowing with a flourish. If there was a Chinese question, was he not perhaps the embodied answer?

His Western clothes, he concluded later, must have saved him, for by the time he understood what kind of a meeting he'd joined, he'd already insinuated himself far into the crowd, too far to exit swiftly. Or rather the crowd

had congealed around him; when he'd arrived it had seemed looser, knots of Irish here, English there, French by their accents to one side, Deutsch by their build to another. There were no other Chinese, and he felt a flash of irritation that none had bothered to appear, vindicated that he had. Of course, he should have known by their absence, but he lingered in the vicinity of some Portugeezers (he recognized their language from the flower boat with a pang of nostalgia—sailors who'd jumped ship and turned miners, he guessed), and gradually the spaces between the groups had filled, the knots of men tautening, until leaving would have required him to draw attention, elbowing his way out of the mass, until finally the crowd closed tight as the speaker—a liverish redhead in a fustian jacket—climbed up onto a splintery buckboard and called out over the corral in his broad brogue.

"They're a plague on us, a *blight* indeed! For have they not blighted our prospects, those of my Fenian brothers and our brave sisters of Erin? They take our jobs on the iron road and their jobs at the hob and hearth." An answering buzz rose from the corral, along with the dusty stench of aged manure. "And how is it natural that they can do both a man's *and* a woman's work? What species of creature are they to upend the order of things? Cipher that if ye can. They work harder than us, some say. Oh, really? Who thinks they're stronger 'an me?" He had shrugged his jacket off and pushed up his sleeves as he warmed to his theme. Now he flexed his arm mightily until the rolled cuff seemed to tighten on it like a tourniquet and the pale flesh swelled red. "So why are they hired? Because they work for *less*—less pay, less food,

less dignity. And what does that make 'em? Less *men!* Lesser to be sure, but heed me, also *more*—in their poised and waiting *millions,* so many more. And I tell ye" —he jabbed a stubby finger at the crowd—"they won't stop with me and mine. Nay! They'll come for *your* work —Dutchman, Swede, native-born, yea, even you English —and your pay afore long. Can ye doubt it? Can ye *afford* it?" And the crowd bayed as one, some throwing their hats in the air so it seemed as if the roar had blown them off. To Ling it seemed the mass of men had come to a rolling boil.

"Exclusion!" the speaker was bawling, as if into a gale. "Exclusion by act of law, or *expulsion* by strength of arms!"

Ling felt himself crushed in the fist of the throng, his breath coming in shallow pants. He wormed a hand up between himself and his neighbor to keep his hat tugged tight to his head—to lose one would be to lose the other, he feared. He kept being thrust into the back of the sour-smelling fellow before him, his collar so wilted and greasy it seemed embroidered with filth. A man, he thought pityingly, who couldn't even afford laundry—another to his left, one more to his right, men whose shirts he itched to boil—and then it came to him that they were boycotting the laundries. Only when the crowd dispersed, bumping and jostling him as they drained down the alleys toward the slough to smash windows and set fires, did he feel he could breathe again, as if he'd been held underwater. From behind, watching them go, all he could make out was the pallid skin of their napes in the gloaming, cleaner than their grimy linens.

8.

And all that was two years ago. Two years and eighty miles of track, Ling thought as the train pressed forward, engine thudding like a heart, as if into the future. By now ten thousand Chinese were working on Crocker's "Celestial Railroad," as the papers were calling it. And they owed it all to him (even if now, in line behind other Chinese, he'd learned to wait in silence as they struggled with the language, only making sure, when it was his turn, to speak as distinctly as possible).

It was as if, like the Monkey King, he'd plucked the very hairs from his head and created an army. Though he still sometimes imagined his queue attached, reached back instinctively to sweep it aside when he sat, waited for it to bump his back when he halted.

But now they were striking. Crocker had told him the news two days earlier, his face wrung tight with consternation. "Chinese don't strike; they *break* strikes." He stared at Ling, as if expecting him to contradict the provoking telegram in his fist, but Ling kept his eyes down. It came to him that he was the only Chinese Crocker knew, to the extent that he knew him at all. All those thousands were judged by his standard—not just the strength of his back but his loyalty. For he was loyal to Crocker. Not just because Crocker was his employer, his route to riches and a comfortable life, but out of pride. (He *was* proud; Ng had been right.) He had been proud that Crocker had backed him against his partners that day in the yard. That was why he held fast as they stacked him higher and higher with firewood. He'd been proud to prove himself better

than the ghosts' opinions, to prove the Chinese better than they thought. Proud that they should all be measured by his standard. Except now, before Crocker's affronted gaze, the measure was reversed—*he* was being judged according to *their* worth.

He felt a momentary instinct to protect Crocker, as if his faith, his naive trust in the Chinese was in danger. Or perhaps he just didn't want Crocker's look of astonishment to become one of recrimination: *You deceived me.* And in turn he felt his own anger at the Chinese, for letting down not Crocker but himself, Ling. *Ingrates,* he thought, almost before he knew it.

How he yearned, then, to tell Crocker he was half white. He'd even imagined it: the look of perplexity, followed by one of gratified recognition, lighting up the big man's face like a paper lantern. He never had, of course—out of shame, at first, about his sordid origins—but now it came to him that he never could, not after that day in the yard, for fear that Crocker would think he had gulled him, misrepresented himself as Chinese.

The train had paused to take on water. The shouts of the engineers as they went about their work seemed thin and distant compared to the deep throbbing of the engine itself. In the stillness, Crocker began to stir.

"Where are we?"

Ling eyed his map. "Colfax?"

Crocker nodded, pulled out his watch, big as a saucer, and studied it owlishly.

"Good time." He looked at Ling. "You've been partaking of the scenery."

"Yessir." As if it were an order.

"Wait'll you see this." Crocker beckoned.

He led him out to the rear platform, open to the sky. Ling could smell the sappy scent of the pines around them, mixed with hot oil and singed air.

"There," Crocker was saying. He was at the edge of the platform, looking up along the train and the track to come. "See it?"

He caught Ling's arm and drew him close. The platform was narrow and the iron rail low, and for a moment Ling feared being jostled off it by Crocker's bulk. A curl of steam swam past overhead, dizzying him.

"Cape Horn," Crocker said, pointing to a buttress of rock. "They said we couldn't lay track there, sheer as it was. But your boys did it." He slapped Ling's back as if he'd carved the way himself, making him clutch the filigree railing.

The train gave a lurch and Ling felt himself stagger into Crocker's girth, and then the big man righted him. "Luncheon, I think," Crocker declared, as if reminded by the pressure on his stomach, and Ling followed him back inside, grateful to be of service.

He busied himself in the cramped galley among the victuals packed by Cook that morning—half a dozen baskets of cold meats, bread, cheese, one composed entirely of apples, shiny as shoes, and a bucket filled with bobbing, jostling beer bottles.

When he went back in to set the table, Crocker was nowhere to be seen. Taking the air, Ling guessed, but when he peered out he saw his employer on the rear platform, sighting along a rifle, hunting, Ling supposed, his body

tensing for the report. Yet by the time he returned with food Crocker hadn't fired a shot, and the big man was at the table, tucking a napkin into his shirt collar, the rifle stowed.

Ling himself ate standing up in the galley, and when he went in to clear Crocker was asleep again, hands laced over his stomach, mouth ajar.

Outside, the narrow walls of Bloomer Cut closed in—the engine's hammering echoing back off the stone—then receded, and the train seemed to climb into the air. Ahead the hillsides, speckled with snow, looked piebald. Steam from the locomotive— *The Governor Stanford,* Ling had noted with a sanctimonious thrill as they'd boarded—whipped past the windows, and it was as if they were entering the very clouds. The track snaked along a precipice, and when he looked down there was only air between him and the distant bristling treetops, the silver wink of a river far below. It made him giddy, but if he stared ahead the sensation was of flying, or rather of riding a bird, one of those—were they eagles?—lazily circling the updrafts before him. So this was the famous Cape Horn. Men had been lowered in woven baskets to blast out this ledge, so the papers said, the wind spinning them like tops, then swatting them against the rockface. It was one of the most celebrated achievements of the Chinese on the line, and Ling had expected to feel pride, had imagined fatuously bursting into applause, but instead he felt his heart filling with fear. How many times had he built this very scene playing with the Crocker boys, getting down on the floor of the nursery with them to lay the track for their tin train up inclines of primers and three-volume novels, all under

Crocker's indulgent eye, only for the boys to stage gleeful, clattering wrecks? Ling pressed himself back into the plush upholstery now and stared at Crocker, counting his breaths until the track curved like a slow brushstroke into a tunnel, and he sat in darkness for so long he felt the damp chill penetrating his bones. When they did finally emerge it was to the searing brightness of snow all around.

Even the sun seemed to shiver here through the spruce branches, throwing lacy shadows on the snow, as if the mountains were draped with the same antimacassars adorning the furniture at the Crocker home.

The dappled sunlight grew stronger as they rose above the feathery treetops, onto the Secrettown trestle, the panting engine drowned out by the percussive clatter of the wooden bridge. Ling had overheard Crocker telling his Associates at a recent meeting that the rickety trestle, all eleven hundred feet of it, would eventually be buried beneath tons of earth—a precaution against fire—to make a permanent embankment. *As if it were a secret itself,* Ling thought, the spidery lattice of stilts and crossbeams too frightening for passengers to behold, though he recalled Ng telling him the place was originally named, satirically, for a gold strike that local miners tried unsuccessfully to hush up.

For a moment there was nothing but blue on either side, and then the rails met earth again in the form of a sharp ridge curving off to the left. Below and beside the track Ling made out small cairns of rock dotted among the trees, and as the land rose like a slow wave to enclose the train again he saw them come closer until they stood within a few yards of the track. Mile markers? But they

were too irregularly spaced. Something to do with the construction? Spare ballast for the grading? And then the isolated ones gave way to a little cluster, laid out together side by side in a clearing, and he realized they were graves.

Crocker had told him that around a dozen men had been buried in an avalanche near Alta the previous winter and their bodies only found in the spring, still upright, still gripping their tools, frozen as if by Wu Kong's magic. Crocker had reported it as a marvel—"cigarettes still in their dang mouths"—and yet Ling had noticed that he couldn't recall the exact number of Chinese—"ten or fifteen, supposedly"—and this from a man who could tell you the price of a shovel in 1854 (fifty dollars— admittedly a memorably fabulous sum). Where had Ling been during such disasters? he asked himself. In Sacramento watching the trains pull into the depot with a load of snow for the local boys to have powdery snow-ball fights.

The dead, he'd heard, were buried with a bottle along-side them, a scrap of paper or cloth with their name and home village inside it. Some of these graves contained the remains of men blown to bits in the blasting, "and not all of them found," as the papers related. Ling shuddered at the thought of their not being buried whole. Someone from their clan or district association, whichever of the Six Companies they paid into, would eventually come to claim their bones and send them home, perhaps on the same ships that had brought them.

Once, as he'd filled buckets at the laundry, a drowned body had floated past him along the slough, a man's,

judging by the queue that trailed it like a water snake, though the flesh was so pale and puffed that Ling had taken it at first to be a clump of laundry. It had drifted silently into the early-morning mist before he could think to snag it, but he'd seen the face later that day in his own tub just beneath the soap scum, a wound like a dark stain on the brow, and thrust it back down with his paddle, thumping and splashing to cover his sobs.

Before that, on the voyage out, Ling had found his own bunkmate—a fellow so seasick that Ling had thanked the flower boat for his own sea legs—cold and stiff one dawn. Not wanting to fail the man's spirit and blight his own enterprise before it began, he'd gone to the captain and pleaded with him not to bury the body at sea.

"What d'you suggest? That we pickle it? Salt-cure 'im?"

And so the body had been sewn into a sack, weighted with a length of rusty chain, and tipped over the side into water the color of long-worn jade. Ling had watched it go, his queue hanging down toward the spray like a fishing line. And moments later the sailor's cry of *Floating gold!* went up, the ambergris spied bobbing beneath a mob of gulls, their wings flecking the sky like breakers. A wondrous occurrence, Ling would realize later, which at the time seemed no stranger than burying a man in water. That night he had had a berth to himself, but he slept poorly, tossing and turning as he dreamt of the dead man's bones gnawed by fish, swirling and bouncing across the sandy ocean floor. He imagined the spirit out there in the waves, slapping the wooden hull, trying to get in, trying to tell Ling it was his turn to lie down.

Outside, the earth rose up once more on either side of the tracks, another deep cut, sharp as an arrowhead, and the train was plunged into gloom again.

They had paused again at Cisco, the great engine huffing as if to catch its breath, the town so new it still stank sweetly of cut lumber. Crocker sat up, rolled his head on his neck with a crack, and pushed himself to his feet. He set his shoulders so that Ling knew to drop his topcoat about them, but when Ling moved to follow him out, the big man raised a hand. "Won't be needing you here."

Ling watched him lower himself heavily from the platform and talk to a couple of men who had stepped out of the sharp shadows of the depot. Their words were drowned by the pecking echo of hammers, but each shook Crocker's hand and bobbed his head emphatically at something the big man said, their nodding exaggerated by their collarless throats. Crocker turned and clambered back aboard, but one of the men had spotted Ling at the window, and as he watched the fellow pulled a face and gave a little caper. "Ching Chong, Chinaman, sitting on a rail," he crooned. "Along comes a white man to chop off his tail!" A childish ditty, but this was a grown man. Beside him, his companion's teeth were gritted, yellow as nuggets in his dark beard, and this more than the other's prancing doggerel made Ling uneasy.

Crocker barreled in, and when Ling looked again the pair had vanished, though whether back into the shade or elsewhere he couldn't have said. The train was already shrugging to life again, the depot scarcely fallen behind before Crocker was snoring lustily once more. A smut

from the smokestack had settled on his shirt front, Ling noted sorrowfully. He licked his finger, bent close to dab it away, vacillated. The train was trembling so much he'd only smear it. He made himself lean back, look away, let his eye follow the telegraph lines, swooping like swallows alongside the track.

Past Cisco the ascent slowed. Brilliant flecks of snow flung against the windows like rice. Along the track Ling could see the muffled forms of men, bundled in quilted coats over their baggy homespun, sacks and scarves wrapped around their faces and hands. Some were trudging along the line, picks and shovels on their backs, bent against the wind as much as the weight of the tools; others sat on logs before oilcloth tents, hunched over smoky fires. One bent to scoop a handful of snow to his mouth, the crystals shining in his thin beard. Another knelt beside a stream of runoff tumbling alongside the roadbed, washing his hands, the water in the sunlight rippling and sparkling like a cascade of coins.

As the train passed, the men's heads rose for a second, so that when Ling looked back, their faces were like a wave, rising and then falling. And each face he saw was Chinese. He lost count of how many, and then he stopped counting, and then he stopped looking at all, sat back from the window in the shadows of the carriage, almost as dizzy as when he'd looked over Cape Horn. It was a long time since he'd been in the company of so many Chinese—he used to have his forehead shaved each week by a Chinatown barber, but since he'd lost his queue he'd let his hair grow in—and he found himself suddenly shy. And something else: ashamed to come before these men

dressed like a dude, bathed, and well fed while they trudged through the smutty snow or bent over cooking pots, though what they might be eating he couldn't guess. Crocker had had their supplies — the rice, dried cuttlefish, and smoked sausage shipped from China — stopped in Sacramento. "Even the opium and women," he bragged to Ling, drawing a line across his throat.

It made Ling think of Little Sister. Of course he'd had girls since, though never the same one twice, always wondering if he might find her again, always wounded not to. He'd heard by then "going to see the elephant" used as a euphemism for a visit to a brothel, an echo of something Little Sister had once told him. He even knew of a bawdyhouse called the Elephantine, the El for short, or sometimes simply Hell. Once in a humor half daring, half despairing — his escape from the anti-Chinese rally had endowed him with a reckless, magical faith in his new appearance — he'd even tried a ghost whore by the irresistible name of Miss Ellie. He got as far as her room in his Western clothes, with his hat low over his eyes, but when he took it off she balked. "I have the money," he said, holding it out like a talisman, but she spat back, "Not for all the tea in China, nor the opium neither!" and he'd found himself, despite himself, admiring her scruples. He'd beaten a hasty retreat, but her harangue had followed him even after he gained the street. "The nerve on ye! To turf me out of my own 'onest work and then buy me with the proceeds like some 'eathen 'ore!" He'd slunk into the shadows even as she stood framed against the light, her arms clutching her bare breasts to her chest like a pair of bulging laundry sacks. Only later, his heart slowing, did

he wonder if under the caked and greasy makeup, the talc-y bosom, and despite her name, he hadn't recognized the woman. Wasn't it Bridey herself? She hadn't seemed to know him at first, with his hair cut and wearing a suit. Or perhaps she just couldn't tell him apart from other Chinese, as he'd heard whites complain.

Then again, he reflected much later, perhaps it hadn't been her at all and it was he who struggled to tell one Irish girl from the next.

Crocker had taken him along to a brothel once. He had started taking Ling about on business in the last year or so, even teaching him how to drive a surrey, liking the idea of traveling with a manservant. Not that Crocker was any kind of fop or dandy; being a valet to Charles Crocker, it was to be understood, was manly labor. Perhaps in this spirit, Crocker arranged for Ling to attend him one evening at a bawdyhouse. They were in San Francisco, the first time Ling had been back since his debarkation.

"I can trust your discretion, I know," Crocker breathed. "Not as a servant but as another man, yes?"

Ling nodded, puffed by the confidence, by the thought of Crocker and himself as equals.

"Mrs. Crocker just can't take it," the big man disclosed, his hands drawing a curve before himself to indicate another pregnancy, though for a moment Ling thought he meant his own swollen girth, as if the poor woman couldn't withstand his bulk.

The brothel was a renowned one, as plush and brocaded, swagged and damasked in Ling's memory as the palace car. In Chinatown the cribs Ling frequented brought back his home—the thick, ripe scent of naked flesh, a warm

stink of crowding and confinement, as if the girls were livestock in a pen. So vivid was the recall that he half felt the sluggish sway of the old flower boat beneath his feet. But this was different, not the memory of a brothel but a dream of one.

The madam was the famous Ah Toy, once famous for her beauty—"Men would ride two days just to behold her," Crocker had told him in the cab over—now for her business acumen. "Risen from whore to madam," according to Crocker. "And rich as Croesus," he added approvingly. As if money had purified her, as if he would welcome her as an investor. Ling remembered Little Sister speaking of her in almost the same tone of admiration. It was reckoned she'd slept with ten thousand men.

"Prolific cunny," Crocker marveled. "Yet still snug as a virgin, if what your sages say about foot-binding is to be believed, eh?" The swaying gait resulting from bound feet was rumored to strengthen the muscles of the *hai*. "Tight," Ling agreed hurriedly, "as . . . ah . . . a fist." He blushed furiously.

The madam had greeted them in the parlor, a sinuous silk presence, rustling and fragrant, daintily leaning forward on her porcelain shoes to kiss Crocker on each cheek—no easy task, given the capaciousness of his beard —and calling him, purringly, "Charles." He had clasped her gloved hand in his and actually bowed. Ling had found himself beaming, heart brimful, at such a display of warmth. He held his breath in anticipation of their withdrawal, but Ah Toy had clapped lightly and waved her girls (all of them Chinese) forward and Crocker, after lingering consideration, had taken one of them by the

hand and led her away—Ling had glanced at Ah Toy, as if there'd been some mistake, but she was smiling lustrously —leaving Ling in the perfumed parlor to wait, leaving him moreover with a curt "Stay here" uttered before the assembled whores and their madam.

He had stood by the wall, brow furrowed, until one of the girls offered him tea. He sat with them then, and they had been friendly, even playful, one of them drawing a hank of hair across her upper lip like a mustache to make the rest laugh, another slipping off the flowerpot shoes she wore to simulate the tottering walk of bound feet (he had finally smirked at that subterfuge), until one after another—*Zhen! Jia!*—they had been summoned by the madam for her customers. After forty minutes it was just him and Ah Toy.

"You like my girls?" she asked him now in Chinese, but he put on a show of disdain.

"They're nice enough for whores."

"Nice enough to you, because they know you don't have the money to buy them. You're safe to them, like a brother." She smiled demurely. "Or a eunuch in the Forbidden City."

He flushed. "I have money."

"Maybe." She smiled sweetly again. "But not the balls to spend it."

He searched her painted face for some sign of the coarseness of what she'd just said, as if for some blemish in the perfection.

"How much?" he demanded hotly.

"They're all gone." She shrugged, her silks rustling. "You missed your chance."

"How much for you?"

She eyed him placidly, ignoring the impudence. He stared back, trying to guess her age, but her makeup— rice-powdered cheeks, penciled eyebrows, rouged lips— was like an embroidered screen. Only the dry claws protruding from her fingerless lace gloves gave her away.

"Bolder than you look. And a flatterer!" Only she used the Chinese euphemism "horse fart spirit." "But I'm not for sale. Not anymore. Unlike some."

"Meaning me?"

"You work for him, he pays you. The girls he pays to fuck, and you he pays to . . . wait, yes?"

"For now."

"Ah!" She pointed a long enameled fingernail at him. "Ambition! Very good. What will it get you?"

What indeed? he pondered.

"Will you build railroads of your own? Have servants of your own? *Chinese* servants?"

"I just want to be rich," he said quietly. "Never mind how."

"Rich, rich." She clapped her hands, and her bracelets rang. "Everyone wants to be rich. The *only* question is how."

"What about you? Did you always know you wanted to be a whore, a madam?"

"A whore, no. No woman wants to be a whore, or be called one. I prefer *haam-sui-mui,* myself." He blinked. "But a madam? Well, every whore wants to be a madam. I was the first, you know, the very first Chinese whore in this town. Why do you think I became so famous? I created the market for these girls. They'd none of them be here without me."

He stared at her. She was not so unlike Aunty Bao, for all her finery.

"You're proud of it."

"It's business. I treat them well—well enough. Better than I ever was."

"And how do they feel about you?"

She was staring at the teapot before them, and slowly, as if it were a great weight, he found himself lifting it, refilling her cup. She nodded.

"Oh, they hate me, naturally. Every last one. What do you think? They'd thank me? Only their fathers thank me." She peered at him. "You think I should be a mother to them, love them, spare them. Do I look like a mother?" He caught his breath, but she didn't seem to expect an answer. "They've had enough of filial duty, wouldn't you say?"

But he was lost in a memory of his own mother, in a silk dress, a red cheongsam, not unlike Toy's, so smooth and slippery that when she sat him in her lap—he couldn't recall how old he was, but not much more than a babe in arms—he kept sliding from her grasp. He remembered her laughter, but to him the slipping was terrifying. He cried, and when once he slid all the way to the floor, landing in a heap at her feet, he screamed all the harder trying to climb back up her silken leg, so slick, almost wet to the touch, that he couldn't get any purchase on her, felt her warmth beneath the red but kept losing his grip and sliding to the floor. And all the time he wanted her to pick him up, just pick him up, but she wouldn't, just kept laughing. It was so vivid—he had to fight the desire to grasp a bunched fistful of Toy's dress—only it couldn't be a memory, he knew; she'd died bearing him.

"If not me," Madame Toy added, dabbing her lips, "some man would own them."

"They might marry."

"Ownership under a different name. Work without pay. Slavery is what that is. They fought a war in this country to end it!"

"So they're better off as saltwater girls?"

"Shows what you know!" she retorted, finally provoked. "*Haam-sui-mui* doesn't mean that. It's not Chinese. It's from English—*hand-so-me,* what the ghosts called us. Means beautiful."

She believed it, Ling could see, by the way she thrust her chin, and for his mother's sake he wanted to as well.

"But it's shameful."

"Is not! These girls sacrifice their honor for their families. They should be proud, rather. It's only men who are ashamed for women. Ashamed for themselves more like, for not being able to save us."

Ling colored.

"Ai-ya!" She sighed. "It's not the worst life. I tell the girls they could always be squeezing fish balls instead!"

He started at the reference. As a child he'd been mesmerized by old Tanka women at that work, squatting over a tub of fish paste, mashing it in their fists until the little white balls swelled like bubbles between thumb and first finger before dropping like milky pearls into a bucket of water.

Madame Toy poked a bony beringed finger in his chest.

"We're not so different, you and I. Oh, I know about you. Crocker's 'pet'—the one he brags about—the first

pet, first among thousands, but still a pet. And he's not bragging about you. He's boasting of himself, his vision."

He caught her hand in his, and held fast when she made to pull away.

"A joke between friends," she whispered. He caught a whiff of sweat beneath her perfume. "Let me find you a nice girl."

She looked at him intently, painted eyes widening. "Ah, I see it now. You're a mixed seed. Of course." He gripped harder, warning, but she continued serenely. "That explains it. Half-breeds are always trying to be twice other men." She pursed her lips. "And you hate whores because your mother was one."

He felt her fist relax and he loosened his own grip and they held hands almost tenderly for a moment.

"I don't hate them," he muttered. Then: "Did you ever hear of a girl called Little Sister?"

"Sure." He leaned forward. "They're all *someone's* little sister." She shook her head ruefully. "But now I see what you want. Like other men, after all. The same thing, the one thing. Love. The only thing you can't have, poor Chinaman, not on Gold Mountain."

"Can I ask?" he began. "What would you—you or one of your girls—what would you do with a child?"

She sat very still. "I wouldn't have one."

"But if you did?"

"Even if I did, I wouldn't," she told him flintily.

A couple of the girls had drifted back in, and behind them Crocker, slightly flushed but otherwise just as when he left, smoothing his hands down his ample vest front.

"Dressed himself, I see," Ah Toy murmured to Ling, with a final squeeze of his hand. "Careful. You could be out of a job." Together they watched Crocker down a glass of rye standing up, one foot propped on a silk hassock as if it were something he'd just shot.

Ling had felt a qualm for Mrs. Crocker afterward. Felt some obscure kinship—both of them shamed somehow. She was such a refined figure, dressed in long gowns, her pale skin glowing against the dark fabrics, all gliding serenity next to Crocker's bustling, bristling energy. But Ling must have betrayed something—bowed too deeply or too long, allowed some softness to steal into his voice —for she summoned him to her chamber a few days later. Crocker was at his office, the children at their lessons.

"I felt you should know," she said brusquely, squaring her shoulders under her lace shawl, "that I'm well aware of my husband's occasional evenings."

Ling started to say something, but she cut him off.

"Please don't. *He* can deny it. Between a husband and wife there may be necessary mendacities. But *you* are not to think you know what I do not. Understood?"

"Yes, ma'am," he murmured. He recalled Crocker confiding in him once his intention to name a town along the railroad after his wife.

"Very well." She seemed to Ling as stiff and unyielding as the tightly stuffed and buttoned horsehair chair she sat upon. "These are Chinese girls, I assume?"

Ling nodded wretchedly.

"Well, that's something. Your sort have a reputation for cleanliness, at least. And a Chinese girl displays a certain discretion. He could hardly fall in love with one, after all.

And none would be so presumptuous as to try and make a claim on him."

She looked at Ling and waited until he said quietly, "No, ma'am."

He was jolted now by the train's braking, the long caw of steel on steel drowning out the thrum of the wheels. He felt a sliding sensation in the pit of his stomach, as if something were loose inside him, as if his body wanted to keep going rather than stop. But it was the end of the line. He feared Crocker might roll off the divan and was about to reach out a hand when the big man grunted and stirred, catching himself. He sat up at once—the speed with which he moved his massive frame often made Ling want to jump—planted his feet, and looked about him for his hat. Ling offered it to him, and Crocker ran a palm over his head to smooth his hair and pulled it on tightly.

"Right!" he declared, spirits revived. "This is it. The front. Summit Tunnel."

9.

Crocker stepped out onto the platform at the rear of the carriage as if onto a balcony. The train had pulled up on a narrow shelf next to a rough-hewn shack—the foreman's office—resting akimbo on a railroad flatbed, the wheels sunk into stiff mud. Below, the land sloped away slowly and then more steeply to a narrow cut in the mountain through which the rails receded. The ground around the office was bare, churned by foot- and hoofprints and wagon ruts, dotted here and there by gnarled tree stumps,

but downslope, fanning out from the rails that ran like a line of stitches through their midst, was a small city of tents like a miniature range of snowy mountains, smudges of smoke rising up between the peaks into the porcelain-blue sky. And between the train and the tents, filling every foot of ground with the exception of the track itself, were Chinese.

Ling had been ascending for so many hours now that looking downhill he felt as if he were toppling, had to put out a hand to steady himself for fear of pitching forward. He would have hung back in the doorway, but the big man wanted his buffalo fur—the snow had turned feathery and finally stopped and the sun come out, but in the shade it was still raw at this elevation—and Ling came forward to drape it over his shoulders, straining on tiptoes to lift it. On the hook beneath the robe he'd seen the rifle in its deerskin scabbard. "Will that be all?" he murmured, smoothing the collar over the pale roll of fat, splintery with stubble, at Crocker's nape. He was hoping to withdraw from both the cold and the cold inquiry of the faces lifted to them, but Crocker shook his head, drew him forward. "Take a look, my boy. Take it all in! None of this would have been possible without your fine example."

The big man's basso seemed oddly muffled to Ling—it made him wonder if he'd been deafened by the engine—so instead of perusing the crowd he turned to Crocker, only to find his employer gazing back at him with a look of appraisal, his eyes as flat as in the old tintype portrait of him hanging at the mansion (the photographer had drawn them in because the exposure took too long for

anyone not to blink). And then Ling's ears popped and sound, like cold air, flooded into his head once more.

Ling was almost relieved when the foreman, Strobridge with his eye patch, strode toward them. He was wearing a moleskin coat, a pick handle swinging jauntily in his hand as if it were a walking stick.

"I'd have thought they'd be back at it afore now, Stro."

Strobridge pulled himself up the ladder with one hand, spitting with gusto from the new elevation. "Oh, they're feeling it, all right," he noted grimly, his one good eye seemingly aimed at Ling.

He was accompanied by a chargeman called Kurtz, sporting a tightly curled imperial, and a dozen Irish crew chiefs, who ranged themselves around the rear of the palace car, all of them with picks or shovels on their shoulders as if ready to take up the work of the strikers. Just the kind of men the Chinese had displaced, now set over them. Ling overheard one of them, his beard streaked from one corner of his mouth with tobacco chaw, introduce himself to Crocker: "Name o' Bill, sir, but you can call me Bill-in-a-China-shop, if you catch me drift." The lopsided brown stain exaggerated his smirk grotesquely.

"Well, bring them up." Crocker sighed irascibly. "And you," he told Ling, "you translate."

So that's why he was here, Ling thought as he watched half a dozen Chinese approach the car at Strobridge's wave: "These claim to speak for the rest."

"By what right?" Crocker asked, and the foreman shrugged. "They've got the thickest heads." To Ling, the men, most bareheaded, their shaved brows pale above the

tan lines where their hats normally rested, looked break-able as eggs, even with the mass of workers arrayed behind them. He adjusted his own derby nervously, first tugging it low over his eyes, then tilting it back to cover his bare neck.

It wasn't that the men didn't speak English (albeit a pidgin version), Ling found, but that Crocker wanted to be sure of what they meant, as if he thought they might not really know the meaning of the word *strike*. The Chinese were belligerent — Ling wondered if their hostil-ity was magnified by his presence, or if it was even for his benefit — and he found himself speaking their demands softly to Crocker, as if by mumbling he might lessen them. But it only made Crocker bark at him "Speak up!" and Ling blushed to be chastised by a ghost in front of these others. Not that Crocker didn't yell at them too, inveigh against their duplicity. "We had a deal," he blustered, the Irishmen chomping on their beards like horses at the bit around him. "You took the job at the wage we quoted. No one obliged you."

Ling had barely translated these words — quietly, but forcefully, he hoped — when one of the men bawled back in English, "Ten hour a day good for white man, forty dollar a day good for white man, all the same good for *China*man." The striker, a fellow with a nose so broad his nostrils seemed permanently flared in anger, glared at Ling until he turned to Crocker.

"They say . . ." he relayed haltingly, as someone else behind him added, "Same beatings as white workers, also!" "They say," Ling continued, "that they wish equal . . . terms with other laborers on the line."

"Tell him we don't work to make him fatter!" another man, face shadowed under the brim of his hat, yelled in Chinese, to flickering laughter.

"I can't tell him that," Ling hissed.

The man pushed his conical bamboo hat back off his forehead, his face opening wide like an eye beneath a lid. Ignoring Ling, he pressed on in accented but dogged English.

"We no work for make you fat! We work for make we rich. We use mine gold, now we mine nothing. That's what is tunnel: no-thing! We mine air only. *You* must give gold. No gold. No work."

"No work? No food!" Crocker thundered, slipping into pidgin himself at the sheer impertinence. "You tell 'em that," he snapped at Ling, who passed it along with an air of wretched redundancy, the strikers having already turned to each other to confer.

"Try to fuck me," Crocker was growling, "I'll fuck 'em right back." But fortunately he didn't seem to expect Ling to translate this odd threat. Ling had heard it before, of course. Men so starved of women, he could only suppose, had somehow mistaken sex for fighting.

Strobridge, smacking the ax handle into his palm as if applauding, leaned in to Crocker. "Shall we persuade them otherwise?" There was a general uncrossing of arms among the Irish.

Crocker surveyed the mass of Chinese, his thumbs thrust so firmly into his vest pockets Ling feared the stitches would give, and shook his jowls slightly at Strobridge. "Tell 'em if they go back tomorrow morning I'll pay 'em for the time lost. If not, I'll dock every man

jack for each day wasted. And any man obstructing another from returning will answer to Mr. Strobridge here. I'll not stand for intimidation, you tell 'em." And after a long moment Ling did, clenching his teeth to stop his voice cracking with hypocrisy.

Another man stepped forward, an older fellow the others seemed to defer to. He gave a long sniff — Ling feared he was going to hawk — and shrugged. "We strike," he reiterated before adding, as if this clinched something, "We strike it *rich!*"

"I'll give him a strike, by God," Strobridge snarled as the men dispersed. "That'll bring 'em to heel, mark you."

"It better," Crocker muttered. "At this rate we'll need to hire niggers, and after them, who knows? Mexicans." He shook his massive head at the calamity of it. "We must stop the rot here. I'm the author of this road, goddamnit! You and your men are armed?"

"A score of us bossing thousands of them? Always."

"Very well. The posse from Cisco should be along after sunup."

Strobridge spat one last time in the mud, followed by half his men, as if loosing their first volley.

Ling looked away across the valley as if to feign indifference. The scattered trees on the distant hillsides looked like a crowd of tall, thin men, another army, stilled and silent, watching them.

10.

Ling had dutifully climbed back aboard the train behind Crocker and helped him to the cold supper Cook had

packed that morning. Crocker was silent, aside from the tearing of his chicken. Afterward he paddled his fingers in the bowl Ling held for him, dabbed a napkin to his greasy lips. "Fetch me down the locked case." There was a pair of pistols inside, nestled in burgundy velvet like a heavy necklace. Their arrangement—barrel to handle, the curved trigger guards innermost—reminded Ling of something, but only when he lifted one out and proffered it to Crocker did he see what the layout resembled, a single shining gun mirrored by the shadowy absence of the other: the *taijitu*, the yin-yang symbol.

A gun belt was coiled in Crocker's carpetbag; Ling helped him buckle it, kneeling to cinch the tie around his leg. Above him, Crocker's paunch, girded by leather, bulged firm as a muscle. The big man slid the pistol into and out of the holster a few times until he was satisfied. Ling cast another glance at the second revolver, still snug in its case, weighing whether it was for him, but Crocker dismissed him with a curt wave when he asked if he needed anything further. Ling had seen him in such spleen before, though never at the Chinese; he knew to make himself scarce.

All he could think about was what the strikers had demanded: not just more money—he'd expected that— but *equal* pay with white workers. It wasn't a vast disparity; the main difference, as Ling understood it, was that the white workers had their board included in their salary, the Chinese had to pay for their food out of theirs. But for Ling it changed everything. His pride was founded on proving Chinese men equal to, if not better than, whites. Now it turned out they were just cheaper. The same as

Chinese food, Chinese laundry, Chinese whores, Chinese lives. *Of course,* he thought dully.

He stepped back out onto the rear platform and watched the dusk come down on the mountains like the lid of a pot. Behind him the mouth of the unfinished tunnel yawned open, jagged and dark. Even the engine, cool and silent, seemed to cower before it. Ling tried to imagine walking in there—bad enough in daylight, but he knew the men worked in shifts around the clock. Though perhaps it would be easier to pass from darkness to darkness, he reflected. As it was, it seemed as if the night emanated from the tunnel, blackness pouring forth from it as from a pipe. Beneath him he could just make out men perched on upturned buckets and barrels clustered around fires and candles outside their tents, smoking and drinking tea. He might have imagined it, but there seemed a holiday atmosphere. Men stretching their legs before the fire, arching bent backs. Ling could hear them chattering, the Cantonese carried on the wind to him along with the scents of tobacco and tea, and a floral note of . . . yes, opium.

He had felt ashamed to come before them in his Western garb and haircut, but something else too: a freak. He'd seen it in the faces of the crowd, marveling at him, not as a traitor or a toady—or not only, he realized—but also as a wonder, a phenomenon.

It made him think of Chang and Eng, the famous Siamese twins of the traveling show. He'd met them once, accompanying Crocker to the opera house. He'd stood in the shadows of the box watching them play table tennis and juggle, conversing all the while in perfect English he

could only envy. Crocker was fascinated. He'd seen other such shows, he said: years earlier, back East, a Chinese lady with tiny feet eating with chopsticks and using an abacus; more recently in Woodward Gardens, the Giant Woo, so tall he could light his cigar from a gas lamp. But these twins were extraordinary. Crocker was especially struck by their strength, as they lifted weights and then members of the audience overhead. "Are there many more like them at home?" he asked Ling. "Can you imagine? One could spike, the other swing the maul!"

After the show Crocker had insisted on going backstage and drawn Ling along. The twins were in their dressing room, each with a glass in his hand, one—the one on the left; Ling couldn't recall which was Chang, which Eng—of water, the other of wine. Crocker shook hands with each, his fleshy clasp engulfing first one and then another hand: "Pleased to meet you, pleased to meet you." They had twitted him gently over the delays in completing the railroad—"The passage via the isthmus is *so* wearisome!" —and as if suddenly reminded, Crocker had added, "Allow me to present my manservant, Ling. Ling, my manservant. Quite a prodigy in his own right."

Ling had been stunned. He'd never been introduced before, not once, let alone twice, though something about the repetition seemed ludicrous. All he could do now was bow, once and again, in greeting. The twins were dressed in evening wear, their hair cut short in the Western fashion. Ling couldn't stop staring between them at the point their chests met, wondering at the flesh that united them but also at the linen of their shirts, which met so ingeniously.

"Oh, really," one of the twins said — the face on the left — while the other looked away impatiently. Their bodies seemed to lean away from each other, perhaps for balance, yet giving the impression that they'd rather go in different directions. Their brows were filmy with sweat from the heat of the footlights. "And what is so remarkable about Mr. Ling?" Left asked, blotting his temple with a lace handkerchief.

"Why, he's a model of industry. I go further, a *muse* of industry, of capital and labor. Were it not for his shining example, we of the Central Pacific should never have thought to hire so many thousands of your countrymen."

"We've heard of your Chinese army," Left replied, using the plural pronoun even though Right looked utterly indifferent. "Storming the Sierra, is it?"

"Indeed, sirs, and this is the very man. The first among ten thousand!" And Crocker raised Ling's arm as if he were a prize fighter and pinched the muscles there.

"Quite the sensation," Left noted, looking Ling up and down. "An honor." He held out a hand, and Ling took it gingerly.

"First of your kind, eh?" Right asked, thrusting his own hand forward and drawing Ling close enough to whisper. "The real trick is to be one of a kind." And how peculiar, Ling thought, for this twin to be talking about uniqueness. To Crocker, Right added, "You might be chary of first impressions, though. When we were originally exhibited, you know, quite a few of your countrymen thought all Chinese came in pairs. We're not all alike, you know. Even if we look it."

Crocker chuckled amiably, as if this were all part of the show.

"Perhaps you should talk to Mr. Barnum," Left went on smoothly, "have Mr. Ling exhibited. Send him about the country . . . by train, of course. If you can spare him, that is?" Both were staring at him now, and Ling felt caught between their gazes as if between two chopsticks.

They were mocking him, these odd urbane monsters—one directly, the other more subtly—and mocking Crocker too, though his boss was immune to it, unable to conceive of a Chinese ragging him, let alone two grotesques. But Ling had heard that the twins had toured Europe, met royalty and presidents. "Baron" Crocker must seem nearer to Barnum, that bloated showman, than to all the dignitaries they'd met.

Ling wanted to tell them how he'd once been mocked in their name. How would they feel about that? Irked or abashed? And how did he feel toward them—resentful that they'd made Chineseness part and parcel of freakery?

It seemed to him that Left might at least feign regret but Right would likely deny it gruffly. Strange, he thought, to be yoked together so, each other's brother and burden, and yet be so different, even after a life of shared experience. Had they always been different, he mulled, or grown apart in temperament, like figures in a mirror—the one raising his left hand, the other his right? Was it an innate contrariness or some fundamental lust to be different, distinct from the other who was so close in every physical sense—an insistence on individuality?

Someone coughed behind them.

"You'll excuse us, sirs," Left lamented. "The gentlemen of the local medical establishment are here to examine us."

"You're not in poor health, I hope?" Crocker asked.

They shook their heads in unison, to giddying effect.

"Not since debarking from the steamer, thank god. The doctors visit only to ensure no fraud, to examine us—"

"To poke and prod us—"

"To ensure no chicanery."

"That we are what we say we are."

"Siamese, he means." The one on the right winked at Ling.

"Well, good luck to you, joining the nation," Left called over his shoulder. "Or should I say conjoining?"

"What a pair," Crocker muttered afterward, in perplexity.

Ling himself had felt a nagging disappointment, though at the time he attributed it more to the letdown of discovering that the circus had not included, as widely rumored, an elephant among its wonders.

It was almost full night now, yet on the platform Ling felt as if he were perched on a stage. It was all for show, after all. The grand palace car, his own servile presence. Crocker typically traveled more modestly, had never brought Ling to the front before. A show of strength, then, but not only a show. He laid his hand on the chill metal of the railing and thought of Crocker's gun, the polished weight of it as he had lifted it from the velvet-lined rosewood box and handed it across, the slight pause as Crocker held out his

hand for it and it seemed to hang in the air between them, along with the sickly scent of oiled metal.

Did the strike leaders know what they were doing? Did they truly represent these men?

Far below across the plain he thought he made out distant fireworks, soundless from this distance. Some celebration, but of what and by whom? And then he realized it was lightning, flashing in the low clouds.

He ducked back into the carriage, to the closet that was his berth, and changed into the work clothes wrapped in his bedroll, kneeling to tie his trousers at the ankles before stepping off the train. "How's Crocker reckon all Chinese are like you when you don't even look Chinese no more?" he recalled Little Sister asking him once.

The men, when he moved among them, were gambling —dice here, fan-tan there—heads bowed close to their fires. Many, he saw, had their queues coiled tightly around their foreheads, in some cases around their hats, to keep them out of the way while they labored. In the firelight the dark braids looked like chains. When he stopped to watch a game of dominoes, someone offered him tea and he accepted, feeling the warmth of the liquid through the china cup, amazed to find such a delicate thing here, so far from home. Then the players invited him to sit in for a game. It was such a tonic to hear Chinese spoken again that only when they had emptied his pockets of loose change did he catch on that they knew who he was. Belatedly he recognized a couple of the strike leaders among the firelit faces. "You're a credit to your race," someone joked, and he knew they must have conspired against him somehow, and yet he only smiled. He owed

them this, he figured, and the losing came as a kind of relief, the money sliding from his fingertips.

Afterward he asked the men about their lives, where they were from, the work they did.

"Digging," offered an older man. His queue was down, and he was puffing on a stubby cigar. He'd been the last of the strike leaders to speak. The man's face was a web of lines except over his cheekbones, where the skin was pulled tight and smooth, shiny as polished wooden knobs. "Digging, digging, digging. All day, all night, you can hear the picks and awls ringing from underground. The only difference is if you dig east or west."

"East or west?"

"We dig from both sides of the mountain to go faster," the old man explained. He nodded to one of the younger faces flickering in the firelight. "Ah Ho has a brother on the other crew. The bosses call him Eastward Ho, his brother Westward Ho."

"I tell him we go up the mountain's cunt, him up her ass," the young man added, wagging a railroad spike between his legs. "He says *we* go up the ass."

"Who can tell in the dark?" someone asked morosely. "Who even remembers the difference?"

"Either way she's a tight bitch!"

There wasn't a woman for fifty miles in any direction, Ling thought. Just men, men, men, as Little Sister had prophesied.

Others were superstitious about the work. It was terrible feng shui to build a straight line through the mountains, they told him, hands held out to the fire as if in prayer. Everyone knew demons liked to travel in straight

lines; evil liked to come quickly. At funerals scraps of paper, each with a tiny hole in it, were scattered along the route to the cemetery; any demons would have to pass through each hole before pursuing the living or the dead. But now the men were making a way for the straight line of track, doing the demons' work for them. That, they told Ling, was why so many had died.

The demons struck at them in many ways. In falls from cliff sides, in avalanches, in blasts that took a man's head from his shoulders. Track layers tried to pin the demons down, driving spikes into them, but the demons always wiggled free, slipping like sunlight over the polished rails. There were two demons, some men said, left demon and right demon—the devil of violence and the devil of greed—in a race with each other across the continent. The right demon wanted to get ahead, so he killed men working on the left; the left demon retaliated by maiming the men on the right. This was the race the men cared about, not the one between them and the ghosts from the east. Some thought that the demons were twins; others said they were male and female, lovers who yearned for each other. By day they squabbled to the ringing of hammer and spike. But at night they lay together, side by side, silently. And sometimes an errant blast or a landslide would twist them together into an inextricable knot of steel. When the lines were finally joined, one man warned, demons would be able to fly from one side of the country to the other in clouds of sparks and smoke, bellowing, shrieking, fiery-eyed and fiery-bellied.

To protect them the men had invented new gods to pray to. The god of the hammer, the god of the spike, the

squeaking god of the wheelbarrow, and, the greatest of all, the black powder god, whose blasts scared off any demon, just like firecrackers at New Year.

The senior man ignored this talk serenely, leaning back on his stool, the tip of his dangling queue tracing illegible characters in the sandy dust behind him as he rocked back and forth. "Sometimes," he said finally, screwing the cigar into the corner of his mouth, his fingers as stubby as the cheroot, "I think I'm going to grow old in there, die and be buried in there, and then it'll turn out I was digging my own grave all along." He produced a little bag from the collar of his tunic, secured by a leather thong around his neck. It rattled when he shook it—"Finger joints." He grinned. "I mean to be buried whole"—and Ling saw that he was missing the tips of two digits, to frostbite or accident.

"Other days," the man continued, "I let myself dream maybe the tunnel will go all the way home to China. The last tunnel we finished, when we met in the middle, it was like that. Like we'd dug up Chinese. I was there when a hand thrust through the hole, out of the darkness." He held out his seamed, stunted hand, and Ling almost grasped it.

"So here we sit at the top of the world," someone murmured. "Next to the deepest hole in it."

"But aren't you proud at all?" Ling pressed them. "Of what you've achieved? What about Cape Horn?" he reminded them. "The whites couldn't have built that except for Chinese skill." He had heard that the men had woven their own baskets, after an old Chinese practice, to be lowered in down the sheer rockface. But they just

looked at him with bemused impatience. Baskets? They didn't know anything of baskets. Men on ropes? Who would be so foolhardy as to dangle over a cliff? "They're not paying us enough for that!" Such modesty, Ling thought at first. He remonstrated with them. The feat was famous; they were celebrated for it as far afield as San Francisco! It had been in the newspapers!

"Lies." The old man shrugged. "I was there. That's just a story made up by the bosses."

"But why?"

"To justify hiring us over their own, probably."

It made Ling consider queasily if even his own role hadn't been a fiction, another story made up by Mister Charley. The possibility yawned vertiginously: his whole life an invention of others.

In turn the men asked him eagerly about Crocker, what he was like.

"I just do his laundry." Ling blew across his tea to cool it. "Wait at his table. Set out his clothes." *I'm his servant,* he thought, his head bowed. These men were workers. He and Crocker had mistaken one for the other.

"They treat us like dogs," someone—the man who'd called Crocker fat—said, spitting into the embers, "and say we're his pets." Ling nodded slowly. He'd heard it too, him the loyalest of dogs.

He felt his old pride rise up in him for a moment, like a knot in his throat. Had he truly been proud to show Crocker and his cronies what the Chinese could do? Or was he just proud to prove he was better than other Chinese? The exception, not the rule.

He swallowed it down now, this pride like vomit.

"They'll shoot you like dogs too," he said hoarsely.

"We're willing to die," the other said.

"And you speak for everyone?"

There was a pause while they looked around the fire at the glowing faces.

"Well, why not?" the man asked at length.

Ling just stared at the older fellow. "But don't you see?" he finally managed, his voice thick with despair. "That's how it starts."

After he left them, he stood for a long while before the tunnel. Up close it wasn't much more than a rough-hewn cave fanged with rock, like a shark's mouth he had seen once, rows and rows of teeth angled every which way. Meltwater ran down the walls, glazing the rock, and dripped from overhead like a slow pulse. This close, the darkness was so dense the starlight seemed to fall in shafts from the night sky behind him, the stars like bullet holes in a blanket. The tunnel's blackness, by contrast, was so palpable he felt he might reach out and caress it. *One more step and I'll be gone.* He felt his body summon itself, lean in, and then a chill tear tapped him heavily on the neck and he pulled up short. "It rains in there," one of the men had told him, but to Ling, breath held tight between his teeth, the pattering sounded like nothing so much as laundry dripping.

Or blood, he thought, turning away with a shiver. A powder man, they'd told him, had been blown to bits just the week before, nothing left of him but his boot heels.

When he climbed back into the palace car he found Crocker sitting up in the dark. He was in his shirtsleeves,

collar and cuffs undone, a crystal tumbler in hand, peering out into the night, a revolver at his elbow. For a moment Ling imagined the gun was smoking, and then he saw the stub of cigar in the ashtray beside it.

"Do you need me, sir?" he asked, holding up a taper.

"Oh, is it you?" The big man took a long swallow, the whiskey the color of gold in the candlelight. "No, that's all right," he murmured. "I was just thinking. I crossed these mountains myself, not far from here—twenty year ago, nigh on." He shook his head slightly, as if it hurt to remember. "What we'd have given then for a railroad. Three cussed months it took us."

Ling's own passage from China had lasted but five weeks; strange to think his home, measured thus, was closer than Crocker's own.

"And we were the lucky ones, not like those Donner wretches and all the rest of them, starved or froze or scalped along the way."

Ling gave a shudder at the memory of Uncle Ng's story, but Crocker paid no heed.

"This road will save lives one day, my boy. You mark my words. This is history we're riding, civilization. Excursionists will be picnicking at Donner Lake within two years."

Ling tried to picture the dark landscape sliding past, as if the train were already under way. How he wished they could go back. But all he could see in the window was Crocker's waxen face perfectly reflected, as if he were peering in on them from another carriage alongside. His great beard was coming in white, Ling noticed, as if he were snorting forth twin plumes of steam. Ling could just

make out his own form dimly mirrored behind Crocker's, alongside the scroll-top desk, but his face was obscured, too dark to be reflected. Crocker took another sip, and Ling remembered Uncle Ng warning him off whiskey: "Looks like gold, tastes like gold—bitter."

"Yessir," he whispered. "Goodnight, sir."

Crocker just shook his head again—"Twenty years and forty pounds ago"—and reached for the decanter.

11.

Ling had lain awake that night, tossing and turning, his shoulders bumping the wall beside the narrow cot, the narrowest he'd slept in since his passage from Hong Kong. Then, though, he'd been hemmed in on all sides by other Chinese; now he was alone in a box not much bigger than a coffin. It made him think of the dead president again —"Emperor Lin Con," as Uncle Ng called him. Ling knew foreign devils didn't practice ancestor worship, but the body's journey home had moved him and he'd found himself weeping for the slain man, though at the time of his death he'd been in the country no more than a few months. Now he contemplated his own bones, where they'd lie at last. He paid his dues to his district company, which would see his remains returned home if he died, but he couldn't imagine it suddenly. Besides, who would worship him, whose ancestor would he be, growing old among all these bachelors? He felt himself a hungry spirit already, rattling in his own jar, gnawing on his own bones. He missed home, he thought, wherever it was.

* * *

In the morning he brewed coffee for Crocker, laid out his dressing gown beside his berth. He felt himself sway with tiredness, almost as if the train were already in motion. He caught himself longing for his bed back in the attic of the Crocker home and shook his head to clear it.

Strobridge brought the news just past sunup. The Chinese were back at work. *They had listened!* Ling thought. He felt jolted with joy, as if the train had lurched forward. But then outside he heard their Irish foremen jeering at them: "Welcome back, boys. Good of ye to join us."

He pushed past Strobridge, down the steps and away from the carriage, watching the lines of workers draining into the tunnel. One man, slight in dark pants and a filthy shirt that might once have been white, paused crossing the tracks and turned to face the locomotive, buckets of tools dangling pendulously from each hand. For a moment it seemed as if he were barring the way, staring the engine down, as if it couldn't flatten him beneath its wheels. The man raised a hand as if to wave it away, bucket flailing, but Ling was too far off to hear what he called, and then two of his fellows hustled him away.

Mounted men, their horses stepping daintily among the rocks as if not to wake the rifles cradled in their riders' arms, ringed the encampment.

Strobridge was smoking on the rear platform when Ling climbed back onboard. The foreman was gazing into the dark socket of the tunnel, and yet Ling had the uncanny sense of the man's ruined eye, behind the patch, following his movements.

"Tell the boss when he wakes," Strobridge reminded him, and Ling, startled for a second to think they shared the same boss, nodded once, feeling it as a great burden.

He broke it to Crocker when he delivered his egg.

"I won't be returning to Sacramento, sir."

"Why, whatever for?"

"I thought I'd hire on the line."

Crocker shook his massive head, his beard rasping on the brocade collar of his dressing gown.

"You shouldn't listen to those harsh words I had for the others, you know. They're not meant for you. Why, you're practically one of the family. The children wouldn't hear of me letting you go."

Ling thought of the Crocker boys, laying pennies on the rails with them one day when they were seeing their father off, and marveling together after the train had passed at how the coins had been warped under the wheels, the Indian head smeared and obliterated. "But are they still worth anything?" little William had asked querulously.

"Please to convey my sincerest apologies to them, sir."

Crocker gave him a pinched look.

"You reckon I'll give you a raise when I wouldn't give that lot one? It's hardly a sound bargaining position to threaten to leave for a poorer-paying post, my boy!"

"No, sir. That's not what I want."

"You really mean it." Crocker sighed. "You'd trade this for that?"

"Yes."

The big man was tapping around his egg with a knife, cracking the shell neatly.

"You think I treat these men harshly, is that it? That I endorse, even authorize, Stro's methods?"

"Yessir."

"Well, perhaps I do. Though never with you, you agree?"

"That's true."

Crocker pried open the top of the egg, releasing a thin column of steam. "So, just to be clear, you leave me on point of principle."

Ling nodded.

"What is it you reckon you owe these men exactly?" Crocker took a sip of his coffee, dabbed his lips. "And here I was thinking I was the one who was paying them." The cup, Ling saw, was from England, the blue willow pattern a ghost's dream of China.

"What the deuce has gotten in to you?" Crocker set the cup back in its saucer with a clack, slopping a little coffee on the tablecloth, and Ling had to stop himself from reaching forward to blot it. All that sustained him was that the Chinese had already kowtowed to Crocker once that day. "It's *business,* you know. Nothing personal."

Ling stared at the stain on the linen between them as if memorizing it.

"My," Crocker said at last. "You have pride. I would not have featured it." He whistled softly. "What a continuous marvel you people are."

Ling bowed infinitesimally.

"Talk about seeing the elephant! Very well. I'll tell Strobridge. He won't give you any special treatment, you know."

"I understand."

"Then you're dismissed." Crocker shoveled a spoonful of egg into his mouth, spoke around it. Only the pallor of his cheeks betrayed his fury. "Just don't come crawling back. It would be such a letdown."

Ling bundled his few possessions in his bedroll. He took a last look at the folded suit and the white shirt hanging on the back of the door. He'd never felt entirely at ease in them, ever conscious of the clean linen, anxious not to soil the clothes, to preserve them as long as possible in their pristine state. He always tried to sit carefully so as not to crease them, to remain as calm as possible so as not to perspire. He'd wanted to avoid any sign on them of contact with the world—a smudge of ash from a pipe or the fire, or, worse, an ink or food stain. But he'd also aspired to leave no mark on them himself. He sniffed the underarms of his shirt each night, studied his cuffs, judging if they might serve another day. And it gave him a particular sense of satisfaction—no, *relief*, really—to see his collar still pristine now, as if unused, as if he'd somehow moved the whole day within its stiff circumference but never quite touched it.

He had thought he was just uneasy at the notion of someone else washing his clothes. There seemed something shameful in having another Chinese do his laundry (the Crocker linen had eventually gone to one of Ng's competitors). But now he realized it was because he'd known the clothes were never truly his.

He recalled the new product Crocker's store had begun to stock: celluloid collars. "Celluloid?" he'd asked. "Oh, it's the coming thing," the importunate clerk had assured him. "The future! Don't need no starch, you see." Ling

had been admiring one when the clerk placed the advertising handbill under his nose, with a line drawing of a caricatured laundryman and his customer.

Chinaman: *No tickee, no washee!*
White: *No washee, no Chinee! So long, John!*

Ling shook his head mournfully at the memory, allowed himself to smooth with his forearm, one last time, the velvety crown of his derby before setting it atop the pile.

Later he stood on the tracks watching the train depart. He listened to each long sigh of the engine as if it were waiting for him to change his mind. And then finally—reluctantly, it seemed—it shrugged into motion, backing slowly down the track, and then faster and faster. A solitary pine, etched against the sky, seemed to point the way.

He watched the locomotive dwindle and finally twist out of sight—the carriage and freight wagon which had trailed them like a queue, he realized belatedly, now going before—and then he followed the great gouts of steam, gashing the sky until he couldn't distinguish them from the clouds above anymore and there was nothing left of the train except a rainbow-sheened puddle of oil and the glossy coil of a turd resting neatly in the center of a tie.

Crocker, busy winding his watch, had walked past him without a glance when he boarded, as if Ling, his forehead freshly shaven, were invisible. *As I might as well be,* he reckoned, though not unhappily, among the hundreds of other Chinese lined up for work. He'd thought for so long that he needed to be better to belong. But he'd never really

wanted to be special, it seemed to him now, the realization stinging like the cold air on his raw scalp, only the same. The big man had got it wrong. Ling wasn't proud. What good was pride without women around, after all? Who were you to be proud for? He pictured Crocker, asleep already, probably, his slumbering weight carrying the train careening downhill. You dream your railroad will annihilate distance, bring everything closer, Ling wanted to tell him, but what if it only carries us farther and farther apart? *Father and father,* he thought with a shudder, wondering ruefully at the apt poverty of English, all those toneless words sounding the same, meaning something different.

The crowd began to shuffle toward the tunnel, but he hesitated for a moment, staring at the empty track, the two silver lines drawing away dully toward a third, the horizon; above it the soaring speck of a bird—an eagle, for sure this time—tawny wings spread stiffly in the sun.

Too late he recalled the gold piece in his waistcoat pocket. He'd left it nestled there when he took the suit off, and now it was gone, down the mountain, as if it had never existed. Someone bumped him and he stumbled into the long, lurching line of men jostling into the darkness.

12.

Crocker had seen the elephant, he'd said. *Have I?* Ling pondered. Seen it all, or at least his fill? Or was he still hoping for more? It was a question he'd continue to ask himself for years to come, long after his queue had grown back (though he continued to tuck it into his collar to disguise its length).

The men had been slow to accept him at first. "I quit Crocker," he told them, and they looked about them and said, "How? Why?" But when Strobridge had tapped him for work as a powder man—"Don't look so scared. Didn't your lot invent fireworks?"—he'd gained their grudging regard. He grew adept at tamping the charges, paying out the fuse, uncoiling it behind him with a flick of the wrist as if he were sowing rice. The other men let him bathe first, or gave him an extra portion of rice, like an offering, because he went back into the darkness when a fuse failed, as it often did in the damp. He'd get slowly back to his feet and, while the rest watched from cover, as if in ambush, retrace the fuse down the tunnel toward the rockface, looking for a break, all the time fearing that the fuse was still live, the charge about to go off. All under the singular stare of Strobridge, who had lost his own eye in a blasting accident and who stood now as warning to any of them.

He'd not expected to survive the job, nor cared overmuch if he didn't. But it seemed he was lucky in this. Later he'd work with nitro, and even the bosses would creep softly about him—China-shop Bill backing away, hands up, head bent, so that the men started calling him Kowtow Bill instead. It was as if Ling himself were an unstable compound, ready to erupt at the slightest provocation. He enjoyed the deference, though in truth what he thought of as he stepped gently along with the nitro in hand was how he'd served Crocker, his gliding way of moving around the big man.

Had he seen it all, then? he wondered, watching nitro reduce bosses to obeisance and mountains to dust. Or later, when he helped lay ten miles of track in a single day?

Or later still, witnessing Crocker's old associate Leland Stanford (who had lately revised his opinion of the Chinese upward as "quiet, peaceable, patient, industrious, and economical") raise a hammer to strike the final golden spike into the railroad . . . and miss his swing. But perhaps that was no stranger than a man driving a long fang of gold back *into* the earth—though of course it was swiftly drawn out again and an iron spike inserted in its place.

But even then, apparently, there was more to see. The road completed, work was scarce suddenly, thousands of men unemployed. Ling hired on with the Six Companies as a bone-scraper, working his way back along the line he'd helped lay, exhuming the bodies buried beside the road, gathering their bones to be shipped home to China. It was just another kind of mining: sifting the soil, sometimes with chopsticks, for every one of the 206 bones in a human body, the tiny white pebbles of wrists and ankles, fingers and toes winking from the dirt in his sieve, each to be checked off on a list, each hand and foot bagged in its own pouch and nestled in a box among the other polished bones. Just another kind of laundry too—every bone scrubbed of dirt and flesh, boiled and rubbed with a solution of Chinese wine and water until it shone, cleansed of its mortality.

The boiling was the worst, he found, the soupy smell obliging him to sit upwind. He lit joss sticks to mask it, saying a prayer for the dead men, and for Uncle Ng and Little Sister for good measure.

Just once he turned up a small piece of gold among the bones, as if it too were one of the remains. He rolled the heavy nut of it in his fingers, wondering where it fit in a

body. He couldn't imagine anyone leaving it there, but then it came to him that the dead man must have swallowed it, perhaps over and over to keep it secret. Ling had already pocketed it, but he slipped it back among the small bones of the wrist, giving the bag a little shake until the nugget sank out of sight. He didn't believe in spirits anymore, but he didn't want any trouble from them either.

He found the work peaceful, apart from those moments when a train scythed through the air nearby, though he always had warning from the singing rails and took care to cover his work from the eyes of passengers with an unfurled umbrella. It was more awkward in the towns he stopped in along the route to ship the bones back to the coast, a first and last ride on the rails they'd laid for most of the men in his care. Townspeople were suspicious of him, some hostile. When they learned of his work some would say "Good riddance," while others seemed resentful that their country wasn't a fit place to be buried. Ling ignored them, though once he reluctantly allowed a local undertaker and once an insistent doctor to accompany him on his doleful work. The undertaker, after taking a spill on the silky carpet of pine needles, sat in the shade drinking and gawping—*Here's me planting 'em and you digging 'em up. Truth is, I always speculated what become of 'em under the dirt*—until he fell asleep. The doctor studied the bodies, twisting the ends of his mustache between thumb and forefinger as if turning a key, and offered opinions as to what they'd died from—malnutrition, disease, or violent accident (the latter, including falls and explosions, wasn't hard to spot)—though to Ling the cause of death was in each case simple: the railroad.

Eventually he found himself back in San Francisco at the very dock he'd arrived on twenty years earlier, delivering the last remains in his charge and deliberating whether it was time to follow them home. The Exclusion Act, barring further Chinese immigration, had finally been passed (the last in a long line of anti-Chinese laws dating back to a ban on carry poles). No more Chinamen. No more women for those already there.

At the foot of the gangway, an old tar, so leathery his race was indeterminate, asked him if the bones were bound for doctors in China. "I 'member when we used to ship 'em up from Panama, bodies of them what died of yellow fever building that there railroad 'cross the isthmus, skeletons for the medical gentlemen, even some poor devils pickled in barrels for surgeons to practice on. That railroad, they say, was paid for by the fees for those bodies."

"I wouldn't be a bit surprised," Ling said mildly. He remembered Crocker's spluttering indignation when the Panama Railroad — all forty-eight miles of it! — had been referred to in his hearing as the *first* transcontinental.

So *had* he seen the elephant at last? Ling asked himself a little later, lighting his pipe, staring out over the expanse of the bay, the water gray and wrinkled with chop.

By then he'd learned the expression, before it was adopted by miners, had originated with troopers on their way to the front. "Going to see the elephant," meaning the great gray army of the Confederacy. That war had almost torn the country in two, but the railroad, men said, had bound it back together, the tracks and ties like sutures to a wound, now fading to a scar.

Or perhaps just stitches to mend a rip, Ling thought. If he'd once been proud and later ashamed, he'd now grown bitter. The railroad finished, the Chinese had scattered across the West, thousands of them looking for work and willing to do it for less than most ghosts. That plus the influx of new labor from the East, over the very tracks the Chinese had laid, had made competition for jobs even fiercer and resentment among the ghosts more pronounced. This was the season of the sandlot riots, of *The Chinese Must Go!* The Chinese might have physically united the country by building a railroad across it, but now they were uniting it in another sense, binding the quarreling tribes of Irish and English, French and Germans, Swedes and Italians together against a common enemy.

We made them white, Ling thought. Just like Uncle Ng said. Just like bluing. Whiter than any laundry.

The Chinese were singled out for their race, their peculiar ways—blacks came in for the same treatment, of course, but the country had almost come asunder fighting over Negroes, and the Chinese, for the time at least, seemed an altogether simpler target—but also because, unique among all immigrants, they were the ones who looked to leave, to take their wealth home with them. It offended settlers, this sojourner attitude, exemplified by the very bones Ling helped to send back to China.

And now he might go aboard one of those ships as a passenger himself. He had enough saved to buy a ticket home, and he had certainly come to envy the peace of the men in his care, their silence, their stillness, their eventual homecoming. He was old, even Gold Mountain was old;

Australia was the new Gum Shan. And yet . . . there was still the matter of the elephant.

A part of him, younger and more innocent, still hoped the phrase might refer to a real elephant; circuses were all the rage then, after all. He'd heard of Jumbo, the star attraction, made famous in part by the railroads, which allowed him to be shipped from city to city, traveling as the papers said in a palace car of his very own. It made Ling smile to picture it—the elephant reposing like Mister Charley, the man's voluminous beard grown into a flowing trunk—and he yearned to see the beast, but the nearest he'd come was being passed once, somewhere in Nevada, by a circus train, a giraffe's great neck stretching above the treetops, its tiny ears pinned back in the wind. *They'd better have it lie down before the Sierra tunnels,* he thought. He could hear the roaring of lions, the chatter of monkeys, and, he fancied, the bellow of an elephant over the engine. He found himself waving at the train like any child.

But lately he'd read that the famous pachyderm had been killed, struck and crushed by a train, of all things. All that was left was its skeleton, on display in a museum in Washington, and he'd seen enough bones. In another paper he'd learned of the death of the Bunker twins, Chang and Eng, their bones buried in North Carolina but their shared liver pickled and on show in a museum back East.

Now on the docks what came to mind at last was the old Chinese fable of the blind men and the elephant. How one flapped its ear and said it was like a fan, and another grasped its tail and said it was like a snake, a third rubbed

its trunk and proclaimed it like bamboo. And so on and so forth. It's how he felt about his life, about Gold Mountain, like one of those blind men finding an elephant but not knowing what he held.

And yet, looking out across the roadstead to the famous gap of the Golden Gate, Ling resisted being driven out. If what distinguished the Chinese from the rest was that they didn't mean to stay, well then, some of them *must* stay, and why shouldn't he be one? Him and all the whores, he thought, summoning up Little Sister for the first time in years. *They* couldn't go home for shame, but if he did, he'd still be Tanka or Eurasian, the stains he'd hoped to wash away with wealth. On Gold Mountain, at least, they were all simply Chinese.

It reminded him of a dirty version of the old story told to him by a whore—maybe Little Sister herself, though after so much time and so many whores he couldn't be sure. He'd met her again, years later, alive and well, if more ample than before, madam of her own establishment, albeit one in a dusty backwater he passed through on one of his bone-gathering trips.

He hadn't known her at first. She was in a Western dress, dark watered silk and flounced crinoline—very seemly, if a little dated. He recalled Mrs. Crocker in similar styles, and when the woman called him by name he'd had the odd thought at first that it was her, his former mistress. And then he'd recognized Little Sister's wanton grin.

"Well, if I ain't seen the elephant!" she'd exclaimed. He'd been tempted to turn on his heel, look behind him. She meant him, of course, and yet he wanted to deny it, as

if it were an accusation. She held him at arm's length to study him—he could feel the dirt under his nails, in the seams of his clothes and flesh—and then embraced him, and even though he knew she pitied him, it felt as if she'd lifted a yoke from his shoulders.

She was calling herself Madame Celeste these days and partnered with a robust old highbinder who went by the name of Sam Gum—a play on Gum Shan—though whether he had chosen the name or had it bestowed upon him, Ling never knew. He reveled in it, though, styling himself Missa Gold in expansive moods, though he was certainly called other names by those he beat at the poker table in the corner of the brothel. He reveled in those too, though as if they were so many laurels, going so far in latter days, after the fame of Bret Harte's poem "The Heathen Chinee," about a couple of whites gulled by a Chinese gambler, as to call his place the Heathen Café. The poem's fame, despite the dim light in which it showed his kind, brought him customers by the bushel, though he was sure to sit down to the table in only a vest, his arms bare to the shoulders, so no man could accuse him of cheating like the Chink in the poem, the cards secreted in the folds of his voluminous sleeves.

And through it all he kept winning—not always, but often and steadily. Ling had stayed for a few days, scouting the tracks in and out of town for bodies, so he had a chance to observe him most evenings and overhear the gossip about him. Many were the theories as to how Ah Sam managed it. Cheating was ascribed to him—strategically placed mirrors on the walls, the collusion of waiters and the hurdy-gurdy dancers twirling across the floor

—but he was always willing to change his seat, to sit with his back to the dance floor or bar. Some suggested that such was his Oriental inscrutability that he had a natural advantage in bluffing. Still others ascribed his success to sobriety, it being said that the bottle he swigged from at his elbow was filled with cold tea and not whiskey—a trick he may have learned from the hurdy girls, or learned them himself—which gave him another edge over most of his rivals. If appealed to directly, he would only say, "No trickee, no cheatee! Luckee!"

"He speaks perfectly good Melican," Little Sister assured Ling, hawking into a spittoon. (She'd taken up chewing tobacco in the intervening years, as if to keep her aim in, though when he asked, she grimaced: "Takes away the taste of cum.") "He just likes to Chink it up," she noted. She wanted Ling to think well of him, he thought, and he was touched.

"At least he's luckier than poor Ng," he told her, and she rolled her eyes.

In truth, Ling had already guessed it wasn't luck but the very opposite that served Sam so well. "Don't believe in fortune," the gambler opined contemptuously after the suckers had cleared out. The two of them were having a drink together, Little Sister hovering sleepily. Sam seemed to need to explain himself, but Ling found he already liked the man, was happy for Little Sister. "Didn't I put in my years scratching around the mother lode?" Sam asked. He'd not struck it rich there, and he knew moreover from bitter experience what a Chinaman's chance meant—none at all. He'd been run off claims, he'd seen his fellow Celestials gunned down for sport. (The story sounded so

much like Ng's that Ling wondered if he'd cribbed it from Little Sister, or if the similarity had drawn her to him.)

"You know we can't testify against devils in law?" Ling nodded. "Best thing that ever happened," Sam grunted.

"How d'you figure?"

"Chinese can't testify, devil reckons he can do anything bad—whoring, dope, drink, gamble—around Chinese. He feels easy here! Good for business."

"I guess so."

"And, no, I don't believe in luck," Sam declared, banging his glass onto the table. And that was his edge when playing men—white men—who to a soul cherished, like a hand cupped around a flickering candle, a belief in it. Hadn't they come out West on the basis of it? These men were quintessential Americans, believers in the main chance, certain they deserved better than their lot, that the world, the earth, owed them its treasures. (Ling thought those men believed in something else too—their superiority to a Chinaman—but he nodded along.) Such men, on aggregate, Sam was saying, stayed in a hand past their time, hoping, hoping, always hoping for the right card, or at least the wrong one for their opponent. "But I don't believe in such stuff," he asserted with a belligerent little puff of his chest. He bet on the cards he had, not the ones he wished for. That's what the West had taught *him*. "My candle went out long ago, but I can see all the better in the dark for want of it."

"He doesn't believe in love either." Little Sister smiled ruefully when the gambler had scraped his winnings into his hat and taken himself off to bed. "No more than I. It's why we get along so tolerably well. A gambler who doesn't

believe in luck and a whore who doesn't believe in love. It's the secret of our success!" She looked at him shrewdly. "And what about you, bone scraper, do you believe in the afterlife?"

He shook his head slowly. "I've no ancestors, no descendants. I've no use for an afterlife."

"Well, good for you!" She raised her glass. "All those credulous fools dreaming of going home even when they're dead, paying good money for the privilege. Money that could get them fucked in this life if they spent it wisely. Oh, I know, they think women have no souls. What a lonely afterlife for them! I have no soul, so I make the most of my life here and now. Besides, who's to say the soul resides in bones? Why not in the flesh? Any whore might tell you that."

"But what *do* you believe in?" he asked her.

"Gold!" She grinned crookedly. "Still gold. I'm faithful! And you?"

"I believe," he sighed, "you were pregnant. I didn't want to at first."

He stared at her steadily until she met his eyes.

"Were you?"

"But you never came looking for me!"

"I heard you were dead. Besides, I never knew your name."

"Sure you did."

"Your real name."

"Mei Mei, Little Sister. That's the name he gave me, even though I was the eldest."

Ling stared at her.

"I guess he wanted to honor her."

He nodded slowly.

"You didn't answer my question, though."

"Oh, who can remember? Who wants to? All the pregnancies and miscarriages, stillbirths, and worse."

"I'm sorry."

She shrugged. "Some live." She gestured toward a girl sleeping on the bar. "My eldest. Goldie, they call her, though I named her Jin, on account her cradle was an old prospector's rocker. Her sister is around here someplace too." She smiled wanly. "How do you think I started my own business?"

He took a drink, shuddered only a little as he swallowed.

"They're half?" he asked while she poured him another, and she nodded.

"But *their* children will be more white than not. They'll be something. Storekeepers. Teachers!"

They were silent for a long time. He laid his hand on hers, and after a moment she turned it over, squeezed his back. She rose and pulled him up from the table.

"No charge," she whispered.

"Now *I've* seen the elephant."

She set her hands on her hips. "What are you suggesting?"

"I meant the money," he said hastily, but she winked.

"I know what you mean. Just don't go telling everyone. Bad for business, lah. Besides, Ah Sam wouldn't like it."

"He's jealous."

"Not so long as there's gold involved."

"I won't tell a soul," he promised, and she grinned.

"They'd never believe you anyway."

He had been joking, but as he watched her disrobe, he wondered if he hadn't really seen the elephant, seen it years ago, that first morning at Ng's as she knelt in the tub to bathe.

When she was naked she stretched out a hand to caress his cheek and reach for his neck, not to pull him close for a kiss, as he thought, but to slowly draw his queue forth from his collar and smooth it over his shoulder.

Afterward, in bed, as he licked the taste of her tobacco off his lips, she told him her version of the elephant story.

The beast, in her variant, is approached not by blind men but by blind women. "One grabs his tail," Little Sister said, making a gesture with her fist, "another his trunk. Ah, an elephant is like a penis, the first cries. And the second says, I'm keeping this elephant!" And they cupped their hands to each other's mouth to catch their laughter as if it were spit.

Silver

Your Name in Chinese

The truth is always exciting. Speak it, then.
Life is dull without it.

—*Pearl S. Buck*

Riveting

In 1926, after the first spadeful of earth was turned with a golden shovel, she had the honor of driving the first rivet for Grauman's Chinese Theatre. She'd starred alongside one of the theater's backers, Douglas Fairbanks, in *The Thief of Bagdad* two years earlier. In yellowing press clippings she can be seen posing for photographers with a ball-peen hammer perched jauntily on her shoulder as if it were a golf club or parasol (though after she struck the first symbolic blows—"Chink, chink," some card joked —a worker with a pneumatic hammer moved in to finish the job). The next day the caption in *Variety* called her a "riveting beauty." She was twenty-one years old.

Fifty Million Frenchmen

In Yokohama the newspapers catch up with their ship, with a juicy bit of Hollywood gossip. It's 1935. Clark Gable's *Parnell* is a bust, except in China of all places, and Carole Lombard has had some fun dropping fliers from a biplane over the MGM lot saying, "Fifty Million Chinese Can't Be Wrong!" a reference to the Broadway smash of ten years earlier, *Fifty Million Frenchmen*, and its hit song.

It's a coup. "Typical Carole," she observes over the rim of her highball when people ask, though she envies Lombard her wit, and Gable a lover to make light of humiliation. If only she'd had someone. If only she'd thought to fly a plane over the studio. And what would she have dropped? A bomb, probably.

It thrills her fellow passengers, she can see, that they know her and she knows Carole Lombard, and it dismays her too, this reflected starlight that dims her own pallid glow.

Instead she makes a joke of it. It starts to do the rounds.

"Fifty million seagulls can't be wrong," someone kids at the rail; a flock hovers off the stern, taut as kites.

"Fifty million snowflakes can't be wrong," says another, flapping at his face, though snow hadn't featured in any of their imaginings of Japan. But then it is January. If you squint, offers a wag, they look like cherry blossoms.

"Fifty million Japanese," says someone else, staring out over the city, but what *they* can't be is left unsaid, out of deference to her, perhaps. Fifty million Japanese can't conquer China, she thinks to herself.

"Fifty million waves," she offers gamely. In the steel-gray distance they seem as still as a photograph, waiting to be counted.

But most often she finds herself returning to those fifty million American moviegoers left in her wake. What can't they? she wonders. See her kiss.

Darkness, Invisible

She bought her first movie ticket at ten, with the tips she earned making deliveries for her father's laundry. This was Los Angeles—*Lo Sang* in Chinese—her birthplace. Cutting school, she walked for miles in the heat to avoid being seen by anyone she knew. Only when she hadn't passed another Chinese face for blocks did she duck into a theater—a Biograph, she later recalled. The ticket-seller gave her a narrow look, inspected the Indian head on the coin she held out as if it were a passport (this when Nickelodeons still cost a nickel), and waved her through. The ticket stub is preserved on the inside cover of her scrapbook.

At first she felt self-conscious, being the only Chinese, and a young girl at that, in the audience. She hid in the bathroom, terrified and lonely, tracing the pattern on the tin ceiling, until she heard the organist start up, and then she slipped in and took a seat. But in the cool darkness she found herself relaxing, laughing with the rest at the short subjects, weeping with everyone else during the feature, emotions she would never have betrayed on the street and which even here she glanced around furtively before giving vent to. But no one was watching her; all their faces upturned toward the screen, each one lit with the same silvery glaze. No one, not even she, could tell the difference. It was the first place she felt like an American.

When he found out her father made her kneel and beat her with the broom.

But she kept going, sometimes seeking out movie houses so far from home that the intertitles were in Spanish. Pearl

White in *The Perils of Pauline* was a favorite—perils that included villains called Wu Fang and Long Sin. Her own villainy included forging notes from her father to give to her teachers in an English he couldn't write, getting whipped first by him and then by them when discovered.

In the beginning it was the theaters' thrill of invisibility that she craved, that she couldn't get enough of, tired as she was of being stared at in the street, picked on in school. Outside, even the sun seemed to glare at her; inside, it was all chill shadows. The flickers were the one place she didn't feel watched, the one place where she could watch others. Later, though, she came to envy those faces and figures on the screen before her. Not to be stared at was one thing, but to be stared at as they were stared at, with love and awe, was something else again. She wanted to be like them. Every face on the screen was white, but in the dreaming darkness anything seemed possible. At home in the mirror she practiced their expressions and poses awkwardly. But in the dark she made their faces her own.

Orientally Yours

She turns heads on the boat deck. She turns heads on the lido deck, reclining beside the saltwater pool. She signs autographs in the beauty shop, at the soda fountain, at the bar. "Orientally yours," she writes, then her name, Anna May Wong, in English and Chinese, Wong Liu Tsong. She's the only Chinese in the First Cabin. She turns heads at the captain's table. She turns heads in the salon. The ballroom is as big as a soundstage. Men scramble to pull out chairs for her. She's a dab hand at quoits.

A woman in furs is reading *The Good Earth* on the promenade deck. Would she sign it? A passing steward proffers a pen. She pushes up her sunglasses, fogged with salt rime. "I heard Pearl Buck wanted you for the part," the woman says, and she nods as if this matters. "Good Earth, Better Sea!" she inscribes gaily on the flyleaf.

The ship is the SS *President Hoover,* named for the thirty-first president, a one-time manager of the Chinese Engineering and Mining Company. Mr. Hoover served honorably in the defense of Tientsin during the Boxer Rebellion. Later he helped ship fifty thousand coolies to South African mines. It is said the president and first lady spoke Mandarin in the White House whenever they wanted to communicate privately. Their portrait hangs over the grand staircase of the steamliner.

Out of Yokohama she visits steerage and finds it filled with Chinese, stacked in bunks, many of them old, their faces freckled and pouchy, on their way home after a lifetime away. She tells them she is visiting her father, who has moved back to his ancestral village, and they smile

toothlessly, nod in approval. They are bringing home treasures. They show her radios, bicycles, wristwatches. They show her the prized canaries they are bringing as gifts for family, the birds cowering mutely on their perches like their owners on the edge of their bunks. Through the hull she can just make out the dull reports of first-class passengers shooting skeet off the stern. One younger man clutches a box tightly to his chest, and when she asks what's in it, he tells her the bones of his father. She signs autographs for them but omits the "Orientally yours."

Later, alone in her suite de luxe, she sips her nightcap, lies back on satin pillows plumped by the maid, loses herself in the lustrous grain of the burled, inlaid ceiling, while her fingers trace the mazy scrollwork of the dado rail.

Wong Liu Tsong means "Frosted Yellow Willow." Her father asked her once what Anna May meant. "Me," she said simply.

Rubbernecks

Her father still remembered the excursion buses, horse-drawn and open-topped, that had toured Chinatown at the start of the century. Sightseers in straw skimmers led by a talker with a horn for a mouth calling *Lookee here, lookee there,* directing their attention hither and thither, earning them the name "rubbernecks."

It was a racy fad, she learned later — a vogue started in San Francisco and New York that had spread to Los Angeles, driven by exotic photographs and the seamy, salacious reputation of Chinatown. Yet as a child she never believed her father's stories. A man with a horn coming out of his mouth? She pictured a single arcing tusk, like an elephant's. Besides, and almost as improbably, when were Chinese so interesting to whites? She wasn't sure they were so interesting to her, even.

But at eleven she'd spotted a crowd on a street corner presided over by a man with a megaphone (the "horn" her father referred to was a speaking trumpet, of course) and hurried up to see if the rubbernecks had returned, only to find it was a movie crew. She tarried to watch the stars emerge from their parked limousines for a take and then retreat back to the curtained splendor of their gleaming automobiles. The leading lady, Mae Murray (from whom she would later adopt part of her English name), wore a fur, shrugging it daintily on and off her shoulders between takes like a cape, but beneath it she was dressed in diaphanous rags. It was a costume, of course, but the girl was disappointed, thought a star should dress like those at the premieres she'd seen in newsreels. This was *acting,* she

told herself. Even in rags Mae Murray was beautiful, her skin and hair lustrous. And how she moved! Stalking gracefully from car to scene, gliding in the midst of so much busy energy. Just from her walk you could tell she was something.

The girl tried to walk home like that, on the balls of her feet like a dancer, one leg reaching out in front of the other as if on an invisible tightrope.

Within two months, already tall for her age, she had begun to model fur coats in newspaper advertisements for a customer who'd been impressed by her posture when she delivered laundry. She tried to give the money to her father, but he didn't like the pose she struck. He was ironing. "A disgrace," he called her. "Do you know no shame?" He doused the linen with his brass sprayer. She tried to tell him it was acting, but the distinction was lost on him. "Who acts like a whore? I ask you. Whores, that's who!" He pushed the money away. "I'm no pimp."

He was wrong; she knew all about shame. Hadn't she'd grown up washing and ironing other people's "unmentionables"? She once told an interviewer she changed the spelling from M-A-E to M-A-Y "to give myself permission." "Permission for what?" "Why, everything!"

Another time her father caught her applying "makeup." She had collected her lucky red packets from New Year's, moistened the paper, and rubbed it against her cheeks as rouge, used burnt matches for kohl. He scrubbed her face with a cloth until her cheeks were raw. "Our business is *cleaning*! How do you think it looks if the laundry girl is dirty?"

But she didn't want to be in the family business.

"It's my fault," her mother whispered later. "He always wanted a son. He didn't come home for days after you were born."

Her mother dressed her as a boy for early baby photographs. She was a tomboy as a girl. Years later, in cabaret, she'd perform in top hat and tails.

Chinese Rubbernecks was also the name of an early short set in a laundry — she saw it once as a child — featuring a fantastical tussle between two Chinese during which one grabs the other's head and stretches his neck across the frame before releasing it to snap back into place.

Ten Doors

The family laundry—home until she was six—was on
Flower Street, a block north of Chinatown, the
Laundrymen's Association having decreed that laundries
had to be at least ten doors apart to regulate competition.
The new family home on Figueroa was three blocks
further removed from the bachelor society of Chinatown
in a mixed neighborhood of Mexicans, Irish, and recent
Eastern European immigrants. She grew up, she later told
friends, with one foot in Chinatown, one foot in America.

"Everyone comes to Los Angeles to be a star," she said
once. "I was born there, but you could say I still came
farther than most."

The Role of a Lifetime

Turned down for the role of a lifetime—O-lan in *The Good Earth,* a Chinese female lead; how many of those will she ever see?—and turned down for a white actress. It's a public humiliation, a famous snub. A loss of face, she's still Chinese enough to think.

She'd been tipped for the role in the press for years; "born to play it," they said. It was what she'd be waiting for all this time. But she'd known she wouldn't get it as soon as they cast Paul Muni, *Scarface* himself, in the lead. The Hays Code forbade the portrayal of interracial relations onscreen, even when white actors were playing in yellowface. "You're just not the type" was how producer Irving Thalberg explained in awkward apology. "You're *too* Chinese." (By contrast, Muni, when Thalberg offered him the role, joked, "I'm about as Chinese as Herbert Hoover.") The part of O-lan went instead to the German actress Luise Rainer.

"I'm in the business of creating illusions," Thalberg added. As if she weren't.

At parties she made light of it. "The role of a lifetime? Horsefeathers! Besides," she added coquettishly, "isn't that what Doug Fairbanks used to promise all the girls? The *roll* of a lifetime? It wasn't true then either!"

But a public humiliation requires a public response. Which is why she's sailing to China. If she can't have the role of a lifetime, she'll take the trip of a lifetime, a visit to the homeland she's never set foot in. Her father moved back two years earlier, after selling up, and her plan is to meet him in the family village. He has never approved of

her career — it's hard to escape the suspicion that he left the U.S. to get away from her notoriety — and their estrangement was cemented when she failed to return from New York, where she was appearing on Broadway, for her mother's funeral five years ago. She had fought for her little sister, doe-eyed Mary, to be her understudy — she balked at a yellowface stand-in — but if they had both attended the burial, the theater would have gone dark. There was a moment when they both realized it, and she saw her sister's face flicker with the understudy's avid gleam.

"*You* must go for both of us," she told Mary. "You'll regret it forever if you don't."

"But what about you?"

It's the bigger part, she wanted to say, *the grieving daughter. You'll be taking over from me in* that *role.* Instead she declared tightly, "The show must go on."

Mary had always been their father's favorite anyway, born after he already had sons. It was why she'd promised to aid Mary in her acting career: to spite him. He'd hoped the younger sister would chaperone the older, but she'd bribed Mary to look the other way with walk-ons and bit parts.

Now, as she circles the deck of the *Hoover,* she's hoping for a prodigal's return of sorts, a reconciliation. Never mind that her father has moved back in with his first wife and son, her mother being technically the "little wife," the concubine.

But she also has another vindication in mind. She's arranged for her visit to be filmed for Hearst Metrotone News. If she can't star in *The Good Earth,* she'll star in

her own movie, and perhaps along the way remind audiences of the *real* China, not the Hollywood version. A cameraman has been assigned to meet her in Shanghai and accompany her on her travels for the purpose. The show *will* go on.

See, See, See

They called her the C.C.C. She had begun to hang out around movie crews, wherever there was a shoot. The Curious Chinese Child. *Queue-rious*, someone cracked, tugging on her braid playfully. She didn't mind. She could picture the credit:

Curious Chinese ChildWong Liu Tsong

The long line of dots like a string of pearls.

One day they herded her into a crowd of Chinese extras. She was thirteen. *Only you have to stop ogling the stars,* someone told her. They paid her seven dollars and fifty cents, more money than she'd ever seen. Chinese extras made a buck fifty more than whites because of their rarity (one of the very few times she'd make more than white performers). She gave seven to her father and he left the broom in the corner. She saved the rest to take herself and two school friends, Jia and Zhen, to the California Theater on Main Street when the picture opened. She needed witnesses. She was so excited to see herself, her face hot and tight as if stretched before a projector bulb. But she couldn't find herself on the screen. There was the street scene, there were the stars, there was the crowd, but she couldn't see herself in it. Couldn't find herself among all those other Chinese faces. *That's me,* she whispered to the girl next to her in the balcony. *There I am!* But it was a lie. She couldn't believe she could disappear on film, she who'd felt so self-conscious, so incandescently aware of herself. When she stepped out into the matinee sunlight,

her eyes stung, and she blinked away tears. Her friends didn't even mind, just giggled and thanked her for the tickets. "Let us know when you're in another movie." It shocked her less that others couldn't see her — she knew she was only an extra — than that she couldn't find herself. It was like looking in a mirror and not recognizing yourself. What good was the silver screen if it didn't reflect you?

She went back alone the next day and sat through show after show, searching the edges of the frame, but she was as invisible on film as she had been in the audience. She felt cheated. Four hours walking up and down before the camera, and nothing to show for it! She yearned to have the projectionist halt the reel, or run it in reverse. She pictured the crowd bobbing back up the street, carefully planting each backward step with a kind of exaggerated nonchalance. How well they kept their straight faces. *Get out of the way*, she wanted to call to them. She wanted to reach out and push them aside. She thought perhaps they would step back and reveal her, still walking forward, but no, she must have walked backward herself, down off the curb, back across the street, and up onto the other side without tripping. She imagined herself pausing with the others, as if to catch her breath, after the director called "Action" and the boy with the clapperboard jumped out of the way, the crowd of them milling about, smoking and chatting, then drifting away in twos and threes until they thinned out. She saw herself alone striding home backward on the balls of her feet, slipping into her room past her mother, plucking her cheeks pale in the mirror, tousling her hair with the brush, holding a towel to her face, and

then catching water in her hands, laying it back in the basin, backing at last into her bed and lying there, eyes bright as the light faded.

Within three years she would receive her first screen credit—"A credit to your race," he called it—in Marshall Neilan's *Bits of Life*. She was sixteen. Neilan, fifteen years older, would be her first lover. What was the brassy backstage gag? She pictured it as a sepia intertitle:

It ain't rape if
he's a director . . .
It's your big break!

Though to herself she whispered, *It ain't rape . . . if he's white.* Neilan told her he would leave his wife for her, but when he did, it was to marry the silent star Blanche Sweet. He was just the first of many who deserted her. "Men!" she used to toast sardonically. "They're just so damned scrutable!"

Pre-Code

Even earlier in her career, before the Code, when the rules against the depiction of miscegenation were not absolute and she could have white lovers onscreen, prevailing attitudes—particularly of audiences in the southern states—meant that her romantic roles were constrained. She never kissed one of her leading men in Hollywood. Whenever their lips approached, something would intervene—a train whistle, a shot, a scream, once the clamor of a huge gong. Her onscreen white lovers invariably threw her over in the end, and her character would usually die—by her own hand if she was an innocent, as in her first starring role, in *The Toll of the Sea,* or by another's if she was some scheming seductress. She could be Butterfly or Dragon Lady, it didn't much matter in the end.

I yearned to play O-lan, she confides in her diary as the ship steams west, *because the character was a mother.* When she looks back at the journal years later, she'll be puzzled by a single blank page, until she recalls it was the day they lost crossing the date line.

Critical Reception

Reviewers praised her as "naturally Chinese" and "an exquisite crier, without the need for glycerine." She was possessed of a "porcelain pulchritude."

Toll of the Sea was the first Hollywood feature shot in Technicolor; critics called it a short-lived fad, sure to go the way of Kinemacolor, and Prizmacolor before it.

Now at the stern she hears people extolling the "Technicolor sunset" over the shuddering throb of the twin screws. Pewter water stretches away unbroken in every direction, the ship at the center like the last glass proffered on a vast tray.

Female Parts

She recalls her mother hardly ever setting foot outside the house. Even when her father took the children to see the touring opera troupes, her mother stayed behind. Her father told her that all the women onstage were played by men, and she would stare at them, trying to see if he was telling the truth.

When she was little she thought her mother was scared. When she was older she understood that respectable wives did not show themselves in the street. "Public women" was a euphemism for whores. But she still thought her mother was scared of something. "The poor woman did have seven children over twenty years," her eldest sister told her once. "What chance did she have to get out?"

Their mother was married at sixteen to a man almost thirty years her senior. Her film-star daughter was seventeen years older than her youngest brother. When their mother died she would care for him as a son. Her sibling could have been her child, her mother a sibling. (And was it amid all those children that she first yearned to stand out? She wasn't the eldest, the youngest, or a son, after all.)

In a census of 1910 there were seventy-seven females in Chinatown to over two thousand men; they were a minority's minority.

The women she did spy on the streets as she went to and from school or about her laundry deliveries were prostitutes, or so she guessed. They told her she was beautiful — *ho leng*. They told her to hurry home.

Her mother saw her once acting in front of the mirror in her bedroom, re-creating some melodrama, hands to

her face, then tearing at her hair, her mouth open in a silent wail. Perhaps it was that silence, but her mother had said nothing either, just held her eyes in the mirror for a moment and turned away. They never spoke of it; her mother can't have told her father. He would have beaten them both if she had.

Her maternal grandfather had been a cigar-maker in San Francisco, and sometimes her mother would roll a short cigar and smoke by the window. Sometimes, after she started acting, she would join her and they would smoke together in silence.

Years later, when she heard that her mother had been killed by a car, she couldn't believe it. What was she doing in the street? Secretly she blamed her father for keeping the woman cooped up all those years. If only her mother had been more used to the streets, she might have known to look out for a car.

Ancestor Worship

Her father had been born in a gold camp called Michigan Bluffs. She liked to imagine her grandfather coming to America to seek gold the way she sought fame. But her father corrected her. "He was a merchant, a storekeep, not some gold-digger." *Like me,* he meant, *not you.* She watched him light joss sticks, press them between his palms, bow deeply before the family altar.

Later he told her, "In that same camp at the same time Mr. Leland Stanford also started his first business." He nodded portentously.

"Actually, I'm not sure that comparison reflects so well on Grandfather," she observed. The place was a ghost town by then anyway.

The Gold Cure

She's never been seasick a day in her life, likes to take the air at the prow even in rough chop, watch the rabid waves flinging themselves at the hull. The night sky over the Pacific, though, so dark and deep compared to Los Angeles' with its haze and city lights, makes her dizzy. The stars seem so many and so bright, yet unattainably distant.

In her teens she suffered a nervous breakdown—Saint Vitus' dance, some have speculated—and she would endure spells of depression (often fueled by drinking) throughout her life. As a child she was "cured" by a Chinese doctor who scratched a gold coin down her arm repeatedly until she bled. The graze, a long white tail ending in an angry red welt, looked like a comet. She asked if she could keep the coin, but the apothecary shook his head. It was an antique, he said. Besides, the gold was already in her blood now.

The real cure was her father's reluctant agreement to let her pursue acting. He had wanted her to be a secretary, but she was hopeless at shorthand.

"I'll be famous," she promised him.

"What is that, fame?"

"Like *face*," she explained. "I'll make you proud."

And he'd shaken his head grimly. "Famous, maybe. Proud, no." Actors, he explained, were lower than coolies in China. How could you be a famous coolie? As for actresses, what was lower than a coolie? A harlot. Who would want to be a famous harlot?

"Fame is not face," he concluded. "You get famous, I lose face. Ill fame, more like."

"Rich, then," she vowed angrily. "I'll get rich. Isn't that the same as face?"

He tried to marry her off, but no respectable Chinese would have her. "Perhaps marriage is not her fortune," her mother suggested. In interviews she would put her unmarried state down to the fact that Chinese men preferred traditional wives.

In the end her father was only persuaded to let her appear in *The Thief of Bagdad* when Douglas Fairbanks came to the laundry and said he'd personally chaperone her on set. Doug called her a "modest little person," even promised to lock her in her dressing room between takes. Her father believed him, she is sure. He could no more imagine his daughter taking a white lover than taking one himself. *Amalgamation* (as he called miscegenation) was "no good for nobody."

At night, through the slit blinds of the hotel window, the new sign in the hills flashed steadily above the palms: holly. wood. land.

Her land, she thought fiercely.

"What is it, love?"

"*Horry*wood," she giggled, leaning into Doug's chest.

In bed he called her the *Chink in my amour*. On set he liked to twirl the key to her dressing room on his finger.

His wife and founding partner in United Artists, Mary Pickford, was known as "America's Sweetheart," "Blondilocks" (though she'd also been among the first to don yellowface as Madame Butterfly in an early silent). "Her real name is Gladys," Doug whispered around his cigarette. "You couldn't even pronounce mine," she scolded him.

Pickford and Fairbanks never had children together; they named their famous mansion Pickfair.

$

The *Hoover* is part of the Dollar Steamship Line, its twin black funnels banded in red, emblazoned with bright white dollar signs. When smoke billows from them she imagines the stokers below shoveling piles of greenbacks into the boilers like spirit money burned for the dead.

She always had a head for business. She kept the books for the laundry long after she became a star. When invited to be the celebrity host of a mahjong game at a local theater, she refused unless she also got to keep her winnings. She invested in real estate and later, in lean times, lived off her income as a landlady. Her contract with Hearst is paying for this trip to China.

Still, her father considered her a fool—and unfilial—for sending out her own laundry when he and the family would have done it for free.

As a rule he refused all her offers of financial help, but he was happy to let her pay for her siblings' education. The only one she declined to support was her older half-brother in China. As a student in Japan he'd seen one of her movies and written to his father that he should stop her from disgracing the family. When her mother had sent a newspaper clipping of her modeling furs, her half-brother had asked them to send him the wristwatch advertised on the reverse. Ever since she was a child she'd resented the money her father sent back to his family in China, money she, her brothers and sisters and mother helped earn through their labor at the laundry (though of course in later years her generosity to her siblings enabled her father to send even more to China). What

had that money bought? she wonders. Food? Clothes? Love?

Now there's a new man's watch in her steamer trunk. A Hamilton Tonneau in white gold. She sets it on the dressing table in her stateroom, watches it glide back and forth with the swell.

The High Hat

She styled herself a flapper, in beaded dresses and cloche hats. Bobbed hair became her trademark, and the skinny, boyish silhouette—she was five-foot-seven, a tennis player—suited her small chest. In the lingo of the day she was the monkey's eyebrows, the kitten's ankles, the goat's whiskers, the duck's quack, the cat's particulars. A tomato, a biscuit, a Sheba; the darb, the berries, the limit. With her keen chassis and swell stilts, she could dance the Charleston—and how! The trick was applying rouge to your knees.

A *dapper* was a flapper's father.

Prohibition was all wet. She would come home ossified, spifflicated, oiled, and owled, and her father, the Gimlet, that Airedale, would scream at her to "talk American!"

"Oh, for the love of Mike! Says *you!*"

"Who this Mike?" he demanded.

Her second lover, the director Tod Browning, was twenty-five years her senior, a Father Time in the parlance. She called him Daddy, told him his whiskbroom tickled. He was good in the feathers, but he had a fire bell at home and refused to drop the pilot. It was all balled up. Eventually she told him the bank was closed and found herself a new big six in Douglas Fairbanks, twenty-two years her senior ("big six" being a reference to a six-cylinder engine, like that in her own Willys-Knight roadster; Doug actually drove the straight-eight Duesenberg, appropriately enough, she told him, since he was a real Duesie!).

She once said she went a decade without having to light her own cigarettes. But she was never a gold-digger, nor goofy for any forty-niners, the male equivalent. Her many

admirers she dismissed as grubbers and duds, pikers and pills, highjohns and hoppers. Men were divided into cake eaters and corn shredders, Smith brothers, hiphounds, and flatwheelers. She was nobody's blue serge. Engagement rings were handcuffs, marriage was a line.

To be given the high hat, in the jargon, was to be snubbed.

Siamese

"She never wanted to be just famous," Browning said once. "She wanted to be white. I told her she was going to have to settle for being famous for being Chinese."

Tod went on to make *Dracula* with Bela Lugosi, but his career had been all but ended by *Freaks,* his gothic circus melodrama featuring real sideshow performers, including a pair of Siamese twins.

She'd heard he'd considered Myrna Loy, Jean Harlow for the lead, but he'd never called his former lover. The Siamese twins were played by the Hilton sisters, Daisy and Violet, originally from Brighton, England. At parties, when she heard others express their outrage about the picture—one woman was suing MGM, claiming it had caused her miscarriage—she nodded, kidded, *They couldn't even get real Siamese!*

Scrapes

Browning was her second lover but the first to knock her up. A "flusher," the whore in Chinatown she paid for penny-royal pills called it. In England it was known as a "scrape," back East "riding the Lightning" a reference to the notorious roller coaster. In France was best, she thought. There you saw the *faiseuse d'anges,* the angel-maker. But after that one, she was only able to get pregnant in movies.

There is a point on the sundeck, above the children's playroom with its sandbox and slide, rocking horses all in a row, where she likes to linger, listening to their happy shrieks.

Queue

Her earliest memory was her father cutting off his queue. She was six. They were still in the house on Flower Street where she was born. News of the 1911 revolution was spreading through Chinatown. Three years earlier her father had given money to Sun Yat-sen, Father of the new Nation, at a rally. She cried when he cut it off, thought he was hurt, but he laughed, teeth bared, and told her he didn't need it to go home any longer. *Home?* she said, and he said *China,* and she cried again because she thought he was leaving.

He'd taken, for a time, to wearing the fez of the fraternal order of laundrymen. She used to marvel at how he balanced it, wanted desperately to stroke the golden tassel.

She wore her own hair in braids as a child. In school, she told Doug, the boy sitting behind her used to dunk the tips in his inkwell, stick pushpins in her, tell her she had dirty ears.

"It ain't your ears they're going to be looking at now!" Doug beamed his famous grin.

She was smacked by her teachers if she spoke Chinese, but her father enrolled her in Chinese school when classes let out. Ten hours of studies each day.

"No wonder I played hooky, what?"

"Bad girl. You should be spanked."

By then she was wearing her hair in the Child Flower style, lustrous bangs covering her forehead. It was to become her look, her take on the flapper's bob. She wore it long past the point when she lost the virginity it traditionally denoted.

Combing it now before bed in the round vanity mirror that makes her look like she's staring out a porthole, she recalls an even earlier memory: her father playing with her as a child, holding the tip of his queue to his lips, fluttering his fingers over it as if it were a flute, whistling music while she clapped, delighted. She searches the mirror for a trace of that child, but it's as if she's been smoothed away with cold cream.

She returns to her brushing, static sparking around her head as if in answer to the flicker of lightning on the dark horizon.

Costars

It's hard to be a leading lady without leading men, and there were no Asian leading men. But over a thirty-year career she worked on stage and screen and radio in the U.S., England, and Germany with Douglas Fairbanks, Laurence Olivier, Orson Welles, and Lon Chaney, "man of a thousand faces." She made a short with Laurel and Hardy and played vaudeville with Jack Benny. Alfred Hitchcock once threw a pie in her face. She taught Myrna Loy how to use chopsticks. She met Sinclair Lewis, Zora Neale Hurston, Somerset Maugham, Walter Benjamin (who described her hair, let down, as like "a dragon romping in water"), and the Prince of Wales. She stayed at the Algonquin at the same time as Gertrude Stein. She taught Constance Talmadge how to use chopsticks. Man Ray took her portrait. Cecil Beaton photographed her for *Vanity Fair*. Her supposed lovers included Fairbanks, Vincent Price, Tod Browning, Marlene Dietrich, and Leni Riefenstahl. Men and women, all white. She taught Loretta Young how to use chopsticks. When rumored to be engaged to the Korean contract player Philip Ahn, she said that "kissing him was like kissing her brother." (Chinese boys, it seems, felt the same about kissing her, she was such a tomboy at school.) She never married. It would have been illegal for her to marry a white under California's anti-miscegenation laws. "The only happiness is with one's own race," she affirmed in interviews. She taught Renée Adorée how to use chopsticks.

"Chinese in movies aren't inscrutable," she lamented drily. "They're un*screw*able." But in life the ban on mixed marriage made her the perfect mistress, one who could never expect to wed her lovers.

Truth and Beauty

Such was the interest in her love life that she used to open press conferences by calling out over the reporter's clamor, "It's not true!" — a witticism that became her catchphrase. At premieres she'd climb out of her limousine and fans and reporters alike would chorus her name, just to hear her deliver the line. Searchlights scissored overhead. Like chopsticks, she thought, about to pinch up the morsel of the moon.

"We have a lot in common," she used to kid the reporters. "My family business was dirty laundry too."

Foolish Things

On their last night aboard, they beg her to sing with the band. *Any requests?* she asks, accepting another drink, and someone calls, "These Foolish Things." It's said it was written for her by a lover, the screenwriter and lyricist Eric Maschwitz. But she pouts, tells them she can't quite recall the words.

> *A cigarette that bears a lipstick's traces*
> *A something, something, something, some-thing*
> *something*
> *Oh how the ghost of you clings*
> *These foolish things remind me of you*

In bed one bright morning, Eric had told her the sun through the slit blinds ruled her skin like staff paper. He had written on her with his index finger.

But she knows the bawdy parodies and fears others do too:

> *Lipstick traces on an old French letter*
> *A bout of pox that won't get better*
> *Oh, when I piss it stings*
> *These foolish things remind me of you*

Instead she offers them Noël Coward's "Half-Caste Woman," a staple of her cabaret act. The next morning they'll dock in Shanghai and she'll set foot in China for the first time.

Abroad

She took a trip like this the last time her career stalled. That time to Europe. It was the making of her. "Everyone comes to Los Angeles to become a star," she said on another occasion. "I had to leave."

She met Paul Robeson and Josephine Baker.

She saw her first white prostitutes on the streets of Berlin.

She got to kiss her leading man on film.

She loved Europe, she concluded, because she found "absolutely no race prejudice" there.

She was photographed by Alfred Eisenstaedt at the Berlin Press Ball alongside Marlene Dietrich, cigarette holder clamped between the teeth of her smile, and Leni Riefenstahl.

The kiss was later cut "on moral grounds."

There were fewer than eight hundred Chinese in Germany at the time, less than a thousand in England and France. Fewer in all three countries combined than at home in Los Angeles. She was less bound by stereotypes, more free to create her own.

The "Wong haircut" became all the rage. English girls tinted their faces with ocher to get the "Wong complexion." Embroidered "coolie coats" were the height of that season's fashion, though she herself sported the finest French designs.

She burned incense in her hotel rooms before interviews. "To ward off bad press," she joked.

In Germany and France and England she was still Chinese, of course, but also glamorously American. When the English reviewers complained about her Yankee

squeak in a play, she laughed in delight (though she noted they offered no criticism of her costar Olivier's "Chinese" accent) but made sure to take elocution lessons from a Cambridge tutor. *I should play Eliza Doolittle*, she wrote in her diary.

She filmed her first talkie in three languages, German, French, and English, reshooting each scene thrice over, each in a different language.

When she returned to the States, reporters marveled at her classy accent. *London was divine, practically a second home, though the weather was perfectly beastly.* She described it, self-deprecatingly, as her two hundred guineas' worth of English, but it was worth every penny just for the dumbfounded looks she got, a Chinese with a British accent. One interviewer noted she preferred English tea to Chinese now, and went so far as to say she no longer looked quite Oriental. Her voice also ensured she had a career in talking pictures, unlike Constance Talmadge, Blanche Sweet, Mae Murray, Douglas Fairbanks, and Mary Pickford (who compared adding sound to movies to "putting lipstick on the Venus de Milo").

She herself had viewed the Venus de Milo in the Louvre with Josephine Baker, the "Bronze Venus." Baker hailed the statue, *Sister!*

She was twenty-five and had begun to lie about her age (in part to defuse questions about her unmarried state). If challenged, she put the discrepancy down to the Chinese way of counting age. A baby was considered one at birth, and years added not on birthdays but at the start of the lunar new year, so that a Chinese could be two years younger by Western reckoning.

Newsreel

Her cameraman films her coming down the gangway in her mink. When he emerges from behind the lens to wind the camera, she sees he's in his thirties, handsome. Hat pushed back, neat pencil mustache, dark double-breasted suit. Good linen, she thinks approvingly. He cranks the key in his strong fingers, swiftly and emphatically. His name, he tells her, is also Wong. The most common surname in China, he adds as if in apology. He has to lean close — she's wearing a hat with a tiger motif, specially designed for her in London — and shout over the cheers of the crowd, the answering blasts of the ship's whistle. He smells richly of hair oil.

She gives him her hand. "Mr. Wong."

"Hai-sheng," he says, "but you can call me Newsreel. They all do. Newsreel Wong." He explains how his bureau chief had called his hotel once but hadn't remembered — or known how to pronounce — his name. After that it stuck. He's thinking of having it changed legally.

A stage name for a cameraman, she thinks. Whatever next?

"What does that make me?" she drolls. "Hollywood Wong? Film Star Wong?"

But he is already filming again, the camera between them, covering his face.

"Well, all right," she tells him airily. "Newsreel it is!"

At least it's better than what the grips call her friend the cameraman James Wong Howe — Phil Ming (though wisely never to his face, mindful of Jimmie's early career as a bantamweight fighter). And, she prefers "Newsreel"

to plain old "Mr. Wong." Too much room for confusion there. Already, in her very first interview—a few enterprising reporters had come out to the ship by launch the night before to make their deadline—she's been asked about her love life. She only shrugged, parried ("I'm married to my art"), but the story that greets her on landing says she's accompanied on her trip by her beloved husband, Arthur.

When asked about her single status, she liked to deadpan, "'A flower need not love, but only be loved,'" a line from *Daughter of the Dragon*.

Native

She speaks Cantonese—with an American accent, her father has always said—but no Mandarin or Shanghainese. Now she requires an interpreter to tell her hosts how delighted she is to visit her homeland. It's just as well the newsreel is silent, she thinks, the announcer's voice-over to be added later. Besides, didn't she do some of her best work in silent pictures?

Newsreel films her at Yu Gardens framed by a moon gate. He films her on the Nanking Road, shopping and turning heads. In the Sincere Department Store she is delighted to learn that the onomatopoeic Chinese word for the pneumatic tube system is *pung*. He films her on the Bund pointing out junks, rubbing the paw of the bronze lion outside the Hong Kong and Shanghai Bank for luck. There are more cars than she expected—though she must try a rickshaw—more telephones, more streetlights. Overhead the telegraph lines make a net against the sky.

"I'd pictured rubble, ruins. We'd heard Shanghai was bombed."

Newsreel nods. "In '32. But not the foreign concessions. The Japanese wouldn't dare."

A pair of trams cross in front of her, parting like curtains. She marvels blithely at the modernity. "Why, it reminds me of Berlin. I was expecting old Cathay! But it looks nothing like Grauman's Theatre."

Mostly, though, there are more Chinese than she ever imagined—compradors in tang jackets, black-and-white amahs, monks in their yellow robes—crowding every-where, more than she's ever seen. And this she keeps to

herself: secretly she feels like an extra again, is glad of her chic Western wardrobe, Chanel suits, for helping her stand out.

The Mayfair Mannequin Academy of New York named her "the World's Best-Dressed Woman" in 1934. *Not bad for a laundryman's daughter,* she wrote to her father at the time, but he didn't reply.

She finds herself waiting for Newsreel to say "Action!" Pausing at the edge of the frame, her weight tipped forward, but catching herself. They laugh when she explains it to him. Yet she still wants him to tell her what to do. "Was that good?" she asks after a take, and he says, "Sure." She feels naked without stage makeup, lighting. She asks to redo a moment when she bumps into someone. "If you like." She repeats a particular gesture, a little turn of the wrist as if she's presenting the scene around her, practicing between takes and then repeating it to make sure he captures it, until he looks up and over the camera and asks, "What are you doing?"

Newsreel's Eyemo camera runs for twenty seconds, fully wound, and she begins pacing her movements to his rhythms. From the taxi to the hotel lobby, twenty seconds. Greeting a fan, twenty seconds. Admiring a bolt of silk, twenty seconds. And then it's time to change the reel.

She feels as if he's winding her up like a tin toy.

Finally she leans on a rail overlooking the river, waiting for him, and when he raises up, she lifts her own Leica to take a picture of him.

"You look like a tourist," he tells her, and she frowns. On the Whangpoo the sails of junks unfurl like fans, raised as if in modesty to hide them from gaze.

She outfits herself with a new wardrobe. She sheds her Western dresses and suits for sleek qipao. The milky-eyed tailor who measures her wraps a knotted string around her bust and waist and hips. She used to work as a seamstress at her father's laundry when she was a child, she says, and he nods when someone translates. Afterward she shows off her new gowns for the camera, accessorizes with a jade cigarette holder. "Going native," she tells Newsreel. He touches a finger to the knot of his bow tie as if it were a button.

She blends in better, at least until people address her in Mandarin. She can't recall the last time she felt invisible like this. But she fears getting lost in the crowd. She relies on Newsreel to pick her out, on the camera to make her stand out.

In later years she'll wear those dresses in movies and charge the studios an extra fee to rent her wardrobe.

Life and Art

The decision to make a movie of her own life proves ill-starred. While greeted warmly at first in Shanghai—one newspaper, describing her beauty, speaks of her eyebrows like "tender moth caterpillars," her eyes "like kernels of apricots"—and feted by high society, flashbulbs sizzling in her wake, there have long been disparaging murmurs, often from Nationalist critics, about her roles and their depiction of the Chinese. She is most famous for playing a prostitute in *Shanghai Express,* notorious for her scanty costume in *The Thief of Bagdad*. Both have been subsequently banned in China, denounced as "ghost films."

Those were only roles, she tries to explain. The only ones she could get. It was acting.

But it's a difficult distinction to make while a newsreel camera follows her everywhere, whirring gently in the background.

Shameless, they call her at a film board banquet in Peking. Lewd. A disgrace to Chinese womanhood. A Yankee puppet.

She nods politely, smiles shyly, unsure of their Mandarin.

"Too American," Newsreel translates tactfully.

Her familial disgrace is now a national one.

"It's just acting," she repeats, but it's a difficult distinction to make to a newsreel man.

"People believe what they see." He shrugs. "I'd be out of work otherwise."

She tries to tell him that she refused a different role in *The Good Earth,* that of Lotus, the teahouse dancer, another young seducer. He is loading a new canister of

film. "I told them, 'You're asking me as a Chinese to play the only unsympathetic character in the movie!'" But the truth is she wasn't offered it, despite testing for it. Already at thirty she was too old for the part. Perhaps it was for the best, she tells herself. She's not sure she could have borne it. To stand so close, day after day on set, to the role she craved. Her sister Mary had no such qualms. She happily took the minor role of Little Bride. "It could be *my* big break!" She'd never known how much her sister coveted her career, nor how much she could covet her sister's youth (if not her flat nose). "Have you no shame?" she'd retorted. *No loyalty?* she meant. "They're just using you." She bit her tongue. In a more conciliatory spirit she had offered this trip as a lure to tempt Mary away, just as she'd once invited her along to Europe. But the girl had shaken it off petulantly. "It's *your* turn to play daughter."

"It's true," she tells Newsreel abruptly. "I am a bad example."

Beneath the camera, all she can see of him is his mouth, the cigarette jutting to one side so that smoke doesn't float in front of the lens. It twitches slightly.

Spirit Way

At the Ming tombs outside Peking, a guide encourages her to toss a rock up onto the curved back of one of the stone elephants along the Spirit Way. *For luck,* the guide says, clapping when she lands one. Later Newsreel tells her, *It's for fertility,* and she wishes she had the cool dry heft of it in her hand still.

Dan

Back in Shanghai she meets the Chinese star Butterfly Wu, the so-called Empress of Cinema. They exchange autographs while the cameras roll. "Can you read Chinese?" Wu asks sweetly beneath her breath as she inscribes a photo.

She meets Mei Lanfang, the great *dan* actor of female roles. He explains the different kinds of *dan* in the opera. *Hua dan,* vivacious young women. "Like you," he says, giggling. *Daoma dan* and *wu dan,* the warrior women. *Lao dan,* the older women. *Cai dan,* the female clowns. "And which are you?" she asks. He specializes in *guimen dan,* he explains, virtuous ladies. "Though I have played the others too." She nods. They compare hands—hers have been called the most beautiful in Hollywood—but she envies his elegant fingers, delicate wrists.

Butterfly Wu's great rival in the Shanghai film world, Ruan Lingyu, will commit suicide later that year, driven to it in part by vicious press coverage of her unhappy love life. Wu is rumored to have laughed on hearing the news.

Intermission

Newsreel attends an open-air cinema with her. "Where the stars compete with the stars," she quips. "Where the Chinese go to the pictures," he says.

The film is in Mandarin and she leans in close to hear his whispered translation until someone hisses, *Xu!* "Hush," Newsreel murmurs, and she giggles, leaves her shoulder pressed against his.

At the intermission he sits up straight and she does the same. He snaps his fingers for the cigarette girl. She tells him, "It's chilly. I'd like to leave now."

Footage

"What happens if you run out of film at a crucial moment?" she asks once while he reloads.

"Sometimes I carry two cameras. Though I don't always load them both," he admits.

"Why not?"

"Some people just want to be filmed. Generals, mostly."

"Generals!" she says, because she can see he wants to impress her.

But what she wonders is if there's anything in the camera now. If any of this is actually happening if it isn't being filmed.

He raises the Eyemo again.

"Say, when are we going to see some footage?" she asks.

He blinks. "Oh, I don't get to see it. I shoot it, I send it off. Someone else edits it, writes the voice-over. Often the only time I see it is in the lens finder."

The clockwork of the camera starts to tick down.

"Sounds like the movies," she tells him. "We shoot scenes out of sequence, so we don't even know how the stories will turn out when we're making them."

"Sounds like life," he says, and she laughs.

"I guess."

Still, it unnerves her somehow. Not getting to see herself. What has he captured? The cameras and cameramen she's used to make her look good (even when she's being bad), but this time she's not so sure. What is he seeing through that lens? It makes her self-conscious suddenly, for the first time in years.

This is not why she became an actress; this is not why she became famous.

"Stop staring," she whispers, but he can't hear her over the mechanism.

Make Love to the Camera

If you're trying to seduce a nation you have to start somewhere.

She walks toward him as he films, and pouts.

She walks toward him and stares into the lens, one eye squinted closed as if trying to peer through it at him. "You're too close to pull focus," he complains, backing up. She follows and blows a kiss. He wipes the fogged glass, starts over.

She walks toward him and smooches the lens. He rubs it clean, patiently. "I can't use this."

After they sleep together, she thinks it'll be easier, but he looks at her over his cigarette as if he's expected it.

"Was it all you imagined?" she asks him in the mirror of her dressing table.

"I didn't imagine it," he says.

"Really?" She flares her eyes to apply makeup. "Yet my films are so lewd."

"I've never seen any of your films." He closes his eyes against the smoke. One finger scratches at the seam of an eyelid. "Only read about them."

For a moment she looks at him with unfeigned aston-ishment, and then she slips back between the sheets, presses herself against him.

She is the first Chinese movie star. He is her first Chinese lover.

When in Rome, she thinks. And in fact his penis, rest-ing on his testicles as if on a pillow, is exactly the propor-tion of Greek and Roman statuary she's seen in the muse-ums of Europe. The ideal of male beauty. His torso is as

hairless as those statues too, smooth and cool to the touch.

He stirs beneath her. But she's not in Rome, she thinks with a smirk.

"What?" he asks.

"Nothing. I was just thinking, I've finally come home."

But he doesn't get the double-entendre, and she doesn't care to explain it.

"'It's a long journey and a lonely one,'" she quotes instead from *Shanghai Express*, sinking into him.

Beside her the needle rides the waves of the gramophone like a ship on a starlit sea. A fan spins endlessly on the nightstand. She feels dizzy.

Marlene

As Tiger Lily she'd kissed Betty Bronson as Peter Pan (the movie inheriting the stage convention of Peter being played by a woman) on the cheek.

But it was her first time with a woman.

"So?" Marlene bobbed her bare shoulders. "It's my first time with a Chinese."

On the vanity, two still champagne coupes, lipstick-printed. It was Berlin, the golden twenties; everyone was daring something, and she'd always been fashionable. Still, she swore Dietrich to secrecy.

"But of course, darling. We have to have secrets, so we can tell when we're acting."

"Self-combed women" was how her father referred to lesbians.

When the rumors got out anyway, Marlene made a little moue. "So? Now the public will just know what great actresses we are."

Later she asks herself, *Is that why I did it? All the scandalous behavior, the lesbian lovers, the white lovers, to distinguish myself from the characters I played. Or to copy them?*

And were the lesbian rumors, she wonders, the reason she could never marry?

Annas

There are real whores, she has heard, back in Chinatown who style themselves after her, with funny names like Anna May Well and Anna Mae East.

Anna May. Anna Might. Anna Better.

Anna Won't. Anna Don't. "Anna—!"

They bob their hair like hers, dress like her, pose like her. Some are quite convincing lookalikes. Once, years ago, a young man stopped her in the street for a moment, took her arm, called her by name.

"Do I know you?"

"It's John," he said. "Jake." But then his friend pulled him away, flashed a badge.

"Excuse him. He's confused. Thought you were someone else."

"Someone he loved?" she ventured, searching the fellow's face.

"Someone he lost."

His friend pulled him away. "Jeezamarooni," she overheard. And, "I think that was the real McCoy!" And, "C'mon, Jake. It's Chinatown."

Her father always said she looked like a whore. She wants to stamp her foot: "No. They all look like *me!*" But really, is that better or worse?

In Shanghai, it's said, there are fifty thousand taxi dancers and sing-song girls, mostly in the French Concession. She's fascinated. "I played a Shanghai prostitute, after all. I'm famous for it." She asks Newsreel to take her one night to the "flowery world," as it's politely called. "In the spirit of research. Besides, I can practice my French."

"I guess some stereotypes are true," she says archly as their car slides through the night streets under the bare plane trees. Girls call out to the car. "Perhaps they all are in a nation of five hundred million."

"Just not the only truth," he offers, leaning forward to draw the curtains.

The too-sweet smell of warm rot rises off the river as they cross a bridge.

He takes her to a club, at her insistence, so that she can see the taxi dancers. He has joined her for tea dances at her hotel—he possesses a smooth, sauntering foxtrot—but he won't dance with her here. Over the brassy strains of "yellow music," the local jazz, she tells him she's shocked by how many white prostitutes there are alongside the Chinese. They glow even paler in the light of the ballroom spotlight.

"Russians," Newsreel explains, tamping a cigarette on his case. He has added a one-point pocket square to his suit, she sees, and a pair of celluloid sunglasses. Their tinted round lenses make her feel she's still looking into his camera.

"I didn't think there were that many foreigners in Shanghai."

He shakes his head. "Very popular with Chinese men too."

"Really? Do you ever come here?" she asks him. She wants to refold the handkerchief in a triple crown and tuck it back in place, patting his heart.

He ducks his head to light his cigarette, his oiled, combed hair sleek as a '78. "In Chinese, the expression is 'driving a nail.'" He illustrates by swinging an invisible hammer.

Behind him the saxophone player raises his instrument to his lips as if swigging from a giant bottle.

She is fast becoming a type herself, a type unto herself. "The Anna May Wong type," reads the stage direction for a character in a late Pearl Buck radio drama.

Dim Sum

In Hong Kong, perhaps drunk, perhaps feeling the strain, she forgets that the birdcage microphone is on, insults the delegation that comes out to welcome her. A near-riot ensues. A banner proclaiming her "the flower of film" is torn down. Garlands are crushed underfoot; their heavy scent rises over the jostling crowd.

Chicken! the mob bays (in Cantonese now, so she knows they're calling her a whore). *Rotten cunt!*

It's Newsreel who pulls her away and hustles her into a cab.

"Thank you," she tells him. For just a moment she had seen he was torn, debating whether to keep filming.

"It's nothing. I've been in worse scrapes. In this business you learn to move fast. To protect your camera." He cradles it in his lap. "I'm sorry," he says.

"For what?"

"The mob. The name-calling."

"Oh, that. I've been calling myself names since I was ten."

"Nicer ones, I hope."

The taxi hurtles through the streets, scattering bicycles.

She sings a little ditty to herself.

"What's that?" Newsreel asks.

"Just a silly number I used to perform at parties: *Anna May Wong / From Olde Hong Kong / She Can't Be Wrong!*"

"I didn't know you'd been to Hong Kong before," he says politely.

"I haven't."

He offers her a cigarette, snaps his lighter in her face, snips it closed.

"They say you got your nickname in Jinan," she tells him, exhaling. "Covering the massacre?"

He nods.

"I saw that footage. Two thousand Chinese civilians, by the Imperial Japanese Army." She shakes her head. "And now you're filming me."

Outside, coppery light filters through the banyans. In the breeze their leaves shimmer like sequins on a dress.

Subsequently she is warned by the Nationalist authorities not to travel inland to see her father until tempers cool. He is warned not to receive her, on pain of deportation.

Her friend and costar in several pictures, Warner Oland, is also in town. He played her father, Fu Manchu, in *Daughter of the Dragon* years earlier, and still calls her daughter (though when he played her coercive lover in *Shanghai Express* he observed, "This is all getting a bit incestuous, no?"). If she can't see her real father, she tells Newsreel glibly, she'll settle for her movie father. The show must go on.

But she hopes Oland will help her too. He is the star of the Charlie Chan series, the most popular movies in China, and has been feted on his own tour, despite—an irony that pierces her to the quick—playing his most famous role in yellowface; he's a Swede, among friends goes by Jack, short for his real name, Johann. But the Chinese don't seem to mind, or even to notice. They love Charlie Chan, as a positive portrayal of a Chinese, no matter by whom, and in Oland's case it doesn't hurt that

he stays in character for interviews and appearances, answering to "Mr. Chan" and speaking of his pleasure "at visiting home of venerable ancestors." *My bloody line,* she thinks viciously.

She should resent him, but he's been kind to her in the past, run lines with her and helped her hit her marks, and she respects him. He's classically trained, has performed Shakespeare onstage and his own translations of Strindberg. She's hopeful he'll put in a good word for her with the authorities, help her on her way to her father.

She arranges to meet him for dim sum. Oland, despite the boast that he's known as "one-take Warner," is a famed drunk. The producers on the Charlie Chan pictures are said to encourage his boozing, thinking it adds to his character's air of serene geniality. So Warner claims, at least. He calls it his method; his favorite toast is "Action!" She thinks dim sum will be too early for him to be drunk, but she's only half right. He arrives sober enough, in a natty cravat and houndstooth suit, but proceeds to drink through lunch, filling his teacup from a silver flask. "Let's get in character," he says, raising it to Newsreel's camera.

"Rotten luck," he tells her, "about *The Good Earth*. They say Luise will win the Academy Award for *The Great Ziegfeld,* you know. They're calling her the 'Viennese teardrop.'"

"Well, that's just ducky. She'll probably win it for *The Good Earth* too."

He is concentrating on his chopsticks. "Could be."

"That should be my award!" Doug, as the original president of the academy, had presided over the first ceremony, in 1929. Mary Pickford, Irving Thalberg, and Sid Grauman

had been among the other founding members. She's never been invited to join.

Jack laughs. "But you wouldn't win it, daughter."

"Why not? I'd be better in the role than her."

He chases a slippery dumpling around his plate. "Of course. And that's why you wouldn't win. Don't you see? If she wins, it'll be for *acting* Chinese. You *are* Chinese! Take it from me. The people here don't hold it against me that I played Fu Manchu. That was acting. But you, they revile for playing his daughter." He gives a sidelong glance around the restaurant at the other patrons, staring at them.

"I act!" she hisses, remembering how once at a party someone had asked her if inscrutability and acting weren't mutually exclusive.

"No, daughter. No. *You* are a star. What you always wanted to be, yes? To see your name in electric lights? Then don't complain. Stars don't act, they play themselves. Gable is Gable, Lombard is Lombard. Onscreen and off, for the most part. That's why we love them, not just because they're the same but because they seem real, not fake. What do you think all the movie magazines are for? You can't blame people for confusing you and your parts. And very lovely parts they are, by the way. Ah!" He finally spears the dumpling with his chopsticks.

She pauses demurely for the waiter to bring the next dish. He lifts the lids of the bamboo steamers with a little flourish, like doffing a hat.

"But what about you, Jack? Aren't you a star?"

"Oh my dear, how kind of you." He dabs his greasy lips. "But no. They don't cast stars in yellowface, don't you know. It spoils the illusion. Why do you think they use so many Europeans? We're not so recognizable. Besides,

honorable Mr. Chan is star, I only humble servant. You no believe? I can be replaced like——." He snaps his fingers, and a waiter looks over. She waves him off. "Already there's talk of a Chinese-language version of Chan. True, true. I met the fellow who will play him—play *me,* I should say, since he plans to impersonate my performance."

She has heard of a Chinese remake of *The Thief of Bagdad* called *The Flying Bandit.* She wonders about the Chinese they got to play her.

"A Chinaman playing a Swede playing a Chinaman!" Jack guffaws. "What'll they think of next?" He played Al Jolson's disapproving father in *The Jazz Singer,* she recalls suddenly. Jewface, he called it once.

He applies himself to his dim sum. His cheeks are flushed, shiny—from the steam or more likely the drink (*Why can't he just hold it?*)—and his cravat spotted. Shumai, he declares, remind him of Swedish meatballs, but he struggles to eat them. He's never mastered chopsticks ("Mr. Chan too busy detecting to eat!"). At one point he looks up at her across the table, steepling his fingers, "Channing it up," as she's heard him describe it: "Ah, vely cunning plan, daughter. To remind fellow diners that Chan actor not real Chinese. One might almost think you wish him lose face." He toasts her. "Or yellowface, at least."

She denies it, but he has the sleepily satisfied look of a man who's cracked the case, the look that has made him an icon.

In interviews later on his tour, when asked about his lunch with her, "Mr. Chan" will smile and bow and call her his "number-one daughter." *Gee, Pops,* she says to herself, but she knows he's only trying to help.

Celestial Body

She isn't a star, she thinks later. Or an actress. But something in between. The first Chinese star, they call her, and it's the qualifications that are crucial. First. Chinese. A star may play only him- or herself, but she is supposed to play a race. How can she be herself and represent millions, both at once? And who does she represent them to? To themselves or others? *Who does she think she is?* an outraged Nationalist critic has demanded. She wishes she could say.

Not a star, then. A star gives off its own light. Another celestial body, a moon, reflecting others' light.

Yellowface

Her pal Jimmie Wong Howe (Newsreel is an admirer of his namesake's work; she likes to drop his name) calls them "sticky-tape" actors on account of the makeup people's trick for slanting their eyes. "Only Warner has never needed it," she tells Newsreel. He's gathering his clothes; he never spends the night in her room. Sparing her the gossip, she thinks, though it's a bit late for that.

"Something to do with his Lapp ancestry, supposedly," she goes on. "At least that's what Jack tells the movie magazines. He just trims his eyebrows and smoothes down the tips of his mustache and he's passable."

Newsreel looks dubious. He's a reporter, after all; his business is with the real, not the fake. But then what is he doing with her?

"You'd be surprised," she tells him, just prattling now to make him stay. Once on the set of *Shanghai Express* a wizened grandpa, an extra, approached to ask if Jack had grown up in such-and-such a village in Canton, as if they might be old chums. She translated for them, explaining politely that Warner was Swedish, explaining politely what Swedish was, Jack all the time nodding and bowing and twinkling with amusement. *Acting!* he'd crowed afterward.

That old grandpa was probably half blind, she thinks now, though at the time she had marveled at Warner, the alchemy of performance.

Newsreel shakes his head. Nearly dressed now. He's forgone his usual Western attire lately for a Zhongshan suit, she notices. She reaches for him, but he shakes his head again.

"Not acting," he says. "Not sticky tape or trimmed eyebrows. It's you."

"Me?" She smiles coyly, anticipating a gallantry.

"You make him Chinese. He stands next to you, he looks Chinese. *You're* his yellowface."

His, she will think after Newsreel leaves, and Olivier's, and Lon Chaney's, and Orson Welles's (even on radio, a white played Chinese). Once, years earlier, Jimmie had shown her a grainy print of one of the very earliest films, Edison's *Chinese Laundry Scene* from 1894, a slapstick short featuring a Chinese (played in yellowface) fleeing a policeman.

"At least Jack must have talked to the Nationalists," she tells Newsreel the next day. A telegram has arrived from the capital. She has at last gotten permission to visit her father. "That was me," Newsreel admits. He has influential friends who appreciate his work reporting on Japanese aggression in Mongolia.

"Thank you," she tells him, with a stiff little bow to the camera. "And do you share your friends' opinion of my acting?" she muses loftily.

"I told you, I've not seen your movies. But do you think," he asks wearily, setting the Eyemo aside, "even if you were the best actress in the world, you would be allowed to play white roles?"

She does not remark the few occasions she's been cast to play non-Asians, twice as "red Indians," once as an Eskimo. *Picturegoer* recently reported the offer of a plastic surgeon, and self-confessed fan, to "fix"—gratis—the slant of her eyes, meaning the fold of her lids, so that she could play European roles. She politely declined, saying, "It's a bit more permanent than sticky tape!"

Edison had died in 1931, and the nation marked his passing by turning off the lights for a minute. Obits called him the Father of Motion Pictures, but Jimmie told her the inventor only began work on his kinetoscope after a meeting with Eadweard Muybridge, who'd pioneered chronophotography with his "horse in motion" study for Leland Stanford (the original goal of which was to establish definitively that horses engaged in "unsupported transit," which is to say, took all four feet off the ground at the gallop). "And Stanford, see," Jimmie went on, warming to his subject, "made his money — to buy horses, to hire Muybridge — from a railroad built by Chinese. Meaning without us, maybe no movies."

But all she'd recall later was that Edison's favorite actress was Mary Pickford.

China City

Her father had moved home two years earlier. Old Chinatown had finally been razed to make way for Union Station. She used to joke he was old enough to have seen (and be soured on movies by) the Lumière Brothers' short *Arrival of a Train,* which according to legend had panicked early audiences, who thought a real train was bearing down on them. But the joke wasn't so funny anymore. She pictured the train tracks running through her old home, herself strapped to them in her childhood bed like an old silent-era damsel in distress.

She had tried to persuade him to stay. He said he was going home, but it felt as if he was leaving her, getting as far from her as possible. "But *this* is home," she tried to tell him, and he shook his head. It didn't help that he had another family in China, another wife, a son. She felt disowned. *Little Orphan Anna,* she derided herself.

She had tried to persuade him to move the business. There was talk of a New Chinatown, and of a competing location called China City, the former to be run by Chinese businessmen, the latter the brainchild of a white socialite, Christine Sterling, who'd previous developed the Olvera Street Mexican market as a tourist attraction and who was courting her for her support. But her father balked at China City when he heard that the shopkeepers there were expected to work in costume and speak pidgin. There were plans for rickshaw rides and something called a Chinaburger. "Chinese Movieland," he called the development scornfully, and she soured on the project herself, throwing in with the New Chinatown developers, appearing at their grand

opening to plant a willow tree, when she heard that China City was to feature the leftover sets from *The Good Earth* and other Chinese-themed movies. It was like a graveyard of her career, she thought. (The place went up in smoke ten years later, and she felt a wicked thrill at the news, a shiver of happy spite.) New Chinatown was the authentic Chinatown, she told him. But her father wouldn't move there either. "What for," he asked, "when I can have the real thing?"

So now she was coming to him, and bringing a cameraman with her.

"Don't worry," her father had told her when she bade him a tearful goodbye in L.A. "This way you won't have to come to my funeral."

Face

The night before she sees her father she dreams she's lost face, literally. That she has no face, just a smooth art deco mask, the features streamlined and silvered. It feels hard and cold to the touch. When she tries to take it off, she sees it's riveted at the temples and along the jawline. Her hair, her trademark bangs cut just a little longer in the center of her forehead to make her face heart-shaped, is a steely coif.

When people come up and stare, all they see are their own faces shining back.

Makeup, she thinks, but all she can find to hand are some red packets for lucky money. Just as she had as a girl, she moistens the paper and rubs it on her burnished cheeks for rouge. But it won't stick. In the mirror she sees herself reflected and reflecting, so that she seems to recede infinitely into her own sleek features.

In *Daughter of the Dragon*, her character threatened to disfigure the white heroine, her rival, telling her lover huskily, "You will have the torture of seeing her beauty eaten slowly away by this hungry acid."

"Villains," Vincent Price would tell her roguishly, "are always the best parts. It's *so* good to be bad."

Rails

On the train inland Newsreel tries to interest her in the fact that the line they're traveling on was laid by the same Chinese who'd previously built the transcontinental railroad. She wonders how they were welcomed home. The track, as she stares at it stretching into the distance, looks like a long strip of celluloid. It even sounds — *clackety-clack, clackety-clack* — like film through a gate.

"Now who's mixing up life and movies?" Newsreel mocks.

"It's different," she snaps. "My life *is* movies."

Home

She isn't certain how she'll be received by the villagers, so she sends word ahead and her father meets them in the lane outside, leaning on a malacca cane. His neck has thickened, his hair receded; his face seems too small for his head. She runs to him and they embrace, but the camera jams, so they have to do it again. Already she has nothing left to say to him when he releases her from his second stiff embrace. For his part, he only repeats, *Welcome, welcome,* as if absentmindedly, as if he'd seen her just the week before instead of two years ago.

The dust of the road settles on their feet.

"And how is Mary?" he asks.

"Fine." Still the favorite, then, after the boys, at least. "Of all you girls," he told her once, "Mary takes after your mother the most."

And yet how she has missed this disapproval! It shielded her from the world's.

When Newsreel asks for a third take, they shake hands and refuse to do it over. The sun is as bright as a follow-spot, she complains, squinting. Her father's face is more lined and liver-spotted than she remembers; it dawns on her that he's come home to die. "I don't want to get wrinkles," she says with a sniff.

She introduces them fatuously. "Mr. Wong, Mr. Wong. I call him Newsreel."

They bow, greet each other as "Cousin," in reference to their shared clan name.

"Hai-sheng," Newsreel says, gripping her father's hand. "Sam Sing," her father replies.

"My old pappy," she'll call him in the voice-over for *Bold Journey,* a 1950s ABC special cut together from Newsreel's footage.

She stays for ten days. Newsreel films father and daughter strolling around the village in bright sunlight, catching the wondering faces of locals looking on. Some of them have seen her onscreen at the local town and act as if she isn't real. Not as if she isn't Chinese, but as if she isn't human. They want to pinch her and prod her. When she speaks they compliment her on her Chinese, as if she weren't a native speaker. Even the mules stop to stare.

For her part, she tries to play the role of the good daughter, both while the camera is rolling and when it's silent, but it's all an act. She bows to her stepmother, bows to her half-brother. ("You're older than I thought," he tells her; "You're exactly as I imagined," she replies, proffering the watch.) Her father expects her to stay. He has plans to marry her off finally. "What about him?" he whispers, glancing at Newsreel. She flushes. For some, she knows—old-timers, country folks—there remains a whiff of incest to marriage between people with the same clan name. That's how Chinese he is. That's how desperate.

The pause stretches out until the camera ticks to a stop. Her father cocks his head, as if waiting for an alarm to go off.

In Shanghai she had attended a mass wedding at the invitation of the mayor: the brides in pastels (white being a funeral color), their veils made of mosquito netting. All those young men and women paired up and arrayed before her, as far as the eye could see. Newsreel's camera panned slowly from her stricken face over the crowd. She edged a

little closer to him, the pair of them on the dais like a couple on a cake.

"Mr. Wong," she whispers now, "are you ready?" He raises the camera like a mask.

"This is what we Chinese do," her father continues. "We go to Gold Mountain, get wealthy, come home. It doesn't matter how you make money. I tell them I was a big-shot merchant, not a laundryman. There I was nothing, here I live like a king." It's true, she sees. He's a respected and famous figure in the village, resplendent in his long silk changshan and plush homburg (at home he'd favored Western shirts and pants, figured his customers would trust him with their clothes if he wore the same as them), and she's happy for him, understands why he's returned.

For a moment it all makes sense. Why come so far, after all, if not to stay? If Hollywood has rejected her, why not reject Hollywood? But she can't. Filial devotion has its limits. *There,* she thinks, *I'm still a star, if a little tarnished; here I'm a daughter.*

"But you're Chinese," her father insists, pressing the ferrule of his cane into the dirt. They are standing on a dike above a paddy field, silhouetted against the sky. "Don't you ever get homesick?"

"Always," she sobs.

"Well, this is where you belong."

But she shakes her head. "There I'm Chinese, here I'm American." Her homesickness is incurable. "*You're* supposed to be my home," she whispers.

They both look away, into the camera, until it winds down. And even then, in the silence, Newsreel keeps it pressed to his face.

At night she lies awake, listening to the sizzling buzz of insects. Newsreel won't come to her in her father's house. At least she's brought a flask.

When it's time to leave, she stages a little scene: father and daughter holding hands, moving apart, arms extended until finally contact is broken. And walking backward out of frame.

"Cut," Newsreel says. She sighs, shakes out her arms. She misses the stark theatricality of silent pictures.

"You were great," she tells her father, and he looks confused.

She pushes the tears away with the heel of her hand. "They used to say I was the best crier in pictures," she tells Newsreel. A prized talent in the silent era. "People used to crowd onto the set just to watch me weep."

At the station, waiting in the flickering shade of a ginkgo tree, her father takes Newsreel's hand. "Thank you for taking good care of this daughter." He bows stiffly; she notices that the tips of his bushy eyebrows are silvering.

"Sorry about that," she murmurs afterward, leaning against Newsreel in the compartment. "It's just that he sees us together all the time. He doesn't understand. I hope you weren't offended."

"Oh, that?" Newsreel says. His cheeks hollow as he draws on his cigarette. "No. Not at all."

"Ah," she says, straightening. It's suddenly spelled out like a title card in a silent picture. "You never told me you were married. No wonder you think I'm a slut."

There's a clatter of applause, and a formation of wild ducks rises from the marshes along the tracks, flies into the sun.

Public

They spend their last two days in Hong Kong, avoiding each other. But back in Shanghai, she insists Newsreel accompany her to the Public Garden in the International Settlement. Its English lawn is said to be as tightly trimmed as the nap on a billiard table. She wants to see the carp pond, the band pavilion, the infamous NO DOGS OR CHINESE sign. She wants him to film her beside it, flouting it. When he balks, she tells him, "Oh, don't fret, they won't arrest me. I may be a bitch, but I don't think it applies. Do you?" She twirls her scalloped parasol nonchalantly.

No footage survives, if the excursion ever took place.

Wong

She says goodbye to Newsreel at the docks — "Thank you, Hai-sheng," she whispers — but he continues to film her as she waves from midship, from behind a veil of red-white-and-blue streamers. She blows him a kiss.

She has grown fond of him. They've enjoyed a few laughs. Between them, she and Newsreel have heard them all.

Wong time.

Wong place.

Wong number.

When she introduces him, they take it in turns, after a beat, to add, "No relation."

"Newsreel Wong and Film Star Wong — we could be a double act."

Except she is also Shameless Wong, Spinster Wong, Stinking Whore Wong, American Wong.

"You *really* never saw one of my pictures?" she teased him in the taxi to the ship.

"Some were banned, as you know. And, to be frank . . ." He shrugged. "I don't really care for movies, make-believe."

"Now it can be told!"

"But which ones should I see? To remember you by. My friends at the studio can get prints."

"Oh." She squeezed his hand, smiled wanly. "None of them."

She plucked the pocket square from his breast before they parted, "to remember *you* by"; flourishes it flailingly now from the deck.

"Fifty million Chinese," she shouts down to him over the ship's horn.

"What?" he yells from behind the Eyemo. She wishes he'd put it down, let her see his face one last time.

"Fifty million Chinese," she tries again. He cups a hand to his ear. "Fifty million Chinese can't be Wong!" But he just keeps filming.

And Wong can't be fifty million Chinese, she thinks ruefully as she watches the crowded pier, sailors and stevedores, dwindle into the distance. She waves until he is out of sight, then presses the handkerchief hard to the corner of each eye in turn, as if to stanch a wound.

It's her one and only visit to China.

Half-Caste Woman

The first night onboard, she sings in the lounge—*Drink a bit, laugh a bit, love a little more*—leaning into the curve of the white piano. If Americans think her Chinese and Chinese think her American, the British understand her as Eurasian.

Half-caste woman, what are your slanting eyes
Waiting and hoping to see?

She met Noël Coward once at a club in London. He'd famously written *Private Lives* while recuperating from flu in Shanghai. She told him how strange it felt to have English hotel staff pressing her gowns, chanced a sally: "Is that what you'd call iron-y?" "What say?" he asked absently, simpering at someone across the room. "Quite so. Irony," he affirmed, correcting her pronunciation.

Scanning the far horizon,
Wondering what the end will be.

Later, on deck, tumbler in hand, she'll crane over the rail. She searches the moonlit distance for a funnel, for a spout. For a husband, she thinks, but all of *them* might as well be lined up at the Long Bar, longest in the world—*naturally!*—at the men-only Shanghai Club. Plenty more fish in the ocean, ha! Flecked with moonlight, the waves glint like teeth, rings of them radiating outward like the maw of a shark. She hangs further out, gazing down into the water rushing past, trying to imagine those jade

depths. What would it be like to dive in? To lie back and watch the towering hull slide past on the screen of the sky and slowly sink into the velvety dark? And yet it's the surface, as ever, waves shimmering like scales, that beguiles her. The chop clapping the hull, the lacy veils of spray, the whirling foam wreaths. And why not? she thinks. We live on the surface, after all. The surface supports us, cradles us, buoys us up. She spies, suddenly, the sleek curves of dolphins running alongside, their dark, shining backs rising and falling, turning like film on a spool. She lets her glass drop into the darkness, brings her gloved hands together in silent applause.

Spurned by a man, spurned by a country. She's not about to kill herself for either.

Gong

It storms for four straight days. In the depths of each trough she's pressed into her mattress springs as if by a lover; at the crest of each wave she feels momentarily weightless, as if her spirit were rising out of her flesh. And then it's calm again. The distant dinner gong summons her like a cue.

Home Again

The *Hoover* steams under the partially constructed Golden Gate Bridge into San Francisco on October 16, 1935. There's still no roadway, but the first long swoops of cable have recently been draped across the bay like a garland. "Welcome home!" passengers call to one other. Beyond the bridge, everyone clusters to starboard to watch the white city rising up Telegraph Hill like a cloud of fog around another new marvel, the Coit Tower. Only she stands to port, studying Angel Island, the immigration station where thousands of Chinese have been detained over the past three decades, as it slips astern. It's as close as many of them have come, she knows: able to see Gold Mountain but never touch it.

The great ship beneath her slows and settles into a filigree scum of froth.

215

Dreams

Throughout her career she'd occasionally steal into theaters to watch her own movies with an audience. She liked to sit toward the front and side near the organ. The Mighty Wurlitzer at the Chinese Theatre was decked out in red and gold to match the decor, the curved tiers of keys like stalls and circle and balcony in miniature, and she would imagine the crowd settling into their velvet seats behind and above her. And then when the lights went down she would turn and watch their faces. She enjoyed their looks of shock when the house lights came up and they recognized her, but even better was the moment of confusion just before that, before they placed her, when they smiled, half consciously knowing they knew her but not from where. They looked so shyly vulnerable for a moment, as if they thought she knew something about them. She felt like she was waking them from a dream.

But in later years, in smaller roles, she could stand in the gilded lobby of the Chinese Theatre as they filed out and not a single person would glance at her as they hurried out into the night. She might as well have been one of the art deco figures adorning the walls, their smooth mirrored faces stoically blank. By then the organ had been removed. She missed the terraced keyboard, the neat black-and-white ranks like a tuxedoed audience for a premiere.

Once, in 1936, she goes incognito, in turban and sunglasses, to attend a screening of her old acquaintance Leni Riefenstahl's *Triumph of the Will,* and while she knows better than to advertise their relationship, she finds herself secretly envying Leni her ecstatic patriotism.

And the Winner Is . . .

Luise Rainer accepts the 1936 Academy Award for Best Actress for her role in *The Great Ziegfeld*. Luise Rainer accepts the 1937 Academy Award for Best Actress for her role in *The Good Earth*.

Rumor has it that Rainer was so sure she wouldn't win a second time she stayed home in her pajamas. Called with the news of her win, she dashed to the ceremony without even putting on makeup, but fought with husband Clifford Odets on the way and had to pace five times around the Biltmore before she was steady enough to enter and receive her award.

Between 1936 and 1937 the Rape of Nanking, among other atrocities, has put acting prizes in proper perspective. Yet still it stings when Madame Chiang Kai-shek, wife of the Nationalist leader, remarks after a specially arranged screening that she can't believe Rainer isn't Chinese.

"Bloody Saturday"

During the bombing of Shanghai in 1937, Newsreel Wong will take one of the most famous images of the war: a baby, bloodied and crying, in the ruins of the railroad station. "My shoes were soaked in blood," he'll recall later. By the time *Life* reprints it in October, an estimated 140 million people will have seen it. Eventually it will be credited with turning the tide of Western public opinion against Japan. For years afterward rumors will swirl that the photo was posed, the image manipulated.

All in a good cause, she'll think, though how could he have stood to take it and not immediately scoop up the wailing infant?

The fate of the crying baby, an orphan—or *warphan*, in the famous coinage of the childless Madame Chiang—is unknown.

The next year MGM will release a film called *Too Hot to Handle*, about a newsreel cameraman in China faking footage of an aerial attack. Starring Clark Gable and Myrna Loy.

Fathers

Warner was right about Luise, but she'll never have the chance to tell him. He'll walk off the set of *Charlie Chan at Ringside,* his eighteenth Chan film, in 1938. After disappearing on a weeks-long bender, followed by a spell in a drying-out hospital and an acrimonious divorce, he'll leave the country, reemerge months later in his native Sweden, only to succumb to pneumonia.

At least he died at home, her father will note. *His* sojourn in China will last only a year beyond her visit. He'll be forced to return to Los Angeles after the Japanese invasion of China, forced to leave her stepmother, her half-brother. She'll greet him off the gangway — *Welcome home!* — and he'll look at her as if it's her fault. She'll throw her arms around him anyway.

Gold Mountain was only ever where he planned to live and work until he got rich. But he'll die there, in 1949, and she'll attend his funeral and arrange his interment beside her mother, whose bones had never been sent to China. She won't go out to Rosedale to visit them as often as she should, but sometimes she'll sit in the vast, cool barn of the waiting room at Union Station, thinking of them and the home they made nearby, listening to the click of heels on the terra-cotta tiles echoing back off the travertine walls (a temple to trains, her father called it once) until she grows self-conscious about having no one to meet, no train to catch.

Near the end of their affair, when she was blue, Doug used to call her Sum Ting Wong; at the start, he'd told her she was really something. When he dies, in 1939, she'll

read that his real name was Douglas Ullman. His last words: "I've never felt better."

Irving Thalberg hadn't lived to see *The Good Earth* open.

Walter Benjamin, who wrote that her name unfolded like "a moon-filled blossom in a cup of tea" but also misspelled it as Anne May Wong, committed suicide in 1940 rather than fall into Nazi hands.

Even Carole Lombard, the profane angel, will die: in a plane crash in 1942.

Only Charlie Chan will live on, a new yellowface actor, Sidney Toler, taking on the role vacated by Warner. Even the footage from *Charlie Chan at Ringside* will enjoy a second life, Warner's scenes reshot with Peter Lorre in yellowface as the Japanese detective Mr. Moto, the film released as *Mr. Moto's Gamble*.

Poor Warner was right about that too. He was never the star.

The Understudy

In 1940 her younger sister, Mary, will hang herself in her garage—out of despair at her stalled acting career, it's rumored. Another butterfly killing herself for unrequited love.

"She always wanted my roles."

"She always wanted to *be* you," her father accuses. It's true, she thinks (even though she's always suspected that Mary took her name from Mary Pickford to spite her). Once, tipsy in Berlin, the girl had crashed the car and given her famous sister's name to the *polizei*.

"I'll never forgive you for encouraging her," her father says.

"For once," she tells him, "we agree."

They bury her next to her mother, the same gravesite where Mary took her part years earlier.

"How can you bear it?" Mary asked her once.

"What?"

"Any of it. All of it."

Mary waves her arms about too much, she thought critically.

She sighed. "You know when you're doing a scene and it's near the end, and the take is a good one, and you need to sneeze or you have an itch, or you think you might corpse?" *Corpsing* being British theater slang for breaking character, laughing.

"Oh yes! That happens to you?"

"No. I just tell myself I can get through it for another few seconds. And I do. That's how I bear it. One take at a time. You can always make it to the end of the scene."

Mary, almost wailing: "And the next and the next?"

So melodramatic; no wonder she fails.

"That's acting, darling. That's *art*. It's why what's unbearable in life—loss, heartbreak, despair—is bearable on the screen: because we know the picture will end."

But if Mary was just playing her, who was the worse actress?

It's just another scene, she tells herself at the funeral, another scene that will eventually—

Mary, she recalls suddenly, had always wondered about their mother's death. How could she just step in front of an automobile? Why would she?

Exclusion

After her trip, partly by choice but also because China is now an ally, she starts to take "better" parts in lesser movies. No more dragon ladies, no more butterflies, no more prostitutes. Partly by choice, partly as a function of her increasing age and receding fame, she wears longer gowns that cover her legs—those great gams. She wears her hair in the traditional styles of married women, like *lid of teapot*, combed forward in a smooth dark slab.

She collects money for China relief, appears at fundraisers, donates her salary, auctions her dresses for orphans and medicine.

At New Year's 1941 she stands under a sign: your name in chinese 10¢. A calligrapher writes out the names she bestows on tourists. Lotus Moon. Lucky Flower. Sage Tiger. (*Are you naming people or restaurants?* the calligrapher cackles in Chinese.)

"And what does *your* name mean?" a square-jawed fellow asks, laying a dime in her palm, and she smiles, leans in to tell him. "Phew!" a heavy young woman interjects, taking his arm. "I bet she could help us with baby monikers."

Her smile freezes as if in a photo. "Congratulations," she offers, and then, with a little bow to the mother-to-be, "Golden Peach."

She is the guest of honor at the Moon Festival parade of 1942, which marks the opening of the new East Gate of Chinatown, the Gate of Maternal Virtue, riding in an open-top car beside the Chinese consul, lantern-bearers and a corps of Chinese majorettes to the front of them, camels and even an elephant to the rear.

But in 1943, when Madame Chiang Kai-shek, American-educated, third wife of the successor to Sun Yat-sen, the Nationalist generalissimo (the *Missimo* to his *Gissimo,* as they're popularly known), tours the U.S., speaks to a joint session of Congress, and holds a benefit rally at the Hollywood Bowl, she isn't invited. Rita Hayworth is there, Barbara Stanwyck and Greer Garson, Ingrid Bergman and Loretta Young are there. Even Mary Pickford, despite having retired ten years earlier, at the end of the silent era. Thirty thousand people in total. But the closest she'll get is a newsreel.

It's another grand snub, but she takes it in stride. "It's of no consequence." Even though she has raised funds for the general, defended him against those who call him "Cash My Check," say China will never repay its debts. Even though she has expressed her admiration for Madame Chiang in interviews, privately lobbied producers to play her in a biopic. *The role of a lifetime. Born to play it.* But she knows how the Nationalists feel about her, how the Chinese elite look down on the overseas Chinese. Besides, there's room for only one Chinese star in Hollywood at a time.

As recently as 1938 she was acclaimed as "The World's Most Beautiful Chinese Girl" in the pages of *Look*.

She sits instead in a restaurant in Chinatown. She's a regular; they know her usual, keep a table for her, though tonight she could have any. Chinatown has emptied to see Madame Chiang at the "Rice Bowl," as the wags are calling it. Her siblings have even taken her father, a great admirer of China's first lady. The old laundryman woke early to press his suit fresh, even though she pays to send

his laundry out. She would go with him herself, but she's afraid she'll be recognized, afraid she won't be. Afraid, most of all, of seeing her father applauding another.

She orders chop suey. A dish invented in America for Americans, she knows. But made and sold by Chinese. Which surely should count for something. It's not that she represents the Chinese badly, she thinks. It's that she represents something else entirely. Chop suey! *Chinese American*. That's the new name she's started to hear. A gift of the war, now that boys from Chinatown can fight for America.

Madame Chiang's visit is credited for paving the way for the end of Chinese exclusion in December of that year. It will take five years for California to repeal its anti-miscegenation laws. The Supreme Court will finally rule all such laws unconstitutional in 1967.

Anna May Wong will die in 1961, aged fifty-six, of cirrhosis, two days after her final TV appearance, on *The Barbara Stanwyck Show*. She'd been looking forward to a big screen comeback as Madame Liang in *Flower Drum Song*. She will never have married, never had a child, though she will have finally played a mother on TV in *The Life and Legend of Wyatt Earp,* and her youngest brother, Richard, will still be living with her at the time of her death. He'll bury her beside her mother, her father, and her sister Mary, under her Chinese name. (She'd reassumed it, after a fashion, a decade earlier for the lead character of a short-lived series, a Chinese detective named Madame Liu Tsong. No episodes survive, and thus no copies of the title sequence with its circular credit: "Anna May Wong as Madame Liu Tsong.") *Time*'s obituary will note that she

"died a thousand deaths" onscreen. Several others will quote her father's apocryphal advice to her: "Don't be photographed too much or you'll lose your soul."

She'll live to see Newsreel one more time — in a photo, kneeling beside Madame Chiang in September of 1945 to film her reading a newspaper account of the Japanese surrender. Madame once said of herself, "The only thing Oriental about me is my face." *Life* called her "the most powerful woman in the world," *Liberty* "the real brains and boss of the Chinese government." Hemingway dubbed her "the empress."

Just another dragon lady after all. Newsreel's pose, she notes, is one of supplication, kowtowing — no, *proposing*, the camera proffered like an oversized ring box.

Four years later the Missimo will retreat to Taiwan, renamed the Republic of China, her husband's Nationalists, spent from their struggle against the Japanese, no match for the Communists now. Newsreel himself will eventually retire there. Madame Chiang will never set foot in mainland China again. Instead she'll move to the United States after the generalissimo's death (he was eleven years her senior) and live in New York until her own passing, aged 105. She and Luise Rainer will have kept up a correspondence for seventy years.

The first Chinese American to win an Oscar will be James Wong Howe, in 1955, for black-and-white cinematography. "Life's a heckuva lot simpler behind the camera," he told her once, way back when, on the set of *Peter Pan*.

And somewhere in there Anna will realize what's finally made them Chinese American. It's the revolution, the victory of the Communists over the American-backed

government of General Chiang. After which no sojourner can make his fortune on Gold Mountain and take it home. Not if he wants to keep it. They—all of them—are Chinese American now, not just because America has finally, begrudgingly, allowed them to be, but because China has closed to them.

The closest she'll get is a newsreel . . .

And yet there in the dreaming dark, watching Madame Chiang waving through the ticker tape, doesn't she recognize something in the cock of the Missimo's head, the set of her shoulders, the turn of her wrist? Gestures copied from the movies. *Why, that's me,* she'll think. *There I am after all.*

Jade

Tell It Slant

There was funky Billie Chin and little Sammy Chong...
— "Kung Fu Fighting," *Carl Douglas*

Soon it'll be three decades. A ceremony is planned, a memorial. A plaque to be unveiled. It's more than a year away yet, but I already have an invitation. To attend, to say a few words, to share my recollections. It's tucked in the frame of my dresser mirror, his yearbook picture looking back at me. *Never forget*, it says. *Always remember. Keep his memory alive.* And at the bottom, in italics: *Save the day.* A typo, though I must have read it three times before I even noticed. Now it's all I can think of, that malapropism. Maybe it's why I've not written back yet to decline, as I've declined all such invitations for years. It's a mistake my father might have made, his mother, anyone of their immigrant generation. I wonder if the letter writer is older, or, more likely, someone still hearing an elder's voice in his head.

In the photo he is still young. In the mirror my face could be his father's.

What do I remember? What does anyone remember after all this time?

If you remember it at all, if you were around in the eighties, say, what you remember is a Chinese guy being beaten

to death in Detroit by two white auto workers who mistook him for a Japanese. This at the height of the import scare, when Japanese manufacturers were being blamed for the collapse of the Big Three U.S. auto companies.

Maybe you remember it happened outside a club where the Chinese guy—actually a Chinese American named Vincent Chin—was celebrating his bachelor party. Maybe you remember he was buried on what should have been his wedding day.

But perhaps you thought it was just an urban legend, a bad joke come to life.

Chinaman and a Jew walk into a bar. They order drinks, get to chatting, then out of nowhere the Jew turns round and sucker-punches the Chinaman.

"What the hell was that for?" splutters the Chinaman, and the Jew tells him, "Pearl Harbor."

"But that was the Japanese—I'm Chinese!"

"Oy! Sorry," the Jew goes. "You've all got that black hair, those slanty eyes. It was an honest mistake."

(Stop me if you've heard this one before.)

"Well, all right," Chinaman says, dusting himself off, and they shake, order another round.

Only five minutes later the Chinaman rears back, cold-cocks the Jew.

"What the hell was that for?" the Jew asks, picking himself up.

"Titanic," Chinaman says sternly.

"The Titanic!" the Jew cries. "That was a fucking iceberg."

"Iceberg, Goldberg, Steinberg." The Chinaman shrugs. "Honest mistake!"

Only that night it wasn't a Chinaman and a Jew, it was two Chinamen, Vincent and me. And it wasn't a bar but a strip club. And we were with a couple of white friends, Mike and Jerry. But still.

I don't know about an honest mistake, but it was an easy one. It was dark in there, filmed with smoke, lit only by the snowy static of glitter balls. One of the girls used a fog machine in her routine; another flickered in a strobe. I'm not sure *I* could have told Chinese from Japanese in that light. But I knew the pair across the stage — one silvering, the other mustachioed — were white. And they knew we weren't.

He wasn't a saint, Vincent, though he always figured he might have been named for one. The newspapers all reported he was there for his bachelor party, and sure, that was the occasion, but "bachelor party" makes it sound like a one-off, like *we* took *him* there, when it was his idea and a regular haunt of his, his *turf*. The Fancy Pants Lounge in Highland Park. The girls all knew him; he was a favorite. Contrary to the stereotype — which is why I say it — he wasn't a eunuch.

The only thing that was different about that night, then? It was supposed to be his last time. He told me his mother had given him the ultimatum (*she* knew about the club, his mom, though not his fiancée, Vicki; for her it was almost as shocking as his death). He'd promised he'd quit going after he married. *It's the last time, Ma.* I remember because he said she didn't like that, him saying *last time*. She was superstitious that way, said it was bad luck. "Can't

win," is what he shouted over the music, his breath warm in my ear. Me, I didn't believe him anyway, figured he'd be back the week after the honeymoon.

Maybe I even hoped so secretly. It was the first time he'd asked me along since I moved home after college, my first time ever in a strip club. I'd dressed preppy—pastel polo over khakis and Topsiders. Jerry in his mullet and acid-washed jeans laughed when I got in the car.

"It's not a disco, man! The girls dance *for* you, not *with* you."

"Ah, lay off him."

I was working toward my CPA back then. Vincent had come straight from the restaurant, still in his black slacks and white shirt, but he'd slipped on his Members Only jacket. He was riding shotgun, and from the back seat I watched him spread the wings of his collar in the visor mirror to reveal a thin gold chain.

The papers also said what a filial son he was, working two jobs—draftsman by day, waiter by night—to support his poor widowed mother as well as save for his wedding. They made him out to be a model citizen of the model minority. Saint and stereotype. But think. That night he must have had fifty bucks in smoothed-out singles on him—"Tips, baby!"—so what exactly was he working so hard for? Two jobs to pay for two lives, maybe.

So, no saint.

Our generation's Bruce Lee, someone once called him. Meaning our generation's tragic martyr. Such an American concept (see Lincoln, Abe; Kennedys, assorted; Doctor

King; not to mention James Dean, Marilyn Monroe). But Bruce Lee, for all that he was born in the U.S., always felt more Chinese than Chinese American and was at least as popular with whites and blacks. Plus his death—from an allergic reaction to medication—lacked a bad guy (one reason rumors of triad plots or drug abuse, shades of those old Chinatown evils, abounded).

But now we had our own martyr.

I always wondered how I was supposed to feel about that. I was the friend, after all. Could I have saved him? Should I have died with him? But then he wouldn't be a martyr, or perhaps we both would be (though martyrs, like all symbols, come best in ones). Instead I was the witness. In all the newspaper accounts, and now online if you care to look it up, "his friend who ran away."

If you can be a friend and run away.

Without Bruce Lee, though, would two white men have brought a baseball bat to a fight with an Asian? Had they seen his movies? Did they think they were only being smart, evening the odds against some kung-fu fighter? Vincent did look a little like Bruce—that same thick mop of coal-black hair. So did I, for that matter. We didn't look alike, but we looked like Bruce, more like him than each other, probably. We'd spent our teens practicing his sprung stride and sudden, panting punches, flashing his switchblade smile in the mirror.

Horse walks into a bar—You know this one?—*and the bartender asks, "Why the long face?"*

Yeah? How about this one?

*Two Chinamen walk into a bar and the barkeep goes,
"Why the same face?"*

Okay. But we weren't the same. That's my point. *That's*
what got him killed.

On the one hand, he was more Chinese than me and
most of the other Chinese American kids I knew. He was
born there—the mainland, not Taiwan, like my parents
—lived there until he was six before he was adopted (itself
pretty rare back then), didn't even speak English in first
grade. Then again, his parents didn't live in or around
Chinatown like most of ours. They were in Highland
Park, with no Chinese neighbors. Oh, they came to
Chinatown to do their shopping every weekend—I'd see
him around, knew who he was—but Highland Park was
where he lived, where he went to school. With white kids.
Poles, Irish, Italians. (This was before the riots, white
flight.) So he was always more at ease with them, more at
ease with them than we were, for sure, but also maybe
more at ease with them than with *us*. That's where he met
Mike and Jerry, in grade school. I only knew him well in
high school; they always had that first claim on him (the
three of them had gone to see the Grand Prix a couple of
weeks earlier—they were still talking about it in the car
that night, Mike goofing on *grand pricks*. I hadn't been
asked).

It's one reason Vincent liked the Fancy Pants, even
though it was a rat hole—an old grindhouse with rows of
movie seats still in back and the girls up onstage beneath
the peeling gilt proscenium. It meant he got to go back to
Highland Park, back home (his mother remembered

seeing *Flower Drum Song* there when it was still a respect-
able joint). He'd always hated having to leave. *Driven out,*
as he saw it. His dad had been mugged, so they'd moved to
the suburbs and Vincent had finished high school there.
They traded a third-floor walkup for a nice little ranch
with a carport and scalloped aluminum awnings two
blocks over from ours.

We'd been in Oak Park for five years by then, my father
and me. He owned a grocery in Chinatown but made his
fortune from a sideline. He'd always stocked a few rice
cookers, but on a whim he tried some pocket transistor
radios from the same Japanese suppliers, just as the
market for them took off (this was Motown in the sixties,
after all). I can still remember his suspicion when white
and black teens started coming in for them. A few years
later he ditched the bok choy and the scallions for good
and relocated the electronics business to the Westland
mall, where he cashed in on early video game consoles,
Walkmans, and VCRs. But he'd already moved us from
the apartment over the grocery store a couple of months
after the riots in '67.

My father talked about Oak Park like it was the prom-
ised land. But it never sat well with Vincent. "Can't sleep
right," he complained; he missed the shush of traffic at
night. Really, it felt like running away, I think. He didn't
blame his dad—Mr. Chin was an older guy, in his sixties
by then—but Vincent always figured he'd have fought
back if it were him. You could say he'd been spoiling for
that fight for years.

Irony is, he was a great runner. That was his thing in
high school—track. I was heavy as a kid, shy in the

cafeteria, so I'd take my lunch on the bleachers, watch him doing his laps. I told him running suited his name, and he looked at me blankly. *Vincent*, I said, *means winner.* He liked that, as I hoped he would, but it surprised me he hadn't known. Then again, he went by Vince, at school at least, itself unusual among us, our boys' names, even in English, often echoing the two syllables of a Chinese name: Roland or Robin, Henry or Melvin, Eddie or Peter, like me (I even knew a Nixon once). Myself, I used to call him "InVince," because he was invincible, I told him, but also because he was *in*, in a way I never could be. Really I knew "Vince" just meant American.

On the wedding invitation it was "Vincent" in embossed italics. Vincent and Victoria. Both winners. Vicki and Vince, to their friends. As a couple they couldn't have sounded more all-American. They were planning two ceremonies; Vicki had two dresses picked out, one Chinese, one Western. When I asked him that night how the preparations were going, he told me his mother was arguing with Vicki over guests throwing rice. "She says Chinese don't waste food, still remembers going hungry during the war." The wedding was planned for a Monday, when all the Chinese restaurants were closed, so that everyone could attend. Afterward they had tickets for Aruba.

His middle name was Jen, though I only learned it when he died. He never used it, and it only shows as *J.* on his gravestone. I had to ask what it stood for. Jen: the great Confucian virtue of doing unto others as you'd have them do unto you.

* * *

What do I remember? What do you?

If you remember the case at all, if you're Asian American, say, you might recall that the killers, Evans and Pitts, father and stepson (and what father takes his stepson to a strip club?), pleaded manslaughter. It was just a barroom brawl gone wrong, heat-of-the-moment stuff — an honest mistake! — never mind it took them thirty minutes to hunt Vincent down. The victim had thrown the first punch, after all. They got off with probation and fines of $3000 each. Plus court costs.

Less than the price of a used car, people said.

Maybe you remember that the judge had been in a Japanese POW camp during the war.

Remember when Chinese couldn't testify against whites? people said, as if it were yesterday and not a hundred years ago.

It was Vincent's idea. He told me to run. Only he didn't say *run*. He said, "Scram." It was the last word I heard from him in English, so I've given it a lot of thought. *Scram*. It's what you say to a kid, isn't it? A nuisance. Or maybe what naughty kids say to each other after they ring a doorbell. Scram. Not run. *He* was a runner. Running to him meant winning. Running *toward* something. Scram, I think, meant running away. If he'd said *run* we might both have run, but *scram* was for me. Because he didn't scram. He waited for them. He could have gotten away. When Evans hopped out of the car — a Plymouth, for the record — it was still moving. It ran over his foot, for god's sake! It was the Keystone Klan out there! You think Vincent couldn't have outrun these guys? He lettered in

track. But he was done running. He started it at the club, after all. He would have fought in the gravel and dog-shit parking lot outside too if Evans hadn't gone for the bat. He *wanted* to fight them. Maybe he figured he could make Evans drop the bat, shame him into a fair fight. Maybe he figured just two on one they wouldn't feel they needed the bat.

This was on Woodward, under the golden arches there, fluorescent tubes in the sign humming like cicadas.

I didn't run far. To the edge of the light. Just far enough to live, just far enough to watch.

Scram! Who was he to tell me to scram? Who was I to listen?

He was grappling with Pitts when Evans caught him across the knees, as if reaching for a grounder, after which Vincent couldn't have run even if he'd wanted. Then a line drive to the chest—*pop!*—as he went down, two more to the head when he was on all fours. Swinging for the fences.

I ran back, but too late. Before or after the two off-duty cops working security at the Mickey D's drew on Evans? You might wonder. Me too.

Vincent's last words—"It's not fair"—to me, in Chinese, while I cradled his ruined head, blood bubbling from his mouth and nose as he spoke, blood pouring from his ears like oil. His skull felt like rotten fruit. I thought I'd pissed myself, but the warm wetness in my lap was his brains.

The blow to the chest broke a jade charm, a little carved elephant that had been his mother's, that Vincent wore on his chain—a bad omen to Chinese, though you hardly needed an omen to foretell what was coming next.

The ambulance took him to Henry Ford Hospital, the same hospital he used to take his dad for dialysis, where he lingered for a few days, his mother by his bedside, calling him — "Vincent! Mama coming. Vincent! Mama coming" — as if from a great distance, before she finally gave consent to turn him off. The same hospital where they told her thirty years earlier that she'd never have a child.

I couldn't look at his mother at the funeral, or at Vicki beside her, her eyes veiled by oversized shades. Instead I concentrated on this girl I knew called Patty, a friend of Vicki's, standing with them on the other side of the grave. She was a nervous thing, this Patty, loud and fidgety, but stilled now in her grief, her pale skin glowing against her dark blouse (half the mourners were in white, the traditional color of Chinese mourning, half in black). I realized how beautiful she was. I yearned to comfort her, imagined moving to her across the open grave as if I could walk on air. She was going to be a bridesmaid, and Vincent had promised to set me up with her, but I'd been doubtful, wary. "She's *into* you, man," he'd assured me with a nudge. Now she wouldn't meet my eye.

I watched them walk away after, the older woman between the two younger, leaning against each other for balance when their heels sank into the turf. Then I filled a spadeful of earth, watched it slide off the bright steel blade into shadow.

If you remember the case at all (and maybe it's coming back to you?), if you were watching TV back then, you

might recall her, Vincent's mother—Lily—going on *Donahue* (remember him?), or meeting with Jesse Jackson (remember *him*?) at one of his presidential campaign rallies. She put the yellow in the Rainbow Coalition, people said.

She still had one of those comedy Chinglish accents: *What I live for? I don't have happy anymore. I not care my life.* The kind of accent that makes my generation cringe; Vincent used to do a choice imitation of it. But her voice cracked, daring anyone to laugh, daring anyone to feel embarrassed. *Vely hurt my heart.*

To me, watching at home, Phil leaning in solicitously looked disconcertingly like Evans—the same pasty complexion, the same shock of white hair. *Laugh and I'll kill you,* I thought.

Lily. But Mrs. Chin to me, always. Just another mom, but stouter, shriller, fiercer, and more doting than all the rest, so that she seemed somehow like everyone's mother. (Everyone *else's;* mine had died of throat cancer before I turned seven.) When we were kids she always had treats —egg tarts, mooncakes in fall, her homemade prawn crackers—and praised my good appetite. When we grew up she was always asking when I was going to get married, telling Vincent to introduce me to some nice girl (to which he would roll his eyes, though whether for my benefit or hers, I was never quite sure).

All I learned about her life came from the papers. Some of it I doubt even Vincent knew. She'd grown up in Canton. Her family owned a department store. They must have been well-off, but they lost it all in the war. She'd come

from China in '47 to marry his dad, who'd lived here since the twenties and earned his citizenship by enlisting. Mrs. Chin's own father had resisted the match—an ancestor had worked on the railroads and been driven out—but she was sure it would be a better life. She'd seen so much violence in China at the hands of the Japanese, she wanted to start over. She'd have been twenty-seven—old to marry, delayed by the war—and Vincent's dad even older at forty-four. I guess they tried to start a family of their own, but she miscarried and the docs told her she couldn't have kids. It took them more than a decade to adopt Vincent from Hong Kong. His dad was in his late fifties by then, and even Lily in her forties—the oldest parents of anyone I knew.

They worked their whole lives in laundries and restaurants. "For what?" Vincent asked me savagely during his father's final illness. "They never had any fun." We were outside in his drive, smoking, Mrs. Chin framed in the kitchen window washing rice as if panning for gold. I knew what it was to lose a parent; I'd come to pay my respects. I didn't know his father well—what I remember most is his sure-handed ability to pluck out a fish's eyeball with his chopsticks, a deftness that impressed me as a child almost as much as his relish in eating it appalled me —but I knew the answer to Vincent's question. For what? *For you!* It was the same for all of us kids. The debt he could never redeem, no matter how late he sat up rubbing the old man's swollen knuckles when he couldn't sleep.

"If life gives you lemon," Mr. Chin used to joke, "make lemon chicken!" I assumed he made it up till I saw it in a fortune cookie.

First his dad, now Vincent himself. Part of what was so moving was that his mother's desire for justice, her thirst for vengeance, they were ways of forgiving his most unfilial act: dying before her (beside which sneaking off to strip clubs under Vicki's nose was a pale betrayal). The night it happened, when I finally got home from the hospital and told my father everything, he pulled me close and hugged me. I couldn't remember the last time we'd touched. I thought I'd failed my friend, but it turns out I'd been a good son.

Vincent was the same age when he died as his mother had been when she started her new life in America.

After his death, to support herself, she went back to work for a while at a local factory, making those little plastic ice scrapers for windshields.

They called themselves the ACJ, American Citizens for Justice—no mention of Chinese or Asian in the name—and insisted that placards at marches be in English, which may explain the painful, plaintive pun of CHIN UP FOR JUSTICE on one popular sign. But they're the ones—journalists, lawyers, church leaders, and local businessmen—who helped Lily get the case reopened. And their coming together—Chinese and Japanese, those old enemies, as well as Korean, Vietnamese, Filipino—marked the start of a pan-Asian political movement. And me along with the rest, attending meetings, giving interviews, marching beneath a neatly lettered sign. You could say it's when we became Asian American. Two drunk white guys couldn't tell us apart, and we realized we were more alike than we'd thought.

There'd been Asian student coalitions and alliances and collectives when I was in Palo Alto—holdovers from the antiwar movement—but I'd kept my nose in my books (my "political" involvement at Stanford began and ended with my vote for the football team to be called the Robber Barons; the administration shot that one down). Vincent and I had missed the draft by a couple of years, but he'd always said he'd serve if called, "like my Dad" (I always said Canada was a thirty-minute drive).

"Pan-Asian," I could imagine Vincent joking, for Mike or Jerry's benefit. "What is that, like a wok?" "Sure, a melting wok!" I'd say, and we'd all laugh.

The first meetings were held in the Golden Star, the restaurant where Vincent had worked, everyone sitting around the freshly laid tables—vinyl tablecloths and melamine rice bowls—trying not to disturb the settings, looking less angry or sad in that context than hungry. It reminded me of his funeral the previous summer, only these weren't all the same people who'd come then. I didn't know many of them; many of them didn't know Vincent, and yet they spoke of that night as if they'd been there, as if *they'd* been attacked. In a way, I guess, they felt they had, if not by Evans, then by the verdict.

Part of me wanted to say something—*didn't they know who I was?*—but then it came to me that all their talk of a "heinous assault," a "brutal slaying," wasn't the way you'd talk about it if you were there. That wasn't how I remembered it; that was how they imagined it. They weren't talking as if they'd been there but as if they *wished* they had been. What would they have done if they had been? I wondered, and held my peace. It reminded me of

Vincent, the way he told me about his father's mugging. They were spoiling for a fight too.

Back in the kitchen the cooks were preparing dishes for later, hot oil singing in the steel woks.

I didn't say anything in the end, but Lily was there and she spoke last, halting but firm. She wanted justice for Vincent, and we applauded until our hands stung. But a lot of the people in that room also wanted justice for themselves. Me too, I suppose. I had run, but maybe there was still something I could do.

Sometimes now when people tell the story it's a triumph. Something good, something important, coming from tragedy. "The death of a man, the birth of a movement." I guess that's what Vincent was martyred for, even if he didn't know it.

Don't make a federal case out of it. Wasn't that the Chinese American way? Turn the other cheek, look the other way, water off a Peking duck's back. "Take it on the chin," as a sick joke doing the rounds had it. My father had been mistaken for Japanese in the store plenty of times—he was selling Japanese radios, after all—but he knew better than to correct a customer (even if as a boy during the war he wore a button saying CHINESE, NOT JAPANESE.)

But making a federal case is literally what we did—what we had to do to get the case reopened and prosecuted by the Justice Department as a hate crime. Only it had never been done before. Civil rights legislation hadn't been applied to Asians previously; doing so now was a hot topic, a *choice*. Whose lot to throw in with? Blacks, for

whom the legislation had been written, some of whom were suspicious of a possible usurpation, or dilution, as if Asian struggles were equivalent? Or whites, whom many of us aspired to be like?

I sat at the back of those meetings, between the pay phone and the cigarette machine, watching koi gliding silently back and forth in the aquarium. Every so often the talk would be interrupted, hushed really, by someone trying to come in to eat, the irritated exchanges at the door when they were turned away. I couldn't see from where I was, but I imagined they were probably white. It was that kind of restaurant, the kind with Chinese zodiac placemats, the kind where white diners point out the few Chinese to each other and whisper how the food must be "authentic." I wondered what they thought if they glimpsed a crowd of us inside before the door shut on them.

The koi turned, slid back the other way. They were supposed to be lucky fish, good feng shui. Their filter hummed happily. Next to the kitchen was another tank flickering with bass, tilapia, grouper—the unlucky fish, as I deemed them.

As to our question: Were we a minority, or were we honorary members of the majority? I reckon I know what Vincent would have chosen. Vince. But to get justice for him, we chose the other. Later I heard some blacks call us "fleedom riders"; what they meant was "free riders."

So a federal case, and I was called to testify, to say what I'd heard, what I'd seen, what I'd done. What I remembered.

* * *

It *was* a race thing. No doubt. One of the strippers, Lacey, recalled the line, and then we all did. "It's because of you little motherfuckers we're out of work," Evans said, meaning Japanese, even though he wasn't out of work himself, even though Vincent wasn't Japanese.

Pitts *had* been laid off a couple of years earlier, but he was working again, at a furniture store, and attending community college. Both he and Evans, in fact, went back to work the very next morning, though Evans was eventually fired by Chrysler when his felony plea was accepted. Only then would he really be out of work because of Vincent.

But okay, the car business *was* in the crapper, as Vincent very well knew. He was working for an auto supplier, after all. He was *in* the business.

Would it have made a difference if Vincent had said, *I'm Chinese*? That his mother had moved to the U.S. because she couldn't live in China after the war, with her memories of the Japanese bombing? Probably not. Nips, Chinks, gooks, slants—we were all the same to them. Instead he said, "I'm not a little motherfucker," and Evans came back with drunken magnanimity: "Big fucker, little fucker, we're all fuckers." And then Vincent stubbed out his cigarette and went for him. Punches were thrown, a stool. Pitts had his head cut open.

But maybe everyone's a racist in a strip club. Sexist, sure, goes without saying, but racist too. Afterward Evans tried to say it started because Vincent tipped a black dancer badly. I don't know; maybe, though it sounds like a smoke-screen: *we're all racists*. But maybe we all are in a club. The whole point is to pick a girl or girls you like—blond,

brunette, redhead, black, white, Asian. Did Vincent like white girls? In the immortal words of Hong Kong Phooey, *Could be!* I know we both ignored the Asian girls. You want what you can't have, what you don't have. Why else would you be in a place like that? And he already had a nice Chinese girl in Vicki. "Going with another Chinese," he told me sloppily, "would be unfaithful." But he felt okay about a white girl, because he knew they were unattainable outside of a club. Hell, maybe Evans felt the same about black girls. "I don't like seeing people picked on," he said in court. Such chivalry.

Vincent's father, by the way, was mugged by a black guy. Did I say that already? Or did you assume it?

I don't recall the black dancer, but Lacey I remember. I was disappointed in the girls at first—they were older, their skin tanned leathery or oiled in a way that made you conscious of the smell of sweat in the room. Lacey wasn't a beauty either, of course: a dirty blonde with small breasts and a broad pale ass. But those kinds of imperfections, I saw, were part of the appeal of the place. The women were vulnerable, more naked because they were exposing shortcomings. Some of them made a jiggling show of themselves, as if to say they were in on the joke, good sports about it; others cloaked themselves in a tired boredom that I suppose might pass for sultry. But Lacey was still trying, grinding away to "Physical" in a headband and leg warmers and not much else, smiling like it was a good time. When she shook out her mane at the end of the set, I felt a drop of perspiration land on my cheek. Her skin was fever-warm where I tucked a bill in her g-string. Later, on the stand, she called Vince a "nice"

customer, said they were "friendly," and I envied him, even though I knew the defense was trying to suggest some bias, some innuendo, to discredit her. She testified in a prim skirt suit—padded shoulders, blouse buttoned to the throat, still trying—but I remembered her body beneath it.

The thing about racism, I always think, the *worst* thing, okay, is not that someone has made up their mind about you without knowing you, based on the color of your skin, the way you look, some preconception. The worst thing is that they might be right. Stereotypes cling if they have a little truth; they sting by the same token. A lot of us *do* work hard; many of us (those who hail from Canton, anyway) *are* short. Some of us *do* have small dicks. And yes, as Evans's complaint about Vincent's tipping suggests, some of us are cheap (like our food, our goods, our labor). How would you feel if I called you racist? The *white* stereotype. But some of you *are* racist, right? It doesn't mean that what's true of the many has to be true of the one, any more than what's true of the one must be true of the many.

That's why Vincent's case was so empowering. They thought he was *Japanese*! They were manifestly wrong, completely refutable. We didn't all look alike—that old racist fallacy—but even if we did, we weren't.

His name was Chin, for god's sake! As in *China*.

And yet—it has sometimes nagged me—what if Vincent had been Japanese? His death wouldn't have been more or less, just *differently* unfair, I guess. But would it have brought us together? I doubt it.

And what of me? Weren't Vincent and I alike that night? Evans and Pitts chased us outside the club, ignoring Jerry and Mike. Except Vincent fought back, and they killed him. So we're not all alike, though I sometimes feel guilty for not being more like him.

I'm not a motherfucker, he said. And he wasn't. But it's that word that set him off, I think. More than the race thing, even. *That* we heard every day anyhow. But he didn't like *motherfucker.* He was an adoptee, his father had died less than a year earlier, he still lived at home, and he was about to get married. He didn't like that word. It's unfilial, okay? Disrespectful. We worship our ancestors.

I asked him once about his birth parents—he was cooling down after a practice—and he said he didn't know. Dead, he figured, or unmarried, or so poor they had to sell him or give him away. He'd come from Hong Kong, so they might have been refugees from the Communist mainland. He was taking deep breaths, chest rising and falling, beads of sweat in his hair like dew. I don't know what I expected. I might have been probing for vulnerability, looking for an opening to express sympathy. But this was the opposite of self-pity. "I feel bad for them, but it's not like I remember them." Yet what if they'd kept him? I pressed. He had his thumb to his wrist, counting his pulse. "That kid wouldn't have been me, couldn't have been."

I read somewhere once that in China during the Cultural Revolution, they called bashing someone's brains in *opening the flower.*

I wonder sometimes about the odd echoes—an adoptee and his mother, a father and a stepson. Perhaps they

all had something to prove. Evans did say, "I was just defending my boy." He was a superintendant at Chrysler when Pitts was laid off; maybe he felt he owed him. Maybe he loved him like his own. They still played baseball together is why they had the bat in the trunk in the first place. Turns out Evans only took Pitts to the club that night because the boy had just had a fight with his girl-friend. And the day after (the only day either of them ever woke up in a cell)? Father's Day.

Vincent was my friend. So how could I leave him? He *was* my friend, but I didn't always like him. How could I not envy his confidence, his good looks, his fiancée? Even afterward, I hated him a little. Even in death he made me feel like nothing. Worse than nothing. Oh, it wasn't right, those two getting off for killing him. But that's not why I testified at the federal trial. I wanted to stand up, even if belatedly. *I* didn't want to feel like a motherfucker. So I met with Tina, the young Chinese lawyer, and Jerry and Mike, around a cigarette-burned table, and she told us, "You need to get your lines down, agree on what happened, get your stories straight." I was touching my fingertip to each scorch mark in turn. Tina was slim and a little severe, but her long hair shone like Vicki's. Vincent would have called her *fine*, found a way to make her smile. That's when we remembered the racist talk, heard by all of us above the throbbing music, clearly recalled despite all the booze we'd drunk.

And Vincent's last words? Heard only by me, spoken in Chinese so no one else could understand, never mind that his head was already stove in, jaw shattered, and people

wonder how he could even have retained consciousness, let alone spoken. Well, okay, but it *wasn't* fair, was it? None of it. Tell me that's not true.

What did I do? What would you have done?

Evans got twenty-five years.

Out the courtroom window, I watched a jet slowly raise a scar across the sky.

What is truth, anyway? What I testified? This version? What you can read in the papers or online? Chinese whispers, you might say.

Vincent, incidentally, had wanted to be a lawyer when he was a kid. His mother told him no one would believe a Chinese lawyer. He wanted to be a writer too, but she told him he'd never make any money at it. By the time I knew him he was thinking about being a vet, but she reminded him he was scared of blood.

He *was* my friend. But did I like him, or was I just like him?

I couldn't have told you the hits they were playing at the club that night. "Ladies Night." "Centerfold." "Ring My Bell." "Private Eyes." I couldn't have recalled them, but when I hear those songs now I turn the stereo off.

Maybe, just maybe, if you remember the case at all, if you saw the Oscar-nominated documentary, or studied it in school, or read a blog about it, you'll recall that Evans's federal conviction was later appealed.

Lacey's testimony was called into doubt. Had she received consideration for other charges? Maybe you

remember some titillating smear that she wasn't even wearing panties in court. That prim outfit on a stripper invited distrust, I guess.

And the witnesses' testimony—*our* testimony, our *memory* (by this time five years had passed since that night)—was challenged. We'd been coached by our Chinese lawyer, they said.

Maybe you remember that Vincent was partying with white friends, but probably not. Maybe you remember there was a Chinese friend. Maybe you remember his name, but I hope not.

What did I remember? When did I remember it? I don't know. The air conditioning was blasting in court, but my shirt was sticking to me like a Band-Aid. What if I didn't *want* to remember that night? Did anyone think of that?

Maybe you remember that the federal conviction was overturned on appeal.

He never returned my copy of *Jaws*. He lost a tooth chewing taffy. He wore a polka-dot bow tie at the kids' table one Chinese New Year. That's what I remember.

I remember the first time he played me *Sgt. Pepper*. I remember him shoving someone for calling him Yoko. I remember watching the moon landings with him, a crowd of Chinese families gathered in somebody's restaurant. We'd have been thirteen. Some kid at school had tried to spoil my excitement by saying that Aldrin and Armstrong had shot down Chinese MiGs in Korea. It was Vincent who reminded me, "They're gonna be able to see the Great Wall from up there!" I remember him trying to grow a mustache like his hero, Steve Prefontaine; that he owned

the first pair of Nikes I ever saw. I remember lighting fire-crackers on his lawn for Fourth of July.

There was a civil suit everyone forgets. Evans was ordered to pay restitution, but he never did. He barely worked another day in his life. "Can't get blood from a stone," as he put it.

Evans also said of Vincent, "He was no choirboy."

And: "It's too bad, you know, especially for him. At least I'm alive."

And of the beating: "Something just snapped. I don't remember from there on what happened."

He called me "a little pest."

The evening Vincent's life support was switched off Evans was back on the diamond playing ball, taking cuts.

Afterward I couldn't bear to face her—Lily, Mrs. Chin—and she couldn't bear to stay in the U.S. She already had her ticket back to China when the first verdict came down, but it only delayed things. She finally went back forty years after she left. Went home, some might say, to Canton, though by then it was called Guangzhou. She used to say she couldn't remain in a land of injustice, but I always thought it was the vicious ironies that drove her out. She'd left China, after all, to escape her memories of the Japanese invasion, only to have her son killed because he was mistaken for a Japanese, and then to make common cause with Japanese Americans in her search for justice.

I left for a while myself. Not the country, of course, just back to the West Coast. I worked my way from Sacramento to Hayward to Oakland over the course of a

decade — more running, maybe — until my father started having chest pains and asked me to move back and take over the business. He recovered, thanks to a stent, but the store, already losing ground to Radio Shack when I came home, never did. I like to think I at least persuaded him to cut his losses, get out while the getting was good, and the experience has come in useful anyway. I've mostly been doing accounts for small businesses ever since, helping quite a few of them through liquidation or bankruptcy (no shortage of that work in Detroit). I've done a little of everything over the years, though, even a spell as a finance guy at a Toyota dealership. (Less of a gesture than I imagined: most Japanese cars are made here now anyway, down South in Kentucky, Alabama, Mississippi, and across the Midwest in Ohio and Indiana, though never Michigan.)

TOYOTA, DATSUN, HONDA . . . PEARL HARBOR, went a popular Detroit bumper sticker back in the day. Ten years after Vincent's death, Lee Iacocca, Chrysler's president and pitchman, was still complaining that the Japanese were "beating our brains in." Recently I read that Buick was a bestseller in China.

I wonder how Mrs. Chin might have felt seeing American cars on the roads there. She lived in China another twenty years but came back to the States for cancer treatment at the end of her life. The Asian American Rosa Parks, the obits called her. She's buried between Vincent and his father.

They asked me to her funeral too, as they've asked me faithfully to anniversaries and conferences and rallies down the years, as they've asked me to this latest

memorial. I appreciate the sentiment. They forgive me—
for lying or not lying well enough, either way. If only I
could forgive myself. But it's too late for the truth now.
You can't say all this stuff at an unveiling, in a documen-
tary or an interview. You can't say all this when someone
calls you a motherfucker.

I RSVPed my regrets this morning. I can't, and never
could, save the day.

Lily used to say, *Vincent still be live if I not adopt him.*
I should have talked to her; we were the two who felt most
guilty, the ones who most wanted someone else to pay.
This afternoon at least I went to her grave, all their graves,
cleaned the stones, left oranges and lit joss. Thought of
my own father, long retired to Florida (we sold the house
in Oak Park; I rent in Ferndale now). The sod over Vincent
and his father is a shade greener than that over his moth-
er's more recent plot, like jade that darkens from
wearing.

That Bicentennial summer of '76 our two families
visited the Freedom Train when it stopped in Detroit.
Vincent was at Lawrence Tech by then; I was a sophomore
in Palo Alto. We saw the Constitution, Lincoln's stovepipe
hat, a moon rock, an Oscar, Hank Aaron's home-run
record bat. Vincent's mother read aloud proudly from the
program, "Orientals arrive to build rail beds and remain
to build new lives." His father marveled at the 1904 Olds,
"first car to drive across the country," mine at the moon
buggy, "wheels by GM." For Vincent, though, the high-
light was Jesse Owens's medals.

There's a Canton near Detroit, as it happens (pronounced
with the emphasis on the first syllable; that's why I didn't

think about it for years). You pass signs for it on the way to the cemetery. A little research tells me there used to be a local Pekin and a Nankin too, all named in the 1830s, when the nation was fascinated by all things Chinese, before any Chinese had arrived. Nankin, in fact, became Westland only a few years before my father opened shop there. There are Cantons dating from the same period all across the country, in Ohio, Mississippi, Georgia, Kansas, Texas— the latter two named because their founders came from still other Cantons. The Canton in South Dakota was said to be on the exact other side of the world from its namesake.

When Vincent first came to Oak Park I thought I'd look out for him, the new kid, even though I only knew him slightly then. I felt protective of him, but he never needed me, fit in so much better than me that I occasionally feared my friendship was a liability (some kids, I knew, called us Ching and Chong behind our backs), that he tolerated it only out of pity. I was careful not to presume on it, seeking him out mostly when he was alone.

Ling-Ling and Sing-Sing was another of their names for us—those kids who'd pull the corners of their eyes back when we passed—after the famous panda pair who'd come back from China with Nixon. The same kids who snickered when I got called on to read Emily Dickenson's "Tell all the truth but tell it slant" in tenth grade English. For a while we tried calling ourselves Billie and Sammy, after the funky Chinamen in "Kung Fu Fighting," a hit our senior year. But of course only one of us was fast as lightning.

Sometimes I wonder if anything might have been different if I hadn't gone along that night. Different for me, of course — how I've wished I was never there — but also for him. I'd never been to the Fancy Pants with him before, but I'd heard about it. It was one reason I jumped at the chance. Why hadn't he asked me along before? He'd taken Jerry and Mike. He might have been worried I'd blab, tell mutual friends, that it'd get back to Vicki, I guess, but it's not like he didn't brag about it. No, I think, it was something else. I wasn't as cool as him, you might say, and I wasn't, but really any Chinese is less cool alongside another. Maybe we lose our exoticism. More likely it's that alone, we can define ourselves; with another, we invite all the stereotypes. Alone, or especially with Jerry or Mike, he was Vince. Next to me he was Vincent, Asian. So, I have to ask, would Evans have called us names if there'd only been one of us? "It's because of you . . ." he said, and he meant us, *you* plural. One isn't a threat, two or more . . . well, we were *them*. And would Vincent have gotten so angry if I hadn't been there? Perhaps; probably. But just maybe he felt he had to represent, answer back. He knew I wouldn't — later, when the bouncers intervened, I even tried to apologize to Evans, play peacemaker — so Vincent may have figured it fell to him to uphold our honor, even protect *me*. Then again, maybe he just didn't want to be like me. Maybe he yelled back, threw the first punch, to prove we weren't the same. "I'm not a motherfucker," he said. He didn't say, "*We're* not."

Then again, Evans may have said, "It's because of little motherfuckers *like you* . . ." Accounts vary. Memories differ.

There's a name for it, okay, this idea that we all look alike. It's been studied, documented. *Cross-race bias,* they call it. It's true of how whites see blacks, even how other races see whites. But with Asians the sameness is magnified. There are so many of us! Squeezed together in our overcrowded cities. And we all have the same names! And dress alike, wear glasses (I kept mine on to look at the girls; Vincent wore contacts). Even the things we make are copies—cheap knockoffs, poor imitations. We may all look alike, but when we try to copy you . . . well, the differences are obvious (and if they're not, it just means we're getting trickier, not to be trusted). Maybe to Evans and Pitts, Vincent was just a pale imitation. Maybe the reason they killed him is not that he was like me but that he was trying to be like them.

If I had a gun I'd shoot you now, I told Evans while we waited for the ambulance, but I didn't, of course.

And what about all the other what-ifs? Ten thousand of them, as Evans said. What if none of us had gone that night? Or not gotten so drunk? Not cared what a couple of assholes said? What if I hadn't run? And what if the judge had locked those guys up after the first trial? What if justice was seen to be done? Vincent is still dead, Lily still goes back to China, Vicki is still alone, I'm still yellow. It's a tragedy, but a small one, forgotten in time. But the verdict, the paltry fines, that's what made travesty of tragedy, "rubbed insult into injury," as my father said. Shit, it's a tossup which was more racist, the crime or the verdict. But it's the injustice that lives on, the unfairness that ensures Vincent's death will be remembered. And

alongside it, always and forever, my part, like a bass line, a footnote, minor but essential. His friend who ran away. Martyrs and saints, you see, they have to be brave. Otherwise they're just victims. Vincent could have run away. That's what my life proves. He chose not to (though some say he slipped). Never mind that he *should* have run. He had a mother to care for, a wife to live for. Never mind that he was a hothead who didn't give any more thought to his loved ones than he had in the club. No. He stood up before he was knocked down. And I ran.

Yin to his yang (if you want to fit it in a fortune cookie).

He's a symbol now. His yearbook picture on T-shirts, posters, his name a rallying cry. And yet he can't symbolize *me*. For him to mean what he means, he and I have to be different.

As the old joke goes:

Two Chinamen going down the street.

One of them walks into a club.

The other one ducks.

Not funny? Maybe it's the way I tell 'em.

Yellow is what whites call us, of course, and mean it as a slur—skin color symbolizing character. But in fact Chinese started calling ourselves that first, way back around the time of the Opium Wars, to distinguish ourselves from white and black, when the connotations to us (the Yellow Emperor, the Yellow River) were positive.

We'd been sitting outside the McDonald's on Woodward, perched on a raised planter made out of old railroad ties, our panting turning to laughter. We figured we'd lost

them. "Your face when he pulled out that bat!" "I thought I was gonna shit myself, okay?" It was becoming a story. I could see us telling it at the wedding. I could see us joking about it for years to come. And it was just the two of us, something we'd always share. Evans and Pitts had ignored Jerry and Mike, after all. They only chased us. We sat shoulder to shoulder, sharing a smoke. In a minute I was going to suggest a Big Mac and fries (Vincent would likely counter with a Coney Dog from Red Hots up the block, another old haunt).

Saturday night, ten something, sidewalks still warm from the sun. Six lanes of traffic came and went in the intersection before us, exhaust rising redly in the taillights.

"First car in Detroit drove down this street," he said.

"First mile of concrete paving in the country," I recited from some high school field trip. "First assembly line rolled 'em out right over there."

"Highland Park Hummingbird!" we chorused, nick-name of the famous Chrysler starter motor.

He blew smoke out the side of his mouth. "My dad used to bring me down here to watch the cruising when I was a kid, teach me the names of all the marques. He could still remember the streetcars running. Now I can remember when it was all elms along here."

The last time I'd seen him, I realized, was at his father's funeral. His father, who'd moved to Detroit, like all our parents, because it was a boomtown.

"I don't even want a Jap car," he said. "It'd be like a Jew buying a Beamer!"

"Me either."

"What would you drive if you could have any car?"

I actually wanted an Audi, but what I said was, "Trans Am."

"Sally Fields in the passenger seat?" he teased. "You always loved them pony cars."

"What about you?"

Cars were stopping in the intersection again, close enough to smell the hot metal breath of their engines.

"Porsche, man! Black 911 Turbo Carrera. What else?"

We were still laughing when they spotted us. "Sitting there and laughing," Evans said in court. "It must have been real funny to them." A joke at his expense, I guess he figured.

Or maybe we were just talking about girls? How fast they were. Their curves. Oil changes and joy rides. Headlights and trunks. I don't remember.

I haven't bought an American car in thirty years. I've never been to a baseball game. I have been back to a strip club once. The night after the final acquittal. This was in Cincinnati. Evans's lawyers had successfully petitioned for a change of venue. It would be impossible to get a fair trial in Detroit after all the publicity about the case— interviews Lily had given, they argued, were "prejudicial" —even though publicity was the only reason the case had gotten reopened in the first place. At jury selection, I'd heard, fewer than 10 percent of possible Cincinnati jurors said they'd ever met an Asian American.

The place was called Sin City. Nicer than the Fancy Pants, it smelled of Windex and warm vinyl, a chemical new-car whiff, but I figured I could still get in trouble

there. I was the one spoiling for a fight now, fantasizing about Evans and Pitts walking in to celebrate, tightening my grip on the neck of my beer, feeling the pulse in my fist. I watched the girls—one reminded me a little of Lacey—and I watched the men watching them. But no one seemed to notice me. The mood was mild—sappy, even. Worn, lonely men in rumpled sport coats, eyes wide and watery from drink, grinning like kids on Christmas. I wondered, could that have been Vincent if he'd lived? Lacey had said he was always smiling. By contrast, I was the one sourpuss in there, and the girls seemed to know to steer clear. If anyone was going to start something in there, it was going to be me, but I understood after a while I'd simply be too embarrassed to make a scene. The rowdiest it got was some joker waving his lighter in the air, shouting *Freebird!* until a bouncer shushed him primly, a finger to his lips. The crowd was mostly white, the bouncers all black, the girls a mix, even one Asian girl dancing to "Turning Japanese" (a euphemism for masturbation, so I'd heard, though it might have been BS). She came out like a geisha, mincing in a shiny kimono; by the end all she was wearing was white makeup and bright red lipstick. I found myself blushing for her, unable to watch except out of the corner of my eye, but then it came to me I was ashamed for myself, praying she wouldn't see *me,* come over. Expose me.

She couldn't have made me out in the gloom, I told myself. We men must have just been a constellation of cigarette tips from the stage.

Thirty minutes later she was back, this time in a thigh-length cheongsam and sleek black bob but dancing to the

same song, I thought—both start with that cheesy Oriental riff just like "Kung Fu Fighting"—until I recognized Bowie's "China Girl." And then I did study her, her face, trying to decide.

Toward the end of the set, when she was naked, she met my eyes and I realized she'd known I was there all along, had seen me during her first set, or from backstage. Afterward she came up to me at the bar, wrapped in a short robe, nipples showing through like rivets. I shivered, reminded of how chilled the place was. "Don't I know you, hun?" I swallowed my drink, shook my head, made to leave, but she put her hand on my arm. "What's your name?"

"Vincent." It just came out in my panic. I might have flinched, but if she noticed, it was only because she was used to people lying.

"Well, Vinny, I'm Cindy. Wanna buy me a drink?"

"Can I ask, are you Chinese or Japanese?"

"Whatever you want me to be, baby."

"No, really. Tell me."

"You wanna guess?" she asked, still teasing.

"No!"

"Okay, baby, okay." She was calculating, I thought, trying to decide what I wanted to hear, even though I didn't know myself. And something else—as reluctant to reveal herself as she'd be to tell me her real name.

I tried to imagine Vincent in my place: older, a little paunchy maybe, hairline receding. And suddenly I didn't want her to have to lie.

"It's fine," I told her, finishing my drink. "It doesn't matter."

But she smiled, put a hand on my arm. "All-American, baby. We're all American here."

It felt like something to cover ourselves in, that word, its warm anonymity. And I nodded, sank back on my stool, bought her that drink.

Pearl

Disorientation

The world is yours, as well as ours, but in the last
analysis, it is yours. You young people, full of vigor
and vitality, are in the bloom of life, like the sun at
eight or nine in the morning . . . The world belongs to
you. China's future belongs to you.

— *Mao Zedong*

It's a little before one a.m. by John's watch. *Gotcha Day!*
as it's listed on the agency itinerary, the day they'll get
their baby. Mei Mei, he reminds himself. This is likely to
be his last uninterrupted night's sleep for a while, but
one a.m. in Guangzhou is one p.m. in Michigan and he's
wide awake. Ancient Chinese cities, he's learned on their
trip, had a bell tower and a drum tower to announce the
hours—the bell for the morning hours, the drum for
evening. Or was it the other way around? All he knows is
he's hearing bells instead of drums, drums instead of
bells.

In fact, his pulse in the scratchy hotel pillow sounds like
nothing so much as footsteps in snow.

Beside him, Nola has earplugs, an eyeshade, her bite
splint in. Her breath stinks of melatonin. He wants to
wake her, out of loneliness or spite, he's not sure which,
but when he presses against her she shrugs him off with

an irritated mewl. He touches himself halfheartedly instead.

In the corner the minibar gives a little glassy shiver.

Gotcha Day. There's been some murmured debate among their group of parents-to-be about the phrase. Stan and Bev, who already have an adopted daughter, use it unself-consciously. Lily, their eldest, back home in Knoxville with "Paw-paw" and "Ma-mee" (John recoils from the infantilization of such terms, swears he won't be the kind of parent who slips into baby talk), just adores Gotcha Day. It's like a birthday and Christmas all rolled into one, and only adopted kids get to celebrate it. "Their birthdays are just guesstimates anyway," Bev explained on their river cruise earlier that evening. "Last year Lily tied a big red ribbon in her hair and had me undo it. 'Like you're opening a present!' Of course, then she wanted to open her own presents."

Others are less easy with the term. Alice says it makes her think of her daughter as a thing, a possession, something bought and sold, which is what many of them feel, though they wish Alice wouldn't be so blunt about it. "She's so militant about everything," Nola says when they're alone. "But she never calls her daughter by her Chinese name, do you notice, always Gertie." Short for Gertrude, Alice likes to note meaningfully, waiting heavily, like the adjunct professor of English she is, for people to get the reference. (There's a Lost Generation gag to be made here, but John has resisted.) Alice has a photo of Gertie printed on a T-shirt which she wears every day (perhaps she has several, the group hopes). It's not much

worse than the rest of them, with their laminated photos on lanyards or in wallets, though she does have a disconcerting habit of yanking her windbreaker open to reveal the picture whenever she mentions Gertie. "It's a bird, it's a plane . . ." John whispers when they see her across the hotel lobby.

John and Nola, like most of the others in their party, are careful to refer to Mei Mei by her Chinese name, though they all have Western names picked out, ready to bestow. Anna, in their case, though they'll keep Mei as her middle name.

And yet why don't they use them, these new names? he ponders. Out of respect? To *curry flavor*, in his mother's malapropism? (Some old line—*How do Chinese parents name their children? They toss crockery out the window: ching! chong! chang!*—flits through his wired mind.) Or more likely some cringing deference toward the Chinese authorities? Some tiptoeing sense that they don't own their children yet? Or perhaps out of some reserve, some hesitation to fully possess them?

Probably they're just embarrassed by their choices, he tells Nola.

Such as?

Connie! Or Amy. No, no Vera and Maya. Maxine!

Maybe, Nola suggests mildly, it's just the same superstition that makes biological parents not share a name with others before the birth.

It puts John in mind of the Chinese tradition of calling children by derogatory nicknames—Little Pig, Ugly Dog—endearments intended to disguise how precious a child is from the demons that might steal it away.

Though aren't we those very demons?

And this is why he doesn't like "Gotcha Day" as a name. This whole experience feels like an elaborate trick, some setup, just waiting for that gotcha moment when the rug of their hopes will be pulled out from under, the flood-lights illuminating the city turned glaringly on them.

But then, he reminds himself, they wouldn't be here—he, Nola, most of their party—if fate hadn't already had a laugh at their expense.

They had found themselves in their midthirties, secure and, if not quite content, then cheerfully resigned to their lot. Nola was a preschool teacher by then, John a writer. He'd published a few stories in decent journals, sold a collection entitled *Ancient Chinese Secrets* not long after graduate school, and secured a college teaching job on the basis of it. But then the historical novel he'd promised his publisher about the building of the transcontinental railroad got bogged down. *It's taking longer to finish than the railroad took to build,* he used to joke, *though to be fair, there were more Chinese working on the railroad.* But the joke stopped being funny when the publisher canceled his contract. The trouble—more intractable than the twelve-foot snowdrifts or the granite outcrop-pings the railroad encountered—was a reading he'd given at his new college, a year or so after his first book had come out. He had thought it went well, been flattered by a good turnout (though he gathered afterward it was the last reading of the semester and all the undergrads were belatedly satisfying a requirement). A Chinese student, crisp white shirt buttoned to the throat and

wrists, had raised his hand during the Q&A. "In your lecture," he began, and John had smiled into the microphone and corrected him — "Story" — and the student had nodded and proceeded to list instances of Chinese words John had misused or mispronounced in his story. A long list. There'd been a murmur of amusement, then silence spreading through the crowd like a stain. "Also, please, this one word, *gu gu jai* — it does mean penis," the student said with as much distaste as he might handle one, "but I think is *baby* penis, what you call baby talk, what a mother say, not so . . . *romantic* between two lovers."

John had flushed darkly, managed to thank the student civilly. The host's "If there are no more questions . . ." had been drowned out by simpering giggles.

It had been nothing, really. (He'd blamed his mother, who'd taught him the term and neglected to correct it when he showed her the manuscript, but that turned out to be even more mortifying: *I thought you knew! I certainly never called it that after you were a baby. I thought you meant it*. Meant it! *You know I don't understand your stories. I thought it was supposed to be something . . . kinky*.) Nothing, and everything. He knew he'd been a diversity hire, suspected that the hiring committee had looked past better-qualified candidates. Now he sat in classrooms, in faculty meetings, feeling like a fraud, or worse — a minstrel show. He'd played around after that with a project about Anna May Wong, the early Chinese American movie star trying to make it in the era of yellowface. She'd had her own Chinese critics, but after a couple of years the work hadn't advanced much beyond copious

notes (even their choice of Anna as a name for Mei was only coincidental; they'd had Nola's grandmother in mind) when he'd been offered an unlikely lifeline. He'd been making money, if not a reputation, for several years now writing faux dime-store novelizations of the old TV series *Kung Fu*. The sheer bogusness of the show, the very reason the publishers had sought out an Asian American writer, afforded him an ironic distance from his anxieties of authenticity and enabled him to write again, albeit under the pseudonym Jack Ling—his mother's maiden name, his own middle one, John Smith in her view being too common. (He couldn't very well tell colleagues about these new books anyway. As far as they were concerned he was working on a novel about the Vincent Chin case, and he suspected he'd only secured tenure because the college had had to settle a discrimination suit the year before.) And yet at the same time he felt enough real affinity for the half-white, half-Chinese central character to find some secret satisfaction in the books, even if Nola considered it hack work. (When they'd met in graduate school, she'd wanted to be a poet, but she had given up—in the face of his early success, he sometimes feared.) He'd written half a dozen of them over the past four years and had recently pitched the publisher the idea of starting a new series of Charlie Chan novels.

So they were comfortable, and although neither of them had yearned for a child—*I have enough of them at school,* Nola quipped—it seemed that one might give their lives focus. They could afford one, John could remember thinking, just as a few years earlier they could afford a house, and a few years before that a car. And so

they had tried, experimentally at first, trusting to chance, and then a little more determinedly until Nola had gotten pregnant.

And then things had started to go wrong.

Just past her thirty-seventh birthday, Nola was considered of "advanced maternal age," meaning that a regime of tests and monitoring was recommended, as a result of which they learned from a genetic counselor that their fetus was subject to a chromosomal abnormality. "Mongolism?" John blurted. He couldn't help calling it by the old racially tinged term, realized he'd felt a subconscious dread of the diagnosis, as if what was wrong were an excess of Chineseness. "No," the counselor said evenly. "Not Down Syndrome. Another trisomy, known as Edwards." And amid the despair, John had felt a moment of furtive relief, as if it weren't his fault.

They'd had the procedure. They knew their own limits. But afterward, in a way they couldn't anticipate, they were changed. Or at least Nola was. Whereas before she'd seemed relaxed about motherhood, not one of "those women," as she said herself, now she seemed driven. To her, gently, John suggested it was just the sense of wanting something more when you couldn't—maybe (the condition wasn't inherited, but the risks did increase with age) —have it. "Like poetry?" she asked mordantly, and he dropped it. Secretly, though, he feared her desire was driven by guilt. Nola's family was Irish American, and while her Catholicism was long lapsed, he sensed an atavistic anguish. It was hard, after all, to deny family history when you were trying to create some of your own. So after a decent interval of mourning (if it even *was*

decent to mourn something you'd killed), they had tried
again. He'd been wary, worried about putting themselves
through the rigmarole (his word) again, a process that
now seemed so fraught that their younger selves—only a
year younger—seemed as naive as teenagers embarking
on it, but Nola's desire brought a new fervor to their
efforts.

Frankly, it was the best sex of John's life, more erotic, if
anything, for the suspicion that Nola didn't want him so
much as a child. There was a sense of her using him, of
her taking control, that stirred him. In retrospect, he
wished it had lasted longer, this second effort, but she was
pregnant again within a couple of months, and within a
couple of months more had miscarried, likely as the result
of another chromosomal event. If the first time had been
bad, the second time was worse—more hopeless, more
inevitable. More final. They were just very unlucky, the
genetic counselor commiserated. But it felt like a diagno-
sis, a medical opinion. John knew they wouldn't be trying
again. Nola handed in her notice. She said she couldn't
face the kids. She'd gone back after her leave of absence,
but when she picked up their ongoing chapter book to
read to them, she realized she had no idea what had come
before in the story. "I couldn't make any sense of it," she
told him. "They were all calling out explanations, asking
me to read on, but I just had to close the book." John held
her tightly, told her she didn't have to go back.

They spent a wary year, shying from pregnant friends,
bridling at antiabortion bumper stickers, and most of all
circling each other. They celebrated their tenth anniver-
sary in muted fashion, oppressed by the prospect of their

future together, the years like something to climb. They hadn't had sex for months. John found himself noticing the young women in his classes for the first time in years (while at the same time realizing that they weren't likely to notice him back). He found himself masturbating like a teenager (the sound of one hand clapping, as he called it to himself, very Zen). At the suggestion of a colleague, he started to talk about taking a trip, an adventure. He surfed the Web, brought home guidebooks and spread out maps. He had in mind something reckless, romantic. Nola seemed neutral, until one night she told him, "You gave me the idea really, with all your maps. We can go to China, adopt a baby."

So here they were, even though China had never featured among his suggested destinations, even though he'd never been before.

Nola confessed tearfully that she'd secretly looked into domestic adoption but been put off. "Ironically enough, there are fewer U.S. kids up for adoption since *Roe v. Wade*." She'd got as far as answering an ad and talking to a pregnant freshman thinking of giving up her baby. "But she wanted to know why I couldn't have a baby of my own, and when I told her what happened, she never called back." The idea that she'd done that behind his back, had had to go through that alone, had persuaded him.

1:51.

He's cuddling up to Nola again, nudging his dick into the soft cleft of her ass (the "crack of doom" as they call it, in reference to the moment she's promised to let him fuck her there).

The bedside phone rings, and John starts, snatches it up, heart racing, presses the receiver back into the cradle without answering. In the dark he feels for the cord, unplugs it.

They've been in China for—what? he figures—four days, three sleepless nights since they landed in Beijing. Their first evening, when they were both still jittery with jet lag, he'd sidled up to Nola—hotel rooms had always turned her on—but she'd pushed him away. He hadn't brought any condoms. "You never know," he'd whispered. "It might be fate. Wouldn't that be ironic? 'Only Nixon' or something."

Nola had put a cool hand on his chest, and just for a moment he'd thought she was yielding. "I'd say we're way past fucking irony by now, wouldn't you? I've certainly had my fill of it."

He'd lain awake for hours after that, missed his chance to catch up on his sleep. Time has felt slippery ever since, past and present sliding around inside his head.

There'd followed a day of sightseeing, John so tired he slumped into a doze on every bus ride as if gassed by the diesel fumes. He felt agoraphobic in Tiananmen Square, dizzy on the Great Wall, contemplating its undulating length, like a spiny dragon's tail laid out across the land. When he turned his head to track a guide's pointing finger, he felt his brain sloshing in his skull, inertia making it turn just a little slower than his eyes. The scale of China seemed all wrong to him, at once existentially vast yet so crowded it was hard to breathe (though that might have been the smog hovering overhead like cigarette smoke below a ceiling). It was like being squeezed

between the vinyl covers of Mao's Little Red Book (of which their party had bought several souvenir copies, along with dozens of calligraphy scrolls, oilpaper umbrellas, assorted porcelain, jade, silks, pearls — Mao's book, as far as John could tell, being perhaps the only thing they couldn't have found on any street in San Francisco's Chinatown).

Now they're in Guangzhou to get their children. "Time for get best souvenir of trip," as their young female guide, Napoleon, joked on the bus after one of their "factory" tours, jade or silk or terra cotta. ("For get souvenir" sounded just right to John in his state of bleary stupefaction.) She delivered her English in strings of short, crisp syllables, sounding each distinctly — a familiar singsong cadence it took John a moment to place. Then he remembered mocking his mother's pronunciation of vehicle: *vee-hee-cull*.

Napoleon's real name is Ng Poh Lian. She introduced herself at Beijing airport. "But Nah-po-lee-on if you prefer. Like emperor!" She'd said it with a glowing smile, and John imagined it'd gotten a laugh from previous groups, along with the bent elbow cocked over her waist. But this time the gesture only served to accentuate the swell of her stomach. It was subtle still, John supposed, but not to a group of men and women who had been trying and failing to conceive or carry a pregnancy to term for years, and at dinner that night there was much whispered grumbling about insensitivity or, worse, a sly effort to shame the Westerners. "Very Chinese," someone murmured, and then looked awkwardly at John and added, "No offense."

He'd yawned so deeply he'd thought he'd inhale the room. "None taken," he assured the woman. This was Jeannine, who power-walked through airports, did curls with her wheelie bag, ran a thudding 5K every morning on the hotel treadmill, as if parenting were a triathlon.

Most of the others decline to call their guide Napoleon, settling for "Miss Ng" or "Poh Lian," eager to work on their pronunciation. Only John uses the nickname, smiling at her as if in on the joke. It suits her, he's told Nola. The young woman is diminutive in her black capris and pastel tops but fierce with taxi drivers and hotel porters, shaking her head until her long black hair flies. "She even has the potbelly," he's joked, but Nola shushed him. Mostly he's relieved to have someone in charge, just as he'd once put his faith in doctors and nurses.

No one had mentioned Napoleon's pregnancy—a slight, John couldn't help feeling—and he made a point of asking when she was due, offering her a seat, but she just looked embarrassed. He had to stop himself asking, as he might have back home, if she knew the gender. It was illegal in China to disclose those results from an ultrasound, but he'd heard the technicians could be bribed (he'd heard *everyone* in China could be bribed). And yet he couldn't help wondering if she'd keep the child if it was a girl, or give it up for adoption. But how to ask such questions? What he really wanted was to lay his hands on her stomach, span the soft swell of it, feel the kick of life, but he couldn't very well ask that either. *Unless I bribe her,* he thought facetiously.

Nola was always adamant that she'd never want another man touching her like that. "Especially when the woman's

really big, with the belly button distended, it looks like the men are groping a huge tit!" John had joked about the baby coming to her rescue, kung-fu kicking those hands away. But that was before, of course . . . though in the midst of his jet lag he can't shake the feeling that just as it's the middle of the previous afternoon where he lives, somewhere else on earth, impossibly distant, his past is taking place simultaneously.

And this is also a decidedly Chinese disorientation. It's not just the physical scale of China that has John reeling but the temporal too — the ancient history and the frenetic pace of modernization, cheek by jowl, both such sources of national pride. Napoleon toggles between the two without missing a beat, one moment favorably comparing the achievements of the first emperor — the wall, the terra-cotta warriors — with those of his contemporary, Alexander (referred to, with ingenuous condescension, as Alex), the next rattling off statistics about the towering new skylines (the speed of the elevators, the number of floors, the megawattage to light them all). It makes John's head swim, as if he's years — whole eras and epochs — not mere hours off the pace.

Their second night in Beijing he might have slept. Nola was already out, and he had felt himself nodding off when the phone jangled to life. He'd snatched it up almost guiltily, whispered into it, "Hello?"

"Mister Smith, sir?" A woman's voice, bright accented English.

"Yes?"

"Do you need anything, Mr. Smith?"

"Need?"

"Such as extra pillows? Such as special guest service? Anything at all you desire?"

"No, no, nothing."

He'd hung up but lain there befuddled with fury — good service was one thing, but calling in the middle of the night! — until he remembered an entry from his guidebook. A prostitute, he thought, a so-called ding-dong girl. He'd unplugged the phone, but by then he was wide awake. He'd gotten up, left Nola to sleep while he sat at the window gazing out at the city — drab and dusty by day, now shimmering with light — through the plate glass.

He tried to work out a new *Kung Fu* plot, something about Chinese railroad workers staging a train robbery, using their expertise with nitro to blow the safe, the loot smuggled back to China amid the bones of the dead, but the details refused to gel; worse, the idea seemed somehow glib here. He'd actually been thinking of naming a character Eastwood Ho.

He shook his head. The opposite of fast asleep, he decided, must be slow awake.

He should have slept on the flight out, god knows, but he never slept on planes. He made an effort to have a couple of drinks this time but succeeded only in getting buzzed and keeping Nola up. "*Falling* asleep just feels wrong on a plane," he told her. The heavy head drop jarred him awake in a panic. It's not that he's afraid of flying. He flies all the time without anxiety. It's sleeping on planes he's afraid of.

His father, John Smith Sr., had been a pilot (a Korean war veteran), his mother a stewardess (an original

Singapore Girl)—they'd met on a layover in the mid-sixties, and she still occasionally referred to her husband affectionately as the Captain—so staying alert in the air was genetic, John claimed. That and his father, who'd taught flying out of his local airport into his seventies, always liked to regale him with tales from "the hairy edge" of everything that could go wrong in the air. The Captain had called his shakier students "Chinese aces" after the old air force joke about Chinese landings—"One Wing Low"—and he'd always considered it a professional affront that so many routes to and from China incorporated the lucky 8's into their flight numbers: "This is your captain speaking . . . cross your fingers!" The old man had died two years earlier, and John wondered what he'd think of their flying China Air.

As they climbed over San Francisco, he felt the shudder of the undercarriage retracting and imagined the wheels like giant balls being drawn back into an abdomen. He made the mistake of telling Nola, but she only gave him a look of forbearance. Everything's about sex with him now, she's noted. He's tried to rationalize it. Friends with kids have said they never have sex anymore, they're too tired. "That's because they have *babies*," Nola reminded him. "Newborns. It's not like I'll be breastfeeding."

Still, he can't escape a feeling of something ending, a nostalgia for the life they've lived up to now, for themselves, which has manifested itself as desire. He's tried to make a joke of it, if only to pull the sting of her condescension. On the highway to the airport they passed a sign for an Oriental spa and he lisped, "Me wub you wong

time." "Wrong time is right," she told him, taking his hand off her knee and then patting it.

"You're already acting like a mom," he complained.

On the plane he'd tried to stop talking about sex, stared out the window instead as California receded. Below, the winter sun rippled across the windshields of a parking lot like sequins on a dress. A little farther over there was a municipal lot, yellow school buses lined up like pencils in a case. *Is that the reason they're yellow?* he mused. He knew why pencils were that color. Supposedly China was where the best pencil lead had come from in the nineteenth century. His fourth-grade teacher, Mr. Beasley, told him that, proudly — though whether he was proud of his knowledge or thought John should be proud of Chinese lead wasn't quite clear. "I hear you put the lead in yellow pencils," Jordison, the bully, sneered in the playground at recess. "And I thought you all had teeny dicks," his sidekick Farley yapped. John shrugged. "I guess I'm not as knowledgeable about dicks as you."

When he's in the hotel bar in Xi'an drinking with Eric and his partner, Scott, two more prospective parents, he'll feel guilty for this line, the deflection of racism with homophobia, and reckon he probably deserved the bloody nose the bullies gave him (a nosebleed, he'd told his mother). Then again, considering that technically only Eric is adopting, Scott, as far as the Chinese authorities are concerned, only along as a "friend," they've likely encountered worse. Maybe, John will reflect, he just feels self-conscious about the size of his dick sitting with two gay men. (He asked Nola once, and she gripped him and

leered, "It gets the job done," which wasn't altogether reassuring, actually.)

"I don't even know what an Oriental massage is," he'd told her on the plane. "And is that the last remaining use of *Oriental*?"

"Perhaps they mean shiatsu," she offered, slicking through her magazine.

"Is that the one where they rub you with little dogs?"

"Shih tzu," she corrected.

"Bless you!"

She'd rolled her eyes, taken her Ambien.

But she's obsessed too, he knows. Hours later, when the pilot had announced, "We're starting our descent," she'd nudged him, rested and gleeful: "Us too!"

He was filling out their landing card. Their flight number, 88, was especially auspicious, since it looked like the characters for double happiness, but as much as he believed in bad luck, he wasn't yet sure of good fortune.

Somewhere behind his head a child — perhaps several, a whole nursery, coals to Newcastle — had begun wailing, and he leaned into Nola, whispered, "Mayday! Mayday! We're going down."

May Day. Gotcha Day. Gotcha Mei. This is the form his insomnia takes, words chasing around his head.

It makes him think of the little girl he'd read about in one of the adoption books who, asked where she was from, proudly announced, "My mommy's Va-china."

Where are you from? It's a question he's heard all his life. It's the question they all get, he knows, Asian Americans, and John has taken some comfort in this shared burden

down the years, but this trip is reminding him that they don't always share the answer. He felt it in Chinatown in San Francisco. They'd laid over for a day between flights. It had been his idea, a little fling before parenthood, and Nola had gone along. But once they were there, she had wanted to go to Chinatown for dim sum. Back in Michigan they used to drive over the Ambassador Bridge into Windsor, Ontario, for cheap dim sum, but they'd skipped it since the border crossing became more involved after 9/11. He'd tried to dissuade her— "We're on our way to *China-China*"—but she said it would get them "in the mood." Maybe it worked for her—all the Chinese faces, the flavors and smells of the food—but it made John feel uneasy, out of place. People spoke to him in Chinese and he shrugged, a pantomime of idiocy. When he tried to order dishes by name and the waitress returned the same shrug, it still felt like his failing. She flipped the laminated menu in front of him and pointed to unappetizing, overexposed pictures while he nodded like a tourist.

Outside, at one point they heard cymbals and drums and then a lion danced past the storefront. A new business was opening next door. Lion dances, with their lunging and shivering of the great paper head, always made him imagine the lion was rabid. He knew the performance was meant to scare away demons, but as a young child he'd burst into tears the one time his mother had taken him to see a Chinese New Year parade. "He thought the lion was the demon," his mother had laughed afterward, exasperated. This lion was accompanied by firecrackers, which shook the plate glass beside them and set car

alarms blaring up and down the street long after the last explosion.

And that's me, John thinks in bed, his limbs tingling with tiredness. One of those car alarms—answering the call, but not understanding it, reacting defensively.

2:23. Another half hour gone. Nola snoring like a train puffing uphill.

What's the opposite of wide awake? He gazes into the grainy darkness. Thin sleep? He'd settle for that now.

"You're like a groom before the wedding," Nola said before she nodded off tonight. "It's just cold feet." He wanted to tell her he hadn't had cold feet before he married her, but she already had her earplugs in. All his thwarted desire, he wanted to tell her, it was loyalty. He rests his hand in the warm valley between her hip and belly, aches to stroke the silky curl of pubic hair over her clitoris, makes himself roll away.

He stares at the phone beside him, sits up heavily. It's no use. He feels for his clothes in the dark, his sweater sparking with static as he draws it on. If he stays here, he knows he'll eventually wake Nola, and they'll fight. He's not sure whether he's leaving to spare her or himself. Either way, it's not how he wants to start Gotcha Day. He has a walk in mind, but at the last moment he slides a book from the bedside table—*Quotations from Chairman Mao*—and tucks it in his pocket.

He tiptoes past all the other doors on their floor, imagining all the other prospective—never *expectant*—parents sleeping behind them (the agency has a block booking). It's a long corridor, and by the end he's

sprinting—lightly on the balls of his feet, calves still tight from the steep slopes of the Great Wall—as if to outrun the fear of waking anyone. He pauses to catch his breath by the elevators, looking out at the city, feeling somehow as if he's guarding them all. From what, though? Everything, nothing. What if, he thinks, this—this watchfulness, this free-floating anxiety—is what being a parent is?

They're on a high floor above the drifting veil of smog. He glimpses a floodlit snippet of river between two nearby buildings but searches in vain for the other sights they saw on the tour today—the petals of the flower pagoda, the lissom twist of the half-complete Canton Tower. Instead, overhead, he fixes on a plane ascending, a silver needle flashing in and out of the darkness. He is a child of the jet age, his mother told him once, meaning that their family —*he*—couldn't have existed before easy international travel. "Your father and I would never have met." She was from a wealthy, traditional family, the black sheep owing to her job, and even disowned briefly for marrying his father. Nice girls didn't marry white men; only tramps married across races (*back then,* she added, for Nola's benefit).

When he'd told his mother about their plans, she had pursed her lips and nodded. "Not a son, but at least Chinese. No one need know she's adopted." She'd feared, she confessed, that they would adopt from Central America.

My mother's an aspirational racist, he told Nola.

The Captain, by contrast, had been a casual, even jocular racist, the kind who used phrases like "Chinese fire

drill" and called them "sayings" if challenged, or told lame jokes to "lighten the mood" and "see if people had a sense of humor." Sometime in the eighties he'd developed a line of multiethnic jokes that he thought were PC. *Heard about the new German Chinese restaurant? The food is great, but half an hour later you're hungry for power.* Or, *Hear the one about the Chinese godfather? He'll make you an offer you can't understand.* Or, *What do you call a guy who's half Mexican and half Chinese and only wears one sneaker? Juan Chu!* Like a lot of kidders, he couldn't take a joke himself; the movie *Airplane!* had incensed him, and John, in his teens, had taken to calling him Roger.

"How does every Chinese joke start?" the Captain asked once, and John made the mistake of thinking he was really asking. It went back to the Gold Rush, the building of the transcontinental, he began. But his father's eyes just glittered with amusement. "By looking over your shoulder!"

How they all started, John decides now, is that some asshole came up with them. An author of sorts, even if they weren't written down. And yet no one claimed such jokes. They disowned them, rather. Orphans of another sort. Mind you, John has told the hungry-for-power joke himself more than once, whenever anyone has raised the old canard about Chinese food leaving you hungry. *I can tell it,* he figured, but then that was probably what the Captain thought too. John's heard a theory somewhere that it's only true of Chinese American food anyway, a corollary of Westerners not eating enough rice with the dishes. If so, it seems oddly fitting to him, this dissatisfaction, this hunger at the heart of Chinese American life.

He is distracted by movement. Down the corridor, in the opposite direction from his room, a young man in a suit is bowing as if in prayer before each room. Slipping bills under doors, John realizes.

He takes one more look out over the glistering city, the colorfully lit towers crowded together like stacks of poker chips, emblems of the new gold rush, and pushes the call button for the elevator.

He'd pointed out to his mother once that the enemies his father had flown sorties against in Korea were Chinese, but she'd just shrugged. "Different kind of Chinese," she said. "Mandarin-speakers?" he asked. "No, silly. Communists!"

John understands Nola's desire to visit Chinatown now in the context of the others in their party, some of whom seem here to adopt not just children but a whole culture. Several are already taking Chinese lessons and speak more of the language than John (though that's not hard). Others are reading Chinese literature. While they've waited for flights he's seen everything from Pearl Buck (who, Nola has informed him, established the very first adoption program from China, after *her* first child was diagnosed with a genetic disorder) to *The Dream of the Red Chamber,* names and titles he recognizes but has never read.

It's not just the jet lag that has him feeling numbed and out of sync.

Nola tells him it ought to impress him, all this interest in China and the Chinese, and he knows what she means. It's startling to see so many white people paying attention

to China. In junior high, he recalls, kids were shocked that he was Chinese but didn't come from China, that there were multiple dialects, that China had fought alongside the United States against the Japanese. This latter had especially surprised people who continuously confused Chinese and Japanese, not to mention Koreans and Vietnamese. "They fought with or against all of us in the past fifty years and they still can't tell us apart. And they wonder why they lost some of those wars," his friend Ken Takamura used to say. "Shit, they can tell our restaurants apart more easily than us." When he and Ken had to explain it to other kids at the start of each school year, Ken would roar, "*Orient*-ation, Holmes! I'm sushi, he's chop suey." But John wasn't so sure; even now when he heard Chairman Mao referred to as "the Great Helmsman" he pictured Mr. Sulu from *Star Trek*. "We're both chopsticks and rice and noodles," he told Ken. (They were friends, after all—John didn't have that many—he'd rather emphasize what they had in common.) He didn't bother pointing out that chop suey was as Chinese as California roll was Japanese. When Ken lost patience he used to tell the white kids, "You nuked my folks; his are going to nuke you. Figure it out."

The solution, as it turned out, was for Ken's dad to get a job in Silicon Valley, leaving John as the only Asian in his class. Except back then he was still called "Oriental."

None of his fellow parents-to-be would make such mistakes now, of course, and he should be happy. It's social progress, right, albeit their group is hardly representative. And yet it grates a little. He gets the underlying logic, to be sure. They're doing it for their future children.

They want to be able to bring those kids up with a connection to China, feeling proud of their heritage. The idea is that their biological parents may have given them up, may have been obliged to because of the social policies of their government, but there's still a parent *culture* they can connect to.

I probably just envy them, John thinks bitterly, but he's also suspicious of the parents. Isn't there some liberal guilt at play here? Some disowning of ownership? *We're going to take you away from your home but also keep you connected to it.* The Chinese government encourages the idea; so do the adoption agencies. That's the purported reason why in-country adoptions are required, why these trips include a sightseeing element. "It's not a vacation, it's a cultural education," as Nola has explained it. "And let's not forget the foreign exchange," John replied, but that was going too far. Money—the expenses already incurred, and in particular the bricks of fresh bills in their suitcase (China's being a cash economy, and the Chinese preferring clean bills), which they'll hand over to the orphanage tomorrow—is off-limits or referred to only euphemistically as a donation, *lucky money.*

"Well, how do you think they pay for the care of the other orphans?" Nola had snapped at him when he'd tried to articulate his unease. But the "other" orphans are almost as taboo as the question of money. They—all of them—are engaged in a careful calibration of selfishness. It helps that they're "saving" the children from poverty and lovelessness rather than just filling wants in their own lives, but . . . what about all those they can't save?

* * *

In the elevator he stares at the panel for a vacant moment, trying to figure out what's wrong. There's no fourth floor, no fourteenth, no thirteenth—the number four, *si*, he recalls, which sounds like the word for "death," being unlucky in Chinese, the number thirteen omitted for the sake of Western guests. He appreciates the sentiment. And yet as the elevator falls he can't help imagining those unlucky floors—dark, empty, unfinished—beyond the walls of the elevator shaft.

He knows the adoptees are sometimes known in Chinese as the lucky ones, but as most of the parents are honest enough to acknowledge, *they're* the lucky ones.

"Except what if we're just the rich ones?" John has wondered.

"Oh, don't get all postcolonial on me," Nola told him. "I've actually read Said." (Once when he applied for a job that required an interest in postcolonial studies, she'd reassured him, "You don't need to have studied it, you are it!" He'd always considered himself more of an expert on *dis*orientalism.)

"*That's* not what's bugging you."

"No?"

"No."

He had dared her to say it . . . and she'd shrugged. They had to raise a child together, after all. But he knew what she meant.

Once, years earlier, in high school, he'd experimented with being more Chinese. He'd hosted a Chinese New Year's party. What seventeen-year-old doesn't want an excuse for a party? Suddenly his Chineseness seemed

advantageous. It helped that Chinese New Year that year fell the week of spring break. His father had been on duty, and his mother had helped him prepare and then gone out to celebrate with friends. He made his guests "steamboat," a hotpot made from a soup base warmed in a rice cooker into which diners added shrimp and meat, dumplings, fish balls, noodles, and vegetables. The noodles were for long life, he explained. He was wearing a musty Mao jacket of his father's, left over from the Beatles era, which stank more and more of mothballs as the night went on. What about the tofu? a blonde called Helen asked, and he said, "Luck, I think," not wanting to disappoint her. "What about the shrimp?" she asked. Fertility, he thought, but he wasn't sure he could tell her that (not when the curled pink shrimp were making him think of a penis), so he offered, "Money, fortune, prosperity." "Isn't fortune the same as luck?" someone else asked. They were looking at him a little skeptically now, so when his friend Evan asked with a smirk, "And how about fish balls? They don't seem so lucky, for the fish at least!" John snapped, "They mean, *Fuck you, white boy*." The table had laughed, but the party hadn't gone so well—at least, he'd failed to hook up with Helen. Later in school he heard someone call him "Fish Balls" behind his back.

He'd gone to Caltech the following fall (Stanford, his first choice, turned him down; he always fretted about checking the Asian American box amid persistent rumors of admissions quotas). There, as a freshman, he'd first heard the derogatory term *banana*, meaning yellow on the outside, white on the inside, but he'd secretly welcomed

its aptness. As far as he was concerned, his skin had always been something to trip on.

But now he was ashamed that these whites, from Boise and Athens, Knoxville and Reno, knew more about Chinese culture than he did. Being in China gave him the same sense of shame as going to a Chinese restaurant with colleagues who wanted him to tell them "what's good." He'd actually blushed when people on the trip had deferred to him and he'd had to explain that he didn't speak Chinese.

"And you've never been to China before?" they ask him at least once a day, as if in amazement, as if waiting for him to change his story. (*That's right,* slapping his forehead, *how could I forget?* I'm *the Manchurian candidate.*)

These decent, kindly people remind him of why he hates American Buddhists, could never become one. He couldn't stand the thought of having some white person teach it to him. It's the same reason he's never learned martial arts. ("Gertie's going to learn gung fu," Alice says. "She has to be able to stand up to bullies." But in John's memory the bullies were the ones who knew kung fu.) As a child he'd hated losing at Chinese checkers too.

John's list of things you couldn't do if you were Asian American: play ping-pong, play piano, wear glasses (he had saved up for Lasik the summer of his junior year), wear a camera round your neck, ride a bike, drive an import, grow a mustache (or, if female, streak your hair), wear a sweatband, drink beer, ace tests, sing karaoke (though deep down he'd always dreamed of singing the old Johnny Rivers number "Secret Agent Man" as "Secret

Asian Man," but then, wasn't that every Asian American's dream, to sing karaoke and somehow still look cool?). He'd actually emailed this list to his old friend Ken a few years back, when they'd briefly reconnected after John's book came out. Ken—now going by Kensuke—was working for an Asian American social media startup out of Palo Alto: *Yello!* Maybe that's why he no longer had a sense of humor. "But if you reject every stereotype," he'd written back, "what do you have in common with other Asians?"

And now John wants to scandalize these well-meaning souls on the tour by telling them how much he loves chop suey, General Tso's chicken, and all those other fake Chinese dishes. Takeout, after all, was the only Chinese food he'd known growing up (his father had taught his mother simple Western dishes, but she didn't cook Chinese, her family having always had servants to cook for them). It was his comfort food, and he never failed to miss it when he walked into authentic Chinese restaurants. His favorite meal on the trip had been on a flight, the tinfoil container reminding him of takeout. He even loved fortune cookies, the stupider and more ungrammatical the better. (*Recent plants will work out fine; Something long desired is about to happy.* "You only like the ones that *can't* come true," Nola scolded him. "But that's why you add *in bed* to the end," he reminded her.) He wants to tell them that when he was a kid *Kung Fu* was his favorite show, even with white David Carradine in the lead (even after he knew that Bruce Lee had been passed over for the role because of his accent). And why not? he'd once fumed at a dinner with college friends.

The character was supposed to be half white, after all. He was on a quest to find his white stepbrother, for crying out loud. But all anyone remembered was the blind monk calling him "Glasshopper." (*Grass*hopper, *grass*hopper, *grass*hopper, John had muttered under his breath.) Kids had whispered it whenever a teacher called on him in class, cracking up at their desks, and still he loved the show. The character spoke to him, and it infuriated John to have to be ashamed of that, to have his white friends question his authenticity. *Whatever I am is authentically me, isn't it?* he wanted to shout. But he wasn't always sure.

Once when he'd asked Napoleon if they might see Peking Man—that shared ancestor—someone had piped up, "*Beijing* man." The site was too far from the city, Napoleon explained apologetically, and besides, the actual bones were missing, lost or stolen during the evacuation before the Japanese invasion. At least, to John's immoderate satisfaction, according to his guidebook Peking Man and Peking duck still went by their old romanized names.

"They don't mean anything by it," Nola had tried to tell him the night before, after yet another group discussion of the importance of Chinese culture.

Jeannine has been taking Chinese cooking classes. *I want her to know what it really tastes like, without the MSG.* Eric and Scott have already found a Chinese tutor in San Francisco. Alice is applying for a TESL job in Shanghai —she wants to come back and live in China with her daughter. *I want it to be real for her.* "And we're all going to keep the babies in traditional split pants rather than diapers, right?" John asks to shut them up. It's like they're

wrestling over a lazy Susan, everyone else spinning it one way, he the other.

"They make me feel like there's something wrong with me, with the way I was brought up," he told Nola.

"There's something wrong with the way we were *all* brought up," she said. "If you believe the parenting books. None of us are going to parent like our parents."

"Thanks for the sympathy."

"Come on, John! Maybe you should write about it if you care so much. At least it'd be . . ."

"What?" He glared at her.

"I don't know! Real."

"It'd be real if I wrote about feeling inauthentic?"

"Honest, then."

He thought about wounding her. *And what about you? What are you writing?* "Nothing" has been the answer for so long that he's long stopped asking, but now he suspects she's started again in secret, since the abortion, and he realizes he's scared of what she might answer.

John hesitates in the lobby. He's not set foot outside the hotel alone. He has some premonition, some fear that if he does, he'll never come back, that he'll disappear into the crowd. It's ridiculous, but he remembers a story about some uncle who'd returned to China from Singapore on a visit as a child — it must have been in the thirties — and almost been kidnapped. John can't recall the details; probably there weren't any. The uncle would have been a small boy at the time (*Of course, no one would kidnap a girl,* he'd assured his daughter, John's cousin); perhaps he just imagined it. And yet there it is,

some irrational fear, the same anxiety that has kept John away all these years. It's probably fueled by his own childhood images of China: crowds in Mao suits waving Little Red Books. Back then the Communist countries —China, the Soviet Union—seemed like prisons for their citizens. He went to a Halloween party once as the Tank Man, the unknown and likely disappeared fellow who'd faced down the tanks in Tiananmen Square. White shirt, black pants, laden with plastic bags in each hand. No one got it. The most iconic Chinese figure of the decade, and no one recognized him. The nearest anyone guessed was "Delivery guy?" Several of his friends seemed puzzled that he'd come as another Chinese, as if it weren't a costume.

Mostly, though, there's some essential math at play here. How do you expect to take one of theirs without them taking one of yours? *Gotcha!* indeed.

He's relieved when he sees the hotel bar still open, hurries into its hushed, shadowy embrace.

As much as he resents the other adopters, he knows they resent him too.

Bev suggested as much, albeit wistfully, when she confided in him over dinner one night, "Oh, how I envy you, John, and little Mei Mei. You'll be able to take her out to the park, and parties, the mall, and not have everyone know she's adopted. Even if you and Nola are together, people will think the little one is your own flesh and blood. That'll make a difference, I reckon."

(Bev told him another time that Lily loved helping out around the home. "Her favorite thing when she first came

home with us was folding laundry. Imagine! My little Chinese laundry, I call her!" She laughed, and then covered her mouth as if to catch the words.)

John had nodded along with others around the table, and remembering it now, he finally grasps that all their study of things Chinese—all their acquisitions of scrolls and knickknacks (Eric and Scott have arranged for a rosewood dresser to be shipped to them in Seattle for their daughter's room), which make him think of pet supplies to furnish a habitat—is a compensation for what he has: looking the part. And they know it too, and resent him for how easily it comes. In particular, he's felt it when people ask how long the process has been for him and Nola.

Nine months, Nola says, proud of the symmetry. But everyone else has been waiting a year, eighteen months, two years in one case. "Serendipity, I guess," Nola says, and it may be—a fluke of timing—but he knows the others suspect they got special treatment because he's Chinese.

The only couple less liked on the tour are Norman and Amanda. They're "preferential adopters," as they're quick to point out. "We could have kids of our own," Amanda begins. "But why bring another life onto this overcrowded planet?" Norman finishes for her. It makes a kind of sense —John doesn't disagree with them on the issue of over-population—and yet Norman's righteousness grates. Other couples on the trip, after all, have tried very hard, gone to extreme lengths, to bring another life onto the planet. "It's egotism, plain and simple," Norman said the

first night, "to want to perpetuate our own genes, and suicidal on a planetary, species-wide level."

"Egotism indeed!" Nola fumed later in their room.

"Ignore him," John counseled (the man has a receding hairline *and* a ponytail). But he can't take his own advice. Norman fascinates him. Their fate, after all, is his *choice*, his principle.

"You share the Chinese government's position on population then, the one-child policy?" he asked one morning over breakfast (toast for John, rice porridge for Norman), and Norman nodded sagely. "A regrettable necessity." But this is a tricky response. They—their group as a whole—are beneficiaries, indirectly, of the policy, even if they mostly deplore it. Chinese families who can have only one child get rid of their girls—sometimes to orphanages, but sometimes by killing them, aborting them, or abandoning them after birth. The policy is in large part why they're here, these Westerners, yet it's also a source of heartbreak, broken homes and families. They are already practicing what they will tell the children they haven't even received yet when they ask about their biological parents. For the sake of the kids, they don't want to make these shadowy figures into villains (you can't tell them they didn't love them or didn't want them, you have to say that they couldn't keep them, the adoption books advise). Much easier to make the law the villain, the government. If they're saving these children from something, it's from the consequences of this law, and yet here they are, about to gain from it.

It's a moral knot, but one that in Norman's big hands seems to unravel, and the rest of them envy him this bluff confidence more than anything.

But John can't let it lie. For him, the law isn't the problem per se. The problem is that Chinese families want boys, a cultural phenomenon (albeit one hardly unique to the Chinese).

"But if you make Chinese culture the bad guy," Nola observed back in their room — Norman having gone off exploring with Amanda — "you run the risk of alienating the girls from their heritage and potentially damaging their self-image."

"But why," John wanted to know, "should they have to maintain any connection with a culture that devalues them and has cast them out? Because they *look* Chinese is why," he answered his own question. "Because we know they will look different and be treated as if they're different in *our* society. We're giving them something to fall back on when they're discriminated against."

"Oh, come on," Nola hissed. "It's not that bad." (Nola, who had felt the need to warn her mother before she met John that he was half Chinese.)

"Really? You think if we were all in Romania now we'd be talking about keeping our kids connected to Romanian culture?" (*Are you sure he isn't black?* her mother replied.)

They'd fought in fierce whispers, not wanting anyone to hear them through the walls, the way they'd have sex if they ever had sex.

The whole "culture" thing, for John, is a defense against racism, an anticipation of it, but also perhaps in some obscure way a perpetuation of it. "If even their parents see them as other, what hope do these babies have of assimilating?"

"If you believe that," Nola wailed, "why are we even here? If you had such a shitty childhood, why are we doing this?"

John wonders himself. Norman, he knows, would call this kind of thinking very Western. "The Chinese," he has pointed out, "are matter-of-fact about adoption. They see it as practical . . . on the parents' part. We need children to look after us in our old age." He and Amanda laughed as if they couldn't imagine ever growing old.

"What do *you* think about all this?" John asked Napoleon over lunch one day. They'd just watched the noodles they were eating being made—oohing and aahing at the show as if at a magic act, the noodles appearing from the twisted, stretched dough as if by sleight of hand—but now they paused in their slurping. Napoleon grinned at them. "Is good! Good for babies, good for mommies and daddies. Also more Chinese girls in America now, for Chinese American boys for marry."

Such guileless, sunny chauvinism! It made John laugh, but only him.

"No offense, Miss Nola," Napoleon said, small head bobbing birdlike on her slender neck. "You so *ho leng*, beautiful. Skin like white jade."

Nola gave her bright, tight smile. "I don't think John ever even dated a Chinese."

"What? Really!" they asked. "Never?" And now, John thought, they were calling *him* racist, offended on behalf of their not-yet, not-quite daughters. "They were always going with white boys," he said with a sour smile. "Aren't all our desires racist in one way or another?"

They paused to watch the cook demonstrating how to make shaved noodles, slicing them off a long loaf of dough and flipping them acrobatically into the boiling water.

"Besides," Norman said, changing the subject magisterially, "all this thinking is very twentieth-century. The pendulum is swinging back. Already boys outnumber girls in Chinese schools. Within a couple of decades the gender imbalance could be as much as twenty percent. What will all those boys do when it comes time to marry?" Eric and Scott exchanged a glance. "Maybe the girls will finally be valued for their scarcity."

The little boys they've seen on the streets, in parks and pavilions, are often only children and plump (or just bundled up), and Jeannine has remarked that the little fatties, round as the blown-sugar animals they clutch, will be lucky to find wives. But John is an only child and was husky as a kid, and he finds himself feeling oddly sympathetic to the piggy-eyed, pink-cheeked brats.

"Do you know what you're going to have?" Norman asked Napoleon. Just like that, John marveled.

She shook her head.

"What are you and your husband hoping for?" Norman pressed, and she blushed.

"Give her a break, Norm," John said, which was enough to stop the questioning. Norman doesn't like being called Norm. Norm is the name of a fat man in a bar. Norman is whippet-thin, tall, a cyclist. John pictures him all in Lycra, skinny and tubular as his bike frame. Behind his back the others call him "Normal." When it thundered

one evening they called it a "dark and normy night." John is responsible for most, if not all, of these lines.

One consequence of the gender imbalance looming in China, John recalls in the bar, is the likelihood of increased prostitution. It's already happening, if the hotel is anything to go by. After dinner, the long rosewood bar was lined with young women. In Beijing they snaked through the lobby in a loose line, as if on the catwalk at a fashion show — "knockouts in knockoffs," as Norman put it — heels clicking on the marble floors like beads on an abacus. Now, even though the bar is almost empty, the girls at work somewhere in the hotel, their absence seems to fill it. He watches one of the stragglers close her phone with a snap, sashay toward the elevators in her mini-cheongsam, her stilettos lean as chopsticks. There's a single girl with a glossy bob left at the end of the bar. He watches her dial, hang up, dial again. He wonders if she was the one who called him. He wonders if he was her first call of the night.

She has set her phone down to take a drink, exchange a few words with the bow-tied bartender. John's curious if she'll approach him, feels obscurely rejected that she's barely cast a glance in his direction. He's used to a kind of sexual invisibility in the U.S., but here he's affronted.

He takes out his Little Red Book, reminds himself he's never been attracted to Chinese girls. He attributes it to being brought up surrounded by images of blondes, Western ideals of beauty. Conditioned. Nola, his "occident waiting to happen," is all sturdy curves, her milky complexion set off by rosy cheeks (and, to his enduring

delight, rosy breasts, rosy thighs, rosy buttocks). By comparison Chinese girls tend to seem, well . . . girlish to him (their efforts at sexiness a kind of vampish dress-up, not to be taken seriously), if not boyish (slim-hipped and flat-chested, though he's dimly aware it's this very quality that makes Chinese men seem effeminate). He considers himself immune to the Western fetish of otherness, even if — perhaps *because* — his father wasn't. And yet he envies these girls too, their desirability. He recalls roommates in college extolling the appeal of Asian girls, calling him a lucky dog. But he didn't feel lucky. White guys chased Asian chicks; white chicks ignored Asian guys. Not for nothing does he jokingly call Nola his trophy wife.

On the plane, looking at the young Chinese stewardesses, so different to the aging attendants on U.S. fleets, he'd tried to picture his mother in her youth. She'd quit her job after she married, and his father had quit long-haul flights, settling for regional routes that meant he could spend two nights out of every three at their new home in Seattle (though he called short-haul trips "milk runs"). John's mother had told him once that the Captain hadn't quit sleeping with stewardesses, though. "Sluts of the skies," she'd told him acridly. In fact, the only time he'd recognized his mother in the Chinese flight attendants was when one of them barked at someone to sit down while they were still taxiing to the gate.

Why aren't Chinese prostitutes popular with American men? (If only, he thinks reflexively.) *Because half an hour later you're horny again.* Was that one of the Captain's? One of Jordison's?

He flicks through his Little Red Book to the section on women. "It has become necessary to arouse the great mass of women . . . to take their place on the labor front." Mao too? In his head he hears the tinny rimshot of an irony more wearying than jet lag.

He steals a glance at the girl along the bar, as if she's heard it too, and catches her uncrossing and crossing her long legs on the barstool. He looks away too quickly. Between them the bartender polishes glasses intently, as if he's trying to will his smudge of downy mustache to thicken.

A memory of Singapore's strict censorship laws, of a part with the famous bans on gum and long hair, occurs to him. This was back in the late eighties. The movie *When Harry Met Sally* was out. John had seen it in the States and then flown to Singapore with his mother to visit family during his summer vacation. He'd been homesick, miserable, had jumped at the chance to go see the movie again when a couple of slightly older female cousins — a lawyer and an accountant, though they were both lovely enough to be local news anchors, the acme of Chinese American beauty, back home — had suggested it. The cousins were thrilled that the movie was even being shown in Singapore. Why? John had wondered; it was an innocuous enough flick (wiseass that he was, he liked to say he'd enjoyed it more the first time he'd seen it, when it was called *Annie Hall*).

"Because of the orgasm!" one cousin had giggled, covering her mouth, referring to the film's famous scene in which Meg Ryan noisily and lengthily fakes an orgasm in a deli. "I bet the censors cut it" was the other cousin's

—the lawyer's—prediction, but lo and behold, when they saw the movie, the scene was still there. Afterward the cousins, while exultant that it had been left in, couldn't see what all the fuss was about: "It wasn't even that funny, lah." John had shrugged, too embarrassed to discuss orgasms with these two beautiful women, at once older and more innocent than he, and yet . . . he could have sworn the scene was funnier in the U.S., funnier and *longer,* which meant, he figured later, that the Singaporean censor had decided . . . what? That faking an orgasm was fine, but for only so long? And what did that say about Chinese women's orgasms? he reflected. (Knowing at the same time that it surely said as much, if not more, about Chinese, probably male censors.)

The bartender asks if John wants another, and he looks at the girl. *I'll have what she's having.* He's in a foreign country, after all, freed from the restraints of home. Plus he's a writer. Everything's research. Hadn't Nola told him to write something real? And besides, what can happen? He can hardly take her back to his room. He nods to the bartender and offers to buy the young woman another, sliding down the bar toward her. It's late enough and he's self-deluded enough to feel like he's doing her a favor, as if she's a wallflower. A couple of days earlier, in Beijing, Napoleon had taken them to a local park and a place called English Corner, where students liked to practice their English with tourists. Only none of them had talked to John; they all clustered around Nola and the others, as if assuming his English must be deficient.

Her name is Pearl, she tells him, with the slightest sigh.

"After the river," he says, nodding eagerly — tired as he is, his head feels as loose on his neck as a bobble head — but she shakes hers.

"No?"

She giggles, covering her mouth, beckons him closer. He feels her breath against his ear. "Pearl Fuck."

She giggles again, maybe at his blushing.

"Very . . . literary," he tells her.

Up close she's heavily made up — rouged cheeks, fuchsia eye shadow, colored in as if with crayon. She reminds him of one of Warhol's *Mao*s.

She asks him where he wants to go, and he says, "Nowhere. Can we just talk?" She shrugs, makes to move, and he hastens to add, "I'll pay for your time." He fears if he goes anywhere private with her he won't be able to stop himself, and it startles him, this unaccustomed lust for a Chinese woman, makes him consider what else he might be capable of. "You could practice your English."

"What wrong with my Ingrish?" She pouts, rolls her eyes, but in the absence of any other potential clients, she lets him buy her a drink.

"Napoleon," she says sulkily, and he thinks for a second she must know their guide, until the bartender brings over a snifter of brandy.

"Same thing?" he asks John.

"Huh? Sure. Why not." He looks at the glass before him, puzzled. He's never liked brandy, but he'd been distracted by the waiter's question, the echo of a terrible joke that someone — an uncle of Nola's — had told at their wedding

reception years earlier. Something about—how did it go?
—Paddy O'Keefe's Chinese Laundry. *How'd it get a name
like that? Why, I asked the Chinese fellow that ran it the
very question. Turns out when he arrived in the country,
he was in line behind an Irish fella called Paddy O'Keefe,
and when the immigration officer asks the Oriental his
name, he says, "Sam Ting."* The point had something to do
with John's last name being Smith.

He shakes his head, watches the girl sip her drink dain-
tily. Would she have dialed his room if his last name were
Ling? he wonders. He asks about her, her family, but she's
evasive, reluctant. "Boring," she says. "You want me ask
about your wife?"

He looks at his ring, shakes his head.

"I'm sorry. It's just I'm a visitor here. I'm curious about
your home. Tell me anything. Why is it called the Pearl
River? Were there ever pearls in it?"

"No pearls! Just one big round rock in river, so smooth
like a pearl. So they named it." She shrugs. "You want
tour guide, I think, not girlfriend. You tourist? Business?
What you do here?"

"You first," he says, and she tells him wearily that she
has no family, as if this were obvious. She's an orphan.
"Your turn, mister."

He takes a mouthful of brandy. His next line comes out
as a croak.

"I'm here to adopt an orphan."

They look at each other and then she laughs. "Too
rate!" (He's almost sure she's exaggerating her accent.)

He wants to know about her orphanage, but she doesn't
want to talk about it. She wants to know about America.

Where he lives. What he does. "Tell me about life your little girl will have."

And he tries to — a dog, a bicycle, Disney World, soccer camp — until he spies the tears, nacreous and iridescent, accreting in the corners of her eyes.

"I'm sorry," he begins, and she shrugs again, shivers in the air conditioning. He wants to put an arm around her for warmth.

"Wait. I know joke." She blots her eyes with the heels of her hands, as if they were tears of laughter. "Two Chinese couple adopt a white baby. What they call it?"

"I don't know, what do they call it?"

"Sum Ting Wong!"

He smiles.

"What? I tell it wrong? My Ingrish no good?"

"No," he tells her. "Very good."

"Sure is good. Joke no good, huh?" He nods. He's heard it before, except then the question was "What do you call a retarded Chinese baby?" Where *do* all these awful jokes come from? The playground? Jordison and Farley and their ilk? Maybe, and maybe it's why he responded in kind, calling Jordison the Big Finnish (though never to his face). Chinese is full of puns, of homonyms, so who knows, perhaps it's a genetic disposition. Perhaps it's even where his interest in language, his life as a writer, began. (Then again, maybe it started in his mother's rare but memorable solecisms . . . and his nasty pleasure in making fun of her for them, his need to distance himself from her.)

The girl takes a sip of her drink. "You know this phrase in Ingrish, 'mother of pearl'?" she asks abruptly.

"Yes."

"But no 'father of pearl'? Is so?"

He nods.

"Same in China. And you?" she says appraisingly. "You Chinese or what?"

"Half," he says. "My mother."

"Ah," she says. "Mother country," and again they fall silent.

A pair of girls enter the bar, tottering slightly on their heels, and she glances at them.

"Time up," she says, tapping the counter. He lays bills before her one after another—Mao's face on each note—until she nods. "You should have fucked me." She leans close. "You could have gotten me pregnant, left little orphan for some other American adopt. Joke!" she says when she pulls back and sees his face. "Besides, in China, it's easy to get abortion." She snaps her fingers. "Hard not to."

She picks up her phone (a "Samsing," he notes) and begins calling again, stabbing at the buttons, until after a while he slides down the bar to finish his drink. Basketball is playing on a TV overhead, the sound so low that the chirping of shoes on hardwood is clearer than the commentary. John squints to make out the teams before he figures out they're local.

Mother country. He's been thinking a lot on this trip, and not too kindly, about his mother. She's excited, has encouraged them, even offered to come with. But now he wonders, shouldn't she have kept him in touch with Chinese culture? And what kind of a name for a Chinese kid is John, anyway? What were they thinking?

"It's hard for you, I know," his mother had told him after that failed New Year's party. She'd come home and found him in a black mood, intuited the trouble. "To look one way and be another. For inside and outside not to match. For Chinese the exterior, the face, is what counts, what is real. But in the West it's the interior that is the true self." She smoothed his hair—very black, very fine, very straight. "And if inside and out don't match, we don't know what we are. One or the other? Or both or neither?" Back then he'd blamed her for his outside, ducked under her hand.

But another time she told him that the Chinese knew the difference between inner and outer. "We go along, do the right thing in public, but we know we don't always mean it. How you think the Chinese survive communism! I knew an Englishman in Singapore—Mr. Phipps, he trained all the stewardesses in deportment, we called him Mr. Hips behind his back. He claimed the Chinese learned that from the British, but I always thought they might have learned it from us."

After his father died, his mother started to talk about moving "home" to Singapore. "'Home'?" John said. "You've lived here twice as long as there by now." But she just shrugged. He found himself resisting, even resenting the idea, and it crosses his mind that he's hoping she'll stay now that she has a grandchild, for his sake even more than Mei's. "Don't worry!" she'd told him when he tried to explain his unease. "I'm not dead yet!" And then she'd patted his arm. "But you know we're all orphans in the end. Don't look so sad. It's better than the alternative. You'll understand when you're a parent."

His mother, for as long as he can recall, has always drunk warm water in preference to coffee, even tea. He's taken it as an individual quirk all these years, but now there's a thermos of warm water by the bed in every hotel room. What he mistook for an eccentricity of hers was true of a billion people, and he's not sure if he knows her more or less for the insight.

Sam Ting, he thinks. And for a second he feels he can glimpse the origins of the joke. If *you* spoke no English and just watched a guy ahead of you in line enter America, wouldn't you claim whatever he just said, even if it was his Irish name?

But then he thinks of his father, and how he, John, doesn't much resemble the Captain, never has. Mei Mei might look like John—as Bev has noted—but it's never occurred to him before how his father might have felt that his son didn't look like him, didn't look like *his*. And now he recalls how often he was introduced, by aunts and uncles, by his grandmother, as *Jack's boy*—an explanation as much as a claim—so much so that he used to pipe up *I'm John!* and make the adults laugh, a laughter that seems stilted in hindsight. But he also remembers his father beside him, big hand on his shoulder or tousling his hair, owning him always.

He feels the bartender's eyes on him now. Through the windows the city lights blink back at him. He realizes he can't bear to see Pearl walk out of the bar, and he swallows quickly, sets his empty glass down too hard.

And yet he can't go back up to the room, to his sleeping wife. He stands in the chill, blazing lobby, catches his

reflection in the glass of the doors, his hair tufted and twisted into cockeyed horns.

The liveried doorman, hands in his sleeves, gives him a questioning look, but John shrugs and the man bows him out into the night. John waves back, the Little Red Book still in hand.

It's not a "dark and normy" night, at least. If it's even night still. He looks at his watch and sees that it's almost five. It's still dark, though, or perhaps just overcast. Neon shimmers in the smog. John knows it comes from the factories and power plants that ring the city—not to mention the scooters that seem to outnumber the bicycles he expected, and the cars (many of them American)—but he can't help thinking it's a byproduct of all the smokers in China. As if the air weren't bad enough for their lungs.

And this too is what they're saving their girls from: pollution. Every Chinese crowd contains its share of people in surgical masks, looking less like doctors somehow than outlaws. John has seen at least one fellow smoking a cigarette through a hole in his mask, several others pulling theirs down to hawk wetly on the sidewalk.

No one, he reflects, slipping the Little Red Book in his pocket, ever says they're saving the girls from communism. They're careful in general not to talk much politics. They've been warned not to by the adoption agency, told not to ask the guides awkward questions that could make them uncomfortable or even get them in hot water. Not one of them has asked about the student protests in Tiananmen Square. The largest square in the world, Napoleon told them, with room for over a million people,

and yet nowhere in that vastness was there room for a mention, let alone a memorial to the protestors. Tank Man was less recognizable in China than in America. That's what he wants to tell Norman and the rest. *And you think* I'm *the inauthentic one?*

Only once, when a line of black Audis, taut as a train of kites, had overtaken them on the highway, each car flying small red flags, had someone—Alice, maybe—asked Napoleon, "Party officials?" But she'd shaken her head, laughed. "Wedding party." They'd watched the cars streak ahead in chastened silence.

A pickup rattles by John now, its bed packed with cages of sleeping chickens on their way to market.

The streets are quiet at this time of day, and John, for a change, can walk without drawing a crowd. Their party as a whole tends to attract attention, but he's hoped that alone, he might blend in, feel for once in his life invisible. This is what he needs, he thinks, to get away from the group, to figure things out for himself. He and Nola don't need to adopt for the same reasons as the rest, in the same way as the others, right? And yet even when he's slipped away from their tour he knows he stands out. His clothes are wrong, of course, but probably there are other little things too. He remembers on another trip to Singapore —he'd taken Nola after they were married—a cousin had pointed out that the gold in his wedding band wasn't yellow enough; the Chinese favored a very bright gold. And that he was too short. Too short! That may be why few people speak to him in Chinese here; the only ones who seem to assume he knows the language are in his own party. Those locals who do talk to him speak louder and

slower, as if he's an idiot. Others seem to feel he's just rude. If anything, he's more stared at than invisible.

In America, growing up, he always felt burdened by his Chinese appearance. Here in China, like a wish granted by an ironic deity, he's white. He thinks enviously of a trip he and Nola took to Ireland a few years ago, how he'd recognized her complexion everywhere. He'd thought it would be like that.

On the empty streets he's free for once at least to look around at his leisure. He's spent so long looking up, over the heads of the crowd, peering at the sights, it's a relief to look around close up, at ground level. Besides, looking up makes him dizzy — the drink working on top of his tiredness. He feels a little like one of those steel balls in a tilting maze. He peers down alleys and into parking lots, at the front stoops of stores, before he grasps what he's doing. Stan had told them that their first daughter, Lily, had been found in a box outside a post office. He and Bev have been back there — to the "finding place," as Bev calls it, dabbing a Kleenex to her eyes — and taken photos to show Lily. They plan to bring her back on their next trip, but they wanted to take photographs in case the buildings are torn down, the area redeveloped. Everywhere they go new towers are rising, cocooned in scaffolding and nets. "China is gonna be great when they finish it," as the joke goes.

John himself has read accounts of babies being found outside stores, in marketplaces, at railway and bus stations, in the lobbies of hotels even. Foundlings, he thinks, the word so oddly Dickensian (and he suddenly recalls, as a child, wishing *he* were an orphan, telling his shocked mother, *They always have the best adventures*). The

locations are taken as signs of love. The parents want the babies found quickly. Many are said to be rural women —it being harder to keep a pregnancy secret in the city —who take a risk coming into the city to leave the child somewhere where it'll be found, as opposed to abandoning it in a remote location to die. The mothers, it is surmised, must often wait, hidden, to make sure their babies are found. One account even has it that adoptive parents have had babies thrust into their arms in parking lots or come across babies under bushes.

And this, John realizes, stopping short, is what he's looking for, why he's out walking at this ungodly hour. He's hoping to catch a glimpse of such a moment . . . and then what? Claim the child? Pursue the mother? And ask her what, even if he could communicate with her? And yet he finds himself holding his breath as he looks into corners and shadows. It's like some treasure hunt. And then it comes to him that what he's really looking for is some sign. This whole process is so managed, so bureaucratic; he's looking for an accident, for fate to intervene. Not that he could even keep any baby he found; he knows that. But still, irrationally, he finds himself looking.

If a Chinese mother pressed her baby into his arms, even if he couldn't keep that baby, he'd feel chosen somehow, as if someone thought he could be a father.

But the only young women who beckon him from the shadows are hookers. One bares her breast as he approaches and he hurries on, floaty with tiredness.

On the way back to the hotel he begins to hear birdsong, the dawn chorus, even if he hasn't detected the change in

the light himself. He tries to look for the birds, to identify the species, but the trees and telegraph lines are empty. And then he locates the sound, coming from the blocks of flats above him; each balcony he sees has a small cage hanging from it, and he remembers the songbird market they saw in Beijing, the tiny birds, little more than chicks, huddled in their bamboo cages.

The sun rises weakly. It seems smaller, more distant through the haze than at home, as if he's not on a different continent but on another planet altogether. In a park he glimpses old people practicing tai chi, singly and in pairs, between the trees, their slow movements so oddly intimate he feels as if he's intruding. A sound like firecrackers makes him jump, but when he looks he sees it's a man whipping a wooden top in a square. The streets begin to grow busy, and he feels self-conscious, like a thief revealed in daylight. He finds himself hurrying back to the hotel, relieved to see its neon signage. Near the entrance there's a row of shop-houses in an arcade. It's meant to look traditional, even though the goods on sale are souvenirs, Western snacks, the prices too high for any locals. A cleaner dozes on his broom in a doorway, and John feels a pang of envy. One of the stores is just opening and John sees the owner, a genial fellow he's heard others refer to as Charlie Chin, on account of the hairy mole sprouting there, setting out his wares. He's hanging packs of disposable diapers from hooks overhead with the help of a pole. Charlie has no English to speak of — he holds up a calculator to show people prices — but his sales pitch is a jovial *Adopt me!* (They've theorized that someone — some earlier new parent — explained their baby as an "adoptee"

and he misheard.) He regales John with it now, a joke that also seems like a greeting, and before he knows it John has called back, "Adopt *me!*" and the man nods and smiles with delight.

John buys the English-language *China Daily* from him, flicks through it as he walks. A photo of a steam engine on page 3 catches his eye. It's a Chinese locomotive in Mongolia — the last steam train in passenger service in the world, apparently — which is finally being retired. It's being sold to the U.S. to run trips for rail buffs. *Must use that somehow,* he thinks, with a little spring in his step.

In the lobby he pauses to glance into the bar, looking for the girl. She's there — still, or again? he wonders, unable to judge from her pale, drawn face. He wants to tell her to get some sleep.

He slips into the room, undresses, curls up behind Nola, nestling his leg between hers, in her yielding bed-baked warmth. For a second he pictures Pearl in her micro-skirt, slender pale legs scissoring like chopsticks, imagines being pincered between them, shivers slightly.

A viscous shaft of daylight, faintly spangled, slips between the curtains, dust motes suspended like gold. He holds his hand in the beam, but they swirl from his grasp.

Memories of their tour slide through his mind, as if he were flipping through them on his phone. The way every building for miles around the Great Wall — gas stations, convenience stores, public bathrooms — was crenellated. The expats (or rather *half pats,* as he's learned they're called) overheard in an airport bar talking about how much longer they need to work in China before they can

go home wealthy—a new breed of sojourners. The terra-cotta army, thousands, probably tens or hundreds of thousands, strong, rank upon rank of men, each with a unique face. "I guess we don't all look alike," he'd whispered to Nola sotto voce, all the time searching for one that looked like him.

He might not know that much Chinese history or culture, but he knows something of the history of Chinese America: all the men without women, the women without husbands. The Chinese without Chinese. And yet he, and others like him, are somehow their descendants. Mongrels and bastards, orphans and warphans. *No wonder we put so much stock in family,* he thinks. We value nothing more than what we don't possess.

Now that it's morning, now that he doesn't have to sleep, he feels himself relax at last.

Nola is agonizing when he wakes up. What do you wear to meet your new baby? It's a moment of some ceremony, on the one hand. On the other, you're very likely to be spat up on. He blinks at her as she holds up blouses. Plus what would the Chinese approve of? Not white, of course, that impractical, funereal color. Probably red—always auspicious (though John views all the red outfits sported by the group as a kind of sucking-up). He kisses her, slips past to the shower.

There is a nervous breakfast, everyone excited, talking in hurried, hushed tones. Bev shows off a sign Lily has made—happy gotcha day little sis!!!, each letter clipped from a magazine. "She's into collage right now. Everything looks like a ransom note!" John smiles, sips

his coffee, glances across into the dark bar, now cavern-
ously empty.

And then Napoleon herds them into a plush function
room, the kind of neutral space where business confer-
ences are held, panels and symposia. Plastic chandeliers
dangle overhead, clacking gently in the air-conditioned
current. The group forms an excited ring around her,
camcorders chiming to life and rising up as if at a press
conference, and she explains that the babies will be
brought in one at a time by their carers. Couples clutch
hands; the singles among them clutch photos of their chil-
dren. Alice performs a slow pirouette, as if dancing alone,
to take a panoramic photo. Stan and Bev lean together,
touching heads—in prayer, John guesses (it occurs to him
suddenly that they're probably pro-life). He turns to Nola,
squeezes her hand. "What?" she asks. "You look good,"
he tells her, and she does, radiant, but her eyes are on the
door. "All our lives are about to change forever," someone
murmurs, and John turns to see who—to argue the point,
reflexively—and as a result he misses the door opening.

"Towson," Napoleon calls. Stan and Bev. It won't be
alphabetical, then. The baby is a tightly bound parcel,
red-faced from the cold, probably, though for a moment
John fears she's too tightly trussed. Bev bursts into happy
laughter, folding her into her arms—"I could eat you up"
—almost at the same moment that the baby begins to
bawl and Stan, behind his camera, melts into snotty tears.
Pandemonium. Flashbulbs, a smattering of applause. And
then the next name, and the next. The babies are heavily
dressed, as soft and plump as the plush toys they're soon
to be surrounded by. If they don't cry, their adoptive

parents do; often so do their carers. The room is dissolving in tears, John thinks, his smile of anticipation stretched tight. Already his lips and cheeks are starting to ache. Another and another. "Knowing our luck, we'll be last," he tells Nola, and she nods stiffly. Jeannine presses her face to the bundle in her arms, croons, "Hi, Celeste." (*Seriously?* John thinks.) Norman throws his new daughter up in the air like a football, catches her, and swoops her around the room while Amanda calls "Careful!" Eric makes unselfconscious baby talk while Scott wrings his hands.

And then everyone has a baby except them and the door is closed and they look at each other and then Napoleon. She's moving through the crowd, counting, lips moving, and then she's before them. A frown crosses her face, and she calls in Chinese for the orphanage official, who appears beside her. There's an animated conversation, Napoleon's voice rising. But in anger, alarm? Chinese has always seemed animated to John, an excitable language, but he's not sure how to read its tones. And then Napoleon turns to them. "So sorry," she says. She takes a breath. "Baby sick this morning, fever. Could not bring. They should have telephone. I call at once and find out more." Her hands rest lightly for a moment on her own stomach, and John has to tear his eyes away from it, look at her face.

"Is she all right?" Nola asks, stricken, and Napoleon gives a frail smile. Her hand hovers between them and she pats the air. "I find out more, okay? Promise."

The news is filtering through the crowd. People have been looking wide-eyed at each other, eager to share their

joy, as if to make it real, and now the giddy tide of feeling has washed up against the quiet couple in the corner. Video cameras, recording all this as if it were the birth itself, turn on them—accusingly, John can't help feeling, as if they've struck a wrong note on this celebratory day.

"It's okay," he says carefully. "They say she wasn't too well this morning. Just a precaution, I expect. Probably didn't want to infect the others." He's making this up, but it seems so plausible he's instantly relieved. Of course that's it. This must happen all the time. Babies get fevers all the time. It's *normal*. But even as he thinks it he sees the runny noses of half the kids, hears the colicky breathing. How sick must Mei Mei be?

They all take a moment to hug them tightly on their way out—Stan and Bev, Alice, Eric and Scott, Jeannine, Norman and Amanda—and by the end John is in tears. "Oh, you poor darlings. If I could give you ours . . ." Bev begins. An impossible, awful offer, but heartfelt, he knows. And yet he bristles at a hidden selfishness amid all the good wishes. They—he and Nola—are everyone's worst fear, he intuits. To come so far and be denied at the last. He detects in their faces some relief in having their fears come true—for someone else. Some things are too good to be true, unless something bad happens to make them real. You can't believe in your own luck unless someone else is unlucky. Some price must be paid to salve their consciences.

They sit with Napoleon in her room, watching her make calls. She barks into the receiver but translates for them in a mild undertone. "Country folks," she says, pursing her lips, though she's told them the orphanage is

only an hour away, on the outskirts of town. "Good with babies, though." Someone at the other end of the line goes to fetch the orphanage administrator. Someone goes to fetch the doctor. Someone else is at lunch. Napoleon is dogged, indefatigable, and John feels a great love for her, wants to bring her a glass of water, make her sit down, ask about her own baby. Friends have told him about this, the deep gratitude to nurses and pediatricians, anyone who fights for your child.

At one point the phone rings and she speaks in unmistakably warm hushed tones that raise their hopes. When she hangs up she is smiling, and they lean forward. "So sorry. My husband," she explains. "I told him call back later."

She tries the orphanage again, and talks for what seems like a long time, angrily and then more softly, leaning into the phone, her hair curtaining her face. When she turns to face them she smiles weakly, holds up a finger.

"I arrange," Napoleon finally tells them, hanging up. "This afternoon we go orphanage, collect her." She nods. "Be resolute!"

This afternoon; they nod in turn. "Still Gotcha Day," Nola says weakly. Just another lag, John tells himself.

They're out of Tylenol. They have plenty of baby Tylenol, but John isn't sure it'll do any good, and Nola doesn't want to waste it on herself anyway. There's so little he can do for her, so little to say (*Are you okay?* he keeps asking, but when she said, *Yes. What about you?* he almost said, *What* about *me?*) that John jumps at the chance to go out and find a drugstore, to enact his love for her. He can

hardly stand to be in the hotel anyway. The building seems to hum with baby energy now. He pictures all the other couples in their rooms with their babies and he wants to get out. He tells her he thought he saw a pharmacy a couple of streets over, and she lies back and covers her eyes, without thinking to ask him when he saw the pharmacy.

In the little park old men play ping-pong on a cement table, across a metal net; old women stir mahjong tiles.

He amazes himself by finding the pharmacy again, but when he steps inside the shelves are lined with unfamiliar boxes with indecipherable labels. The jet lag is catching up with him again. He feels top-heavy with tiredness, brimming with exhaustion, as if he might spill into sleep. He studies the shelves for some clue, but the boxes, brightly colored and tightly packed, covered in Chinese writing, remind him of nothing so much as fireworks.

And how odd to celebrate July Fourth every year with Chinese-made fireworks with names like Golden Peony and Dragon Tail, Dancing Butterfly and Chrysanthemum Glory, Moon Willow and Blossoming Pearl (not to mention that old knee-slapper, Golden Shower). He used to announce them at Independence Day parties, making up a few along the way: Red-Haired Devil, Great Leap Forward, Laundry Bomb, Flying Lice, Wok-et to the Moon, Panda-moan-ium.

Now he stands at the counter, pointing at his head, crossing his eyes — *Thunder Head*, he thinks, *Temple of Fire* — until the shaggy-haired clerk says, "Ah, Ty-Le-Nol," as if he's trying to teach John the pronunciation. He

takes a box off the shelf, turns it around to show the English on the reverse.

On the way back to the hotel John spots a Starbucks, hurries inside. Or rather a "Starlucks," he notices as he stands in line, another one to add to the list of copycat names the group has been trading back and forth: Starcups, MukDonald's (complete with a stylized graphic of Donald Trump in a clown suit), and, everyone's favorite, Dulce and Banana. Is it any wonder none of them mentions communism? It's just capitalism misspelled. But the signs, so glancingly familiar yet so deeply off, only add to his disorientation. *It's as if they're all named by my mother,* he has joked, joining in the general hilarity, albeit uneasily. None of the others would be seen dead in these Western knockoffs (even if John's occasionally found himself salivating at the thought of a burger). Such places aren't "real," the group agrees. Not really American, of course (though there are KFCs on every other corner, real McDonald's side-by-side with the fakes, Western food being as ubiquitous here as Chinese is at home). But also —and this is what they really mean—not Chinese either. Yet what if they're filled, as they are, with real Chinese? What price authenticity, then? And what does that say about where they're taking their new daughters to and from? The girls will grow up Chinese American, John knows, but what will that even mean if China continues to modernize, Westernize? How will it differ, how will it be better, if at all? Still, beyond the group opprobrium, something about these American imitations rankles with him, makes his skin crawl, and he ducks out as soon as he's downed his double espresso (a vast improvement, to be

fair, on the three-in-one mix sachets of Nescafé, whitener, and sugar back in the hotel room). His mother reckons China is turning into Singapore: *Singapore on steroids. Never mind the regime, let's shop!* But that too sounds increasingly American to him.

Only . . . this *isn't* the way back to the hotel. A block beyond the coffee shop he slows, pauses, works his way to one edge of the busy sidewalk, out of the flow of the crowd, and stands on tiptoe to see over their heads, looking for something he recognizes. How can it be? he wonders, aghast. He wandered these streets in the darkness and found his way back without difficulty, but now in full daylight he's—he resists the dread word—lost. It must be the crowds, the traffic—a silver pedicab, looking like an armored scooter, bleats at him as it rushes past—but the explanation doesn't tell him which way to go, and he feels a spasm of panic. He's breaking out in prickling pinheads of sweat. He wants to run to the corner, to look up and down streets, but his path, his view, is impeded by bodies in every direction. He thinks of Nola at the hotel, her bad head. How long has he been gone? She'll start to get worried. And the thought of giving her another worry makes him feel sick. When he should be there comforting her. He starts to push against the current of bodies, released by a traffic light; he starts to push and people shout at him. He should excuse himself, but he doesn't have the words, and something, some fear of unmasking, makes him hesitate to speak English. And yet the terror is rising in him now, the sense of entrapment. The Walk signal overhead blinks hyperactively, the little white figure leaning forward, animated legs strobing. Only when he

shoves and feels the body before him yield, looks down and finds it's a child he's stumbled into, knocked down, a small girl, now wailing, does he stop, try to lift her to her feet. Now he's holding back the crowd, to shield her, bent down, his haunches burning, getting kneed in the head so that for a moment he fears he'll sprawl underfoot, be trampled. But then he gets his balance, forces himself upright, the child in his arms, and a woman is tugging at his, pulling him aside into a doorway. She takes the child from him, sets her on her feet beside him, thanks him— *xie-xie*, a phrase he has memorized from the guidebook, practiced with drivers and guides and hotel maids—and now he's saying it too—*xie-xie, xie-xie*—which seems to puzzle her, this exhausted-looking mother, and the child is still wailing, and the mother, casually, without even looking down, smacks her around the ear, and she stifles her cries, though John can still feel her trembling sobs where her bony shoulder is pressed up against his waist.

Jesus, he breathes, and the woman squints at him and says, "Ingrish?" And he nods—"American"—and she beams. "How do meet you please!"

The hotel is only four blocks away. (In his tiredness he must have left the coffee shop by a different door from the one he entered by, gotten turned around, freaked out when the caffeine hit.) The girl runs ahead, her plastic sandals clapping. Outside, he tells the mother her English is very good, and she blushes. (He thinks of his own mother, how even years after living in the U.S. she'd have described the packed street as *chocolate block* with people.) The child swings on the end of her arm, eyes down and almost hidden by the long bangs curtaining her brow. He wishes

he had something for her. Money seems wrong, but apart from his bag of Tylenol he's empty-handed. He settles for leading them across the street to Charlie Chin's, letting the girl choose some candy. It feels like an offering.

He's still sweating and shaky when he gets to the room, but Nola only gives him a nod, as if she's barely noticed his absence. When he sits with her on the bed, she puts her head on his shoulder and he presses his lips to her hair, inhales her scent. "Your poor head," he says, and she says, "My head? Oh, it's fine." And he understands that she sent him away, must have been as relieved to see him go as he was to leave, but somehow the insight makes him love her more, not less, as if it were some unspoken pact, as if the lie were a gift. A notebook sits on the desk, pencil angled across it. She sees him notice it.

They sit side by side on the edge of the bed, heads touching, arms around each other. He looks at the clock by the bedside. It's still only 1:45. "Are you hungry?" he asks, fearing that she'll send him away again, but she shakes her head gently, rubbing it against his. Two hours to go. Not so long after all this waiting, but it seems an unimaginable, unfillable vastness. She sees him looking at the time and turns her face to his, kisses him.

Thank god, he wants to tell her, thank *you*, but he knows enough to stay silent as they lie back.

"Better?" she asks later, and he nods.

"I feel less like a horny teenager, at least."

She smiles and rolls against him, nestling.

All her refusals, her avoidances, all these weeks and months, he concludes, gazing at the ceiling, have made him feel not just unwanted, frustrated, unattractive, but

more Chinese. And yet . . . He's knows he's an attentive lover, always aiming to please her first, a point of pride and one reason he's been so resentful of her coolness in bed (though, paradoxically, why he so cherished their sex when they conceived). But now he wonders if he's just diligent, polite, wonders if he'd be the same way with a Chinese woman.

Nola opens her eyes, sensing his body tighten.

"And you?" he asks quickly.

"What?"

"Better?"

She smiles weakly, grips his hand.

"Soon. I hope."

In the suitcase, between the packs of diapers, the clothes and toys for the baby, and the gifts for Napoleon, the other agency staff, is the thick envelope of cash. They've been told they need to make a donation (John makes air quotes around the word) of $3000 to the orphanage. These envelopes exchanged hands this morning for most couples, but John is taking theirs with them to the orphanage. He thumbs through one of the stacks, rifling the bills, watching Mao flicker past, expecting him to move as if in a flipbook, to wink or stick out his tongue. "Mousy Tongue," he recalls with a start, a childhood name for the Chairman that made his mother laugh. He tries the bundle in his coat pocket, where it bulges. He's already tried it in his money belt, where it makes him look potbellied. He feels like he needs an attaché case, or a small grip, the kind of bag that cash—ransom money—is exchanged in in the movies. Instead he tucks it into

the diaper bag, next to a plush elephant with a stretchy trunk and crinkly ears.

When he brought the wad of bills home from the bank, more cash than he'd ever held in his hands, he joked that they could skip the baby and just pick up some opium— "Or I could just spread it on the bed and we could roll around on it a little." "I imagine," Nola had told him, "that that's exactly why the Chinese prefer crisp new bills."

It's the money that gives the whole thing its air of illicit-ness, of purchase, even though they're not buying the baby but making a gift for the care of the orphans left behind. He's not sure if that makes it any better. He doesn't like to think of all the thousands of other orphans and what will become of them. And how will Mei feel about them? he asks himself. He imagines these "lucky ones" having a kind of survivor guilt in later life.

The cash certainly makes him feel guilty, and because he feels guilty he expects to be caught, punished, which is probably why he feels such a sense of doom. The cash too makes him fear he's about to get ripped off; it's the same wariness he felt talking with Pearl.

He shakes his head as if to clear it of such doubts. Three thousand, he reminds himself, is also a lucky number, the word for "three" sounding like the character for "birth."

They take the stubby tour bus to the orphanage, just he, Nola, Napoleon, and their white-gloved driver. It feels strange sitting in the almost empty minibus, hemmed in by traffic, in a country that's so crowded. Napoleon intro-duced the driver as Ah Ling (an introduction that means he needs to be tipped). Just a coincidence, John knows.

Chinese call themselves collectively the *baixing,* "the hundred names"; only a hundred or so surnames cover nearly 90 percent of the entire population, compared to many tens of thousands for the same proportion of Americans. Still, he finds himself studying the driver in the rearview mirror, looking for some resemblance beneath the close-cropped hair and straggly goatee, until the man makes eye contact and John turns away, wary of distracting him as he weaves through traffic, seemingly pumping his horn as often as his brakes or gas. (In Beijing and Xi'an, John had nicknamed their drivers Wie! and Wu! for their slithery, hurtling negotiation of the congestion. *Asian drivers,* he'd whispered to Nola.) Behind them the city recedes, the tops of its skyscrapers lost in the purling smog like mountains in cloud, the sky below bisected by cranes. A pair of them almost touch, a trick of perspective, as if forming an arch — the Gate of Eternal Development. He pictures all the high-rises he's seen in China laid out end to end, guesses they'd stretch as far as the Great Wall.

The orphanage is visible from a distance in the dusk, the bright forms of plastic playground equipment dotting its grounds. Up close, the slides and seesaws are worn and rusted, the plastic bleached and frayed. Big children, six or seven or eight or nine — John finds it hard to guess their age — have commandeered rides that seem too small for them, while littler ones — toddlers? surely they should be asleep — scrape and dig with sticks at the dirt. "They look like they're tunneling their way out," John jokes, and Nola gives him a look to shut him up.

He pats the money in his bag for reassurance.

Nurses in white coats oversee the children but from the perimeter, giving them the air of scientists observing an experiment. Or haunting ghosts.

Inside, they're greeted effusively by the director, an older woman with tightly permed hair and cat's-eye glasses. Her white coat creaks with starch as she ushers them into her office, offers them tea. They decline; Nola can't bear the delay, he knows. John can see the director is a little put out, but then Mei Mei is brought forth and handed over to Nola. She's tiny, even parceled in blankets, but John is relieved to see she looks healthy. Pink-cheeked and bright-eyed, with no sign of her recent fever. The recuperative power of babies! He touches her tiny fingers, so improbably small and perfect, and she gives him a stern, warning look. He wants to seal the deal, hand over the cash now, before anyone can change their minds—as if he's just stumbled on an incredible bargain—but something, some residual fear of being taken, some sense that it's the most cash he's ever held in his hands, or perhaps some intuition of something in the orphanage director's manner, so eagerly polite, makes him pause. He looks at the baby again; he pushes back the downy bangs at her temples. He looks at Nola and he knows she knows too. There's a drowning look in her eyes, and he wants to protect her so much that he misreads it.

She wants him to shut up, he realizes a moment after he says, "But this isn't Mei Mei. This isn't the girl in the photograph." He pulls it out to make sure, stuffs the envelope of cash back in the same pocket. There's a birthmark, a small mole on her temple. A beauty spot, they'd called it to each other. He peers hard at the photo, trying to

determine if it's a blemish, but then all at once everything else is wrong—the set of the mouth, the nose. They're already trying to tell him—the director, even Napoleon —that the photo is old, that babies change, but he can see that putting the envelope of money back in his pocket has given him the upper hand here. "It's not, is it?" He looks at Nola and she nods infinitesimally.

Outside the director's window night has fallen, and he can see them all reflected in the dark glass as if on a screen. On her desk John sees a paper surgical mask, still bowed to the shape of the director's face, with a smudge of lipstick in its middle.

"Where's Mei Mei?" he asks. "It's all right if she's sick. We want to see her. We'll wait until she gets better. It's all right."

But even as he says it, he knows it isn't. The director and Napoleon have a hurried exchange. John has never yearned so much to speak Chinese.

"Baby die," Napoleon whispers at last, looking stricken, and he nods, over and over, of course, of course. Baby die. Babies die all the time. It's the most natural thing in the world.

Beside him, Nola's eyes are closed so tight the tears seem squeezed from them.

"When?" John says.

"This morning." While he was out walking, he thinks. Or while everyone else was celebrating? While he was sitting in Starlucks? He always thought those copycat joints made the Chinese seem like flatterers or fools unable to tell the difference. Now he wonders if they're not mock-ery, if the Chinese aren't in on the joke. But the deception

is the least of it. Poor, poor Mei, he despairs, not so lucky after all. He never met her, yet he feels like he's in mourning, so much so that what Nola says next doesn't surprise him, though Napoleon's and the director's faces fall in shock.

"I want to see her."

There's a hurried, tumbling conversation in Chinese.

"It won't do any good," Napoleon begins.

"I want to see her."

"Is the truth," Napoleon assures them, and he believes her, even though he knows she's tried to pass off the new baby as Mei.

"That's not why," he tells her. He looks at the director. "Please, let us see her."

He knows they want him to take the other baby. He knows they want to keep this quiet. He knows they want his money. He knows they'll allow it.

And they do. The baby in Nola's stiff arms is passed to the director, who passes her to a nurse. They're led into the basement, down a long corridor, bare pipes overhead. They pass an open door through which they glimpse huge washing machines, a line of dryers, their windows like a row of portholes on a submarine, and, dwarfed by the equipment, a group of toddlers folding laundry. Tiny shirts and pants. John thinks of little Lily.

At the end of the hall there's a small office, a doctor's, judging from the posters tacked to the walls, and beyond it a bare examining room. Everywhere in China is chilly, he's found (they're here off-season), but the room is frigid —not refrigerated but naturally cold, like a pantry, or a root cellar, or the grave, of course. He folds his arms,

tucks his hands under the cuffs of his rolled shirtsleeves for warmth.

At the threshold Nola puts a hand on Napoleon's arm, shakes her head, and the guide nods, visibly relieved, stands outside, her back to the door, as if on guard.

Mei is bundled up on a metal desk that doubles as an examination table, and John's immediate feeling is how hard the surface looks, how drab and colorless compared to all the cribs he's ever seen. And then he notices her stillness. He's been around sleeping babies before—the children of friends—but the quality of this stillness is different. And then he sees it's not the baby—or not only—but also the adults. Normally we creep around a sleeping baby, hushed, gentle, slow, breath held. Now the director moves brusquely, jaggedly, her feet scraping the floor, not fearful of waking the baby, eager if anything to make a little noise, to affirm her own life. John makes himself inhale, exhale.

A cloth is raised. They look at her face, already faded to gray, as matte as the photo they've cherished. Her mole is a dark period at her temple. He imagines the life draining from it as from a hole.

It comes to him that all this time, all this ambivalence on his part was a kind of fear of this tiny baby, that somehow she would make him less real, less authentic, and he bows his head, begs for her forgiveness.

"Okay," Nola says with a swallow, and John puts his arm around her quickly to steady her, leads her out and up the rough concrete stairs, away from what he can't help thinking of as the death floor.

* * *

Back in the director's office, slumped in low chairs, more Chinese flits over their heads. John has the toy elephant in his hand—no idea when he took it out, how long he's been gripping it. He remembers, absently, the huge elephant statues at the Ming tombs outside Beijing, Napoleon explaining that they were carved before elephants became extinct in China, in the fifteenth century. When he looks up, Napoleon is studying them carefully.

"You must decide, John, Nola. I'm so, so sorry. But will you take the other baby? The director says she's the very best they have. Strong, healthy. And you can have her for less." Napoleon bows her head, tucks a string of hair behind her ear. "She is desperate. If you don't take, there will be questions, trouble for her, I think." *And for you?* John reflects. *Is this your Waterloo? If you lose your job, will you be able to afford a child?*

He appraises these two women who are trying to sell him a baby girl. He hasn't seen a man since he entered the orphanage.

The director says something else in an undertone.

"Come," Napoleon says gently. "Spend some time with her."

There is something indecent in all this, but when John looks at Nola, he knows she feels it too. *We have the diapers,* he wants to say. *What else are we going to do?* So they go along.

And in her eager panic the director ushers them into the ward.

The thick smell first—the cheap scent of wipes and talc and cleaning fluid—then the sound, almost industrial, like a factory floor, until he can begin to process

the uproar of crying with, beneath the wails, an uneven, juddering beat—it takes John a further moment to identify it—of children pulling on crib bars, jumping on mattresses. The cribs are made of a black tubular metal—hence the industrial clamor—and he can't help but think of cages, of cells. When he makes himself banish that thought, the place reminds him of an old maternity ward, all the babies lined up, with perhaps a cigar-smoking dad peering in at them from behind a window, trying to identify his. Only here there's no glass between.

"Here."

The director is holding out the baby to them. John stares at it, making sure it's the same one as before. Its legs are kicking, its face contorted, and for a moment, over-whelmed by the noise, put off by the aggression with which the director pushes the baby at them, both he and Nola freeze. And then Nola takes her into her arms.

The woman calls out in Chinese, and Napoleon, after a brief consultation, whispers tightly, "If you no like this one, she says . . . you can choose. See the others. Take any you want!"

She gestures to the row after row of babies. *Another one in half an hour.* John can suddenly understand why Stan and Bev have come back for a second child. "Like Chinese takeout," Stan had joked. It had seemed crass before, but John gets it now. What will become of all these children? How can they save only one?

The director is reading names off the cribs—Zhen, Jia—hoisting another child in her arms, squeezing her as if to plump her up, or like a vendor attesting to the ripeness

of a melon. In her white coat, she looks suddenly less like a doctor or even a scientist than like a grocer.

"No," John says quickly. "We can't choose!" He looks warningly at Nola. "We can't!" Though he knows for sure only that he can't. It's overwhelming. He looks down the ranks of cribs and feels the way he sometimes feels in big-box stores, Costco, Ikea, even as the comparison revolts him. But then it's not just the sheer multiplicity. He can't choose between even two options. He couldn't choose what to do about their own pregnancy, after all, was only too happy to defer to Nola's right to choose (that's why, he realizes with a shock, she hates him a little bit), before that couldn't, still can't, choose China or America, wants both, which may be to say neither.

And what about the child? To be singled out, to live for all these others. To be one and represent many, and inevitably imperfectly—he knows what that feels like, that burden. There, gleaming darkly, is the germ of inauthenticity.

But Nola is nodding. "We can't choose," she agrees softly. But she's not looking at him. The child has her finger in its tiny grip.

And this is what she wants, what they both want more than anything, not to choose, after all, but to be *chosen*. He by her, she by him, both of them by this child. It's part of why he loves Nola, he thinks, because she, a white American, chose him.

Napoleon looks at them narrowly, perplexed. She has a spray of freckles across the bridge of her nose, John notices for the first time, and then he recognizes how pale she's gone. "Okay, okay. She says, since you Chinese, John, she have a *boy* for you, tomorrow, next day latest."

Baby penis. John shudders.

"I'm not *that* Chinese," he says, and it's true. He's never felt more American. He's finally reached the limit of his Chineseness, the outermost frontier, and it feels like a revelation, like making out the jagged line of the Great Wall from space. "We're taking her."

And Nola pulls the baby close. "She's ours."

And she is. By fate, by fortune, by luck, good or bad or both, which after all, commingled is fate. This man, this woman, this egg, this seed, this country, this town, this room, these people, this baby. The lucky ones.

He'd save them all if he could. But in the end one will have to stand for them all (though he leaves the envelope of money). It's not right, of course. It's fucked up. Many into one won't go. And yet the alternative is worse: to save none, to walk away empty-handed. The only thing worse than choosing is not choosing. And yes, it'll be a burden on the child, an intolerable one perhaps, but perhaps that's also what luck is, what it should be: a burden, a duty, an obligation.

Napoleon smiles with relief, as if she'd been offering them her own child.

On the way back in the bus, he holds the child and she falls asleep on his chest and he curls around her and sleeps himself all the way back to the hotel. But she wakes with him too when they pull up, begins to wail—wet or hungry?—and they hurry inside, John jiggling the plush toy desperately in her face—"See the elephant!"—until Nola takes her. His past self, the self who came in and out of these doors earlier today even, suddenly seems

impossibly distant, another person. The baby's cries pin him to the present.

Napoleon bids them goodnight, reminds them of the morning's itinerary. She'll see them to the station, the train to Hong Kong, where they'll complete the immigration paperwork at the U.S. consulate before flying home in a couple of days. John tries to thank her, show there're no hard feelings, that they can trust each other to keep their secret. "We couldn't have done it without you, any of us. You do incredible work." She smiles tiredly. Dark filaments of hair float about her face like the pencil lines of a sketch. "You're my last group," she confides, not quite able to disguise her relief. "I'm quitting for when baby comes." Her relief, John thinks, and perhaps too her distaste. He wonders if she's always felt that way or only now that she carries her own child. Tomorrow they'll tip her generously, proffer small gifts with both hands (cosmetics from Nola, American candy from John). Poor impersonal offerings. He had wanted to give her a copy of his book, but he knows it's bad luck; *book* in Mandarin also means "loss."

It's late, and across the empty lobby John spies Pearl stepping out of an elevator. She walks toward them, tall in her heels, and he sees her taking them in, him, Nola, the bundle in Nola's arms. Her face is unreadable — inscrutable, he thinks, despite himself — but when she meets them she pauses as if waiting for the last echo of her heels on the marble and gestures to the baby. Napoleon makes as if to shoo her away, but John says, "It's all right." He looks at Nola, and she steps forward. Pearl stares at the child for a long time, not baby-talking,

not smiling, not waving. Waiting for the baby to see her, and still.

"Okay," she says at last. She fixes John with a look and he nods once, the slightest bow. "Take her," Pearl says. "Take her home."

"Who was that?" Nola will ask him in the elevator, and he'll shrug, avoid her eye. But later that night, when they need a name that isn't a dead girl's—not Mei, not Anna, it'd be bad luck—he'll whisper it: *Pearl*. In the dark, sitting beside her, both of them awake now, watching the baby sleep, he'll hear Nola thinking about it, and he'll press his lips to her hair in a kiss—*mother of Pearl*—and feel her ease against him.

"I wonder what she'll be," Nola murmurs a little later. "Listen to me. Typical mom." But he holds her tightly. It's good to be typical for once, to ask a question they haven't allowed themselves for years.

"I'll settle for happy and healthy," he says, because he already aches for her to be successful. Nola stifles a yawn. "Happy and healthy . . . and rich and famous."

"I always wanted to be a rock star," she says, giggling. "Olivia Newton-John."

"What a coincidence. I always wanted you to be Olivia Newton-John too."

She head-butts him softly.

"I always wanted to be an astronaut," he recalls. Specifically, the first Chinese American in space, as he'd announced at the front of some grade-school class (he's startled to think there was a time when he'd innocently embraced his identity, seen it as an advantage).

"Never say never."

"I'm pretty sure there already has been—a couple, at least." Saying it, he dimly recalls one or both of them being asked if they could see the Great Wall from space and that in fact the answer was no (and, even more surprisingly, that the idea itself predated the space program, dating back to turn-of-the-century speculation about canals on Mars). Even if it had been true, he's read recently that huge swaths of China are increasingly invisible from space beneath a blanket of smog.

Still, maybe Pearl could be the first Chinese American on the moon, or even Mars. The Chinese, he knows, have plans for human exploration of space, even if NASA's mission seems to be faltering. He'd done a little research a while back about the Chinese space program, the brainchild of a brilliant scientist called H. S. Tsien, who'd trained at Caltech before the war, helped recruit Werner von Braun to NASA, but been jailed and then deported in the Red scare of the 1950s. The Chinese already have a rudimentary space station on the drawing board—what was it called? Heavenly Palace. And a moon rover called Jade Rabbit. So why not the first Chinese American on the moon, maybe as part of some joint venture.

Nola's weight softens imperceptibly against him; her breath slowly settles.

He pictures Pearl looking back at the earth, wonders what she'll see. A cloudy blue marble, like a cataracted eye? A place of pollution, overpopulation? Or will China's increasing global influence have extended to inspiring (or enforcing?) one-child policies in other countries? Will the draconian salvation of one nation extend to the world?

And will China's own lingering authoritarianism enable the country to belatedly but swiftly curb its emissions?

But really what he wonders is how this future Pearl—this taikonaut!—will think of him and Nola. Will they even be alive still, or still together? Will she resent them for taking her from a resurgent East (at the start of the Chinese century) to a fading West (at the end of the American one)? Or for her name (*Pearl?* Kids will call her Pearl of the Orient, Pearl Harbor, he realizes; she'll have to tell them *I'm not Japanese! or Hawaiian!*)? For her sense of alienation, marginalization?

Or maybe, just maybe, she will belong . . . maybe in 2032, on the fiftieth anniversary of the tragedy, America would declare a Vincent Chin Day to honor the diversity of Asian America. Maybe the other girls—Celeste, Gertie, and the rest—would go on to be athletes and celebrities, justices and presidents (of Amtrak, of GM, of the Academy of Motion Picture Arts and Sciences!).

And maybe she wouldn't look back at the earth anyway but rather at the stars. H. S. Tsien, he recalls now, trained as a railway engineer and ended up as a rocket scientist. Who could possibly tell the future?

Nola is snoring again, her breath gently flaring.

Over her shoulder he sees the clock has slid silently past midnight.

But he's grateful at last for his sleeplessness, glad to be alert, as if standing watch over this new family. Like a terra-cotta warrior. It recalls his dream on the bus back to the hotel of Xi'an, of the terra-cotta army, and of the men —that other army, of artisans—who made them. He'd

imagined the cold clay dense and tacky in his fingers as he tried to summon a face to sculpt, one unlike all the others. Who should it be? A friend, a brother? Who among all the possibilities? The choice had paralyzed him in his dream, or at least he'd woken before he could decide, still with a sense of lingering panic.

He thinks now of all those silent figures, rank upon rank of men, waiting patiently underground, invisible and forgotten ("the original ancient Chinese secret," as Nola whispered) until discovered by local farmers digging a well in the 1970s. John had presumed them buried by time, but in fact they'd been deliberately interred in carefully paved trenches, roofed over with timber and tamped dirt, as if lined up in long lightless tunnels. He'd pictured them being unearthed whole too, but apparently only one among all the thousands had been found intact, all the rest painstakingly reconstructed from pieces and shards sifted and brushed from the soil, the scope of the original undertaking matched only by the scale of the recovery effort.

And what a literal act of representation! Life-sized, and one-to-one, armed with real weapons. That's what really takes the breath away. (That and the megalomania of the first Qin, or Chin, emperor; then again, the country was named after him!) John has seen a handful of touring figures in museums at home, but what he's never appreciated before is how together, en masse, the army—for all the artistry of the individual figures, detailed down to the lines on their hands, the moles on their faces, the weave of their queues—is barely a representation at all, as close to real as possible, each figure standing for precisely one man, representing only himself.

Thousands of figures, maybe hundreds of thousands, crafted by thousands of workers; John suddenly imagines each making a single face. In which case, he thinks, watching Pearl's tiny hands open and close in her sleep and flexing his own in echo, as if to knead the air, imagining the dry clay on his knuckles cracking in gray flakes, what choice but a self-portrait? What else can we represent if not ourselves, however uncertain or contradictory those selves might be? After all, aren't those very contradictions and uncertainties what make us ourselves?

It's just a dream, he knows, based on a tourist's fleeting visit. But this is what he'll tell Pearl first, he thinks, when she asks, as she will ask, as she will *be* asked (*Where are you from?*), about China.

Acknowledgments

My thanks are due to many for their assistance and encouragement in the completion of this project: to Nicholas Delbanco, Marshall Klimasewiski, Zachary Lazar, and Louisa Lim for reading and commenting on various drafts; to Roland Hwang and Frances Kai-Hwa Wang for talking with me about the Vincent Chin case; to Dan Keane and Jennifer Tomscha for their hospitality in Shanghai; to Angela Healy for the inspiration; to the 2015 Kundiman faculty, fellows, and organizers for welcoming me into their community; to the University of Michigan, in particular the Department of English for research funds, the Institute for the Humanities for writing time, and my colleagues and students in the Helen Zell Writers' Program for their fellowship in our shared endeavor; to my agent, Maria Massie, ever my sure guide through the publishing woods; to Janet Silver and Andrea Schulz, for their help along the way; to my U.S. editor, Jenna Johnson, who made this a better book, and to all at Houghton Mifflin Harcourt (Lauren, Pilar, Megan, Carla, Lori, Debbie, Bruce, Ken, Rachael, and Liz) who continue to make their publishing house feel like my home; to Carole Welch, my U.K. editor, for her faith and patience, and to all at Sceptre, my house at home. Lastly, my deepest thanks to Lynne for everything, always, and to Owen for giving me hope for the future of reading.

Numerous books and articles were consulted in the course of writing this novel. What follows is only a partial list.

On the building of the railroads, I'm indebted to David Haward Bain's *Empire Express* and *The Old Iron Road* (and to David's enthusiasm for the project when he heard me read from it in early form at the Bread Loaf Writers' Conference in 2011). Stephen Ambrose's *Nothing Like It in the World* and Richard White's *Railroaded* were also valuable sources.

Bury My Bones in America, by Lani Ah Tye Farkas, and *Canton Footprints,* by Philip P. Choy, were helpful in imagining the experience of early Chinese immigrants in California.

Two biographies in particular, *Perpetually Cool: The Many Lives of Anna May Wong,* by Anthony B. Chan, and *Anna May Wong: From Laundryman's Daughter to Hollywood Legend,* by Graham Russell Gao Hodges, informed my understanding of the actress.

The following greatly contributed to my understanding of the Vincent Chin case: *Asian American Dreams,* by Helen Zia; the documentary *Who Killed Vincent Chin?* directed by Christine Choy and Renee Tajima-Peña; *Building Our Legacy: The Murder of Vincent Chin,* a trial reenactment scripted by the Asian American Bar Association of New York, Dean Frank H. Wu, and the Honorable Denny Chin; and the article "The Man Who Killed Vincent Chin," by Michael Moore in the *Detroit Free Press.*

Adoption texts that were especially informative include *Intercountry Adoption from China: Examining Cultural Heritage and Other Postadoption Issues,* by Jay W.

Rojewski and Jacy L. Rojewski; *The Lucky Ones: Our Stories of Adopting Children from China*, edited by Ann Rauhala; *West Meets East: Americans Adopt Chinese Children*, by Richard Tessler, Gail Gamache, and Liming Liu; and the article "I Met My Daughter at the Wuhan Foundling Hospital," by Bruce Porter, in the *New York Times Magazine*.

Finally, for their resources and holdings I'm grateful to the University of Michigan Library, the Museum of Chinese in America in New York, the Chinese American Museum in Los Angeles, the Chinese Historical Society of America in San Francisco, and the California State Railroad Museum in Sacramento.

None of the above, naturally, are responsible for any inaccuracies in the text or the many fictional liberties I've taken with the material.

PETER HO DAVIES

The Welsh Girl

Longlisted for the Man Booker Prize

Wales, 1944. Captain Rotheram, a Jewish refugee working
for British Intelligence, arrives to interrogate the infamous
captive, Rudolf Hess. In a prison camp near a remote
Snowdonian village, a young German soldier wrestles with
the shame of his surrender. And among the curious locals is
seventeen-year-old Esther Evans, who longs to experience
the wider world. When their paths connect, all three will
come to question their deepest loyalties, as the war irrevo-
cably alters the course of their lives.

Casting fresh light on dark times, *The Welsh Girl* captures
the extraordinary intensity of wartime relationships as it
explores the bonds that hold us to family, country and
ultimately, our fellow man.

'Deeply felt and vividly imagined'
Lionel Shriver, *Daily Telegraph*

'Moving, memorable and beautifully written . . . a gripping
human story . . . it leaves one thinking about the nature of
cowardice and patriotism, identity and roots'
Jessica Mann, *Sunday Telegraph*

'A beautifully crafted, lyrical novel'
Maggie O'Farrell, *Observer* Books of the Year

SCEPTRE

Join a literary community of
like-minded readers who seek out
the best in contemporary writing.

From the thousands of submissions Sceptre
receives each year, our editors select the books
we consider to be outstanding.

We look for distinctive voices, thought-provoking
themes, original ideas, absorbing narratives and
writing of prize-winning quality.

If you want to be the first to hear about our
new discoveries, and would like the chance to
receive advance reading copies of our books
before they are published, visit

www.sceptrebooks.co.uk

 Follow @sceptrebooks

 'Like' SceptreBooks

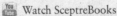 Watch SceptreBooks